HIGH PRAISE FOR JENNIFER ASHLEY AND *PERILS OF THE HEART*!

"Deliciously fun, delightfully entertaining. Featuring impeccably crafted characters and laced with both humor and danger, this historical romance is simply superb."

—*Booklist*

"This is one of those lightning-fast roller-coaster rides loaded with escapades and plot . . . a wonderful escape from a stressful day."

—*Romantic Times*

"*Perils of the Heart* is just plain fun. It has action and adventure, lust, and a sweetly naïve heroine with nerves of steel."

—*All About Romance*

"Jennifer Ashley has written a surprisingly fresh debut novel in *Perils of the Heart*, a delightful romance and intriguing tale."

—*The Romance Reader*

"An incredible first novel that has everything a reader could ask for and more with a story so well told, it's one not to be missed."

—*Romance Reviews Today*

"This is a fun and enjoyable story [with] lively adventure, wonderful characters."

—*Historical Romance Writers*

THE PIRATE'S PRIZE

Alexandra cleared her throat and called upon her haughtiest blue-blooded tones. "Sir, you take a liberty."

Grayson did not look daunted. "No. I licked you. A liberty is a kiss."

"Is it?" She stared at him in confusion. "I do not think there is much difference."

He bent to her again. "You taste like honey."

"You must be out of your head, my lord. Relieved to find yourself alive."

"Perhaps a bit."

"You ought to rest, then. You will feel much more yourself in the morning."

He smoothed a lock of hair from her cheek, drawing fire with his touch. "You should rest, too, Mrs. Alastair. You have had quite a night."

"An astonishing one, yes." To save a man from death and receive the most passionate kiss of one's life certainly qualified as an extraordinary evening.

Would life with a pirate next door always be this exciting?

Other *Leisure* books by Jennifer Ashley:

PERILS OF THE HEART

The Pirate Next Door

JENNIFER ASHLEY

LEISURE BOOKS NEW YORK CITY

LEISURE BOOKS®

October 2003

Published by

Dorchester Publishing Co., Inc.
200 Madison Avenue
New York, NY 10016

ISBN 0-8439-5277-6

Visit us on the web at www.dorchesterpub.com.

ACKNOWLEDGMENTS

Thanks go to my editor, Kate Seaver, and my agent, Bob Mecoy; to Patrick for his button magic; to Nancy, whose music sparks my own creativity; to Gary for being such a loyal fan; to Chris, Elizabeth, and Lizzie for their continued belief in me; to my parents, who gave me my first typewriter as well as much encouragement; to Forrest for his unconditional love and support; and to Hannah, who continually brings me back down to earth.

The Pirate
Next Door

Chapter One

London, June 1810

Alexandra Alastair lay in her slim-posted bed beneath green silk hangings, her hands flat on the coverlet, and debated whether she dared add the viscount next door to her list of eligible suitors.

Grayson Finley, Viscount Stoke.

She and Lady Featherstone knew little about him. He had disappeared from England as a lad and had turned up again only a week ago to take the title of Viscount Stoke, which his second cousin had passed on to him. Lady Featherstone had discovered, through careful research, that the new viscount was thirty-five years of age and unmarried. Very possibly, Lady Featherstone had said, her dark eyes twinkling, he had opened up the house on Grosvenor Street because he wished to seek a wife.

Alexandra's open eyes stared at the carved vines and leaves that wound themselves around the light wood of

1

Jennifer Ashley

the bedposts. She was not as sanguine as Lady Featherstone. It was June, the season nearly ended, and likely
the viscount would only stop in Town for a brief time
before moving on to his country estate.

He was certainly different from the other gentlemen
on the list. Those gentlemen were all polite, all respectable, all likely to make her a quiet and steadfast second
husband. Her first husband had been anything but steadfast, dying finally by falling down the stairs in the house
of one of his mistresses.

Her head throbbed as the humid air of the summer
night touched her burning cheeks. Thoughts of her de-
ceased husband always made her head ache. Which was
why she and Lady Featherstone had so carefully culled
the list, talking and listening and learning about the
shortcomings of each gentleman. The gentlemen who had
succeeded in reaching the list: the Duke of St. Clair, Lord
Hildebrand Caldicott, Mr. Bartholomew—all dependable, trustworthy, respectable. Alexandra squeezed her eyes
shut. And hopelessly dull.

The viscount, on the other hand, was extremely interesting. She'd seen him a few times in passing, usually
when she'd been descending from her carriage just he was
leaving his house next door. He was a most unusual-
looking gentlemen—she refused to use Lady Featherstone's terms, "most splendidly and magnificently
handsome." It was true that he was most unusual for a
Mayfair gentleman. His broad shoulders filled out his coat
quite well, and the small smile he sent her way made her
heartbeat change to a dull thudding. His skin was sun-
bronzed, a tanned color that spoke of lands far from foggy
London. He had hair streaked gold, which he wore unfashionably long and pulled back into a tail. His eyes,
which sometimes lingered on her longer than was polite,

were blue—dark blue like the twilight sky in June.

He did not dress like the other gentlemen on her list either. Sometimes he went out with only a loose greatcoat shrugged on over a shirt and calf-skin breeches, and leather boots that reached above his knees. The carriages and horses he hired were fine; but Annie and Amy, her twin downstairs maids, had told her that he had only opened a few rooms in the house and that everything was dark and dusty.

The viscount had a tall, massive manservant with very dark skin and a bald head creased with ridges of scars. Her own footman, Jeffrey, a big lad, was terrified of the viscount's manservant. Of course, Alexandra conceded, it was difficult to imagine someone Jeffrey was *not* terrified of.

Other gentlemen who came and went included a young man of about her own age who dressed as casually as the viscount, and a short man with a leathery face, a cheerful grin, and an Irish brogue. None of them looked terribly steady and dependable.

But, on the other hand, definitely not dull.

She opened her eyes and took a few deep breaths, trying to still the pounding in her head. She wanted a steady and dependable gentleman, did she not? One who, above all, had a fondness for children. Because if she did not marry one of the steady and dependable gentlemen from the list, Alexandra Alastair would never have children.

Once, long ago, she had borne a child. Her husband had looked almost relieved when the little lad had died, only hours old. Her grief had taken her to a place of darkness, from which she had never quite returned. Theophile had pretty much ignored her after that, and Alexandra had never conceived again.

The night brought a cooling breeze that touched the

3

tears on her wet cheeks. Her bedroom faced the garden, and the scent of new roses drifted to her from the vines that climbed to the windows. Her garden was a mere square patch, but amid the stones of the city, even in elegant Mayfair, the green quiet of the enclosure soothed her. She loved her garden, which had been her retreat, her sanctuary, during her five years of marriage to Theophile Alastair.

From the garden, she heard voices. Male voices.

The ivy at the window rustled like satin skirts in the breeze. The voices came again, sharp, angry, grim. Puzzled, she brushed the tears from her cheeks and sat up.

She realized in a moment that the voices came not from her garden, but from the house next door. The window next to hers must be open, and sounds were floating from one house to the next. Someone was arguing in the room on the other side of the wall.

She silently flipped back the covers and slid from the bed, her feet finding the warmth of her slippers. She snatched up the peignoir that lay on the gold armchair and slid it on, tying the ribbons down the front. She approached the window and pulled back the drape.

She heard a man's voice, drawling and unfamiliar, his vowels liquid and long. "So tell me why a man from the Admiralty visited you today, Finley. If I like your answer, I might just let you live."

Chapter Two

He struggled for breath, the coarse rope tightening around his throat as his feet scrabbled for purchase on the floor. Ropes burned his wrists behind him. The dim, dry part of his mind reflected that he'd survived James Ardmore's near-hanging trick before. That time, Ardmore had relented and cut him down, but only after extracting a terrible promise.

Grayson's toes would not quite take his weight, only enough to keep the rope from entirely cutting off his breath. Ardmore wanted him to struggle, wanted him to almost succeed in saving himself. Until, that is, Grayson grew too tired of fighting his own weight and dropped, choking off his breath and killing himself.

He regarded the dark-haired, grim-faced man who at one time he'd called his friend. The man he had rescued from a cage on a pirate ship, who had joined him in the mutiny that launched the adventures of Ardmore and Finley, co-captains of the *Majesty* and the terror of the seas. They had been all of eighteen years old.

Ardmore's gloved hand held the rope that passed through the heavy ceiling ring and down to encircle Grayson's neck. He drawled in his Charleston accent, "I'm losing patience, Finley. Tell me."

Grayson's lungs burned as if sand grated them. He drew comfort from the thought that Maggie was safe. No matter what happened to him, Maggie was safe, and Oliver and Jacobs would care for her. But if Grayson died too soon, he would not finish the settlements he had begun to ensure that Maggie got all the money he could possibly leave her, to ensure that she grew up a wealthy young woman.

"Go to hell," he said.

The rope jerked. "Tell me. Or Jacobs dies."

Jacobs was lying downstairs, holding his wounded side, two of Ardmore's men pointing pistols at him. Ardmore had burst in this evening with a band of his crew to threaten Grayson's life, breaking their truce. How long before Oliver, Grayson's manservant, could bring help, he could not say. Grayson had sent his own men to fan out from Greenwich to Gravesend after the Admiralty had come calling with their offer of amnesty in exchange for his help.

He could not let Ardmore interrupt his plans yet. Ardmore actually had promised Maggie's mother, Sara, to let Grayson bring the girl back to England. Ardmore had given his word, as Sara lay dying, that her daughter would become the Honorable Miss Maggie Finley and live in a fine house and wear fine clothes and be attended by fine servants. For love of Maggie's mother, Ardmore had stilled his murderous rage and allowed Grayson to return with Maggie to England. For a price.

Ardmore hauled on the rope, and Grayson's feet left

the ground. Black stars danced before his eyes.

"*Tell me.*"

Grayson drew stinging air into his throat. "The French king."

Ardmore's eyes narrowed. "There is no French king."

"In exile. Gone missing."

The rope slackened. Grayson's feet hit the floor. He gulped air, fire flickering the edges of his vision.

"Louis Bourbon?" Ardmore asked in genuine surprise. He brushed his finger over his lip. "The English have lost track of their pet French king? Interesting. What do they expect *you* to do about it?"

Grayson's voice grated. "They think pirates in pay of French agents took him. They believe I will know who is capable of smuggling him back to France." He paused. "Besides you."

Ardmore gave him a long, cold look. "I don't want to play."

"I don't give a damn," Grayson ground out.

Ardmore's eyes were hard green points of hatred. Grayson watched him warily. They had made a bargain, but Ardmore was unpredictable. A tricky bastard, as Ian O'Malley, Ardmore's own first officer, called him. Ardmore played by his own rules.

Ardmore smiled, an ugly, feral smile that made his handsome face bleak. He tied the rope fast to the bedpost, the line tight enough so that Grayson's toes just touched the floor. Ardmore had been tying lines for seventeen years; Grayson knew it would not be weak.

"I'll leave you here to dance," Ardmore said softly. "Maybe your man Oliver will return in time to save you, or maybe he won't. In the meantime, you can hang there and wonder how long it will take for you to die."

Grayson tried to swallow air, tried to lean his head

back to open his throat. Ardmore came close to him, looked up. "It took my brother a long time to die," he said. "Think on that."

His light green eyes were like ice. The trouble between them had started a long-ago, far-away day when Grayson had married the Tahitian woman they had called Sara. That event had led, across years and through the waterways of the world, to this one. To James Ardmore staring up at him and wanting Grayson to die.

Ardmore gave him a final look, then turned and walked away. His footsteps rang in the empty hall. He descended the staircase, and then Grayson heard his curt orders to the men who waited for him below. The front door opened, and, after a moment, closed. Then silence.

The rope creaked from the ring in the ceiling. The ring also supported the chandelier, an iron thing from centuries passed. If Grayson jerked hard enough, he might dislodge the circle of iron. Or he might just snap his neck. Unless the chandelier simply fell and crushed the life out of him. The bed was too far across the room to be of any use, but the straight-backed chair might help. Now to discover if Ardmore had left it just out of reach, or just near enough.

As Grayson walked his toes toward the chair, he damned himself for lowering his guard. Ardmore and his men had overwhelmed him and Jacobs while they'd supped together and pondered the whereabouts of Ardmore's watchdog, Ian O'Malley. Now all was clear. O'Malley had gone to report to Ardmore about Grayson's visit from the Duke of St. Clair, a man with a prominent position in the English Admiralty.

Grayson's foot just reached the chair. He managed to hook his straining toes around the leg of it and jerk the chair toward him. His hold slipped, and he swung heavily against the rope. His vision went black.

He heard voices from the stairs, then a feminine shriek. Pattering footsteps raced toward him, accompanied by a swift rustling of silk. Slim arms wrapped around his legs and tried to lift him.

"Help me," a female voice panted. "Jeffrey, quickly, cut him down."

Another pair of arms, heavier and stronger caught his hips and hoisted him upward. The rope went slack around his throat. He dragged in a great gulp of air, fire dancing before his eyes.

"I don't have a knife, madam," a boyish voice bleated.

A gruff woman answered him. "Take this one."

His vision began to clear. He heard the chair skitter across the floor. Then the frame creaked as a large lad clambered upon it. The boy lifted his arms, bathing Grayson in the smell of his unwashed body. The lad sawed through the rope with the knife, his sinewy hands working fast.

The rope broke. Grayson tumbled down. His tired legs crumpled and he landed flat on his face, his nose digging into the threadbare carpet.

A scent as sweet as summer sunshine drifted over him; a light hand touched his shoulder. "Jeffrey, run after them. Fetch a watchman."

"But they are murderers, madam! I am afraid of murderers!"

Grayson stifled a laugh and dragged in breath after breath, inhaling the stale scent of the rug with as much joy as he would a heady perfume. A cool knife blade touched his wrist, and the ropes loosened. He felt the sting of the knife's edge on his skin, and blood tickled him, but the ropes fell away. His wrists landed at his sides, burning as the blood flowed back to them. He lay there for a moment, enjoying his pain, because pain meant life.

A worried hand touched his shoulder. He lifted his head.

His next-door neighbor knelt over him, her pretty eyes anxious. He had spied the woman a few times in passing since he'd first moved in, and had found her worth a second glance. And worth deliberately inventing a reason to be just leaving his house whenever he saw her carriage depositing her at her front door. He'd ordered Jacobs to find out who she was. His lieutenant reported that she was a widow called Mrs. Alastair. Before that she had been Miss Alexandra Simmington, daughter of Lord Alexis Simmington and granddaughter of a duke. Blue-blooded and well-bred.

And his rescuer. He was in love. Her red-brown hair fell in a riot of curls over her shoulders. Her eyes were brown, flecked with green, cool and calm like the waters of a woodland pond. She wore a feminine and frilly garment of soft green silk that clung to her gently rounded curves. If he could slide open the bows that marched down the front of the gown, perhaps it would part and provide him with a more intimate glimpse of the glories of her body.

She began rubbing his numb hands, pushing the blood back into them. They stung, hot needles pricking his flesh. He wanted to thank her, but words would not come from his aching throat. He rolled himself onto his back, drawing in the air that had been denied him too long.

He slid his burning hand from her grasp and touched her tumbled curls. They felt like crinkled silk. His chest expanded with air, a lovely elixir, bringing with it her feminine perfume.

She was speaking. "We found another man downstairs, hurt."

He heard her without understanding. Her red-brown brows drew together, as if she were studying him in order to write a scientific paper about him. Emboldened, he slid his hands about her waist. Her warm, slippery gown welcomed him, her curves soft and supple beneath it.

Wordless desire welled up in him, spun by the nearness of death and the nearness of *her*. He pulled her closer. Her eyes flickered in nervousness, her long lashes sweeping to hide them. Her face was finely curved, flesh sculpted to bone, and a scattering of freckles dusted her nose. Her chin was a tiny bit plump, and her lips were shell pink, not reddened by artifice. Making a conscious decision, Grayson raised his head and brushed a kiss to her mouth.

She pulled back, her body stiff. Grayson slid his hand to the nape of her neck, kneading softly, gentling his touch. Under his hand she relaxed, just a little. Grayson kissed her again, this time softly, lingering.

After a moment, she gave a little sigh and eased toward him, and he felt a small, answering push of her lips.

Excitement, uncontrolled and uncaring, washed through him. He suddenly wanted her, this lovely, sweet-smelling woman who had lifted him from death. His kiss turned rough. She gave a small cry of surprise, but his body had taken over.

He seamed her mouth with his tongue, and joyfully, arousingly, she did not fight him. Clumsily, she fitted her mouth to his, as if she were unused to opening it to another, unused to accepting such a deep kiss. Her lips grew warm and more passionate beneath his.

Dizziness consumed him, but he did not want to let go. He broke the kiss, but only to roll over, to drag her to the floor beneath him. The lacy, frilled garment was little barrier between himself and her enticing body. He slanted his mouth across hers again, kissing her swollen mouth, scooping up the goodness of her on his tongue.

She made another small noise—of surrender or protest, he could not tell. His arousal was stiff with longing, desire spinning through him. He pressed her thighs apart, molding the thin garment to her, feeling the heat of her through the silk. His fingers fumbled at the little bows, wanting to part the fabric and have at her.

A strong touch landed on his shoulder, pulling him back from the spinning glory that beckoned. "That will be enough of that, young man," a woman's voice said sternly.

He'd forgotten the large, gruff woman and the beefy, terrified boy who'd accompanied his rescuer. He looked up. They stood on each side of him, the woman scowling, the lad open-mouthed with shock and fascination.

Grayson rolled away from Mrs. Alastair's ripe and needing body and curled his arms over his stomach. He drew in a breath of sweet air, and with it came laughter. He laughed for the joy of life and the joy of the beautiful woman on the carpet beside him.

She sat up and stared at him in bewilderment. He lifted his hand and touched the curve of her face.

"Thank you," he whispered. "Thank you."

Grayson Finley, Viscount Stoke, was a very resilient man. He lay flat on his back for less than a quarter hour, drawing deep breaths, before he climbed to his feet. Alexandra watched the animation flow back into his body, which only a moment ago had been content to simply be alive, like water returning to a dry pool. His throat was dark with bruises, but other than that, he seemed little worse for wear. Blue eyes sparkling, he ordered the quaking Jeffrey and Cook downstairs to find the man called Mr. Jacobs. To Alexandra, he said, "Come with me."

No explanation, no waiting, not even dressing himself, for heaven's sake. Well, she conceded, he was half-dressed. He wore leather breeches, a linen shirt opened to his waist, and tall boots, but no collar, no waistcoat, no coat. A white scar ran from the hollow of his throat to disappear in the shadow of muscle under the shirt. Alexandra found herself wanting to tilt her head to trace the path of the scar to its end.

The candles in the hall glinted on his long, sun-streaked hair and shone faintly on the gold bristles of a new beard. Alexandra's late husband had never allowed his beard to appear. The moment he'd spotted a whisker, he'd shouted for his valet to for God's sake come and remove it. He wanted his face perpetually smooth and clean. Alexandra had heard rumors that he liked his women just as bare in certain places. She had never been brave enough to ask if this were true.

The viscount took her hand in his and pulled her up the next flight of stairs. His palm was calloused and hard, very unlike the soft, manicured hands of her husband. The leather of his scarred boots bent and flowed around his joints with the ease of long use. His nose was crooked, as if it had been broken, and a small scar pulled his lower lip slightly downward at the left corner. Not necessarily a perfect face, a fashionably handsome face. But an arresting one all the same.

Despite the candles, the house was dark, the paneling that lined the walls nearly black. The stairs held the patina of age, and creaked under the viscount's tread. Alexandra's light boots barely made a sound. Through open doors she glimpsed rooms where dust sheets had been removed from the furniture. Crates stood about, some without tops, some still shut tightly.

They entered a bedroom on the top floor, which, she calculated, lay just on the other side of the third-floor rooms in her own house. This room had not been aired—the dust sheets remained on what little furniture filled it and the fireplace had long been cold.

He strode unerringly to a panel that looked just like all the other panels lining the room. He touched a piece of raised molding, and the wall swung away to reveal a small, square compartment.

From this, to her amazement, sprang a girl. She was about twelve years old and dressed in a soiled pink silk gown with many ruffles and bows, most of them sadly torn. In her right hand, she held a long and wicked-looking knife. She swept her midnight black hair from her face, revealing sparkling dark eyes under black slanted brows.

"Papa!" she cried. She flung her arms about the viscount's waist, dagger and all. "Are you all right?"

Chapter Three

Alexandra's lips parted in astonishment. The viscount had a *daughter*? None of Lady Featherstone's research had indicated the viscount had a child, let alone one who looked as though she'd sprung from a Pacific island explored by Captain Cook.

The viscount dragged the girl into his arms for a fierce, tight hug. His eyes closed as he pressed a long kiss to her tangled curls. His fingers shook the slightest bit.

"Did he hurt you, Papa?" she asked into his ribcage. "I thought Mr. Ardmore was our friend."

The viscount straightened and gently parted the girl's slim arms from his waist. Alexandra watched him soften his fierce expression to one of studied nonchalance before he answered. "I am perfectly unhurt, sweetheart." He tousled her curls. "Look, this pretty lady rescued me."

Almond-shaped black eyes observed Alexandra with careful interest. The girl had the look of the viscount in the set of her chin, the shape of her lips, the mischievous spark in her eyes, but her skin was dark—the color of milk-laden coffee. She was a beautiful child, but far out of place in elegant and constrained Mayfair.

Questions raced through Alexandra's mind: Where was her mother? Was the viscount married? Her heart thumped. Perhaps she would not be able to include the viscount on her list after all.

But the child was fascinating. Her tight, almost frantic hold on her father told Alexandra that the girl was much relieved to see him still standing. It made her heart ache. But why on earth was she dressed in an unfashionable frilly silk gown more suitable for a ballroom in the middle of the night?

"What is your name?" the girl asked her calmly.

Alexandra looked into the bright eyes and read lively intelligence there. "Mrs. Alastair. From next door."

"A most brave and beautiful lady," the viscount added. He slanted Alexandra a smile over his daughter's head. "She saved me in the nick of time."

The girl looked impressed. The viscount's swarthy hand rested on her shoulder, his grip tight. They made a most bizarre pair.

"May we give her a reward?" the girl asked.

Her blue-eyed papa also scrutinized Alexandra. His casual undress unnerved her. Even her husband, who had dropped his breeches for any woman strolling past, had kept himself well covered. This man's chest, sun-browned and well-muscled, was openly displayed, and he did not even seem to notice.

The combination of both of them looking at her in unspoken admiration was unsettling. Alexandra found herself foundering beyond her depth, her training by several well-paid and very proper governesses proving inadequate.

"Reward?" she stammered. "I do not need anything. Really, I only heard him through the window and ran over to see if I could help—"

The viscount held up his hand. "I have seen the fiercest pirates wet themselves when faced with James Ardmore. You are very brave." His blue eyes darkened. "I have opals that would shine like white fire in your hair. I will have a jeweler set them."

She suddenly pictured his tanned and calloused hands holding the jewels, letting them spill from his fingers to scatter on her hair as she lay beneath him. "I have no need for opals," she said hastily. "Really, for any jewels. Heaven knows my husband bought me plenty."

He gave her a puzzled look, and her face burned. Theo had thrown jewels at her, true, because of course, his wife must be well turned out and not embarrass him. By now, the viscount must have heard all about her humiliating marriage. *Poor Mrs. Alastair*, anyone with a penchant for gossip could have told him. *Her husband was so indiscreet.* Indiscretion was, in her world, a greater sin than infidelity.

She drew a breath. "My lord, I am happy you are unhurt. I will return home now."

"Not yet." He caught her hand and held it loosely. "I must think of some way to reward you."

He lifted her hand to his lips. His kiss was cool and satin-smooth, but the touch of his breath licked heat down her spine. Her mouth still tingled where he'd kissed her. He'd been out of his head, probably not understanding what he did, when he'd held her to the floor and kissed her so passionately. She touched her tongue to her lower lip where his teeth had scraped her. No man had ever kissed her like that. And likely never would again, she thought wistfully, now that he'd come to his senses.

"Papa," the girl said. "Why did Captain Ardmore want to kill you?"

The viscount lowered Alexandra's hand but did not release it. When he looked at his daughter, his expression was guarded. "He was not trying to kill me, Maggie. He was giving me a warning."

Alexandra thought of the words she had heard coming through the window before she'd run upstairs to wake Jeffrey and her cook. She had been startled to learn about the disappearance of the French king, but she had suspected that the enmity between the viscount and the man called Ardmore had little to do with that. The hatred in the stranger's voice had been deep, an anger festered over a long time.

The viscount abruptly changed the subject. He released Alexandra's hand. "We must go and help Lieutenant Jacobs. He is hurt."

The girl's puzzled look turned to one of tight concern. "Oh, dear. Poor Mr. Jacobs. I must see to him. Where is Oliver?" Pushing past her father, she dashed from the room, still clutching the knife, as if she were running off to avenge their enemies.

Alexandra took a step after her, worried she would hurt herself with the dagger, but she was brought up short, like a fish on a hook. She swung around. The viscount held the green silken end of her sash, and he was grinning. "Stay with me, pretty lady."

"But Maggie might be in danger. What if there are more of them? Or if they come back?"

"They won't," he said. "Not tonight."

He certainly seemed calm for a man whose house and been invaded and whose life had been nearly taken. "Who were they? Who is this Mr. Ardmore? You must send for Bow Street."

He toyed with the end of her sash. "It is most important, Mrs. Alastair, that you forget all you heard tonight. Can you do that for me?"

"But what about—"

His gaze became hard. "Trust me when I say that my business is too deadly to drag you or Bow Street into. Go back home and be the pretty lady next door." His expression softened again, and he gave her a small smile, one that made her heart beat a little bit faster. "Perhaps next time we pass, we will not simply nod and go on, but have a small conversation. I think I would like that."

She thought she would definitely like that. "But I cannot let you dismiss this so easily. That man tried to murder you. You must confide in someone. The Admiralty, perhaps."

A crease appeared between his brows, as if he were puzzled she simply did not do as he wished. He possessed the air of one who expected his every request to be obeyed. Took it for granted that it would be. No need to shout when all he had to do was give a look and a word.

Alexandra, on the other hand, had always struggled with obedience. "And what about the French king?"

His face became a careful blank. "What about him?"

"Will this Mr. Ardmore try to stop you finding him? How on earth will you look for him if the Admiralty cannot even help you?"

His eyes chilled the slightest bit. "For your own safety, Mrs. Alastair, and for mine and Maggie's, give me your word you will ask no more questions. I will take care of Mr. Ardmore and the French king in my own way." He looked up, his mouth in so harsh a line that she faltered. "Swear to me. No Bow Street. No questions."

She stared at him, her heart speeding in alarm. "Very well. If you believe your daughter could be harmed, I will not speak of this to anyone besides yourself."

He nodded once, his face still grim.

"However," she said. "I still believe you should tell *me* everything."

He stared at her, his expression amazed. She lifted her chin and added silently, *no, my lord, I will not simply bow to you because you wish it.*

A sudden grin split his face. He placed his hands on her shoulders and leaned in to her. His hot breath touched her mouth. She was reminded of the taste of him when he kissed her on his bedroom floor. Wild, exotic, heady—male. It had been so *satisfying*. It was satisfying now. "Then I will simply have to stop you from asking questions." He closed the inch of space between them and brushed his tongue—ever so lightly—over her lips.

She gasped. The place where his tongue touched burned like the hottest flame, a single point of raw heat. She fought to steady herself and searched desperately for somewhere to rest her nervous gaze. But all she saw before her was his open shirt, his tanned chest, his sandpaper chin. The place her husband had been rumored to like bare became suddenly moist and hot.

She cleared her throat and called upon her haughtiest blue-blooded tones. "Sir, you take a liberty."

He did not look daunted. "No. I licked you. A liberty is a kiss."

"Is it?" She stared at him in confusion. "I do not think there is much difference."

He bent to her again. "You taste like honey."

"You still must be out of your head, my lord. Relieved to find yourself alive."

"Perhaps a bit."

"You ought to rest, then. You will feel much more yourself in the morning."

He smoothed a lock of hair from her cheek, drawing fire with his touch. "You should rest, too, Mrs. Alastair. You have had quite a night."

"An astonishing one, yes." The hollow of his throat was damp, and she had the most dismaying urge to lick it. "How old is your daughter?"

His brows rose at the change of subject. "About twelve, I think."

Did he not know? Alexandra wanted to learn everything about the child. Her heart ached with envy, to have such a beautiful daughter would be wonderful.

"May I—may I ask you one more thing?"

"Be warned. If I don't like the question, I will be forced to take another liberty."

She swallowed. She had to be mad. She ought to run away while she could, escape to the quietude of her house next door. Instead, she let her quavering fingertip hover just above the jagged scar that started at his collarbone. "How far down does that go?"

The smile he turned on her made her whole body hot. He took her fingertip in his hand, kissed it softly, then guided it downward to a point on his breeches, just an inch or so to the right of his groin. "Here," he said. The leather stretched very tight there.

She snatched her shaking hand away. "Was it a duel?"

He shook his head. "A man with a cutlass. I was trying to get between my manservant, Oliver, and someone trying to hit him with a boathook."

"Did you win the fight? And save Mr. Oliver?"

"No, I lost. Oliver saved me."

"Oh." Such violence was foreign to her. Duels happened in her world, yes, but they were civilized and ruleladen, not bathed in out-and-out brutal carnage. "Well."

21

She took a step back. "You must attend to your friends. Good night, my lord."

He only looked at her. He must know that she was babbling because she was trembling all over, her heart racing like a rabbit's. His must know that if he touched her again, she'd melt to the floor like warm pudding and beg for him to lap her up.

Gathering her strength, she managed to turn away and walk out of the room and toward the stairs.

"Mrs. Alastair."

His velvet baritone made her turn back. She clutched the newel post to prevent the pudding from taking over. "Yes?" she asked brightly.

"I ask a favor of you."

She swallowed. "Yes?"

He gave her a long look, his blue eyes gleaming in the dim light. "When you return to your bed tonight—sleep bare."

She clutched the railing beside her, feeling her legs go slack. "I beg your pardon?"

He leaned against the doorframe of the unused room, his gaze warm on her body. "Sleep without clothes when you return to bed. I want to think of you doing so—on the other side of the wall."

Her mind seemed to float, heat sliding up and down her body. "Why?"

He gave her an incredulous look, then slanted her a smile that turned her heart inside out. She pried her hand from the railing and raced down the stairs on shaking legs. His dark laughter floated behind her.

"Alexandra always has the best cakes," Cynthia Waters declared, sinking into the delicate-legged Sheraton chair in Alexandra's front reception room. She plucked a daintily frosted petit-four from the three-tiered tray before her and munched it whole.

Lady Featherstone seated herself next to Alexandra on the Empire settee and squeezed her arm. "Did you decide?" she whispered as Mrs. Waters and Mrs. Tetley conversed about the merits of Alexandra's confections.

"Decide what?" Alexandra asked absently.

"About Viscount Stoke."

Alexandra hid a start. Her late-night adventure had left her tired and sandy-eyed, and she'd actually snapped at Alice—Alexandra, who believed in kindness to all. She gazed at Lady Featherstone's bright face now and winced inwardly. Did everyone *know* she'd lain on Viscount Stoke's bedchamber floor and let him kiss her and kiss her—not to mention later when he'd ever so gently licked her lips.

Or sleeping without clothes for him, which was why she'd snapped at Alice. The maid had entered the room before Alexandra had had the chance to get into her dressing gown and pretend that all was normal. Alice, a well-trained lady's maid, had behaved as if seeing her mistress emerge stark naked from under her blankets was nothing unusual. She'd just said, "Tea, madam," and gone about her business.

"What about him?" Alexandra asked nervously.

"Do we add him to the list?"

Alexandra plucked at her skirt and did not answer. At Christmas at the Featherstones' last year, Alexandra had expressed the wistful desire to marry again and have children. When she'd also expressed the fear that her second husband might be as loathsome as her first, Lady Featherstone, Alexandra's late mother's closest friend, had been understanding itself. The lady had enthusiastically proposed that they draw up a list of the most eligible bachelors in England. They would then observe each carefully and eliminate those not likely to suit.

Alexandra had been hesitant at first, but conceded that Lady Featherstone's plan made sense. If she had been more particular about her choice in the first place, instead of giddily accepting the first gentleman who'd offered for her, her lot might have been much happier. She might even now be surrounded by the children she longed for, and have a husband whose worst crime was tucking his napkin into his waistcoat at supper. She could forgive a little napkin tucking in a gentleman of kindly disposition. Theo had always been immaculately groomed and had possessed perfect manners. Alexandra had mistaken his studied politeness for kindness of spirit. Theo had played his roles so very, very well.

"You must at the very least invite him to the soiree," Lady Featherstone rattled on.

Alexandra hid a sigh. Lady Featherstone had persuaded Alexandra to give the event of the season's end, a soiree that would include everyone who was anyone before they all dispersed for the summer. She felt far too exhausted this afternoon to worry about the details of a party, but Lady Featherstone was smiling eagerly.

"I am not—" she began, but she was interrupted by Jeffrey striding heavily into the room. His wig was crooked.

"Viscount Stoke!" he shouted. Alexandra's three guests looked up eagerly, ceasing their chatter.

Viscount Stoke appeared in the double doorway, looking utterly composed and certainly not as if he'd spent the previous night battling enemies. He wore a coat today, one so dark blue that it was nearly black, but blue enough to highlight the intense twilight color of his eyes. The coat was buttoned over a lawn shirt, and he had pulled his mane of golden hair back into a tail. Instead of a cravat and collar, he'd tied a black scarf about his throat, covering the bruises left by the rope.

Jeffrey bowed and lumbered out, trying to straighten his wig with his beefy hands. The viscount leaned against the doorframe and bathed the room in a half smile. "Good afternoon, ladies."

Chapter Four

Three pairs of eyes widened, three mouths dropped open. Three feminine and giggling voices said, "Good afternoon, my lord."

Alexandra rose to her feet. "My lord." She hoped her voice did not sound all trembly by the time it reached him.

He folded his arms, settling in. He swept his gaze over the room and brought it to rest on Alexandra. His blue eyes were knowing. He'd guessed—he must have—that she had indeed slept in her skin, as he'd suggested. That and she'd dreamed all night of the hot touch of his tongue on her lips.

"I am looking for my daughter," he announced.

Maggie had arrived shortly before Alexandra's first callers with Mr. Oliver, the dark-skinned manservant, in tow. She had greeted Alexandra cheerfully, then asked to see Jeffrey and Cook. Mr. Oliver had led her downstairs. She had discarded the pink frock for boy's breeches, small boots, and a shirt much too big for her.

"Yes, indeed," Alexandra croaked. "She is downstairs, in the kitchens."

"Ah, good. She likes kitchens."

He made no move to explain his strange remark or to leave. His stance was comfortable, as if he meant to lean there all afternoon.

Lady Featherstone, never shy, spoke up. "I was not aware you had a daughter, Lord Stoke. How old is she?"

"She is twelve." No hesitation this time. A spark of pride lit his eye. "And a little hellion."

"Ah, they soon grow out of that," Lady Featherstone said, with the experienced air of one who had raised three daughters. "An excellent governess and a little polish, and they become fine and pleasant young ladies."

The statement did not seem to interest him. He returned his gaze to Alexandra. "Thank you, Mrs. Alastair." He managed to make the simple politeness drip with wickedness. "I will fetch Maggie and go."

Alexandra cast about for something intelligent to say. Something witty. Something that would not make her look like half the fool she felt at present.

His smile deepened, as if he read her thoughts; then he pushed himself from the doorframe, made a half-bow to them all, and turned and strolled away.

Alexandra's sigh blended with those of her three guests. Mrs. Tetley snapped open her fan and waved it rapidly. Mrs. Waters dreamily reached for another petit four.

Alexandra sank to the settee, her legs weak. Lady Featherstone leaned to her and tapped her arm with her fan. "We shall *most certainly* place him on the list."

27

Alexandra opened her mouth to protest, then closed it again. How could she explain why the viscount was not a suitable candidate? Since her husband's death, Alexandra had lived a predictable and unexciting existence, which, after Theo, had been rather restful. Last night had shaken that existence. Gentlemen like Viscount Stoke, who fought with cutlasses and kissed like fire and demanded that she sleep without her clothes, did not enter her world. She was not prepared for such a man, not ready to face anything more exciting than a choice in her morning tea. She had created the list of suitors to ensure that her next marriage would flow along comfortably and predictably. Viscount Stoke had no place on that list.

It had also occurred to her that the viscount's request, coupled with the brazen way he'd licked her lower lip, had effectively stopped her asking him questions. Just as he'd wanted.

Mrs. Waters delicately shook crumbs from her fingertips. "*I* heard, and this is in deepest confidence, ladies—"

Lady Featherstone and Mrs. Tetley leaned forward.

"Mr. Waters imparted to me that someone told *him* that the viscount—" she dropped her voice to a whisper—"used to be a pirate."

Mrs. Tetley's breath hissed. "No!"

"Oh, yes. He certainly looks like a pirate, does he not?"

Mrs. Tetley fanned herself thoughtfully. "He *did* run away to sea when he was a lad, after the tragedy with his parents."

Mrs. Waters looked interested. "Tragedy? I had not heard about this."

Alexandra's curiosity sat up and pricked its ears, though she knew she should stop their gossiping. It was common practice to dissect someone not in the room, but she had never been comfortable with such things. Besides, the viscount was still in the house, and could very well overhear them. He would naturally be angry that his family's dirty linen was being hung out for public scrutiny. She, as hostess, would be to blame.

Before she could speak, Mrs. Tetley went on, "It was horrible, from what I have heard. My sister's husband knew his family in Gloucestershire, and it was quite a scandal at the time. His father, one Mr. Archibald Finley, in a fit of jealous rage, shot his wife, then turned the pistol on himself. The viscount was only a boy at the time. Can you imagine?"

Alexandra's curiosity slunk away and pity took its place. "Oh, the poor man."

"The son of a murderer?" Mrs. Waters asked, eyes wide. "No wonder he became a pirate."

Lady Featherstone looked skeptical. "Would a pirate have a daughter?"

"Hmm." Mrs. Waters stared into space for a moment, and then she brightened. "Perhaps she is the daughter of a maiden he once ravished."

"That would have been a long time ago," Mrs. Tetley said.

Mrs. Waters took on a faraway expression. "Can you imagine if you were a passenger on a ship he had boarded? He'd come to your cabin—" she looked dreamily at the doorway from which he'd departed—"and take liberties with your person. Against the cabin wall, perhaps." The room descended into thoughtful silence, broken only by the sound of carriages and horses passing in the street. "Then he'd tear the jewels from your throat and vanish into the smoke." She let out a long and satisfied sigh.

Lady Featherstone lifted her teacup decisively. "You read far too many novels, Cynthia." She leaned to Alexandra and whispered, "Besides, she must weigh twenty stone."

Alexandra pushed aside the enticing vision of *herself* being taken by the viscount against the wall of a ship's cabin. He would kiss her just as he'd kissed her on the floor of his bedchamber, his lips bruising and commanding. Her hands would rest on his wide shoulders, and he would kiss her and kiss her and kiss her.

When he was finished, he'd lay her, exhausted and weak, on the bunk. He'd come away with her necklace in his hand. "I will keep this to remember you by, dear lady," he would say in a low voice. He would give her a look with his dark blue eyes, press a light kiss to her lips, then turn and sweep away.

She drew a long breath, forcing her fantasy aside. "Be that as it may, we have no proof that he was a pirate." She fanned her hot face. "He is simply a viscount living next door to me. Trying to raise a daughter by himself." She paused. "At least, I do not believe his wife is still living. The house is certainly that of a bachelor."

Lady Featherstone gaped. "You were *inside* his house? When? Why on earth didn't you tell me?"

Alexandra flushed. "Well—"

"What was it like?" Mrs. Waters asked eagerly.

Alexandra foundered. "Well, he has only just moved in, hasn't he? Naturally everything is at sixes and sevens. Much of the old viscount's furniture is still there."

Mrs. Waters looked disappointed. "I heard he brought home boxes of treasure—jewels and silks and exotic things."

Alexandra remembered his words, low and sultry: *I have opals that would shine like white fire in your hair*. Where would he get a handful of loose opals that he wanted to take to the jeweler to set? "Well, of course he must have some mementoes of his travels."

"Visit him again and find out."

Mrs. Tetley joined in. "Yes. Consider it your *duty*, Alexandra, to storm the battlements and find out if he is truly a pirate." She gave a very unmatronly giggle. "And then tell us *everything*."

Alexandra regarded them in dismay. They had fired her own curiosity, but she certainly did not want to snoop and report to them. Besides, if she made a habit of dashing in and out of the viscount's house, people would talk. She must avoid scandal if she was to go on the marriage mart again.

Of course, she would have to venture to speak to him about Maggie's clothes, or rather, her lack of them. Pirate or no, the viscount obviously had no idea how a twelve-year-old girl should be dressed. She could offer her knowledge and assistance in this area. Which meant she would have to take Maggie shopping and help her set up her wardrobe, which would entail any number of visits to the house.

No. Her better self pushed the idea firmly from her mind. She would not poke and pry, and she certainly would not use a little girl as an excuse to do so.

Although Maggie did need clothes. Alexandra knew a dressmaker who did excellent work for younger ladies. And for her governess—of course, Mrs. Fairchild. Her heart leapt. Mrs. Fairchild—the lovely, well-mannered woman who had been Alexandra's last governess, who had given Alexandra her final polish before her debut— would be perfect for Maggie. Mrs. Fairchild had married an Oxford *don* just before Alexandra's wedding, but she was a widow now, and had written Alexandra that she planned to return to tutoring girls.

"Ladies, I—" she began.

She was saved having to explain by a horrible grinding sound of wood on pavement just outside the window. Then came the crash of glass, screams of horses, fervent curses of men, and the frightened cries of passers-by.

Alexandra leapt to her feet. She and her guests hurried to the front window, and Alexandra pulled back the drape. Outside, the summer street scene had changed to chaos. A carriage lay overturned on the stones, its roof inches from the railing that separated the street from her scullery stairs. A delivery wagon lay askew across half the road, and another carriage had spun to collide with it. Horses screamed and struggled in their harnesses, trapped by tethers and chains. A window of the overturned carriage had cracked straight across.

Men scurried toward the wreckage. A few coachmen stood on the boxes of their fine carriages and cursed the delay. An army officer in brilliant infantry red hurried toward the accident. A blond, bespectacled gentleman in a subdued, curate-like suit climbed down from his phaeton, tossed his reins to a boy, and rushed to help.

The viscount emerged from his house and waded into the mess. "Cut the harnesses!" he shouted. "Get them loose."

His daughter scurried out behind him. Nimble in her boy's clothes, she climbed to the top of the overturned carriage and began assisting the coach's shaken footman to pry open the carriage door.

Alexandra turned from the window and snatched up a Turkish shawl from the divan. "People will be hurt."

She hurried from the room, bumping into Jeffrey on the way out. He flailed back, bleated an apology, then dashed to open the door for her.

Grosvenor Street was a busy thoroughfare. Not only

did elegant Mayfair carriages and phaetons trundle up and down it, but delivery wagons, builders' carts, peddlers, men on horseback, and pedestrians used the street as a main route between Bond Street and Grosvenor Square. The congestion made an excellent opportunity for accidents, but Alexandra had not seen one this ugly in a long while. The last had occurred just after her husband's death. On that occasion, she'd had to replace her window, her draperies, and a Hepplewhite console table when a broken timber from a struck cart had sailed into her reception room. No one had been hurt, although Jeffrey had refused to enter the reception room for about six months. But from the frightened sobbing she heard through the now-open carriage door, she feared the worst.

The footman, white to the lips, reached down and lifted out a woman, young and pale-haired, into the sunlight. She had a cut on her forehead and looked about with a dazed expression. Maggie put an arm around her shoulders and helped her sit on the edge of the carriage so that the carter could lift her down.

Alexandra hurried forward and draped the expensive shawl over the poor woman's shoulders. The woman turned to her, unseeing, then pressed a trembling hand to her abdomen. Alexandra recognized the gesture and the slight protrusion in her belly for what it was. The lady was increasing.

She led her away from the wreckage. The carriage blocked the way to Alexandra's front door; they'd have to find some way around it. She surmised the wild-eyed young man Maggie was guiding to the edge of the carriage was the husband. He dropped to the ground and rushed to his wife.

"I knew that coachman was mad," he jabbered. "We

should never had hired him. I knew he'd bring us to grief."

The lady only stared at him, too dazed to respond. Alexandra put her arm around the woman's shoulder and chafed her wrists. She crooned a few words of comfort, but she knew that the lady did not hear her. Doubtless her fears were turned inward, to the child she so precariously carried.

Alexandra certainly knew that fear. A pang touched her as she remembered the weeks and weeks of feeling the growing life inside her, the great protectiveness she'd nurtured for the little being she carried. She had sung to him when she thought no one could hear. When she'd finally borne him, several weeks too early, the pain had been nearly unbearable. The doctors and midwife had watched her somberly, certain both mother and child would die. But Alexandra had lived, forcing herself to survive for the sake of her child. Her little boy had only managed to hold on for one day, then died.

She held the lady's hand a little tighter, wishing she could ensure that the child inside her would never come to harm.

Lady Seton, Alexandra's far neighbor, ran from her front door toward them. "Oh, you poor dears. Come inside. I will give you some tea. And brandy."

Alexandra was about to protest that the pair could certainly come to *her* house, but she realized this was not the time to fight over them. She led the couple to Lady Seton's door, then relinquished them. The gentleman, trying to cover his fear with blustering, went on and on about the damned coachman until Lady Seton's footman closed the door.

Alexandra returned to the wreckage. Fortunately, no one else had been hurt. The viscount and a carter helping him had managed to free the horses. The beasts danced about the street, eyes rolling, heads tossing. The viscount and the carter were now trying to calm them.

The horses from the other two conveyances were being led off out of the way. Maggie stood on the carriage, hands on hips, surveying the mess. It was positively indecent for her to stand out here in breeches, but Alexandra had to admit the girl would not have been able to help had she been hampered by skirts.

Another elegant carriage stopped on the far side of the wreckage. The Duke of St. Clair, one of her expected guests, emerged from it along with Lord Hildebrand Caldicott and his sister. The three of them skirted the debris and met Alexandra at her open front door.

"Good heavens," the duke exclaimed. "Mrs. Alastair, are you all right?"

"I am, yes." She cast a glance at Lady Seton's front windows. "It seems no one was badly hurt, thank heavens." Though there was still a danger to the young woman and her unborn child. Alexandra bit her lip, hoping that the trauma of the accident would not cause the lady to miscarry. Lady Seton was the motherly sort; no doubt she'd insist on the young woman resting a while before trying to return home.

Lord Hildebrand looked anxious. "You ought to go inside, Mrs. Alastair. Those horses don't look safe."

The viscount was holding them now, his broad shoulders taut against his coat. He had calmed the horses considerably.

"Well *I* am going in," Lady Henrietta Caldicott announced. "This has upset me very much." She glanced at Maggie and sniffed. "Look at that urchin child. What is she doing there? They should not allow them into this part of Mayfair."

She is the Honorable Miss Maggie Finley, Alexandra suddenly itched to say. *And her viscount father just heard you insult her*.

Instead, she beckoned to Jeffrey. "Jeffrey, show Lady Henrietta into the reception room and bring more refreshment."

Jeffrey, looking disappointed that he could not remain and ogle the wreckage, bowed haphazardly and pushed himself into the house. Lord Hildebrand drifted after them.

"Is that Viscount Stoke?" the duke asked, shading his eyes.

The viscount relinquished reins to the carriage's white-faced coachman. The coachman looked the horses over anxiously, his scarlet coat smeared with mud and horse droppings. The viscount raised his hand to acknowledge the duke.

The bespectacled gentleman who had stopped to help was moving toward Alexandra and the duke. The duke, not noticing, went to greet the viscount.

What happened next, Alexandra ever after remembered in slow motion. The viscount caught sight of the bespectacled man. A curious look came over his face, a beat of recognition that almost instantly dissolved into pure rage. Maggie, on top of the coach, stared at the bespectacled man in sudden astonishment. "Mr. Henderson!" she called.

The bespectacled gentleman did not answer her. He stepped up to Alexandra. He had a strong face, clear gray eyes, and white-blond hair. His subdued suit made him look rather like a curate or vicar. He was handsome enough that were he a vicar, young ladies would go to chapel simply to stare at him. Their parents would be amazed at their religious fervor.

36

"Mrs. Alastair?" he asked in a polite voice.

It was not proper for a strange gentleman to simply approach a lady, but perhaps the distress of the accident had made him forget his manners. "Yes?"

"Thank you," he said.

Before she could ask, *for what, sir?*, he grabbed a handful of her hair, wrenched her head back, and kissed her hard across the mouth.

Chapter Five

Alexandra struggled. The young man's hand in her hair twisted pain through her scalp. His mouth was brutal and unyielding. This was nothing like the viscount's kisses of the night before. He'd been bruising, yes, but also teasing and playful. This man exuded anger and cared nothing for her struggling beneath him.

With a suddenness that sent her stumbling, he broke the kiss.

The duke was hurrying toward them, his eyes wide with shock. From the vestibule, she heard Lord Hildebrand's voice. "Here, you—"

The viscount strode toward them, his face thunderous. The bespectacled man saw him coming, his eyes widening. He whirled and managed to run a few steps before the viscount's large hand landed on his shoulder and spun him around. The bespectacled man's alarmed look faded.

His lips twisted into a wry smile just before the viscount balled up his huge fist and punched him full in the face.

Grayson strode down Bond Street, Lieutenant Jacobs at his side, bound for Piccadilly and the Majestic Hotel. Anger poured from him in waves. He was surprised it did not wash everyone away down Bond Street.

Henderson had fled in his phaeton, but Grayson had been far too furious to wait for a horse or carriage to be prepared. He had fetched Jacobs and departed on foot in pursuit, knowing where Henderson would go.

Oliver had bandaged up Jacobs's side the night before, and though Jacobs had moaned a bit, he would live. The cut had not been deep. Mrs. Alastair's cook had proved competent in helping Oliver stitch and bandage, and Oliver had been pleased to have the help of such a willing nurse. Not that he said as much—he never would—but he had worn the faintest of smiles.

All of Mrs. Alastair's servants seemed to have seeped into Grayson's house. The lad Jeffrey had taken one look at Jacobs' wound and toppled full-length to the uncarpeted dining room floor. The twin maids, Annie and Amy—at first Grayson had thought he was seeing double—had come running in with a watchman who looked as if he were still in school. Grayson had dismissed the lad. It was hardly fair to send a young and smooth-faced boy after James Ardmore. A prim-faced lady's maid, who said her name was Alice, came after that to fetch the other servants home.

Grayson's rage boiled hotter. He knew damned well who had sent Henderson to perform his little trick this afternoon. He ground his teeth and wished for the cold steel of a cutlass and a pistol in his belt. But this was modern London, and the Majestic Hotel might object to having a lieutenant sliced in half on its drawing room carpet.

But James Ardmore and his band must not be allowed near that beautiful, beautiful woman. She was not a dockside whore or an upper-class courtesan used to dealing with two captains whose exploits had become legendary. She knew nothing about legends. She was a lady, a true lady—one with spun-silk hair and brown-green eyes clear as watercolor. She would be crushed by Ardmore's games.

God certainly must have a sense of humor. When Grayson had had nothing to live for, he'd all the time in the world. Six months before, his life had stretched, bleak and empty, before him. And then he had discovered the existence of Maggie, the daughter he hadn't known he'd had. And now, *now*, he had found the enchanting and heart-stoppingly beautiful Mrs. Alastair, right next door. A lady who tasted like cool wine on a hot summer day. Who looked at him with eyes he could drown in.

Maggie had begun nudging to life the man buried deep inside the notorious Captain Grayson Finley, terror of the Caribbean, scourge of the Pacific. Mrs. Alastair might just reach in and pull that man out kicking and screaming. But now, more than ever, Grayson had to keep that man buried.

The Majestic was a fine Georgian building standing on Piccadilly across from the entrance to St. James's Street. Once a ducal mansion, it had been converted by a butler into an elegant and expensive hotel. Which fit Henderson. The man kept reams of clothes made by the best Bond Street tailors. No Caribbean or Asian needle worker touched his suits; if he tore one, he laid it aside until he had chance to reach England again. Since James Ardmore was a wanted man in Britain, mostly because of his habit of boarding English naval vessels and releasing American press-ganged sailors, Henderson did not see his native England very often.

Even at sea, Henderson tried to keep his hands soft and his manicure perfect. He had finished with honors at Oxford and taken clerical orders, but had gone to sea, disgruntled, because the living he'd expected had been given to someone else. British naval life apparently had not suited him either, because he'd turned up as part of Ardmore's band several years ago.

Jacobs, who had completed Eton and Oxford and came from a lineage as gentle-born as Grayson's own, was nowhere near the snob that Henderson was. Or pretended to be. Grayson had seen glimpses of the steely mind beneath the Henderson who fussed about his perfectly tied cravat. Ardmore put up with him because Henderson was, in fact, a damned good lieutenant.

The man proved to be in the deserted ground-floor sitting room in a wing chair, absorbed in a newspaper. His mouth sported a blackening bruise, which was probably why he'd chosen to repose in a dim corner of an empty room.

Mrs. Alastair also had a bruise on her mouth, Grayson had seen, just to the right of her lower lip. Henderson's mark. She had faintly pressed her handkerchief to it, as if trying to erase it, as the Duke of St. Clair had led her back into the house. Maggie had been very confused by it all. She'd asked in an anxious voice as she'd leapt from the carriage, "Papa, why did Mr. Henderson do that?"

That was what Grayson had come to find out. Mrs. Alastair's guests had hovered around when the duke had taken her back to the reception room to recover. Grayson hadn't liked the look Lord Hildebrand Caldicott had given her, as if he'd envied Henderson his chance. Grayson hadn't been able to get near Mrs. Alastair himself, not to touch her, or take her hand, or tell her dramatically, "I will avenge you."

"Henderson," he said softly.

The newspaper flew up into the air. Henderson leapt from the chair and came to rest on his feet, his eyes wild. He stared at the two men for a frozen moment, then swiftly put the chair between himself and them. "Finley—"

Grayson approached. Henderson lifted his hands. "Finley," he babbled. "You've already hit me once. Ruined my face. See? I had planned to visit a stable of high-flyers tonight, but now that is all a wash."

"Why?" Jacobs asked. "They'll fuss over you."

Henderson brightened. "Do you think so?"

"Henderson," Grayson said.

Just the one word had magical effect. Henderson paled. "Finley, I swear to you, it was not my idea."

"Oh, I know whose idea it was." His voice remained soft—in a deadly sort of way. "What I want to know is why."

Henderson wet his lips, wincing when he touched a bruise. "Captain Ardmore saw her enter your house last night."

"After he went on his wild rampage?" Jacobs interrupted. "I remember him swearing not to kill us."

"Well, he did not kill you, did he?" Henderson raised his hands again. "And I had nothing to with that raid. I didn't know a blessed thing about it until O'Malley told me this morning."

"Is O'Malley here?" Jacobs asked, looking around as if the small man would come popping out of the woodwork.

Henderson snorted. "O'Malley, here? Do you really think they'd let a dingy little Irishman in this place?"

"I'll tell the dingy little Irishman you remembered him

to me," Grayson said dryly. "Go on with your explanation."

Henderson folded his arms, a self-protective gesture. "Ardmore wondered what she meant to you. And O'Malley speculated that if another gentleman kissed her within your sight, we'd know soon enough."

"I see." Grayson still kept his voice quiet, amazed at his own self-control when he really wanted to twist Henderson in half. "You volunteered?"

Henderson let a wry smile touch his lips. "Not so much volunteered as was pressed into service. But I swear to you, my oath on it, that I had no idea she was a—a lady."

Grayson let his voice grow icy. "Have a care, Henderson. What did you think she was?"

Henderson shrugged nervously. "Well, you know—a merry widow. Or a high-flyer. She ran to you, didn't she? What other kind of woman would?"

Grayson kept a rein on his temper, but he felt his control leaking away. In a moment, he'd leap on Henderson and let the Majestic live with having to scrape lieutenant out of the carpet. "She was saving my life, as a matter of fact."

Henderson nervously adjusted his spectacles. "I promise you, I had no idea until I was right next to her. Until I—" He broke off. "And then I realized that Ardmore had made a grave mistake." He hesitated, his eyes concerned. "Is she all right?"

"What the hell do you think?"

Henderson eyed him uncertainly. Grayson was uncertain himself where his anger came from. Not just anger, but raw, consuming rage. She was not his. She was a lady, one who had never learned to kiss. Her soft, innocent lips had fluttered against his, curious, unpracticed. And yet, she'd been married. Her husband must have been a first-rate idiot.

"Know this, Henderson. If you touch her again—if anyone touches her again—I will consider myself free to avenge her honor. On anyone who dares go near her. Tell Ardmore that this includes him. Do you understand?"

Henderson's face was paper white. "Oh, *I* understand. I cannot guarantee anything about my captain."

Grayson's rage churned. He wanted to slam Henderson to the ground and stamp up and down on him. Rip his suit to ribbons and grind his boot heel into that pristine cravat. All for kissing the pretty lady next door who had looked at him in amazement when he'd suggested she sleep without clothes.

She had done it. He'd seen that in her rosy blush when he'd regarded her in her drawing room. She'd been surrounded by middle-aged ladies watching him with bright birdlike eyes, but he had seen only her. She had slept bare for him, and it had embarrassed her. And excited her.

Which excited him. Damn Henderson. His action had made Grayson realize just what would happen if he followed up on his impulses to make her his. Ardmore would think her fair game. Thus complicating the already complicated mess that was Grayson's life.

Murdering Henderson might make him feel better, but Grayson was not foolish enough to think that Ardmore would not retaliate. Jacobs for Henderson, Oliver for O'Malley, perhaps. The vendetta would never end. And Grayson knew that Henderson was a only pawn in Ardmore's games, as were O'Malley, Maggie, and even Grayson himself.

Containing his murderous impulses, he gave Jacobs a nod, turned his back, and started to go.

Henderson's parting shot followed them. "I think you know, Finley, that you've just told me everything Ardmore hoped to learn."

The callers had gone several hours before. Alexandra retreated to her first-floor sitting room; her emotions jumbled. She was to have attended the theatre with Lady Featherstone that evening, but she had begged off before the lady departed. Lady Featherstone offered to stay, but Alexandra had sent her anxious friend away. Alice would bring her a cup of tea, she said, and all would be well.

Alice *had* brought a cup of tea, one liberally laced with brandy. Alexandra now decided she should not have drunk any. Her head felt light and spun slightly. She stared accusingly at the half-full cup near her elbow at the writing table. Her thoughts whirled and leapt, settling on nothing. She reran the string of events several times, seeing again the bespectacled man reaching for her, the viscount's thunderous look, and Maggie's startled cry, "Mr. Henderson?"

Who was the man and why had he decided to kiss her—like *that*—in the street, in front of the world? It had brought mixed reactions from her guests. Lady Featherstone and Mrs. Waters had been horrified and sympathetic. Mrs. Tetley, on the other hand, had looked annoyed that a handsome young gentleman hadn't rudely kissed *her* on the street. And Lady Henrietta Caldicott tossed her head and humphed and seemed very put out, as if Alexandra had created the entire scene, from the accident to the kiss, on purpose to irritate her.

As for the gentleman— She pressed her hands to her eyes. The duke had been kindness itself.

Alexandra raised her head and drew her list from the writing table's drawer. The duke was the first listed. His father had been an old family friend, and he was the first Alexandra had thought of when the words "suitable second husband" had entered her head. The duke was near to thirty. He had been married young, and his wife and one daughter had sadly passed away about five years previously. His younger brother, a naval man, had died at sea just last year, and the duke was now making noises that he needed to produce an heir. Of course, mamas lined up their daughters instantly, but the duke was being careful to choose.

He had been solicitous this afternoon and she'd seen genuine concern in his eyes. Lord Hildebrand, on the other hand, had looked at her most curiously. His polite veneer had thinned, and she'd seen his gaze fix firmly on her lips and the slight mark the bespectacled gentleman had left. Once or twice, she caught him drawing his tongue across his lips. She hadn't liked that.

She drew out a pen, sharpened its nib, opened her ink pot and dipped the pen into the black liquid. Cross Lord Hildebrand off? She hesitated. His odd glances may have meant nothing. She supposed she should discuss it with Lady Featherstone first.

Each gentleman had symbols beside his name in a code only known to her and Lady Featherstone, denoting the answers to particular questions. She entered a tiny hyphen next to Lord Hildebrand's name, the sign that meant the candidate had displayed a slight deficiency.

Now for the question of Lord Stoke. She had promised Lady Featherstone, before that lady had departed, to list him. He was very unlike the others, and few people in London knew anything about him. Which meant she and Lady Featherstone must double their efforts to discover what they could about him. Although she would decidedly *not* report to Mrs. Waters and Mrs. Tetley.

She let the pen trace the shape of his name, the long curve of the *S*, the sharp points of the *k*, the languid roundness of the *e*. She sat still and looked at the name. The stark word did not fit him well. His other name, Grayson Finley, suited him better. She wrote that next to his title. Her hand trembled a little and she moved it before a blot of ink could mar the page.

She closed her eyes and remembered herself returning to her room the night before. She had stood a long time next to her bed, thinking of his command that she sleep without her clothes. The Alexandra Alastair she knew would never do such a thing. But the Alexandra Alastair she knew would not willingly accept the kisses of a pirate.

She must have stood still for nearly thirty minutes. Alice had long since left her and returned to her own bed. The candles were beginning to gutter. And then, slowly, Alexandra had removed her dressing gown. She'd opened her nightdress, one hook at a time, and slid the cloth, warm from her body, down her legs to the floor. She'd stood a moment longer, letting the summer-night air touch her bare skin, and then she'd climbed slowly into her waiting bed.

She remembered still the cool touch of the sheets on her shoulders and calves and belly. The points of her breasts had tightened, tingling as her breath moved them against the sheets. She had pressed the heel of her hand to the hot, aching place at the join of her thighs, trying to suppress the sensations that lingered there. But she had thought only of *his* palm there, and her hand had come away wet.

The dreams she'd had once she'd finally fallen asleep made her face hot even now. She thought again of herself lying in the bed, her bare hips nestled into the mattress.

Except that this time, a pirate lay next to her, his tanned and calloused hand drifting to her hips.

"Lovely lady," he whispered. "May I taste you?"

"Yes," her imaginary self murmured. She braced herself for his mouth on her skin, but instead he laughed, leaned over, and wrenched a diamond necklace—which her fantasy hastily added—from her throat. "Thank you, dear lady."

Then he kissed her, hard, on the mouth, and rose from the bed, gloriously naked. He sauntered away, his taut backside drawing her gaze, and then dissolved into mist.

She opened her eyes and inhaled a long breath. She dipped the pen in ink again and drew another long curve next to the viscount's name, this one of a question mark. She finished it with a precise dot.

Jeffrey's heavy step boomed on the carpet. "Lord Stoke!" he bellowed.

Alexandra jumped, nearly upsetting the inkpot. "Jeffrey, for heaven's sake, do tap or something before you spring into a room like that."

"Sorry, madam," he mumbled. "Lord Stoke is here."

Chapter Six

He was literally there, striding into the room behind Jeffrey. Alexandra sprang to her feet and stepped hastily in front of the writing table.

The viscount gave Jeffrey a dismissing look. Without waiting for Alexandra's directive, Jeffrey tugged his forelock, turned, and fled.

The viscount closed the double doors behind him. Something he should not do. She should not receive a gentleman alone in her sitting room, doors closed, at six in the evening, especially not one who had kissed her so thoroughly the night before. She started to point at the doors, then thought better of it, and lifted the finger to touch her lips instead.

He came to her, his stride quick. Without asking permission, he cupped her face and tilted her head back. He scrutinized the corner of her mouth, and his frown increased. "Damn."

Involuntarily, Alexandra's tongue touched the slight

bruise the bespectacled man had left there. She'd felt it all afternoon, burning her skin like a shameful brand.

The viscount's eyes were hard as blue steel. "He is sorry for what he did. Believe me, he is sorry."

"You know him?" She remembered Maggie's startled exclamation. She had called the man by name. Not only did the viscount know him, but his daughter did as well. That fact stirred her curiosity.

"If you would like him to apologize," the viscount was saying, "I will arrange it."

Alexandra did not want to see the man in spectacles ever again. "No, that is quite all right."

His fingers were points of warmth on her skin. She closed her eyes to it, then opened them again when he spoke. His words were gruff. "I made him know that he is not to accost you again."

"You did?" she asked weakly.

He traced a circle on the side of her mouth, more warmth. "I made them know that I would protect you. That they should leave you in peace."

Who should? she thought wildly. The other pirates? Certainly the ladies and gentlemen of the *ton* would not leave her in peace if he went about proclaiming she was under his protection. *The most curious thing has happened, Your Grace. The pirate next door has made himself my protector.* The response would be shock, curiosity, delighted horror. Ruin.

She could stop this now with a well-placed reproof. She was the granddaughter of a duke, not a lady who was kissed in the street, then avenged. That sort of thing only happened to courtesans and high-born ladies in the demimonde. She smothered a sigh. What interesting lives they must lead. "My lord, truly, I am not hurt."

His blue gaze fixed on her, darkness flickering behind

it. "I have many enemies, Mrs. Alastair." His voice went low. "I wish you were not so difficult to ignore."

She was melting again. She could not do this every time he so much as looked at her, so much as brushed his fingertips over her skin. Where would she be then? She was a respectable widow of five-and-twenty, not a giddy girl who let her head be turned by any handsome man. "You are not easy to ignore yourself, my lord."

His severe frown softened. "That is gratifying."

His lashes were as golden as his hair. They framed his azure eyes, sweeping down to hide the blue as he studied her face.

He said, "My enemies are deadly, and their games are real." His voice turned grim. "It would be better if you were away from here entirely. Do you have a house outside of London, Mrs. Alastair?"

She nodded hesitantly. "My husband left me a small house near Salisbury."

"You should go there. Now."

His severe look made her heart beat faster. She wondered what was wrong. "I cannot possibly now. But I will leave London at the end of June. To spend time in Kent with the Featherstones, as I do every year."

He shook his head. "No. Go now to your little house near Salisbury. Stay there until midsummer at the very least."

Alexandra hated the Salisbury house. It was a perfect little Georgian gilded cage, built in the last century by some aristocrat for his ladybird, sold when the aristocrat's fortunes declined. Theo had liked to install her there during the summer, encouraging her to have dainty tea parties and walks, while he made the rounds of country houses to sleep with other men's wives.

She wet her lips. "It is impossible until the month's

end. I have my soiree next week, and there is much to do."

He looked at her as if soirees were the most unimportant things in the world. His warm fingers lightly stroked the back of her neck, quite distracting her.

She babbled, "The soiree will be one of the largest of the season's end, before we all disperse to the country. Dukes and duchesses have already accepted. I cannot possibly cancel it."

His caressing fingers threaded her hair, and she began not to care about soirees and dukes and duchesses. "You are invited, of course. And your daughter." She bit her lip. "Though she will have to have a proper gown. I did mean to speak to you about her clothes, if you will forgive the liberty, I mean."

Her face grew hot as she recalled their discussion of liberties the night before.

He must have remembered as well. His eyes began to smolder with heat, as if deep inside a fire had been stoked to a furnace glow. "Tell me, Mrs. Alastair," he said. He smoothed a feather-light curl from her cheek. "Did you do as I requested last night?"

She could not breathe. "I did, as a matter of fact."

The corners of his mouth moved upward. "That pleases me."

"You suggested it."

"And would you do everything I suggest?"

"No, of course not."

His brows lifted, his smile deepening. "Then I wonder why you did."

She swallowed. When she spoke, her voice trembled. "To discover what it would feel like."

No other man on her list was this unnervingly masculine. Even the duke, who was near to the handsomest of her possible suitors, was generally always—well, dressed. The viscount's loose shirt let his heat touch her directly. She smelled the warmth of him, his sharp masculine scent.

"And what did it feel like?" he asked.

Glorious. And hot. And strange. And for some reason it had made her crave his hands on her body.

She drew a breath. "We are supposed to be talking about my soiree."

He leaned to her, his body so close that she could no longer speak. "I do not wish to talk about your soiree." He closed the small space between them and brushed a kiss to the corner of her mouth, right over the bruise.

A strange thing happened. All afternoon she had felt the bespectacled gentleman's brutal and invasive mouth on hers. Even when she'd strived not to think of it, she was still aware of his mark, like a burning imprint, a sore she could not soothe. But at the touch of the viscount's lips the hurt and the embarrassment evaporated. Her skin tingled the slightest bit, and then the tingle slowly dissolved, and with it, the hurt.

His lips brushed her like a warm summer breeze. Gone was the assault of the night before—this kiss was healing, gentle, like petals touching her skin. He raised his head slowly, his breath brushing the place where she now felt only his caress.

All thoughts of soirees, Maggie's clothes, and the unnerving events of the afternoon took flight. Awareness narrowed to his lips on her skin, his body so close to hers, his fingertips playing with the soft curls at the base of her neck.

"I should resist you," he whispered, "my beautiful lady next door. But you soothe my heart."

"Oh," she whispered. Daringly, she lifted on her tiptoes and pressed a light kiss on the scar that pulled his lower lip.

He smiled into the kiss. He leaned to her again and nuzzled her neck. The blazing hot line of his tongue traced itself around the shell of her ear. "Lovely lady," he whispered.

He slid his arms all the way around her and held her close. The enveloping embrace made her start. Then her heart swelled with something almost like pain. She had not been held like this, with warm, strong arms cradling her, in a very long time. She had hugged her mother close for the last time years ago, before her mother's illness had advanced and taken her. So long ago. She had longed for children to hold, as her mother had held her, but she had been denied even that simple joy. She had not realized, until this man had put his arms around her, how much she'd needed, and missed, such contact.

She let her head rest on his strong shoulder. How fine it would be to be this man's lady, to be privileged to rest her head thus whenever she needed to. Beneath her cheek, his heart beat hard and slow. His strong hand slid down her spine, stirring warmth beneath his touch. She closed her eyes.

His stance shifted, and she felt him reach for something behind her. Her eyes snapped open. The list. Sitting on the writing table, face up, easily read by any person who cared to glance there.

She made a wild attempt to swing around and snatch up the paper, but his strong arm barred her way. He lifted it from the table.

Her mouth went dry. Drat, why had she not pushed the list into the drawer when he'd come in? The brandy in the tea seemed to have gone to her head. Her head certainly was spinning now.

He scrutinized the paper, then looked at her as he might look at a sailor who'd tried to tie a square knot and ended up with unraveled string. "What is this?"

"It is—" She broke off. She took a step back and tried to find refuge in haughty indignation. "It is private, my lord."

His eyes had cooled. Indeed, they could have chilled a hot room on a summer afternoon. "My name is on it."

Alexandra struggled to find words. She was very bad at lying. She had tried it a few times in her life, and it had never worked. So much easier and heart-soothing it was to babble honesty. The brandy was not helping her either.

"It is a list—"

"I can see that." The temperature in his eyes lowered a few more degrees. "Of what? It is far too short to be the guests for your confounded soiree."

She lifted her hands to her face. "Oh, my lord, please, you must not tell anyone of this. I would be mortified beyond belief!"

The paper began to crumple in his palm. "My silence depends on what it is."

His look was so stern, so completely out of keeping with the silly list of suitors that her curiosity crept in. "What are you afraid it is?"

That, alas, had been the wrong thing to say. His body curved over hers, menace in every inch of him. "I have been threatened with blackmail by the very best in the world, Mrs. Alastair. Some of them I even let leave with their fingers."

She stared in astonishment. "Blackmail? Why on earth should I blackmail you?"

He held the list before her. "Tell me what this is."

His look was fierce, but the truth was so ridiculous. On the other hand, if she did lie to him—and her honest tongue would trip over a lie—what would he do? Throw her through the window? He was certainly strong enough to do so. Or would he—

Their fingers? She curled hers protectively inward.

She drew a breath. If she said it in a rush, maybe it would not sound so silly. "It is a list of potential husbands. Gentlemen who might be interested in marrying me. And whom I would consider marrying." There. She'd said it.

Chapter Seven

Grayson stared at her. He was so used to deviltry and treachery that for a few moments his mind did not grasp what she had said. "Husbands?"

She flushed from the tip of her chin to the line of her hair. "We have narrowed it to seven—er, eight—and plan to pare the list down further by the end of summer."

Honesty sparkled in her eyes, honesty that went all the way down to her lovely, lovely soul. In Grayson's life, he had met many liars. He could count on one hand those he knew who were honest through and through. Ian O'Malley, for instance, never hid his inner self. Neither did Oliver, though the man was naturally taciturn. And now Mrs. Alastair. Delightful Mrs. Alastair, who had rushed to his rescue.

But why did her list contain *his* name? And the name of the Duke of St. Clair and the name of one of the most fearsome villains who had ever walked the earth? The man was supposed to be dead. Ardmore said he'd killed him, and Ardmore was not an idle boaster. Bloody hell.

He released her. She bit her lip, watching him in trepidation.

A list of gentlemen this beautiful creature would consider marrying, with his name by itself at the very bottom. Grayson Finley, Viscount Stoke. Followed by a query mark.

A part of him wanted to laugh. There was merriment in this situation, a veritable chance to tease and play with his lady. At the same time, indignation rose within him. Could she not see he belonged at the top of the list, and all these other callow gentlemen below him?

He laid the paper on the writing table and bent over it. "What are all these stars and crosses and exclamation marks?"

He became aware of her agitated breath on his cheek, of the shimmering curls that just brushed his shoulder. "Nothing, really. They are not important."

He glanced at her sideways. "I had just decided you were one of the few honest souls I had ever met. Do not try to lie."

Her face went crimson. "They mean certain things we know about each gentlemen."

"We?"

"Lady Featherstone and I. The list was more or less her idea."

He exhaled slowly. He imagined Mrs. Alastair and her cohort sizing up the ranks of London's bachelors and quietly discussing their attributes. He was not certain whether the vision pleased or frightened him. He pointed to the name Sir Henry Berkeley. "Why does he have two stars?"

"Stars mean children," she said. "Sir Henry has two. A boy and a girl, ages five and seven. A ready-made family."

The thought seemed to cheer her. Grayson firmly took up the pen that had rolled to the edge of the table and seated himself. He uncapped the ink pot, dipped the pen, and made a neat star next to his own name. "I have a daughter. Another ready-made family."

She watched him worriedly, still nibbling on her lip. She was most fetching when she did that.

He touched the pen nib to the paper. "What do the exclamation marks mean?"

Her flush deepened. "It means—that the gentleman is particularly handsome."

The duke had an exclamation mark. So did, God help him, Zechariah Burchard. But he would get to that.

He drew a careful exclamation mark on the line next to his name. "I have been told I am handsome."

"Yes, indeed."

He turned his head at the shy words. She was gazing at him from under her lashes, her eyes all sparkling.

Common sense suddenly intruded. What was he doing? He had no business including himself on this list, as lush and inviting as this woman was. He had business to conduct, a king to find, Maggie to provide for, and a devil's bargain to keep. He had no time to flirt and play with a lady he could not possibly have. And yet—

Let me, said his thoughts, *just for a little while.* Let me bask in her elegance, in her innocent chatter of soirees and suitors and gowns. Let me stay in this place so removed from my world, just for a little while.

He smiled up at her, then snaked his arm about her waist and pulled her gently down to sit on his knee. She smelled so good, all cinnamon and honeysuckle. He was right about the opals. They would shine white and soft in her red-brown curls. They had been made for her.

His arousal began to request attention. Her soft little

backside on his knee, her sweet-smelling hair brushing his cheek, and her lovely round breasts so near were stimulating him. He was a man, after all, and she was a most intriguing lady. Nothing else seemed important.

But things were important. He made himself return his attention to the list. "What are minuses?"

She shifted a little, which only brushed her softness closer. "Deficiencies in character," she answered.

"I see. Then I will not have any of those. And the crosses?"

Her fingers twitched. "Merits."

"Hmm." The duke, he noted, damn it, had seven. He touched the pen to them. "Why does St. Clair have so many?"

"Well, he is a duke."

"Well, I am a viscount. Excellent." He gave himself a cross. "What else?"

"He is a family friend—"

"I live next door." Another cross to Lord Stoke.

"I have known him a long while, and he has proved his kindness many times."

Grayson contained the snarl that built inside him and continued to make crosses by his own name until he came to the edge of the paper. "I seem to have many merits," he said.

She did not answer. He looked up. She was studying him, her lips pursed, inviting him, though she did not know it, to kiss her. And kiss her.

When she spoke, her voice was very soft. "Are you proposing to me, Lord Stoke?"

He quirked his brow. "Proposing?"

"You are claiming that you are the best candidate on the list. Does that mean you wish to marry me?" Her eyes became quiet, and realms of emotion he'd not seen there before suddenly opened to him. "Or are you mocking me?"

He studied her cool brown-green scrutiny. Somewhere deep inside this woman lay hurt. Grayson had led a brutal existence among brutal people. But that meant only that he had learned to drill down through many layers to find the truth of a person. With Mrs. Alastair, he did not have far to go to find sorrow. His far neighbor, a baronet who obviously loved gossip, had told him that Alexandra's first husband had been little short of cruel. Theo Alastair had dressed Alexandra in silks and jewels and let her adorn polite company while he rampaged through the town making the beast with two backs with everyone from penny prostitutes to the wives of prominent gentlemen. Mr. Alastair had kept several mistresses and did not much care who knew. Most embarrassing for the poor gel, the elderly baronet had explained. Relief when he died, don't you know.

This list meant she was trying to avoid an embarrassing mistake the second time.

He looked into her clear, waiting eyes. "I regret—" he began slowly. He realized, no matter what his arousal was screaming, that he did regret it. Profusely. Why now? *Why did I have to find her now?* "That I cannot marry."

The open spaces inside her suddenly shut with a snap. She closed her mouth, firmed her lips, and seemed to move ten feet away, even though she remained most snugly on his lap. "Then please leave my list alone."

She reached out to draw it away from him. He laid his own, stronger, hand on its edge. "Wait." He lifted the pen and drew a heavy line through the name Zechariah Burchard.

"What are you doing?"

"Do you know Mr. Burchard well?"

"Of course. He is a friend of Lord and Lady Featherstone." She hesitated. "Although, I suppose he is only an acquaintance, really. They have not known him long. But he is a polite gentleman and very forthcoming, and we know absolutely nothing against him."

He let his voice go hard and matter-of-fact. "Zechariah Burchard is a pirate. He deals in any cargo, including slaves, and he will sink all who get in his way—naval frigates, other pirates, pirate hunters. What he does to those he captures from the merchantmen is unspeakable. And he has a bad habit of coming back from the dead."

She blinked. "What on earth does that mean?"

"His death has been rumored at least three times. Each time, he disappears for a while, then appears again. The last time I saw him, James Ardmore had set him on fire."

Her eyes widened. "Set his ship on fire?"

"Set *him* on fire. He got tangled in a piece of his own burning rigging, and then Ardmore shot him. End of Burchard. And now he turns up on your list of eligible suitors."

She looked at the list as if she'd never seen it before. "You must be mistaken. It cannot possibly be the same Zechariah Burchard."

"When did you first meet him?"

"At the beginning of the season."

"Ardmore killed him last November. Plenty of time for him to lay low, recover—however he did it—and take up residence in Mayfair." His eyes narrowed. If anyone were a candidate for making off with a French king, it was Burchard. Why the devil he'd want to, Grayson had no idea, but strange occurrences and Burchard often went together.

This meant that Grayson would have to—damn it—talk to Ardmore. Ardmore and his pirate hunters had been stalking Burchard for years. Grayson would have to break it to him that he'd missed again. He also did not in the least like that Burchard was walking around Mayfair—*meeting with Mrs. Alastair*. Damn, damn, damn.

He did not want to have to search for Burchard and send him either to the grave or to the other side of the world—as far away from his lady as possible—on top of everything else. He had to help the Admiralty hunt a missing French king, and so far, his men had turned up nothing. He had to make certain that Maggie would get as much unentailed money and property as he could possibly leave to her before Ardmore became impatient and returned to his all-out war against Grayson.

He did not want to deal with Burchard and Ardmore and the French king. He wanted to spend time in bed with Mrs. Alastair. She was lonely, she was hungry, and oh, God, he'd never met anyone like her. She had slept naked for him. Inconvenient that he had not been with her at the time, but she had done it. For him. Yes, snuggling under the sheets with this lady for the rest of June appealed to him. Everyone else could go to hell.

Except Maggie, of course. He must keep his senses and keep his head for Maggie.

The vivid vision of the day he had found her suddenly came to him. He remembered the damp Jamaican heat, the slim bones of Sara's wasted hand, and his utter confusion when she'd led him through the house of the missionary couple to a wilted back garden. He had not seen Sara in twelve years, ever since she had deserted him in a port near Siam. How she'd turned up in Jamaica he did not know, but he'd known from the shadow on her face that she was dying. "Her father," Sara had announced to the shocked Methodist man and his wife as she'd paraded Grayson past them. "I bring him."

And there, digging in the dirt with a garden trowel, dressed in a heavy wool skirt and square cotton blouse, had crouched his daughter, Maggie. He remembered with clairty the shock that had coursed through him when she'd glanced up. He'd seen his own mother's eyes staring back at him, the eyes of the woman he had not been able to save from murder. He remembered how he had sunk to his knees, stunned beyond imagining, remembered the hunger in his heart as he looked into her face and had seen his past, his present, and his redemption.

All of this, every single event that had happened since he'd found his beautiful child, he had begun himself, long, long ago when he had decided to accept the advances of his best friend's lady.

A man could be so innocently stupid at twenty-two.

He ever so gently slid Alexandra from his lap. She landed on her feet looking bewildered.

Grayson rose. "Cross him from the list and tell your friends to cut the acquaintance."

Her brow puckered, her lips parted, and ringlets straggled to her flushed face.

Yes, in bed, with her, for the next three weeks.

He decided to leave before he bore her to the floor and shocked her servants silly. Before he ceased caring what the servants thought and simply made her his own.

He put his finger under her chin. "Will you sleep bare for me again tonight?" He found himself unable to keep the longing from his voice.

Her eyes rounded. Outrage? Or fascination? "Sir, you presume."

He really ought to tell her he liked it when she went all haughty. It made him want to erase her irritated expression with a long, dark hour of kisses. He had to satisfy himself now with giving her a wicked smile. "If you change your mind, tap on the wall. To let me know."

She stepped back, blushing hotly. He wanted to laugh. Did she know how beautiful she was, all flustered and bothered like that? If those gentlemen on that list even suspected she was considering them, they would roll over like tame puppies and wave their feet in the air. She would only have to place her hand on the arm of the one she wanted and they'd melt to her.

And then he'd have to break the man's neck. His arousal demanded he take immediate action, but he willed it to silence. He needed to find an icy waterfall somewhere to calm him down.

He satisfied himself by letting his gaze rove once over her delicious body. Then he grinned at her confusion and left her.

Alexandra ran the brush through Maggie's tangled curls, gently sorting them. The girl sat at Alexandra's dressing table, a smock covering her fine new white gown. Alexandra had already dressed in a slip of creamy yellow silk covered by a gown of sheer silver-gray. The skirt shimmered in a pleasing way whenever she moved. Her curls had been caught in a loose knot and twined with pale flowers. A glittering diamond necklace reposed on her breast—ready for a pirate to steal.

It had been nearly a week since the viscount had discovered the list in her sitting room and had teased her with it. She'd been idiotically pleased at first that he had wanted to put himself high on it, and romantic enough to think he'd meant it. And then when she'd blurted her question, he'd turned to her, his eyes subdued, and said, "I regret—"

In other words, no, you silly woman. I am a pirate, I had an exotic island woman as a wife—what would I want with a widow who needs to make a list of stodgy gentlemen so that she can choose her next dull and stay-at-home husband?

And his warning about Mr. Burchard had been most bizarre. Was the story true, or had he been fabricating it to play with her a little more? She had casually dropped the name in conversation with Maggie, but Maggie had never heard of the man.

She had intended, before the viscount had found the list, to have a serious discussion with him about Maggie, and her clothes and education. But after he'd teased her so, then made his second brazen suggestion that she sleep without clothes, she'd not found the courage to approach him.

Of course, that night, she had once again removed her nightrail after Alice had departed and climbed between the cool sheets in her skin. And every night since. She had learned to keep her dressing gown on the bed so that she might cover herself before Alice entered in the morning. Each night she'd chide herself for being so wicked, but then she would remember the heat in the viscount's blue eyes when he'd made the request, the sinful smile he'd sent her way, and she'd be sliding the nightrail from her body before she could stop herself.

Her nightly debate made it more difficult than ever to speak to him about Maggie. Finally she'd written a short note and had Jeffrey deliver it. She first apologized for her liberty of writing him and then for her audacity in suggesting she assist with Maggie. Then she stated that she would be happy to take Maggie shopping for new clothes and that she had a lady in mind who would suit as Maggie's governess.

It had taken her three hours and several drafts to compose the letter. At last as satisfied as she was going to be, she had signed and sealed it and Jeffrey had delivered it.

Ten minutes later had come his reply, scrawled across the back of her painstaking letter: "Do what you like."

She'd stared at the scribbled words for a long time, wondering what they really meant. Was he angry and exasperated and resented her intrusion, or did he simply not care?

She never saw him in the intervening week to ask. She no longer met him going out while she was coming in, but the Duke of St. Clair had been to visit him three times. The duke, she knew, worked closely with the Admiralty. She remembered the viscount's explanation, heard through the window, that the Admiralty wanted his help in finding the missing Louis of France. Her curiosity chafed her, but she had no one to satisfy it.

Maggie's hair was not completely dark, Alexandra observed as she brushed it. Streaks of lighter brown mixed with the black, the legacy of a golden-haired man.

Maggie watched her in the mirror. "My papa thinks you are stunningly beautiful," she observed.

Alexandra jumped slightly, but covered the movement by setting down the brush and picking up a ribbon. "That is very flattering, Maggie," she said when she could control her voice, "but you cannot know that."

"He said, 'Mrs. Alastair is stunningly beautiful.' " Maggie toyed with the brush. "He told me to ask you if you liked emeralds."

"Why on earth does he want to know that?"

"He must want to give you some. He has boxes of jewels. He says they are my legacy, but I do not mind sharing them with you."

Alexandra remembered Mrs. Waters proclaiming that the viscount's house was filled with jewels and silks and exotic things. Maggie and Mr. Oliver were the most exotic things she'd ever seen there, not to mention the viscount himself.

She hastily began winding the ribbon through Maggie's curls. "I do not need any emeralds."

Her eyes were ingenuous. "He wants to give them to you. He usually does what he wants."

"Yes, I'd noticed that."

Maggie was silent a moment, letting Alexandra work. The little girl much intrigued her and continued to the more Alexandra got to know her. She was like her father in many ways, possessing a casual and somewhat careless cheerfulness that was very charming. But Maggie was not a foolish child. She had wells of intelligence in her eyes that fixed with uncanny perception on her listener just before she proclaimed some piece of profound wisdom.

"The missionaries in Jamaica did not want Papa to take me," she said now. "But he did anyway."

Her voice was a monotone, and Alexandra wondered what story the flat words masked. "Did your mama want that too?" she asked, trying not to sound too curious.

Maggie shrugged. "I do not think Mama cared. She often left me with missionaries in whatever place we were and then didn't come back for a long time. She was from Tahiti, and she always tried to go back there, but she mostly just roamed about Jamaica and Martinique. I was happy when Papa came to fetch me. I did not like the missionaries."

Alexandra's heart wrenched. The cry reached her, though Maggie would never say it: *I was unwanted.*

She fell silent while the incredibleness of this whirled in her mind. How could no one want a child? Especially one as lovely and vivacious as Maggie? Her own little son, who had lived but a day, had torn her heart out with his leaving. And here was this child for the taking, and no one had wanted her. The world was a most unbelievable place.

She pulled herself back to the present. Mrs. Fairchild, Alexandra's governess, had always admonished Alexandra that it was wrong to say a hurtful word against anyone, as much as one wanted to. "The missionaries were kind to take you in," she suggested.

Maggie gave Alexandra the pitying look of a twelve-year-old who knows what is what in the world. "The ones in Jamaica always told me how unfortunate I was because my mama and papa were bad people. But my papa was married to my mama. She had a license. She was very proud of it. But they said I should tremble before God and work very hard, because I was the devil's child."

Outrage tumbled to Alexandra's lips. Mrs. Fairchild's lessons flew out the window. "Well of all the—"

She closed her mouth with a snap and picked up her brush again. She silently raged at anyone who could tell this beautiful child she was evil. She raged further at a mother who had left her about all over the world like an unwanted parcel. What had the woman been thinking of?

She firmed her lips and kept her thoughts to herself.

"It's all right," Maggie said, catching her glance. "Papa shouted at them. He said if I was the devil's child, then that meant he was the devil, come to get them. That frightened them a lot." She gave a satisfied smile that exactly mirrored the wicked grin of her father.

Alexandra could imagine the missionary couple, used to a life of severe quiet and obedience, suddenly confronted with a huge, hard-faced pirate with blazing blue eyes and a voice that could drown thunder. She imagined them cowering against the wall while he raged at them. A secret, guilty pleasure touched her.

"Did your mama tell you about your papa when you were young?" Alexandra asked curiously.

"Oh yes. She talked about him a great deal. She said he was tall and had yellow hair and blue eyes. I did not believe her. But when I saw him, I knew he was my papa. I knew it right away. He had a lot of whiskers on his face, but he shaved them off, right after. He said he was sorry he had not come sooner, but he hadn't known about me. Mama was happy that he came to get me. She died just after that."

Alexandra's throat caught. Sincerity and belief shone in Maggie's eyes. Grayson—the *viscount*—must have seemed to her like a hero from a fairy tale, charging in to rescue her from a dark and cold dungeon. Alexandra suddenly wondered what it would be like if such a man would rescue *her*. He would dash in, all handsome, with his shirt open to his waist, slay her enemies, slash the chains from her wrists, catch her into his arms, and sweep her away.

Which was ridiculous. This was Mayfair, and she had no enemies. Unless you could count Theo, but he had not really been an enemy. Just a foolish man who had made her very, very unhappy. There were no dungeons in Mayfair, no chains, no dark enemies. And no pirates. She sighed.

She finished Maggie's hair, and they took Alexandra's carriage all the way to Covent Garden to the theatre. Alexandra had no way of knowing that before she returned again, she *would* confront dangers that even Mayfair could not hide, see for herself a pirate ship, and discover just how much the viscount's enemies hated him.

Chapter Eight

Grayson also was dressing to go out.

"—!" The word was sliced off in his throat.

"Almost finished, sir," Jacobs assured him. The man ceased tying whatever complicated knot he was tying and finally let Grayson lower his head.

Grayson glared at him. "Must you throttle me?"

Jacobs shrugged in his bland, unoffended manner. "It's a cravat, sir. Has to be done."

"The last time I felt this strangled, Ardmore was trying to hang me. Bloody useless piece of —"

Jacobs—his first lieutenant, second in command on board the *Majesty*, and the man he trusted most, despite his relative youth—showed no sympathy. "Fashion, sir. You have to dress to go to a club. Didn't you wear neck cloths when you were a lad?"

"That was twenty-three years ago."

Jacobs gathered up the remaining linens and tossed them to Oliver, who had watched the whole proceeding with enigmatic dark eyes. Grayson irritably settled the knot across his throat. Jacobs, who had grown up in a fashionable family, had been given the task of making Grayson look like a Mayfair gentleman. Thank God he would not have to do this very long.

"St. Clair had better appreciate this," he said darkly.

The Duke of St. Clair had proposed they meet at White's, his club, which would soon be Grayson's. The duke had put Grayson's name forward, and all that remained was the vote. The old viscount had been a member; the new would likely slide in without much trouble, or so St. Clair had said. What St. Clair really wanted tonight was to discuss the search for the French king. Letters of marque had been drawn up, he'd said, retroactively, to condone any and all piratical activity on Grayson's part, but the Admiralty would only grant them when Grayson finished his assigned task. If he did not, Grayson would dangle from a rope, and that would be the end of the viscounts Stoke. St. Clair had never made clear whether Grayson must present the king on a platter or only point them in the right direction. Grayson cynically surmised that the Admiralty would decide what was enough only after he had done it.

He had agreed to meet St. Clair, although he had not much to report. He'd spread a network over the river towns that marched toward the Channel: Greenwich, Blackwall, Gravesend. He had learned some interesting gossip; for instance, he knew that a dock master in Blackwall would take rum, tobacco, slaves, and strangely, pins, for bribes, and that the mistress of the Lord Chancellor was pregnant, probably not with his child. But nothing about the French king. If he were being transported down the Thames, Grayson had not yet found any evidence of it.

But the monarch also had not turned up in France.

St. Clair had spies there as well, and there had been no ransom demands for the corpulent king, nor any gleeful proclamations from the republic that another Bourbon king had been beheaded. Grayson understood from St. Clair that the English were more or less allowing Louis of France and his supporters to remain here in reserve for the day that Napoleon was toppled. But Napoleon had dug himself in pretty deep, and Grayson did not anticipate that date anytime soon.

It was strange to view these political battles from the other side of the water. The war with Napoleon had made the English naval vessels in the Caribbean jittery, not to mention a bloody nuisance. They would fire on and board almost any ship they came across, and press-ganging had reached an astronomical level. He and Jacobs had twice been accosted in taverns by English sailors looking to fill more ranks. He and Jacobs had explained, firmly, that they were busy.

American privateers strolling up and down the waters pounced on ships left alone by the British navy, making things even more dicey. Then there were the pirates. And then there was Ardmore.

All in all, striding through glittering Mayfair searching for a missing king was a walk in the park compared to slipping through all those blockades and dodging the madman, James Ardmore. And, in the end, Grayson had not dodged fast enough. But escaping Ardmore would have entailed abandoning Maggie, and that Grayson knew he would never be able to do.

He remembered with hot clarity the hard planking of Ardmore's deck beneath his knees, the rope burning his neck, the cold sword at his throat. His wrists had been raw with his bonds, his torso bruised where Ardmore and his lieutenants had beaten him. "Why should I not kill you, Finley?" Ardmore had sneered. "Give me a reason not to hang you from the highest yardarm." Grayson remembered his own voice, cracked and desperate, answering, "Because my daughter would miss me."

Jacobs smoothed the black coat over Grayson's broad shoulders, jerking him back to the present.

"Did they get off to the theatre?" he asked.

"They did, Captain. In Mrs. Alastair's carriage. Fine team."

Grayson narrowed his eyes. "With the guard?"

"Priestly is on it, sir."

"Good."

He imagined Mrs. Alastair's pretty eyes going all furious when she discovered that he'd sent along one of his men to keep watch over her, but damned if he was going to let her wander about with his daughter when Burchard was loose.

He had tracked the supposedly dead pirate to lodgings in St. James's, a house of rooms for respectable and slightly wealthy gentlemen. He'd assigned another of his officers the duty of wandering about coffee houses in the area and keeping a surreptitious eye on the lodgings. Grayson had not actually seen Burchard himself, but every instinct told him it was the same man, despite the incongruities.

A rumble of carriage wheels sounded in the street outside, and then the sound of someone thumping on his front door. Grayson moved to the front room and peered out the window. It was not the carriage he had hired, or Ian O'Malley returning. It was a hired hack, however, and the fellow who'd thumped the door now turned back and handed a woman out of the carriage.

"Damn, I forgot about the governess."

"Want me to take care of her, sir?" Jacobs asked, a

bland expression on his face. What he meant was, he knew what to do with servants of the governess' class while Grayson only knew how to command pirates. Grayson scowled. "I will talk to her. She *is* here to teach my daughter."

Oliver had already lumbered down the front stairs to open the door. Grayson strode after him, and Jacobs, with a slight smirk on his face, brought up the rear.

Low, feminine tones met his ear as he stepped off the last stair. Oliver led a woman into the dimly lit hall and went past her to fetch her cases. She began to remove her gloves, and looked up. "Your lordship? I am Mrs. Fairchild. Mrs. Alastair, sent me."

Grayson stopped, his stride arrested. Good lord, *she* had been Alexandra's governess? Alexandra had explained in her coldly polite letter that the woman had taught her and would be excellent for Maggie. Grayson had expected Mrs. Fairchild to be gray, stout, and grandmotherly. What he saw was a woman of about his own age, black-haired with a sculpted face and eyes as dark as midnight. Red lips curved into a polite smile, and sable lashes lowered under his scrutiny.

The rest of her could have made even a man of the most monkish habits go hard in a trice. Her gown was a dull gray, governesslike, but it outlined a body of lush curves, and draped limbs that were long and shapely.

His daughter's governess. The woman who had made Alexandra Alastair what she was today. This could prove interesting.

Grayson pasted on a smile and held out his hand. "Mrs. Fairchild."

She took it, exuding politeness. She looked past him and suddenly went white to the lips.

Grayson studied her, puzzled. The woman had stopped

breathing. She was gazing at something behind him, her eyes wide with shock. He disengaged his hand from hers and turned.

She was looking at Jacobs. He stood three steps up the stairs, and he too had frozen in place, his hand locked around the banister. His face had gone paper white.

Grayson folded his arms and leaned against the newel post. Neither of them moved, not even when Oliver came trundling past with the bags and began climbing the stairs.

Grayson said, "Do you two know each other?"

Jacobs's head snapped up. His face flooded with color and his Adam's apple bobbed with a hard swallow. "Uh, no, sir. Of course not." He looked away.

A blatant lie. Mrs. Fairchild had obviously recognized Jacobs as well. This was becoming more interesting by the minute.

Grayson unfolded himself. "Maggie is at the theatre with Mrs. Alastair tonight, Mrs. Fairchild. You can spend the time unpacking and getting settled. I am going out. If you want tea or anything, ring Oliver."

"Of course, my lord." Her voice was strangled and breathy.

"Good. I will speak to you tomorrow. Good evening, Mrs. Fairchild."

A spark of misery and fear hovered deep in her dark, lovely eyes. Grayson longed to know what this was all about, but he had an appointment with St. Clair and the fashionable dandies of Mayfair. He'd have to pry into the private lives of his lieutenant and his daughter's governess later. He snatched up his hat and went out.

A light comedy was playing when Alexandra arrived with Maggie in tow, all about two sisters, one good, one bad, and their bewildered and countrified parents. The good sister ultimately landed the noble aristocrat's love, plus his hand in marriage, while the bad sister was disgraced. She wept and begged pardon of her stricken parents at the end, and the family was reconciled. Maggie watched this all with great interest.

Of course, much of the play was drowned out by the audience who gossiped, shouted to each other, or called out to the players on stage. A group of young men evidently preferred the wicked sister and kept suggesting that she seduce the noble aristocrat and run away with him. That and to "show us your fine ankles, Nellie."

Lord and Lady Featherstone had joined them in the box, which was comfortably settled with armchairs and a low table on which to place reticules, fans, and cups of tea. Lord Featherstone sipped tea and watched the play with furrowed brows. From time to time, Alexandra caught him giving Lady Featherstone an affectionate glance, and once, under cover of dim lighting, holding her hand. It gave Alexandra a lonely feeling.

After the first offering, the stage lit up again and a few acrobats danced on and commenced tumbling. Maggie turned to Alexandra, her eyes glowing. "The missionaries said all theatre was wicked. But it does not seem wicked."

Lord Featherstone rolled his eyes. "Wesleyans."

Maggie rested her chin on her hand. "But then, I am wicked, so maybe I do not notice."

Alexandra's earlier anger resurfaced. "Maggie, you are *not* wicked."

The Featherstones exchanged a glance. "Indeed not," Lord Featherstone said.

Maggie did not argue. She went on watching the dancing. She had Alexandra's lorgnette in her hand and raised it to her eyes to gaze about the theatre.

Lord Featherstone left the box to pay a visit to some acquaintance, and when he returned, he had a gentleman with him. Alexandra's heart turned over. He'd brought back Mr. Burchard, the one the viscount had so firmly crossed off her list. She had not told Lady Featherstone about this oddity, not knowing what to make of it herself.

But this man could not be the horrible villain Grayson claimed he was. Grayson *must* be talking about a different Zechariah Burchard. This Mr. Burchard was nearing forty, slightly gray at the temples, lean, and tall, though nowhere near as tall as Grayson. He had dark eyes that observed his surroundings quietly, and fine manners. Lady Featherstone had found nothing objectionable about him, though she was waiting on some inquiries she had made about his cousins who apparently lived in Yorkshire.

He bowed to Alexandra and Lady Featherstone, gave Maggie a curious glance, and accepted a chair. Lord Featherstone introduced Maggie as Miss Finley, Viscount Stoke's daughter.

Did Mr. Burchard start at the name, or did Alexandra imagine it?

Conversation began. Mr. Burchard was deferential to Lady Featherstone and attentive to Alexandra without being flirtatious. Maggie had returned her attention to the rest of theatre, and Mr. Burchard did not seem overly interested in her.

Mr. Burchard's unlined face bore no evil taint, and his eyes remained neutral. Too neutral perhaps? Alexandra shook herself. Imagination. There must be more than one Zechariah Burchard in the world.

Lord Featherstone did not say much, probably because Lady Featherstone had gone into full interview mode. She had pried from Mr. Burchard that he had no brothers or sisters, and that his father had left him a house near Scarborough that he planned to open later that year, and that he would be sending invitations for the shooting season.

Lady Featherstone gave Alexandra a look that said she was passing the token to her.

Alexandra touched her tongue to her upper lip and drew on her courage. "Uh—Mr. Burchard. Have you ever been to sea?"

She did not imagine his start that time. His backside left the seat and he bumped back down. But then, it had been a most unusual question. Lady Featherstone gave Alexandra an odd stare.

"To sea?" Burchard's mouth opened and closed a few times.

Lord Featherstone stepped into the awkward gap. "I am often *at* sea," he said, "when seeing the fripperies that are supposed to be fashion nowadays."

Lady Featherstone laughed appropriately, and Alexandra pretended to smile. Lady Featherstone shot her an annoyed look, but took her cue from her husband. The moment smoothed over.

Maggie leaned over the balcony. "Oh look," she cried. "There is Mr. Henderson!"

Alexandra glanced quickly to where she pointed. Indeed, she saw the blond man in spectacles who had so impudently assaulted her the week before. Her heart thumped.

Lady Featherstone had not actually observed the gentleman's rude kiss before Alexandra's house, and Alexandra had not explained to her what she'd learned from Grayson about the incident. Lady Featherstone went on chatting, sensing nothing amiss.

But Mr. Burchard's reaction was unmistakable. His face drained of color, then became a sickly green. He looked at Alexandra and the light in his eyes changed from neutral to alarmed to wary. He knew that she knew that she was sharing her box with a villainous pirate, one who was supposed to have died a horrible and fiery death several months before. Oh, dear heavens.

Chapter Nine

Vanessa Fairchild thought, *If I stay in this room all night and do not come out until I can leave in the morning, I will be all right.* She shivered and hugged herself. The air wafting through the open window held the warmth of summer, but she could not seem to rid herself of chill.

She knew the cold had nothing to do with the temperature out of doors. As soon as she'd seen Robert Jacobs on the stairs, the bottom had dropped out of her snug little world. If only Alexandra had mentioned that Robert lived in the viscount's house, Vanessa would never, never have left Oxfordshire.

But why should Alexandra mention him? Vanessa was to be governess to Viscount Stoke's child, and Mr. Jacobs had nothing to do with that. And Alexandra could not have known the incident between her former governess and Robert Jacobs five years before.

She sipped the cold tea at her side. The dark-skinned man, Mr. Oliver, had brought it for her hours ago, after he had left her here to unpack. Her cases, untouched, still stood in the corner by the old fashioned square-posted bed. To cover her confusion, she had asked Mr. Oliver about himself. The taciturn man had unbent enough to tell her that his mother had been a slave and his father a Spaniard on Santo Domingo. He had known the viscount for nineteen years. Mr. Jacobs had joined them five years ago.

Five years. Right after— What was he doing here? Was he the viscount's secretary? That would make sense; he had taken honors at Oxford. But Mr. Oliver would answer no more questions and had left her to unpack. The tea had long since chilled, but Vanessa would not ring for more.

Someone tapped softly on the door. Her hands clenched, but she forced them to relax. Perhaps Mr. Oliver had decided to bring her more refreshment of his own accord.

"Yes?" she called softly.

The door opened and Robert Jacobs walked in.

She stumbled up from her chair. They stared at each other, unspeaking. Damn him, he had grown even more handsome than she remembered. His hair was as dark, his eyes as chocolate brown, his form as tall and broad. No, broader. He'd filled out, muscle and bone, into a hard-chested, well-framed, delicious picture of masculinity.

She drew a shaking breath. "In the morning, I will explain to the viscount that I cannot stay."

He walked firmly into the room. "Was seeing me again that repulsive to you?"

She blinked. "Repulsive? You?" She wanted to lie and tell him that indeed she had been most annoyed to find him here. Instead, she blurted, "You are just as beautiful as you ever were." *When I was thirty and you were twenty.*

And again now that we are each five years older.

Red stained his cheeks. "As I recall, you could not fly fast enough from that carriage the last time I saw you. Must have been repulsive, a young man declaring himself, and you the respectable wife of an Oxford *don*."

Her breath came in small, dry gasps. After all these years, he still could quell her with one glance of his dark eyes. After all this time, when things should be over and done between them, she still could not face him without trembling. "I was not— But I did not know what to say to you. It was so impossible."

"It was possible until one of us spoke."

She lifted her hands in a supplicating gesture. "No, it was impossible. There would have been disgrace for you, ruin for me."

His lips were white. "And now?"

"Now? There is nothing, now. I must make my way in the world. I have chosen to become a governess, as I was before."

"Your husband left you destitute?"

She twisted her lips into a wry smile. "He had nothing to leave. A tiny income, which does little more than buy my bread."

"Whereas I am heir to a fortune."

Vanessa's heart constricted. She gazed at him hungrily. He had been the only man in her entire life—so ironic, that—who had ever made her feel complete, whole, loved. "What are you saying I ought to have done?"

He regarded her in silence. Five years ago, they'd had no choices. She saw now that their choices were just as narrow. There was longing, wanting, and great regret, but no solutions.

"The viscount deserves to know the truth," she said.

Robert finally bestirred himself. "I will tell him."

"I will. I should not have come in the first place."

His hands clenched at his sides. "No. Captain Finley is not the usual sort of employer. I will explain things to him."

She hesitated, puzzled. "Captain Finley?"

"I mean Lord Stoke. He used to be Captain Finley."

"I see." She did not, but she did not pursue it. The viscount certainly did not look like any other lord she had encountered in her career as a governess or as a don's wife. He looked as though he spent most of his life out-doors. He was much too rugged—that was a good word, rugged—for a fine Mayfair mansion.

Alexandra had not mentioned that he'd been a sea captain, or whatever kind of captain he had been. In her letter she'd referred to him as "the viscount," and all men-tions of him had been oblique at best. But he was un-questionably handsome and had a certain charm. Odd that Alexandra had deliberately not said much about him. Most unlike the girl. Hmm.

"I will speak to him," Robert repeated.

He looked at her for a long time, a scrutinizing, as-sessing look that did not hint of the desire or hunger she felt within herself. But, of course, he was a virile young man, and to the young, five years was a lifetime.

At last he turned from her and left without saying good-night. Vanessa sank her face in her hands and knew she'd never be warm again.

Maggie waved frantically at the blond man beneath their box. "Mr. Henderson!"

Lady Featherstone's cosmetic-darkened eyebrows climbed to her hairline. "Maggie. A young lady does not wave and shout at a gentleman in the theatre."

"I'm not a young lady, yet," Maggie returned. "The governess does not come 'til tomorrow."

"Even so."

Alexandra burst out, her heart hammering hard, "She is right, Maggie. You must sit quietly."

If Maggie did not shout again, perhaps the blond man would not spot them. Alexandra had no desire to see him face to face, and by Mr. Burchard's expression, that gentleman did not wish to either. Fervently.

But alas, alas, the bespectacled man turned, glanced about in a bewildered manner, then tilted his head and gazed unerringly through his spectacles at Maggie, who was still waving her arms. The gleam of spectacles also came to rest on Alexandra. After a moment, he raised a gloved hand in acknowledgment.

Mr. Burchard rose hastily. "Forgive me, your lordship, your ladyship, Mrs.—ah. I must be going."

Lord Featherstone's brows rose in amazement. "Good heavens, is the building on fire?"

"No, I—ah—"

He was hampered from making a quick and discreet exit by the chairs. Alexandra had given Lady Featherstone the best seat in the box, and Mr. Burchard had been placed between her and Alexandra. So he had to stumble past Alexandra's chair, Lord Featherstone's, and Maggie's.

As he pushed past Alexandra, she looked straight into his eyes. She saw a flicker of anger there, rage so black it had taken a life of its own. It drove the man; the man did not control it.

He did not bother to regulate his gaze, he simply pushed past, and Alexandra stumbled back. Below them, Mr. Henderson's astonished stare landed on Mr. Burchard.

His jaw dropped, and *his* face whitened. He gaped for

one moment as if gazing upon the dead come back to life, then snapped around. His ringing words could be heard all through the theatre, even over the din. "Bloody hell. O'Malley!"

Lord Featherstone, spluttering "see here," tried to hold Mr. Burchard back. The man easily threw him aside and sprinted away. The door of the box banged after him and then the bewildered footman outside closed it.

"Well," Lady Featherstone said, settling herself with a thump. "He is definitely *off* the list."

Mr. Henderson waited for them in the lobby below. Or at least Maggie seemed to assume he was. The girl saw him, dropped Alexandra's hand, and darted through the crowd to greet him. Alexandra, her heart thumping, followed the little girl. The small-statured Irishman she'd observed coming and going from the viscount's house on occasion had joined them by the time she reached Maggie.

Maggie wrung Mr. Henderson's hand then turned and threw her arms about the Irishman's middle. "Mr. O'Malley. Why haven't you been to the house of late? I long to play dice, and Mr. Jacobs is not as good as you."

The man returned the hug, a wide grin breaking his leathery face. "Well then, you can always win more money from him, can't you, lass?"

She shot him a wicked smile, reminiscent of her father's. "He's already lost ten guineas to me."

"There you are, then."

"Maggie," Alexandra said sharply. Maggie looked at her, innocently inquiring. Mr. Henderson met Alexandra's gaze, and his cheeks went scarlet.

Maggie babbled, oblivious. "Mrs. Alastair, these are two of my greatest friends, Mr. O'Malley and Mr. Henderson. We rode on the ship with them from Jamaica. This is my new friend, Mrs. Alastair. Is she not beautiful?"

Mr. O'Malley ran an appreciative gaze over Alexandra. His dark eyes twinkled. "Pleased to meet you, madam, that I am."

Mr. Henderson stood as one carved in stone. Maggie rattled on, "Did you catch Mr. Burchard? You were running after him, weren't you? When he saw you, he looked scared enough to piss."

A few matronly stares swiveled to Maggie. Alexandra's face went hot.

"No, the bastard got away," O'Malley said. More matrons gasped. Two raised their lorgnettes. "But we'll catch him. Maggie, lass, let me take you to your carriage. I'll ride home with you."

"There is no need," Alexandra tried. Lord Featherstone had gone out to call her carriage and Lady Featherstone was chatting to some acquaintance on the other side of the room. What they'd think of this Irishman and his language, not to mention Maggie's language, she shuddered to think. She would have to have a talk with Grayson—the *viscount*—on the effect of rough men on his daughter.

Mr. O'Malley looked grave. "There is need. Burchard's running amok out there, and damned if I'm letting him near Maggie. I'll get her to your carriage. You stay here and talk to Henderson. He's dying for a chat."

Henderson shot him a venomous look. Maggie, unnoticing of the nuances, happily took Mr. O'Malley's hand. They scooted off into the crowd before Alexandra could even draw a breath.

Which left her alone with Mr. Henderson. She desperately searched the room for Lady Featherstone, but the woman had disappeared into a crowd of fashionable ladies, lost among a sea of headdresses and shawls.

"Mrs. Alastair."

Mr. Henderson's voice was so contrite, so worried, that she turned back in spite of herself. The blond man was regarding her with a look of sorrow and embarrassment. Despite the fact that he had torn out of the theatre proper not an hour before to pursue Mr. Burchard, he had every hair in place, his clothes were pristine, and his gloves were unblemished. His suit of impeccable black and white hung on a broad frame and long black pantaloons hugged well-shaped legs. The subdued colors made him look the country vicar, but perhaps one with much family money behind him.

He extended his right hand hesitantly, as if afraid to lift it completely. "Mrs. Alastair, please. Let me beg your pardon most humbly. I had no idea you were—you would be—so great a lady. I had no right to approach you, let alone—" He stopped. "I can only say in my defense that I acted on an order, but it was an order I should have disobeyed. I wish I had. The action was meant to be directed at Finley, but I should have realized that you would be the most hurt of all." He moistened his lips, his face growing more red. "Forgive me, I do not have much experience apologizing."

His voice quavered with sincerity. He was completely the country parson now, begging forgiveness for his own sins.

"Mr. Henderson, I am uncertain what to say to you."

His eyes flickered. "I know I do not deserve what I ask. I will only keep hoping for it."

She hesitated. He seemed very contrite and dismayed and embarrassed. She could not help feeling a little bit sorry for him. "I must think it through, sir. You frightened me very much."

Anguish crossed his face. "I know. And for that I most humbly beg your pardon." He adjusted his spectacles with a shaking finger. "It is all Finley's fault, you know. If he did not play his cards so close to his chest, we would have known where things stood all along."

Alexandra frowned. "Why should you need to know where things stand? What things?"

He opened his mouth to answer, then closed it again. "May we adjourn outside? The carriage should arrive soon." He offered Alexandra his arm, with a sidelong glance reminiscent of a dog who expected to be kicked. Her heart softened a trifle. He did look very penitent, and his words rang with sincerity. He knew he'd been wrong, and knew whoever had told him to do such a bizarre thing had been wrong.

She rested her fingertips carefully on his forearm. With a look of vast relief, he led her toward the doors.

Outside, the June night had turned cool. Carriages bottled up King Street as coachmen tried to force their way in for their mistresses and masters. She craned her head to look for Lord Featherstone, but she did not see him. She could not see her own carriage either, nor, more disquieting, Maggie and Mr. O'Malley.

Mr. Henderson walked her a little way from the crowd and stopped in a place where Alexandra was less likely to be bumped or crushed. He kept her on his arm, and tugged a white handkerchief from his pocket.

"I would be honored, Mrs. Alastair," he was saying, "if you would allow me to speak to you again. To see you again. Perhaps for a drive in Hyde Park, or perhaps we could walk in Vauxhall gardens. With your friends, of course," he added hastily.

This was getting awkward. "Mr. Henderson, you did

not begin your acquaintance with me with any measure of trust."

"I know." A large black carriage lumbered toward them, and Alexandra took a little step back to protect her skirts from stray splashes of mud. Mr. Henderson went on, "I wish it for friendship's sake only and to make you know how sorry I am."

"I understand that, sir." Alexandra said, struggling to remember all the politenesses Mrs. Fairchild had lectured into her. She supposed Mrs. Fairchild had not anticipated she would have to soothe the feelings of a gentleman who had forced himself upon her in the street. "Rest assured that should I see you by chance at Vauxhall, I shall not refuse to speak to you."

"I sincerely and truly am sorry. You have no idea." He lifted his handkerchief and sighed deeply. "And I am also very sorry about *this*."

The black carriage stopped next to them. Mr. Henderson brought his hand up and around. Alexandra found her face enveloped in wads of white linen. She tried to take a step back, but suddenly her limbs were weak and would not support her. She had a falling sensation, one that did not stop, and darkness rushed toward her. Dimly she felt an arm around her waist and Mr. Henderson's voice somewhere above her. "No, do not weep, sister. Everything will be all right. Here is our carriage—"

She woke to a slight rocking motion and warm stuffiness. Her eyes felt sandy, and the pinpoint of light from the single lantern seared straight into her brain.

She wanted nothing more than to drift back into silent, dark sleep, but something nagged at her. She needed to remember something, but she could not for the life of her remember what.

She mumbled, "Maggie." She tried to stir, tried to search for the girl.

"She is safe," said a voice. "She is with Ian O'Malley."

At first she thought the voice was Grayson's, and her heart melted with relief. But the timbre was wrong, and the face she saw through half-closed eyes wore spectacles.

"Liar," she said, her tongue feeling thick. "You lied to me."

"I swear to you. She is with Ian, on her way home. Captain Ardmore wanted her, too, but Ian refused. He will help her."

The sentences blurred in her head. "You have no honor," she croaked, her voice failing.

"I know." Mr. Henderson huddled miserably in the seat. "I am a cad and a coward."

She opened her eyes all the way, her whirling, foggy thoughts clarifying. Mr. Henderson sat on the opposite seat of the rather sumptuous coach, twining his fingers and regarding her in sorrow.

"I was just convincing myself to trust you," she said.

He nodded. "I work for a madman. One does not refuse him."

Alexandra made herself sit upright, ready to tell Mr. Henderson what she thought of him and his madman captain. But a blackness rushed at her and she found herself facedown on the seat. She could only lay in a half-stupor, listening to the coach wheels beneath her and Mr. Henderson's fretful voice as he continued to apologize.

Chapter Ten

She smelled water. She came awake when the carriage door opened, and black wind poured over her. "Wh're we?" she mumbled.

"Where we need to go," Mr. Henderson replied, unhelpfully. He had already descended. He lifted her into his arms and scooped her out of the carriage.

He carried her for quite a long way, his boots ringing first on cobbles, then on hollow planking. His fast-beating heart thumped beneath her cheek, and he smelled of cloying perfume.

After a time, he stopped on the edge of the dock and handed her down to the waiting arms of a man she could not see. She was set on a seat, a blanket tossed over her legs. The boat rocked. A wave slapped wood, and chill, moist air rose around her.

Mr. Henderson clambered down and sat next to her.

" 're we goin' t' France?"

Mr. Henderson slid his arm about her waist. "Shh."

The boat silently pushed off. A man in dark clothing took the tiller in the stern, and another manned the oars. They slid through the night. Alexandra sagged against Mr. Henderson, feeling giddy and tired at the same time. The notion that she did not like his suit kept dancing through her head. An odd notion, because the cloth was the softest woven wool, and the cut was perfect. She sighed, wishing it were a midnight-blue coat over a rough linen shirt that Grayson had forgotten to lace up again. She had never known a man's chest could be so handsome.

Mr. Henderson leaned down, startled. "What did you say?"

"Mmm? Nothing."

They went on in silence. Waves whispered against the boat. The smell of mud mixed with a sharp, salty tang. The wind blew chill, though not icy. Alexandra shivered in her light shawl, despite the warmth of Mr. Henderson's arm about her.

Lies. Why did everyone lie? Even Grayson lied, or at least he did not tell all of the truth. Mr. Henderson had certainly lied, and she'd believed him. No, he had not lied about being sorry. She had seen that in his eyes.

Still, here she was in the middle of the Thames near the sea. But no, they could not be near the Channel—they had not traveled far enough, had they? Other boats filled the spaces, lights flickering from lanterns like fireflies on a summer night. She longed for the sweet summer days of her childhood in Kent. Her thoughts surged in that direction, filling her senses with the remembered smells of roses and grass, rain and thunder. White sheep had dotted the emerald fields where she ran, skirts tucked into her sash—don't tell my mother.

How she came to be here in the dead of night, kidnapped, her aching head stuffed with straw, in a smelly little boat who-knew-where on the Thames, she had no idea. It occurred to her fuzzy thinking that if only she'd remained in Kent, she'd never have been married to Theo and her father and mother would still be alive. For one hungry moment, she wanted to go home with all her heart.

Mr. Henderson leaned to her again. "It will not be long. I promise."

"Liar," she murmured.

She noted his frown of discomfort and secretly smiled. She was much too tired and weak to flee, but at least she could rattle him.

She was uncertain how much time had passed when the boat gently bumped the end of a wooden dock. The man at the tiller tied the boat; then up she went again as Mr. Henderson lifted her out. "Can you walk?" he asked.

"No." Her legs shook, and she could barely feel her feet. She sensed that when her head cleared again, she would be very ill indeed.

He cradled her close to keep her upright. The dock was lonely. No lighted ships hovered near, and she could hear little beyond but the hiss of wind in grass.

A ship did moor there, a massive, square-masted ship that rose large in the darkness. A few running lights hung from bow and stern, but otherwise, all was dark. A gangplank extended like a tongue to them from the deck high above.

Mr. Henderson marched with her up into the ship. No one came forward to greet them or demand their business. The men from the boat had not accompanied them. Other than her and her kidnapper, Alexandra saw no one. If Mr. Henderson wanted to go to France in this ship, she certainly hoped he would not expect her to hoist sails or man the tiller.

She started to giggle. She could not seem to stop. The silly thought of her frantically pulling ropes to raise the huge sails while Mr. Henderson shouted orders struck her very funny. Her laughter rang high into the air to be lost in the wind sighing through the rigging.

Mr. Henderson suddenly set her on her feet. She clung to his arm, her other hand pressed across her mouth, trying to stifle her hysteria.

They stood before a door set into the side of the quarterdeck above them. At least, she thought it was called the quarterdeck. She only knew ships from the books in her father's library. She had never actually been on one.

Mr. Henderson rapped on the door. After a long moment, it scraped open. Beyond it stood a very ugly sailor, short and bulky. Alexandra stared at him in shock; then her strange laughter bubbled up and came bursting out.

Mr. Henderson dragged her past the sailor and into the cabin. She found herself inside a square room, built the width of the quarterdeck above. From the low ceiling's painted beams hung two iron lanterns. The entire back wall was lined with windows that looked out into darkness. A lantern hanging outside glittered crookedly through the facets of the glass.

The other two walls of the room were lined with cabinets that fitted around twin doors, one in each wall. The wall behind her held more precisely built cabinets. In the middle of the room stood a long table, and behind it, under the windows, a varnished wooden bench ran from wall to wall. At the table, in a low, square chair, like a prince on his throne, sat the gentleman she'd seen depart Grayson's house the night she'd run to the rescue.

James Ardmore. She had only glimpsed him in the dark

that night, the length of pavement from her front door to Grayson's. Now here he was.

He wore a dark blue coat stretched over shoulders as broad as Grayson's. He had no shirt; the coat was buttoned over his bare, bronzed torso. His breeches and boots were black and his hair was dark as night. His face was swarthy, his tan rendering his lips and cheeks the same color. From this monotone face blazed his eyes, which were chill green like layers and layers of ancient ice.

Here was the man who had put a rope around Grayson's neck and left him to die. The man Grayson had told her was one of the most dangerous in the world.

She clapped her hand to her mouth, trying to stifle her giggles. His green gaze scrutinized her, a gaze that probed her, wanting to know everything about her. She should be so very afraid. She leaned on Mr. Henderson and shook with laughter.

A door to one of the inner rooms opened, and a woman emerged. She was tall, and her dyed red hair, dressed unfashionably high, nearly touched the top of the doorframe. She was neither pretty nor ugly, having a square, plain face and pale eyes that held sharp intelligence. Her mouth was thin, a little severe. Her figure, on the other hand, was the kind Alexandra's husband Theo had favored. Her bosom rounded nicely, and her hips curved under the clinging skirt.

Ardmore glanced at her and extended his hand. She came to him and twined her fingers through his.

Ardmore returned his slow green gaze, colder than January ice, to Alexandra. "Mrs. Alastair. Won't you sit down?"

Mr. Henderson more or less dragged her to the long bench. She plumped to it, holding herself unsteadily. Her giggles shook her.

"I think I gave her too much," Mr. Henderson said worriedly.

Ardmore gestured to the sailor. "Get her some water."

The man ducked into the room from which the woman had emerged, and came back holding a dripping dipper. He brought it to Alexandra.

She'd never drunk from a dipper before. She stared at the thing, mystified. The sailor gave a grunt, lifted the dipper to her lips, and poured the water into her mouth. She spluttered, coughed. Half the water fell in a wet splash to her silk gown.

She wiped her mouth with the back of her hand and regarded herself in dismay. "You've ruined it."

"I will give you the cost of it," Ardmore said.

She looked up. "In jewels?"

He stared at her a beat. "I beg your pardon?"

"*Grayson*—I mean, the viscount—offered me jewels." She gave him a look of disappointment, letting him know that kidnapper or no, he did not measure up to the viscount.

"In exchange for what?"

Alexandra hesitated. Why *had* Grayson offered them? Emeralds, no opals. No, both. She furrowed her brow in thought. Oh, yes. "Because I saved his life. When you tried to kill him. That was very wicked of you, you know."

The cold eyes flickered. "I lost my temper. Sometimes Finley makes me a bit rash."

Alexandra nodded sagely. "I do agree that Grayson— the viscount—can sometimes be a bit provoking."

The woman and Mr. Henderson nodded together. "Yes," the woman said fervently. Her accent was French.

"For example," Alexandra went on, unable to stop the words, "he will decide something must be done, and then go on to do it whether you like it or not. He walks right through your objections as if he does not even see them."

All three of her listeners nodded reflectively.

"Are you going to hang me, too?" she asked Ardmore. "I wish you would not. I have so much to do to plan my soiree. If you hang me, Lady Featherstone will have to finish the menus herself, which would hardly be fair." Tears pricked her eyes.

"I assure you," he answered. "I will do you no harm."

Alexandra chased a drop of water over her lips. She could not seem to catch it. "You have already harmed my dress."

He said nothing. Perhaps he was tired of hearing her bleat about her dress. She felt suddenly sad. Would she ever see Lady Featherstone again? The lady had been so helpful to her, both while Theo was alive and after his death. She was as kind and caring as a mother could have been. Alexandra had no real family anymore. She thought of Grayson and Maggie, and her heart twisted. Perhaps she would never see them again, either. A tear rolled down the side of her nose and dropped onto her wrist.

Ardmore released the red-haired woman's hand. "I will speak to Mrs. Alastair alone."

The woman promptly rose. She dropped a kiss to the crown of Mr. Ardmore's head, then glided out the door to the deck. The ugly sailor followed. Mr. Henderson hesitated. "I do not like to leave her."

Ardmore's gaze remained chill. "Mr. Henderson."

Henderson's hands clenched. "Sir—"

Mr. Ardmore rose. He did not so much get out of his chair as unfold himself in one lithe, long movement, like a leopard rising from its place in the shade. She'd seen a leopard in a menagerie once. Mr. Ardmore reminded her strongly of it.

Mr. Henderson held his ground for a moment. Then he threw a look of apology at Alexandra and glumly marched out the door. Ardmore closed it behind him.

The muted footsteps of the three who had just exited faded into the distance. Above them, pulleys rattled in the wind. A gust creaked open a window near the corner of the room. Mr. Ardmore ignored it.

He moved back to her, then leaned against the table and folded his arms. She returned his look defiantly, wishing she felt well enough to leap from the seat, fling herself past him and run out into the night. She only had the vaguest notion of what she would do after that. Run along the dock searching for refuge? Who would she find out here on the edge of nowhere? Kindly people who would take her in? Or villains in the pay of Captain Ardmore?

He studied her slowly. She wanted to ask him a thousand questions, including who he really was and what he had to do with Grayson, and why on earth had he dragged her out here to his ship?

She opened her mouth and blurted the first question that forced its way out. "Where are you from? Your accent is strange."

"Charleston," he answered, unmoving.

"That is in the South of the United States?"

He inclined his head. "Born and raised a Southern gentleman."

"Do all Southern gentleman become pirates?"

"I am not a pirate. I hunt pirates."

"And you are hunting Grayson?"

"Partly."

She gave him a severe look. "Well, you cannot hunt him, you know. He is a viscount now, an English peer. And the English Admiralty want him to find the French king—Louis or the Comte de Lille or whatever one calls him these days."

His gaze sharpened. "What the devil do you know about that?"

"I heard Grayson tell you. The night you tried to hang him. You left the window open. I heard everything."

He looked bemused. "I see. I had overlooked that."

"It is a mercy you did, or I'd not have known to come and rescue him." She clenched a fold of her sodden gown. "I am most put out with you, Mr. Ardmore. If you had succeeded in killing him, what would have become of Maggie?"

His lips thinned to a straight, hard line. "Maggie would have been taken care of. I would have seen to that." He lifted his gaze to the darkness of the windows. "I will always take care of Maggie. She is the daughter of a woman I loved very deeply, once upon a time."

Alexandra stared. His eyes held a remote softness, one that he would share with no one, one he'd hide if he thought she saw it. "You were in love with Maggie's mother? How could you have been? She was Grayson's wife."

His gaze returned to her, becoming chill once more. "You think that marriage to another creates a barrier against love?"

"No," she said slowly. "It certainly never stopped my husband." Oh, dear, why had she said that? It must be the concoction Mr. Henderson had made her breathe. She would never have mentioned her disgraceful husband to a perfect stranger otherwise. She flushed.

"I know all about your husband, Mrs. Alastair. Who he was, what he did to you. If he were still alive, I would shoot him myself."

Why did that satisfy her? She should not be pleased

with such a violent declaration from a violent man. She should swoon or something ladylike. "Did Grayson threaten to shoot you? Is that why you are angry at him?"

His gaze left her again. "Sara was beautiful. She had slim brown legs, strong from swimming. She had long black hair as sleek as a fall of silk, and breasts full and firm."

Alexandra's face heated. "Mr. Ardmore, you should not mention such things to me."

"Do you know why Finley married her?"

"Why do you call him Finley? He is a viscount now. You should refer to him as His Lordship or Lord Stoke."

"I am an American, Mrs. Alastair. Your damned English titles mean nothing to me. Do you know why Finley married Sara?"

She sensed his growing exasperation. She had better concentrate on what he was saying. "Because she was beautiful?"

"No. Because I loved her. When he discovered this, he stole her from me. He married her—for a joke. And he laughed."

"But—" She touched shaking fingers to her lips. "So you hate him because of this woman?"

His fingers, large and sinewy, tightened on his arms. "That was the beginning. The very first in a long line of reasons why I hate Grayson Finley."

"But that is a very foolish reason."

"Foolish?" His hands balled into fists. There was a deep rage in him she'd never noted in Grayson. And here she was, alone with him in his cabin, her only possible aid being Mr. Henderson outside. Mr. Henderson who had rendered her helpless so he could drag her here in the first place.

She wet her lips and plunged on. "Well, Captain, consider her behavior. She seems to have flitted from you to Grayson very easily, when she must have known you were great friends. If I understand correctly, she then deserted *him*. When she bore Maggie, did she move heaven and earth to find him and tell him the wonderful news? No, indeed. She abandoned Maggie to whatever charitable missionary family happened to be on hand and went gallivanting off. Now, is this a woman you should properly break your heart over?"

His eyes narrowed to green slits behind his black lashes. "I never said I'd broken my heart."

"You must have, or you would not still be so angry. But take my word, Mr. Ardmore, she was not a woman worth falling out over. If she had been steadfast and true to you, and he had stolen her away like a villain, then that would be different, of course. But I am afraid she has simply been very common."

"Common," he said, tight-lipped.

Something deep inside was frantically waving her quiet, but her tongue seemed to keep running of its own accord. "Yes, indeed. I do not think I will ever forgive her for leaving Maggie with people who tried to tell her she was the devil's child. Thank heavens they did not break her spirit."

"The Wesleyans told her that?"

Alexandra ignored him. "And now the poor woman is dead, Maggie tells me."

A muscle moved in his jaw. "She is."

"It was all so very long ago. You ought to put it behind you. I do observe that you have taken up with a new lady, whom you did not introduce, by the by. That was quite rude of you."

"Her name is Madame d'Lorenz, and she is not a suitable acquaintance for a lady."

An idea clicked in her mind. "She is French? Perhaps *she* stole the French king."

Ardmore's eyes narrowed. "She is in exile. Just as he is. An émigré would not hand over the king to Napoleon."

"I see. Do you love her deeply?"

An exasperated look crept into his expression. "Why does this interest you?"

"Because I am attempting to make a point. Do you love Madame d'Lorenz?"

"No."

The word was hard, blunt, final. As if not loving her made him angry.

"There, you see? You ought to release the poor woman at once. It is cruel to make her believe you have affection for her when you do not. What you really ought to do, Mr. Ardmore—" she gave him a chiding look—"is give up paramours altogether and settle upon a wife. One who will look after you." She pointed to his bared chest. "One who will make you wear shirts."

The blaze in his eyes this time had nothing to do with anger. A small, ironic smile twisted his lips. "A wonderful idea, Mrs. Alastair." He reached down and closed one cold hand over hers. "You are a lovely woman. Will you do me the honor?"

She rocked back. "What? Good heavens, no." She struggled for words as she tried to disengage her hand. "I would make a horrid wife for a pirate hunter. I do not even know what a quarterdeck is for heaven's sake. Besides, you are wanted by the English government, and you are a would-be murderer. You could not even be put on the list!"

His brow creased. "List?"

"Even Grayson is on the list. But then, he is a viscount,

and English. He did tamper with things so that he would be the best match on it, and I cannot overlook such blatant cheating, no matter what he thinks." She stopped, deflating. "But he already told me he was not looking to marry, so it does not matter."

Captain Ardmore looked utterly perplexed. "What list, Mrs. Alastair?"

"My list of suitors." She waved her hand before her face. "But you are not interested in that. You want to kidnap me, or ravish me, or sell me to slavers, or whatever it is you will do. I do wish you'd get on with it, and finish it quickly. I am not very brave."

Chapter Eleven

Ardmore gave her an odd, intense look. "No, Mrs. Alastair, I believe you are extremely brave."

She sighed. "At least I did not wet myself. Well, that is, except for the water."

"You did not *what?*"

"Grayson told me that he'd seen fierce pirates wet themselves when faced with you. I admit, he might have been exaggerating, because you do not seem very frightening to me. Of course, that may be because your Mr. Henderson made me breathe that strange concoction, which has made me quite silly."

He pinched the bridge of his nose. "Let us return to this list of suitors. You say you want to marry Finley?"

"It does not matter whether I want to marry him or not. He told me quite plainly that he was not looking for a wife. I imagine that because his first marriage did not go well, he does not wish to try again. I suppose I should cross his name off." She finished wistfully.

"Please do."

She traced her lower lip, back and forth, back and forth. It grew warm. "The duke is still the best candidate, but I imagine he would prefer a debutante to me, a widow rather long in the tooth."

"Only if he is a fool," Ardmore said.

His words flowed and melded like rain on frozen snow. "Mr. Bartholomew, now, he is a quiet and polite gentleman. And really, his stammer is not his fault."

"He sounds most unworthy of you."

She nibbled the tip of her finger. "Mr. Burchard, now, is very odd. Grayson told me he was a dangerous and horrible pirate. And then tonight—"

"*Burchard?*"

His body had gone rigid. "Indeed. Your Mr. Henderson and Mr. O'Malley seemed to think so too. They chased him from the theatre when Lady Featherstone and I were trying to have a conversation with him."

He stood. "Zechariah Burchard is alive?"

"Indeed. Grayson told me you had murdered him, but I suppose you were mistaken." She shivered. "I dislike talking of such things."

"Son of a— Henderson!"

His words were cut off by the sound of something striking the door, hard. The sound rocked the cabin, indeed, the entire ship. Ardmore whirled as the door splintered inward.

The viscount barreled into the cabin, his face thunderous, his eyes blazing blue rage. He could have lit signal fires with the hot fury that poured from him. Henderson and the sailor were hot on his heels. Grayson seized James Ardmore by the lapels of his coat and bore him down to the table. The table, anchored in place, creaked under the onslaught. Ardmore grabbed Grayson's wrists, his own fingers white, but Grayson held him fast.

Panting, Mr. Henderson pointed a pistol at Grayson's head. "Back off, Finley."

Alexandra jumped to her feet. Her legs wobbled. "Please, Mr. Henderson, do not shoot him!"

"I told you," Grayson said to Ardmore, his voice deadly quiet. "Not her."

"Those are your rules," Ardmore returned. "Not mine."

Grayson slammed him against the tabletop. "All of it is your rules. You made this about you and me a long time ago. *You and me.* No one else."

Ardmore's lips drew back. "Were you following the rules when you decided to murder my brother?"

Alexandra gasped. Good heavens. She glanced at the others, but none seemed startled by the announcement. Alexandra wanted to blurt questions, shout to get responses, but words died on her lips.

Henderson's voice shook. "Let him go, Finley. I will drop you where you stand."

The tension in the room made her head ache. Alexandra stumbled to Mr. Henderson's side. "Please, stop this."

Mr. Henderson's gray eyes were hard. "You see, Finley? You are upsetting Mrs. Alastair."

Grayson did not answer. Indeed, he did not seem to notice anyone else in the room but Ardmore.

Alexandra said quickly, "It is all right, my lord. Captain Ardmore and I were only having a conversation."

"A conversation." He directed the words, tight and angry, at Ardmore. "Is that what you call it?"

"You do not deserve this woman, Finley. You are out of your depth."

"You touch her and you will see what is in my depths."

Alexandra watched them, agonized. "He did nothing, Grayson. Actually, Mr. Henderson did all the abducting. Mr. Ardmore only talked to me."

Henderson winced.

Grayson said, "Henderson will be next in line."

"Bloody hell," Henderson said weakly.

Ardmore eased his hands from Grayson's arms. "Put it down, Mr. Henderson."

Henderson stared at his captain for one agonized moment, then stiffly lowered the pistol.

The two men glared at each other, gazes locked, lips tight. "Take her and go," Ardmore said.

Grayson held on a moment longer, then slowly, he released him and stood up. His lips were tight with anger, and he had murder in his eyes.

Ardmore got to his feet. The two men watched each other warily. Mr. Henderson still held the pistol, his fingers white on the trigger. Madame d'Lorenz and the other sailor looked poised to flee.

Alexandra took a tottering step forward and held out her hand to Grayson. "Now, my lord, please, let us sit down and discuss this reasonably—"

Grayson's eyes sparkled like fireworks on a Vauxhall night. "I do not want to discuss it reasonably. I want to rescue you."

"I do not need to be rescued at the moment, my lord. You and Mr. Ardmore should speak. Calmly."

"Damn you, Alexandra, I am rescuing you whether you like it or not." He closed the distance between them in one stride, bent, and hoisted her smoothly over his shoulder.

Her equilibrium went end over tip and she found herself upside down with her nose digging into his damp woolen coat.

"What the devil are you doing?" she heard Mr. Henderson demand.

"Rescuing my lady. Get out of my way."

"Finley—"

The next sound was that of a fist striking flesh. Alexandra winced. Grayson wheeled and began walking fast. Fresh air struck her face, bringing with it the strong smell of brine. She lifted her head, trying to look back the way they'd come.

"You see?" she called. "I am right. He overruns everybody in his way."

Madame d'Lorenz and the sailor had fled. Mr. Henderson, in the lighted cabin, stood as illuminated as an actor on a stage. Scarlet blood dripped to his stark white cravat.

"Why must he always hit me in the face?" he asked plaintively. "Why always the *face?*"

That was only the beginning of the harrowing rescue. Grayson had a boat waiting, with a wide-eyed sailor at the oars. Grayson hoisted Alexandra onto his back and bade her lock her arms and legs about his torso, while he half-climbed, half slid down a rope that was fixed to the rail of Ardmore's ship by a grappling hook.

They went that way because the ship seemed to have moved far from the dock. They floated now in the middle of the river, so wide at this point that the banks were swallowed in darkness and mist.

She looked up at the precarious line that held the weight of them both. "What happens if they cut the rope?" she bleated. "Or loosen the hook?"

"Then we get wet," he answered, his words clipped.

They made it to the boat without any such appalling thing happening. The frightened sailor plied the oars while Grayson steered, which left Alexandra shivering alone in the bow. They rowed, not toward shore, but farther out into the river. Presently, another wet, wooden hull of a ship loomed out of the mist at them.

She was wondering how on earth Grayson expected her to climb aboard, all that long way up the slick sides of the ship, when a sort of harness thing was lowered down to her. Grayson fastened its rope about her waist, explaining that she must hold on with both hands. She was still a bit hazy about it all when her feet abruptly left the ground.

She yelped. The harness began moving upward, bump by bump, hoisted by a pulley manned by a sailor high above. She seized the ropes and held on, squeezing her eyes shut.

A chill wind skimmed the river and cooled her hot skin. Her light skirt crept upward, the fickle wind exposing her stockings, garters, and thighs to anyone who cared to look. She risked a glance down. Grayson was gazing up at her, his white teeth gleaming in lantern light. He was certainly enjoying the sight, she knew it, but she could let go of the harness to preserve her modesty. She could only hope that no one else saw the spectacle of her white limbs dangling from the rigging.

The harness swayed ever upward. Just when she thought she could rise no higher, she floated over the rail. The sailor at the rope grunted as he let her down slowly. At long last, her feet touched the deck, and she pried her hands from the ropes.

The sailor unfastened her from the harness, and she was just beginning to shiver in the breeze when Grayson vaulted over the railing and landed on the deck.

"Why have we come here?" she asked him. "Is this your ship?"

"Welcome aboard the *Majesty*," he said. He waved his

hand at the dark deck, just lit by the faint gray of dawn, but he seemed distracted. He gave orders to the sailors attending them to haul in the boat, then he came to Alexandra. "Come with me."

She tried to take a step toward him, but her legs would not support her. His steady arm kept her from collapsing, and then he swept her into his arms and carried her aft into the stern cabin.

The captain's cabin on this ship was a little different from Ardmore's, she observed, as Grayson made his way to the bunk and laid her gently down.

For one thing, there was only one room, which sloped down a little on either end, and it had no doors leading off into side rooms. His bunk was in this cabin as well, on the left—the port side, she corrected herself. Next to it stood a desk and a chair, and he had no bench beneath his windows.

The bunk's mattress was harder than her own giving featherbed at home, but she could spread her arms and legs a long way before touching the sides. Lying down right now also was preferable to standing up. Things did not move so much when she was lying down.

Grayson watched her test the width of the bunk. His eyes smoldered with the vestiges of the anger that had wrapped him like a cloud of sparks. The tense fury of the two men had frightened her far more than Mr. Henderson's pistol. The aching hatred had filled the entire room, pushing aside all in it. The others had felt it too. They had been bystanders to a battle in which they had no part.

His silence now bothered her. Never since she'd met Grayson Finley had he been silent, unless he had been thinking up something outrageously wicked to say to her.

111

Even then, he would have a mischievous twinkle in his eye. That spark was absent now.

To fill the emptiness, she said, "Captain Ardmore's cabin is bigger than yours."

He turned glittering eyes to her.

She added hastily. "But your bunk is bigger."

His glare did not soften. "Than *his?*"

"I don't know. I meant that your bunk is larger than the bench I was lying on. The bench was far too hard as well. Not comfortable at all."

"What the hell were you doing lying on his bench?"

She blinked at his savage tone. "Because I felt so woozy. From whatever Mr. Henderson gave me."

His face went bleak again. "I am going to throttle Mr. Henderson."

"Oh no, it was not his fault. He was most sorry for it. I believe he is compelled to do whatever Mr. Ardmore tells him."

"I do not share your generosity. He could have defied him. Ian O'Malley did."

Alexandra pushed herself to a sitting position. "He took Maggie. Is she all right?"

He dragged the chair next to the bunk and sat down heavily, resting his elbows on his knees. "He took her home. I saw them. Thank God he is Maggie's devoted slave. Between him and Jacobs and Oliver, she is well protected." He pressed the heel of his hand to his eyes. "Oh, and the governess. She's there too."

Alexandra brightened. "Mrs. Fairchild has arrived? Oh, how splendid! I look forward to seeing her again. She is the best of ladies, my lord, the finest our sex can produce. She will be—"

"*Alexandra.*"

His tired exclamation cut through her eager chatter. "Yes?"

"Did he hurt you?"

He was watching her, leaning forward as if he would bear her down and shake her if he suspected her of lying. Whatever was between him and Ardmore was beyond her comprehending at the moment. She would have to ply him with questions later, when her head stopped feeling as if someone had spun her in place very, very fast. They could have a long talk, and he could explain everything carefully, and she would be able to remember and to understand.

At the moment, she felt the strange urge to either succumb to another fit of giggles or fall fast asleep. "Um, what was the question?" she asked.

He muttered something under his breath that sounded very much like a curse. She ought to remonstrate him on his language. She was, after all, a lady. Or at least she had been, before gentlemen began kidnapping her and kissing her in the street, and commanding her to sleep without her clothes.

Suddenly, he reached to her, closing a viselike grip around her wrists. He dragged her close, then grasped her around the waist and hauled her right out of the bunk and onto the chair with him. Instead of settling her demurely on his knee, he raked her skirts high and pulled her down to straddle him.

Her eyes opened wide. This was a very—interesting and unladylike position. She faced him eye-to-eye, his strong face inches from her own. More unnerving still, nothing existed between her bared thighs and his breeches. A fold of silk gown rested under her backside, but her legs fully hugged the cashmere—not his usual leather. The breeches were a bit damp from their journey to this ship, but she could feel his warmth beneath them. His hands rested on her hips, his fingers pushed under her skirt.

Her breath came fast, and his did, too. She felt the pulse in his fingers and wrists bumping as rapidly as hers.

"You are *my* lady," he said in a low voice. "Tell me you understand."

The scar on his lower lip pulled his mouth down harder than ever. "Actually, I do not understand anything at all."

He cupped her cheek, letting his thumb trace her cheekbone in hard, shaking strokes. "You are mine. He will not have you. Not this time."

She blinked. "Well, of course not. He actually wanted to be added to my list of suitors. Can you imagine? He is not even English."

"I don't give a damn if he's Turkish. He will not take you from me. Not you." His gaze darkened. "Not you."

His hot palm on her thigh rubbed circles on her cold skin. Was he going to kiss her? Her heart fluttered in anticipation. It had been a week since he'd last kissed her, when she'd sat on his lap at her writing table, and he'd teased her about her list.

But he did not kiss her. He studied her so intensely she felt as if his eyes bored all the way to the back of her skull. He was thinking of something else—not her—leaving her behind in a mist of confusion.

Well, she would show him what she thought of that. If he were about to ravish her, he should at least pay her some mind. She settled herself closer to him, then leaned forward and pressed a soft kiss to his lips.

Chapter Twelve

Grayson came out of his contemplation with a start. Eager, soft, innocent kisses caressed his lips, sweet gifts of delight. Oh, Alexandra, a dangerous move.

Her mouth began to explore his, gliding kisses over his lower lip. She gazed up at him from under her lashes in sheer fascination, which made his lower body tighten, calling for immediate attention. No, let it wait. See what she would do.

Her hips rocked a little bit as she unconsciously arched herself to him. He cupped her soft, round hip and found that it just fit into his hand. The vivid vision of her on hands and knees, he behind her came to him. Her lovely hips would rest in his palms, and she would look back at him, eyes heavy with passion, and cry his name.

More tiny kisses brushed his lips. Her fingers found the edge of his shirt, from which he'd ripped the strangling collar and cravat, tossing them who-knew-where in the hired carriage. Several times since he'd met her he had caught her interested gaze riveted to the scar that began just below the hollow of his throat. She was presently most engrossed with that scar. Perhaps he ought to thank Ardmore for laying open his side that day.

She raised her head. "Oh, dear."

"What? Don't stop kissing me." Please, not yet.

Her blush complemented the confusion in her eyes. "I might ruin your fine breeches."

His brow furrowed. "Mm? How is that?"

"It's just that everything is getting a bit damp all of the sudden. I have no idea why. It felt like that when I slept bare, as well. It is most strange."

His black mood moved toward delight. "I can guess why." He slid both hands up to the top of her thighs and let his thumbs dip down into her sweet warmth. A shudder went through her as he touched her, all hot and dark and wet. "You beautiful, beautiful woman."

"How can you say beautiful?" she whispered shyly. "I am such a mess."

"I like you a mess." He withdrew his hand and touched fingers to his lips, then closed his eyes to savor her.

When he opened his eyes again, she was watching him, red lips parted. "Lovely lady," he whispered. "May I taste you?"

She stared at him in pure astonishment. Then she flushed so deeply red her complexion nearly matched her hair. He expected her at any moment to draw herself up, to again become Mrs. Alastair the duke's granddaughter, and ask him how he dared even think such a thing. He waited for it, the end of his pleasant daydream.

"Yes," she whispered. "Oh, yes, please."

Good. The word beat through him. Good, good, good. Where now? he thought, as he scraped her to him for a long, deep kiss. On the bunk? It was a good foot away—so far. No, wait. He would not even have to leave the chair.

He pressed her away from him, sliding her to her clumsy feet before he broke the kiss. His hands wadded the warm silk gown and pushed it above her pale and waiting hips, all the way to the sash that bound it beneath her breasts.

Her hips curved gently from her waist, and in the V between her legs, a soft swirl of dark red hair awaited his fingers. Her belly was the only part of her not perfect. Softly rounded beneath her naval, it contained small puckered pink lines that criss-crossed in uneven directions, curving down her abdomen to the waiting delights below.

He understood what the lines meant. Once upon a time, Mrs. Alastair had carried a child. The evidence was there on her skin. But no child lived in her house, and she'd never once spoken of motherhood. He'd glimpsed a dark pain deep in her eyes, and he understood it now.

That pain made him want to treat her gently. His arousal wanted to be rough and playful. He'd show her both. If he could control himself.

He leaned forward and traced the marks on her belly with his tongue, going over each one with care. Her skin prickled beneath his touch, and the rise and fall of her breath quickened. He bent his head and swirled his tongue over the small tuft of hair between her thighs.

She inhaled sharply. He smiled into her, kissing the warm place, nuzzling it. The scent of her was overwhelming. He wanted to stay here forever, breathing her, kissing her. He flicked his tongue over her, smiling again as her gasps turned to tiny groans of delight.

Her feet moved apart of their own accord, opening herself to him. He nipped at the little bud that rose and swelled at his touch. He had drunk the finest wines in the world, been fed the nectar of kings, but all paled in comparison to the taste of this woman.

And then, to his great delight, she climaxed right before him. She gave a cry and arched to him, seeking his mouth. He obliged. Low throaty moans escaped her, the song of a woman who had found her desire. Her hands furrowed his hair. "Grayson. Please—"

He took her plea for a directive to continue. He drank her hungrily, letting her twist her hands through his long hair. She cried out again, pressing her warm, sweet deliciousness to him—*ah, love, that's the way.*

After a long time, he slowed his plying tongue, drawing from her the last sighs of ecstasy. He carefully withdrew and looked up at her. Her lips parted, her thick lashes shielded her eyes. Her fingers in his hair gentled, smoothing it, hands trembling.

He rose to his feet and gathered her to him. The gossamer dress snagged on a silk fold, bunching up at her waist, leaving her legs bare. He let his hands remain on her smooth hips while he held her close and buried his face in her fragrant hair.

My lady.

His arousal snarled at him, telling him in very basic terms what it thought of him. He held a beautiful woman in his arms, one he'd just brought to climax with his tongue, and what did he do? Throw her to the bunk and complete the deed? No, he simply held her, his face in the curve of her neck. Just held her body against his, learning her fragrance and the feel of her skin.

Mine, he said, in a litany that would not cease. Mine, mine, mine. Never Ardmore's.

In the dozen years after Grayson stole Sara from James Ardmore, James Ardmore had taken every other woman away from Grayson. From a casual fling with a tavern girl to Grayson's more serious affair with a beautiful free black woman in Charleston, James Ardmore had taken them all. He had not done anything so crude as abduction or rape—no, he had employed subtler methods and enticed each one to him willingly, whether their relationship with Grayson was finished or no. Ardmore did not believe in taking revenge and having done. He continued it year after year after bloody year.

Not this time.

Grayson had thought Ardmore would change the rules after making the bargain that allowed Grayson to return with Maggie to England. But Ardmore made his own rules. Grayson would pay the forfeit—he'd given his word—but he would not give him Alexandra.

His lady kissed his ear. He looked down at her. She gave him a tired smile, her eyes smoldering with latent heat. "What happened?"

"You came," he said. "Has that not happened before?"

She shook her head. Her soft hair brushed his cheek. "Never."

Good lord. She was as puzzled as a maiden who'd never been touched, never mind she had borne a child. And when he had kissed her the night she'd rescued him, she had not known how.

Her husband must have been a blind idiot who deserved a kick in the pants. This lady should be savored, taught, coaxed, every response delighted in, like a sip of delicate and potent wine.

"What happens now?" she whispered.

He leaned away from her and pressed her fingers to the front of his too-tight breeches. "*This* wants me to have you. Every bit of you."

Her supple palm molded to him, turning the heat inside him volcanic. "It is quite—" She wet her lips. "Formidable."

His sense of humor returned. "It certainly hates me right now for not getting on with it."

She glided her hand up every agonizing inch. She whispered, "Does this mean you want to take me against the wall?"

He started. There was nothing but innocence in her eyes. Laughter burbled inside him. Thank you, God. Thank you, thank you. How did I find this woman? He put his fist under her chin, tilted her head back. "Against the wall?"

"Is that not customary?"

Good lord, customary for what? Against the wall, hmm. There was not much wall space in his cabin.

"Alexandra, if you want me—" He slid his hands to her hips beneath her dress, lifted her again, and started walking with her toward the line of windows behind the desk "—to take you—" He leaned her back against a wooden slat between the panes, holding his arm between her spine and the hard panel "—against the wall—" He swiftly unbuttoned his breeches and let his very annoyed hardness spill out. "Then my love, I will oblige."

She breathed, "Good."

He lifted her hips to him. She was open and wet, ready. At long last, he slid his very impatient erection straight into her.

Now this— This— He closed his eyes and drew a ragged breath. He belonged there. God, yes.

She kissed his lips. The kiss was clumsy, her breathing unsteady. He answered with a fierce kiss of his own. "Love," he whispered. "Love."

Desire tingled through his body, racing like pins and needles up and down his limbs. Fire curled behind his eyes. She was hot and wet and slippery and yet so tight. She was warm and welcoming and he never wanted to leave.

She whispered incoherently, her lips leaving his to play on his cheekbone, his ear. She lowered her head and nipped his neck. The tiny pain made his arousal jerk and throb. He pressed harder into her, beginning a slow rhythm that his hips knew without instruction. Gently, inexorably, he loved her, faster now, faster.

His climax was coming. He felt it build, felt the clawing darkness seeking release. No, not yet. Not here. Not now.

He lifted her from him, though his erection wept and sobbed at the sudden loss of warmth. He swept her into his arms and laid her back on the bunk, almost falling on top of her in his haste. Her tangling hair swept a wide arc on the blankets. He pressed her against the mattress and nudged her knees apart.

"Are we not finished?" she gasped.

Finished? Was she mad?

"Not yet, sweetheart. Very soon. I promise, with all my heart."

He slid into her, heat and desire and need wrapping itself about him like a warm blanket. She put a shaking hand on his shoulder. "I do not like it—in a bed."

Interesting. A part of his mind filed that away for examination later.

He pinned her wrists above her head and began to love her again. His arousal applauded him. This was more like it.

Her face twisted in desire, her eyes dark and heavy. A red curl straggled across her cheek. "Grayson," she whispered.

"Yes, sweetheart?"

She flexed her fingers but did not try to pull away from his weight on her wrists. "Grayson."

"Alexandra." The name rolled from his tongue as if it belonged there. "Love."

And then he came. Darkness swallowed him and he let it. The instant before his release was complete, he snaked himself out of her and let the blanket take his seed.

She drew a long breath, and her hand came up to weakly stroke his hair. "Oh," she murmured. "That was not so bad."

As if from far away, Alexandra felt cool, still air on her skin. She heard his deep even breathing as he lay, half on and half off her, felt hot bands around her wrists where his hands still pressed her.

A spider spun a web from the underside of beams above, lazily descending a fraction of an inch at a time from an invisible thread. Exhaustion laced her inside and out, and astonishment, and a trembling that began in her belly and would not stop. If she cried, what would he do? Become disgusted, tell her to go? Would he make her row herself back to London alone? She bit her lip and willed the tears to remain hidden.

He released her wrists and kissed her neck. "Mmm."

The thong that bound his hair had come undone, and his sun-streaked locks tumbled down. She trickled her fingers through the rough silk of it.

He raised up to look at her. His lazy smile made her heart speed again. "Not so bad, did you say?"

"No."

His eyes were full of laughter. The anger that had ruled him earlier had fled for now. "I am happy I pleased you, my lady."

She smoothed a lock of hair from his brow. "No, my lord, you are pleased with yourself."

He laughed softly, shaking the mattress. "I damn well am pleased with myself. I am in bed with the most beautiful next-door neighbor a man could want."

"You think me beautiful?" she asked wistfully.

"I never lie about a woman's beauty."

She traced the crooked bump on his nose. "What do you lie about, my lord?"

"An amazing number of things. What do *you* lie about?"

"Nothing." She shook her head against the pillow. "I am very bad at lying, so I try not to practice it."

He gave her a lazy grin. "Practice makes you better." He kissed her skin just beneath the point of the diamond necklace. He touched the jewels. "One of your husband's gifts?"

"Yes." She really did not want to talk about Theo. In fact, in this past week Theo had receded like a half-forgotten dream. His barbed wit, his complete disregard of her wishes, and his blatant infidelity, all the pain and embarrassment they had caused her, had drifted away like mist before a stiff sea wind. A new viscount had moved in next door, and suddenly, everything was different.

He flipped a dangling jewel. "It's hideous."

Anyone with eyes could see that. "It was the best of the lot." She paused. "Are you going to steal it?"

He half-laughed. "What?"

"I thought it was traditional. That is what pirates do."

"Who told you I was a pirate?"

"Are you not?"

His hand drifted from the necklace down to rest, warm, on her bared belly. "I am a viscount. With a daughter."

"That is what Lady Featherstone said."

He blinked. "Lady Featherstone?"

"She said it was unlikely a pirate would have a daughter."

He nodded sagely. "She is wise."

"You have not answered my question."

A crease formed between his brows. "Which question?" he asked cautiously.

"Will you steal my necklace?"

He squeezed his eyes shut and then opened them again. They were blue and dancing. "Why do you want me to?"

"As a memento of the occasion."

He chuckled. "As if the occasion will not be seared into my memory for all eternity."

"Oh," she said, pleased.

He smoothed his hand over her stomach, his gold signet ring cool on her skin. He traced a line over her abdomen, which she knew followed one of the marks left by her pregnancy. "What happened?" he asked softly.

"Nothing happened, my lord. I bore a child. He died."

He did not answer. He leaned down and pressed a long kiss to her belly. Her tongue suddenly loosened. "His name was Jeremy Mark Brenden Alastair. He lived for one afternoon."

Grayson kissed another scar that her gowns hid to all the world except herself, her maid, and now, the viscount next door.

Her emotions were wrung raw, stretched and pulled until she could no longer call upon her habitual control to contain them. A tear leaked from her eye. After a moment another followed. She pressed her hand to her hot cheeks and shook silently.

He drew her to him, cradling her, comforting. "Shh."

She wept on, unable to apologize, unable to stop. She had cried for her son the first day, but had been forced to dry her tears ever after. Theo had not wanted to discuss it; indeed, he seemed to have forgotten all about it by the next week. Alexandra had held in her emotions, gotten on with her life. It spilled out now, the grief, the empty pain, the futile days of going on when she had wanted to die herself.

The viscount's touch tumbled her hair. "Shh."

She wiped her eyes with the back of her hand. "Forgive me."

"Better to cry than to bottle it in. Leave it, and it festers. And then it never goes away."

The pain in his eyes told her that something burned inside him as well, an old grief that he had not been able to release. She rubbed her face against his shirt, amazed she had found someone who actually understood. Even Lady Featherstone, as kind as she'd been, had not been able to offer the comfort she'd needed. She'd found it now with a pirate who had abducted her to his ship to ravish her.

She sniffled. "Are we going somewhere on this boat?"

"Ship," he corrected. "And no."

"I thought maybe we would go to France."

"No, I am not leaving England again. I am here to stay."

She touched his face. His chin was all sandpapery again. Theo Alastair would have gone into shock. "I have never left England."

His brows quirked. "No?"

"My sphere is very small. London and Kent. Your sphere is large." She smiled. "The entire world."

"Not anymore." He flicked her a look she could not decipher. "Not anymore."

He kissed her, as if wanting to halt the discussion before he was forced to explain himself. She decided she did not mind. His tongue lazily circled hers, warm and slow, as if they had all night. Which they did, in a sense. Alexandra was far too tired to climb down the sides of ships and row in little boats back toward London and the West End.

The door burst open. Alexandra jumped. Her teeth scraped Grayson's tongue.

"Ongh!" he said.

"Sir!" Thumping footsteps hastened inside. "McDaniels has arrived. He has news—oh." A young man with sandy blond hair stopped and stared, eyes round. "Sorry, sir. Uh—I'll just be outside. With McDaniels. And his news."

Clearing his throat, his face cherry red, the blond man scuttled back through the door and closed it behind him.

"Damn." Grayson sat up, pushing his hair back. The hard, annoyed expression had returned, driving away his smiles. "I won't be but a minute, love."

Alexandra nodded, finding nothing inside her for speech. Grayson swung his legs off the bed and stood. He took a step; then his breeches pooled around his boots, and he fell forward, a surprised look on his face. He caught himself on the desk just in time.

Alexandra's hand flew to her mouth. Her laughter came out a choked cough.

Grayson snarled something, leaned over, and grabbed his breeches. His backside and hips were pale, she noted, in contrast to his tanned legs. He pulled his pants up and fastened the fly.

"Go ahead and laugh, sweetheart." He shot her an amused smile. "I like it when you laugh." He reached the door, blew her a kiss, and ducked out.

Outside, Mr. McDaniels, Grayson's third officer, waited with Priestly. The man greeted him with a huge grin. "Sorry to interrupt, sir." His *r*'s rolled.

Priestly, who'd made the untimely dash into the cabin, still blushed under the lantern light. "Sorry, sir," he mumbled.

Grayson shot him a severe look. "When you observe me carry a beautiful woman into my cabin, Priestly, don't be so surprised when you find me inside with my pants down." He turned to McDaniels. "What have you got for me?"

McDaniels inclined his had. "Your French king, sir. He did get aboard a ship. Least as far as I can reckon."

Chapter Thirteen

At last, Grayson thought. At long, bloody last. "Tell me."

McDaniels complied. "The Frenchie king lives off in the countryside in a house loaned to him. He pretends it's a little Versailles and they swagger and bow just like they were still in France, except everyone is pretty strained in the pocket."

Grayson nodded impatiently. He knew this. He'd met a few French émigrés through the Duke of St. Clair. They lived meagerly in small houses, or rooms in houses, in the streets between Portman and Cavendish Squares, but pride forced them to behave, as did their king, as if they still had vast wealth, enormous power, and contingents of servants.

"Well, sir," McDaniels went on. "Some of the Frenchies here in London go regular to visit their king, like the Bourbon princes and the Duc de Berri." He pronounced it "Dook dee Berry." "But some of the others, just the normal ladies and gentlemen, and those who have had to earn their own keep, they got to feeling forgotten. So they asked the Frenchie king to travel to London. I hear that it was hard for the king to arrange the visit—politics with our government or some such. I don't know much about that sort of thing."

Grayson nodded. "So he wanted to assure his populace in London that he still loved them."

"Seems like. Came in a carriage with guards and everything."

The émigrés Grayson had met were tired people who by this time had given up ever seeing their beloved France again. The canny ones realized that even if they did return, they would find their country vastly changed, and not the France they had fled.

"So who did the king visit?" Grayson asked. "Did you talk to them?"

"He went to two houses near Marylebone Street. In one, some ladies and their maids occupy themselves making straw hats. In the other, some valet or other has set up a shop selling French trinkets and such for the families who managed to get goods out of France. So the king visits these two houses, and then suddenly climbs back into his carriage and says that's all, he's going home. The other Frenchies were annoyed. They were going to make it a big holiday, have the families come out and see the true king, give him gifts, make speeches, and so on. But off he goes."

Grayson frowned. "Is that all?"

"No, indeed, sir." McDaniels gave him a white-toothed grin. "I talked to all the servants, stood them drinks and so on. You know, some Frenchie wine isn't all that bad, in the right pub. Even met a fellow who can set you up with the best brandy, sans customs." He tapped the side of his nose. "If you want it."

"Kings first, McDaniels. Brandy later."

"Sorry, sir. Anyway, here's an interesting thing. Everyone saw the king go into the second house, but no one really saw him come out. I mean, sir, they saw a fat man in a blue cape, all bundled up, hustling back into the carriage. Why was he all bundled up when the sun was shining hot that day? my fellow wondered. So, the carriages left and that was that."

Grayson's pulse beat faster. "Where are these houses?"

"I can show you. Now my fine fellow in the pub, who lives in the house the other side of the one that sells trinkets, says that early the next morning, the proprietor of this shop gets into a hired hack and goes out. He wonders a bit where he got the ready for the carriage, but didn't think much about it. But later that evening, when he had cause to be down near the river, he sees him again. This time getting out of a boat with a man he's never seen."

Grayson rubbed his upper lip. "Did he get into the carriage alone?"

"My fellow could not say. He saw only the proprietor, but it was early morning and dark."

"That may mean nothing."

"Yes, but I made inquiries up and down the river. Seems he did get into a boat with two large fellows, and when he came back, there was only one. So where did the other fellow go, eh?"

Grayson's blood beat faster. At last, something to get hold of. "Your source is reliable?"

"Sources. Many of them cheeky." McDaniels grinned. "But I put it all together, like."

Grayson nodded. "Good work, McDaniels. Keep an eye on the shop. I want to pay it a visit myself."

"Yes, sir."

He turned over possibilities. "I also want to speak to Madame d'Lorenz. She's always been the expert at what truly is happening in the upper-class French circles. Peel her away from Ardmore; I want to see her alone."

"Yes, sir."

"What do we do now, sir?" Priestly looked expectant. Grayson hid a sigh. His life had suddenly become filled with errands, each one a nuisance. His vision of spending a few days in his cabin locked in Alexandra's arms receded before the Admiralty business.

"Now?" he mused. "Right now I need to talk to Jacobs. To plan how we are going to find that annoying Frenchman in a river full of ships." He eyed Priestly. "I want you and a handful of crew to stay here and look after Mrs. Alastair. She is not to leave. Give her anything she wants, anything at all, but not a boat to get to shore. Understand?"

Priestly clearly did not, but he nodded.

"Good. McDaniels, you will come with me and show me where those houses are." He hesitated. "But there's something I need to do first."

He turned back to his cabin. Behind that door, which the breeze had blown slightly ajar, lay a beautiful, enticing woman, the woman of his dreams. He would have to leave her behind to travel across cold London with an overly jocular, somewhat smelly pirate crew. Life was not fair.

Behind him, Priestly snickered to McDaniels. "How long do you think it will take him, sir? Two minutes?"

"Don't know, lad. Maybe three. He's still fairly robust."

"Should we wager?"

Grayson swung back to them. "I assure you gentlemen, if I planned to do what is in your lewd thoughts, it would be hours. *Hours.* And when this stupid business is finished, I promise you, it will be *days.*"

"Yes, sir," they both said together. The smirks remained.

He turned his back and entered the cabin. Alexandra had burrowed beneath the blankets on the bunk. He shut the door firmly on his men and crossed to her. Her breathing was too swift for sleep, and when he bent down to kiss her, she opened her eyes and responded.

"I have to go for a while, love," he whispered as the kiss ended. "I will return as soon as I can. If you want anything while I'm gone, anything in the world, ask Priestly to get it for you. I'll flog him if he does not. I promise."

"Anything?" she said sleepily.

"Anything, love." Except a ride home, he added silently. She would be safe from Ardmore here. They were in the middle of the Thames; the only way to them was over water. If Ardmore or his men tried to storm the *Majesty,* Ardmore would have a fight to the death on his hands.

He kissed her again, deep and long, savoring her. His arousal, slightly sated now, reminded him how good it had felt to have her squeezing him tight. He ruthlessly tamped down the thought. He ended the kiss, his lips clinging to hers until the last moment.

When he stood up, her diamond necklace dangled from his hand.

Her brown-green eyes widened. She clapped her hand to her bare throat. "What are you doing?"

"Stealing your jewels. It is traditional."

She stared at him in open-mouthed shock, outrage dancing in her eyes, then, suddenly, like the sun emerging from behind a cloud, she smiled.

He clutched that smile to his heart, clutched the diamonds in his hand, and left her.

Across the Thames, aboard the *Argonaut*—whose name had been carefully painted over and rewritten as the *Carolina*—Mr. Henderson toyed with the mother-of-pearl handle of his now empty pistol. Emotion raged inside him, and he did not like emotions. They were inconvenient, a distraction, and a nuisance. And ever since he'd met Mrs. Alastair—if "met" were to proper word for what he'd done—his emotions had plagued him.

On the other side of the table Captain Ardmore read letters, or whatever the hell papers he was perusing.

"Finley's landed on his feet as usual," Henderson observed glumly. "Damn him."

Ardmore did not look up. "What do you mean, on his feet?"

"Mrs. Alastair. If that isn't landing on his feet, I don't know what is." He added reflectively. "I'd be on my knees, personally."

"I agree, Mr. Henderson," Ardmore said in his Southern drawl. "She is an extraordinarily lovely woman."

The usual cold note in Ardmore's voice had actually softened. Interesting. "You are not going to—ah." Henderson rubbed the sides of his mouth, which still hurt from Finley's damned thick fist. "You are going to leave her alone, aren't you?"

Ardmore turned another paper over. "If you mean am I going to force myself upon her, no, I am not. If you mean will I take her away from Finley, yes, I will."

Henderson set his pistol aside, out of temptation's way. "I wish you would leave this one alone, sir."

Ardmore looked up. Henderson stopped himself from flinching. Having James Ardmore give you his full attention was a situation much to be avoided, but he'd stand his ground.

"Why?" Ardmore demanded.

Henderson sighed, then decided he might as well plunge in. It was only his grave after all. "Mrs. Alastair is different. She is a lady. Descended from a duke, for God's sake."

"I come from one of Charleston's first families, myself."

Henderson clenched his hands. When Ardmore chose to be obtuse, it meant he did not want to discuss the matter at hand, and the officer in question should only pursue it at his peril. But Henderson felt reckless tonight. His mouth already throbbed with Finley's punch. What was a little more pain? "I want no part in whatever you intend for Mrs. Alastair," he said. "Finley, I will gladly help you hunt down. He is a pain in the fundament, and I would love to see him get his comeuppance. But Mrs. Alastair—" He broke off. Ardmore was simply watching him, giving him the rope with which to hang himself. "I will no longer help you with Mrs. Alastair, sir," Henderson finished in a rush. "I will not drug her, I will not abduct her, I will not assault her. She deserves none of that, and I am ashamed to have been a part of it."

Ardmore's eyes were as impenetrable as green ice, and just as cold. "Or?" he asked softly.

"Or what?"

"You have proclaimed I and my ideas for Mrs. Alastair can go to hell. On what condition? If I continue to insist, what will you do?"

"I will have to resign, sir."

Ardmore said nothing. The silence stretched, broken only by the soft sigh of wind outside the stern windows, the quiet slap of water against the hull. Henderson was suddenly reminded of the summer day, a few years back, when he'd been visiting Ardmore's Charleston home, where Ardmore's sister, Honoria, lived. Henderson had been walking with Miss Ardmore in the gardens, and to all of his flirtations—she was a beautiful woman, after all—she had simply given him a green-eyed stare and a raised brow. Her clipped tones had told him what she'd thought of him, an Englishman, trying to make up to her. A true ice queen. He decided that the stare Ardmore was giving him now was the classic family signal that the person who received it was lower than worms.

Ardmore finally answered. "You know I cannot let you resign while I am in England. You know why."

Henderson's face heated. "I give you my word, sir, I will not betray you. My quarrel is not with you. I simply do not want anything to happen to Mrs. Ardmore."

Again, the cool stare, the faint look of scorn. "Nothing will happen to her. I do not harm innocents."

"You might this one. Just by being who you are."

Ardmore regarded him for a long, quiet moment. "Your objections are noted, lieutenant." He sat back, steepling his fingers. "Now, tell me more about your chase of Burchard. It looks like we'll have to kill him again."

In other words, subject closed. Completely. Henderson bit back a sigh and launched into his tale, but his inconvenient and troubling emotions still raged inside of him.

"This is the first time I have been on a pirate ship," Alexandra said primly, looking into the flustered face of Mr. Priestly. "So of course I do not know."

Priestly's harried look became more pronounced. He had a narrow face, a shock of brown-blond hair, small blue eyes, and a pinched mouth. Alexandra supposed he made a frightening pirate, but at the moment, he seemed frightened of her. Which was all to the good.

"Mrs. Alastair," he said in a voice stretched thin. "I *really* do not understand what you are asking for."

"It is perfectly simple, Mr. Priestly. I need to know where the lady's retiring rooms are."

"The *what* rooms?"

"Retiring rooms. Where a lady might be private." She leaned toward him and lowered her voice. "For private necessities."

He blinked a few times, and then drew a relieved breath. "Oh, you mean the head."

Alexandra dabbed at her mouth with the almost-white napkin he'd managed to find her. It had been the third napkin he'd brought, and he had almost wilted in relief when she'd said, with slight disappointment, that it would have to do. She'd had a breakfast of bread—fresh, not the stale loaf he'd first produced—hot coffee and fruit. Peaches. Fresh, ripe ones from the market on shore. All served in the captain's cabin on a little folding table covered with a white cloth, no stains. She'd been served on porcelain plates with a silver knife and spoon. Oh, and fresh, cool butter for the bread, please.

She had bade them bring her a bath—hot, Mr. Priestly, not lukewarm—and she'd dressed again in her silk gown. She'd also combed out her hair and gathered it into a tail. Priestly had proudly brought her a silver-backed hairbrush after a two-hour-long search, holding it out to her like a dog expecting a pat. She'd inspected it in his hand and then asked him to please bring her a clean one.

She wiped her hands now while he foundered. Inside her, anger seethed and boiled, anger at none other than that rat, Grayson Finley. She'd heard every word of his conversation with officers McDaniels and Priestly through the opened cabin door, including the order to Mr. Priestly to give Mrs. Alastair everything she wanted, but not to let her off the ship. For any reason.

She needed to return home. She had a soiree to plan. Lady Featherstone would wonder where on earth she'd gotten to. She wanted to see for herself that Maggie had arrived safely home, though she reasoned that Grayson would see to that himself quickly enough. He trusted this Ian O'Malley, though Alexandra was not certain she did.

Jeffrey would bother Cook and not attend to his duties, and Amy and Annie would find excuses to shirk their responsibilities; Alice had said she'd leave if she had to take up where they slackened. Alexandra had a dozen things to attend to, thank you very much Mr. Pirate, even if they did not involve finding a French king and avoiding pirate hunters. Besides, Alexandra had half a dozen possibilities about that French king floating in her head. She really wanted to discuss them with Grayson, and also with Mrs. Fairchild, who knew much about the French and the exiled king. None of which she could do if she were stranded here.

Anything in the world, he had said. Priestly was to cooperate, or risk a flogging. *Well, we shall see about that, Mr. High-and-Mighty Pirate Viscount Stoke.*

Serve him right for making love to her like that, for ripping the cover from her heart and letting emotions she had never intended anyone to see out into the light of day. He had spoken to her the words of her daydream: *Lovely lady, may I taste you?* And then he'd put his mouth on her and stirred fires inside her that she'd never known existed. She felt all stretched and tired and achy and far, far too pleased. Drat him.

"What is the head?" she asked Priestly now, curious.

"It's—ah—in the bows. You go up, and you sit on the

hole—um." He looked her up and down. She waited. "It is outside," he blurted.

She let her brows climb to her hairline. "Outside?"

"Yes," he finished weakly.

"Well, *that* will never do. Do you not have a watering closet or commode anywhere?"

Priestly pointed at the door, his feet already moving to his escape. "I'll just see what I can do, m'lady."

He fled. Alexandra set down her napkin. She had not corrected the "m'lady" to "Mrs." She decided she could only be so cruel.

Chapter Fourteen

McDaniels's shop was unenlightening. By the time he and Grayson reached Marylebone, the sun was high and city traffic was dense. The shop sold little trinkets, snuff boxes, letter boxes, dainty letter openers, and the like, all kept on high shelves on the ground floor behind the proprietor's counter.

The proprietor was not there, but his daughter was, to wait on customers. She was pretty, charming, and very French. Though she was young enough to have been born in England after her parents had made the crossing from France, she spoke with a thick accent and fluttered her eyelashes a great deal. She said "zat is so" or "I zink" every other sentence.

Grayson saw no evidence of a rotund French king stuffed into a back room or looking out of a window next door, but then, he had no chance to search as he liked. He would have to return another time, and either force his way in, or have the Duke of St. Clair charge in with the weight of the Admiralty behind him. The smiling, flirting young woman gave him no clues.

Grayson pretended interest in nothing except purchasing a pretty ink bottle for Maggie. He chose one with an enameled stopper depicting a pair of young lovers chasing each other through a meadow. Their lacy, old-fashioned costumes were splashes of gaudy color on the green landscape. Maggie would like it.

Maggie ran to meet him when he entered his house on Grosvenor Street. She threw her arms about him and he lifted her and hugged her tight. He wondered anew how he'd produced this marvelous and beautiful child. That Maggie had been the result of his callow youth still stunned him.

"Come and see my new governess," she said. "She is most beautiful. I am glad Mrs. Alastair chose a beautiful governess. It will be much easier to pay attention to her lessons in French."

Grayson set her on her feet. "She knows French?"

"Fluently. She also knows Greek. But the letters are all funny, not at all what the missionaries taught me."

Grayson grinned at her. "You ought to see Chinese. They write in tiny little pictures."

Her eyes widened. "Truly? Why can't we write in tiny little pictures? It would be so much easier."

Grayson started to agree, then saw Mrs. Fairchild gliding down the stairs to them. She really was an exquisite woman. If Alexandra had not already wrapped herself around his senses, he might have decided her worth pursuing. But he had Alexandra—

He should be sated, having drunk his fill of her, having driven himself deep inside her. But every memory of her breath on his skin, her scent, her taste, the fires of her touch made his arousal twitch in eager anticipation.

When can we have a go again? it kept asking. When, when?

She was on the *Majesty* in care of Priestly. Grayson had but to travel back down river, climb aboard and—well, climb aboard. Alexandra was a sweet, delicious woman, and he never wanted her to be more than steps away. But he had too many things to take care of first. Life was not fair.

He swallowed his frustration. Mrs. Fairchild reached the ground floor and curtseyed. "My lord," she said in her smooth contralto. "Is Mrs. Alastair safe?"

He inclined his head. "She is. She's staying aboard my ship for a time."

"I see." Her expression told him she did not see, and did not like the situation, but was hesitant to say so.

He went on, trying to think of words an employer might speak to a governess. "Is your chamber to your liking, Mrs. Fairchild? The house is old and dusty, not to mention dismal and dim, but at least the roof does not leak. Is there anything else you need?"

She nodded politely, light catching in her sleek, dark hair. "My chamber is quite adequate. I need nothing more." She hesitated. "However, I would like to speak with you on an important matter."

Grayson stripped off his gloves and tossed them onto a table. "It will have to be later. I have an unfortunate amount of business to attend. Maggie, where is Jacobs?"

"Walking about in the garden," Maggie said promptly. "I cannot imagine why; there are no flowers or anything. Not like Mrs. Alastair's garden. We will have to ask her who made her garden and hire him to do ours."

Grayson nodded absently. "Whatever you like. Mrs. Fairchild, I'll speak to you later."

He strode past them, not missing Mrs. Fairchild's anguished look. He grumbled silently. Why could she not be sixty and have a mustache? Maggie might want a beautiful governess, but the glum way Jacobs was shuffling through the barren garden made Grayson wish for a hideous one. He did not need Jacobs to be distracted just now. Grayson being distracted by Alexandra was bad enough.

He watched Jacobs from the dining room window for a moment, then summoned the young man inside and closed the door.

Jacobs wandered idly about the room, brushing his fingertips to the dark sideboard, the table. "Found the Frenchie king yet, sir?"

"Jacobs."

Jacobs looked up at his sharp tone. It struck Grayson on a sudden just how young his first officer was. Jacobs was twenty-five, and had signed on to the *Majesty* at the tender age of twenty. Because Robert Jacobs possessed great competence and intelligence, as well as a cool head in an emergency, Grayson had come to rely on him in the most complicated and dangerous situations. He had never stopped to think about how little worldly experience the young man actually had.

He continued. "Ardmore is going to try to take me down any way he can, bargain or no. Including using Mrs. Alastair to do it."

The abstracted look left Jacobs's face. "I gathered that, sir. Are you still going to meet him as planned?"

Grayson gave a nod. "Of the outcome of that meeting, I am no longer certain."

"Good, sir. I did not like to see you capitulate so tamely."

"For Maggie, it was necessary. But you see the problem.

You can never be sure what he has in mind. He's always been a tricky bastard."

"You do not have to tell me that, sir," Jacobs said fervently.

"What I do have to tell you is that I want Maggie protected. Always. Ian looks after her, but when all is said and done, he works for Ardmore. I want someone with Maggie I can trust with her life." He stopped. "That is why I am assigning you to stay with her at all times." Jacobs's head jerked up. Grayson went on ruthlessly. "You are to sleep in the room next to hers, take your meals with her, and go with her everywhere, whether it's outings with the governess or shopping for vegetables. I want you her constant companion."

Jacobs had whitened during his speech. "I am not certain I am the best person to protect her, sir."

"There isn't anyone better."

"Oliver—"

"Has much to do. He is busy cooking our meals and looking after us, and besides, I need him for other things." Grayson paused, and then decided to approach the problem head-on. "Whatever is between you and this Fairchild woman, resolve. Understood?"

"Sir." His look was anguished. "She is not just a woman. She is *the* woman."

Ah, here it was. "Explain yourself, lieutenant."

Jacobs stared at the tabletop. "Remember when I first joined you, sir? You asked why a lad fresh out of Oxford wanted to go to sea. And I said, to forget a woman."

Grayson watched him. "Mrs. Fairchild?"

Jacobs blew out his breath. "It was incredible, sir. You have seen her. She is even more beautiful now, if that is possible."

"She was married?" Grayson asked.

Jacobs nodded. "Oh, yes. To a *don*. Hell, he was one of my own tutors. That is how I met her. She was married and ten years older than I."

Grayson chuckled. "Good on you, lad."

Jacobs flashed a smile that told Grayson it had been all that, and more. "I fell devilish hard. You know what it is like when you're that young. You met Sara when you were twenty or so, did you not?"

Grayson nodded. He had been twenty-two when he'd first seen Sara. The South Pacific to him had always been a place of happiness. He remembered the sharp scent of tropical flowers, the warm air on his skin, the tranquil sound of ocean on white sands—all these memories were woven into his first glimpse of Sara. He'd taken one look at her exotic, dark-haired beauty and her flashing, midnight eyes, and fallen hard. Ardmore had introduced her, his arm firmly about her waist, and had given Grayson a look that said see-what-I-caught-you-can't-have-her. When Ardmore and she had strolled away, Sara had looked back at Grayson, sending Grayson a wink and a promising smile. Three days later, while Ardmore was conducting business elsewhere, Sara had climbed into Grayson's bed. When Ardmore had returned, he'd tried to kill Grayson.

Why hadn't the stupid idiot confessed that he'd been madly in love with the woman? If Grayson had known that, he would have left her alone. Maybe. But he'd been young and blind, and Ardmore had been arrogant and proud. Grayson had assumed his friend had been finished with Sara and was handing Grayson his leavings. It would not have been the first time Ardmore had discarded a lady and directed her to Grayson for comfort.

The incident had ended the four-year partnership of Finley and Ardmore, the co-captains of the *Majesty* who feared nothing on the seas. Ardmore had quit him, and Ian O'Malley had gone with him. Oliver, the pirate who had saved Grayson from a cruel pirate captain when he was fifteen, chose loyalty to Grayson and the *Majesty*. So had begun a long and dangerous rivalry, which had escalated to open hatred after the death of Ardmore's younger brother, six years later.

"It is easier to fall when you're young," Grayson agreed, looking into Jacobs's miserable eyes. "But not always sensible."

"Precisely. I damned well wasn't sensible about anything, sir." He made a wry grimace. "*She* broke it off. Not me."

"That was a long time ago."

He shook his head. "Five years, two months, and three days. And still the only music I hear is in her voice."

Grayson exhaled slowly. He sympathized because he knew exactly what Jacobs meant. Alexandra's lovely voice whispering his name had driven him to mad heights of desire. He would never forget it.

"I know," he said. "Some women can turn you inside out, and damned if you know why." He shook his head. "But I need you, Jacobs. You are the only I can trust for this. You know Ardmore; you can anticipate him. But you cannot if you are walking head down in your own misery. Talk to Mrs. Fairchild. Argue it out with her. Give her a good tumble if you have to." He paused. "After you make certain Maggie is safe with Oliver or me, of course."

"She wants to leave, sir. She said she would speak to you about it."

Grayson rubbed his jaw. "Yes, she already tried to corner me for an appointment." What he really wanted was a bath and a change of clothes—that and another few hours in bed with Alexandra. But as ship's captain, he was used to having to solve the personal problems of his crew. A pirate with woman troubles was a sad sight, indeed. Grayson's usual remedy was to pat the man on the back, hand him whatever alcoholic beverage was a specialty of the country they were in, and say, "Have at it, lad."

Jacobs's problems were a little more complex and a lot more troubling. This was the first time the young man had been anything other than his efficient, somewhat ruthless, self.

He said to Jacobs, "Find her and tell her I will speak to her now."

"I will send Oliver for her."

Grayson ground his teeth. "Whatever you like. Just get her here."

Jacobs fled.

Grayson spent the intervening moments staring out into the garden, or what would have been a garden if his tight-fisted predecessor had spent the money to cultivate it. His impatience prodded him to do something, anything, to speed his task to conclusion. He should be back at the shop, shaking the pretty young Frenchwoman until she blurted out where her father had taken King Louis. He should be making an efficient list, like Alexandra's, with little codes next to each item that distinguished its importance. Instead, he drummed his fingers on the windowsill, waited to pry into his first officer's love affairs, and fought off his thoughts of the past.

He had not thought about Sara in a very long time. She had left him—that was that. He'd never expected to hold her anyway. She'd been like a wild tropical bird, an out-of-reach blossom no one could pluck, a creature no one could cage. She'd moved from her native Polynesia across the seas, slipping away from Grayson as easily as she'd slipped away from Ardmore to begin with.

Grayson remembered clearly the last night he'd seen her. They'd put into port and Grayson had stood on his quarterdeck, watching the stars and the weather. She'd come to him and simply told him she would not be traveling on with him. He'd grown angry, but she'd remained firm.

"Sometimes you call me 'bird,'" she'd said in her husky voice. "Give me your hand, Grayson." He'd complied, bemused, and she'd opened his hand flat. With her slim fingers, she'd drawn feather-light lines on his palm. "Bird rests here. You close your hand, try to trap it, what do you do?" She curled his fingers into his palm, pressing them tight. "Poor bird. She dies."

Grayson had looked down at his closed fist, frowning. She gently pried open his hand and touched the palm again. "The bird is here, for a time. Then she flies away. Alive. And free."

"To another hand," he'd said regretfully.

She'd flashed him her beautiful smile. "Perhaps. Or perhaps one day, the bird flies back."

She'd kissed him on the lips, a faint echo of the passionate kisses they'd shared below decks in his cabin, then she was gone, lost to the night.

Now he stood in chilly England, with the sky clouding over and blotting out the sun. He had found a woman who'd made the memory of Sara pale and fade, and what was he doing? Taking her into his arms and showing her the passion that burned and raged inside him? No, here he stood, alone, in this cold and dark house, waiting for Ardmore to make a move, and trying to keep the Admiralty satisfied so they would not arrest him and his crew. His man of business had explained that if he were arrested and convicted of piracy, his title, estate, and money could be seized by the crown, and Maggie would be left destitute. He could not let that happen, even if he had to toady to St. Clair for the rest of his life.

The door opened. Mrs. Fairchild entered, her gown rustling faintly. She closed the door and waited.

Grayson turned to her. She might stand calmly, but trepidation and anxiety flared in her eyes.

"My lord," she said before he could speak. "I have come to give notice. I know I have only just arrived. I will stay until you find someone suitable, if you like."

Chapter Fifteen

Grayson studied her for a time. She stood perfectly composed, the respectful governess speaking to her master, but deep in her eyes flickered a restless anguish that he well recognized. She met his gaze tranquilly, but her right hand clenched until the skin whitened.

At last he said, "Request denied, Mrs. Fairchild."

She blinked. "What? But Robert said he told you everything. Certainly you would not want a woman like me with your daughter. . . ." She trailed off.

Grayson held up his hand. "Mr. Jacobs told me you two once had a steamy and illicit affair. And that you ended it yourself. I am curious. Why?"

She flushed a dull red. "My lord, why do you think? He was young—he did not need me clinging to him, did he, an aging woman who could only drag him into shame?"

"Ah. So you broke his heart for his own good."

She looked panicked. "Broke his heart?"

"These things do not always resolve neatly. I will be blunt. I need you here. I do not have time to look for another governess. I need Jacobs, too, and I need him close to Maggie. I am sorry if you are uncomfortable. You and Jacobs will just have to come to some kind of agreement."

Mrs. Fairchild opened and closed her pretty mouth a few times. "I will find another governess for you, my lord. And stay until she arrives."

Damn it. "No." When she blinked in astonishment, he hurried on. "Look, Mrs. Fairchild, *you* must be Maggie's governess, and only you. Alexandra chose you. She said you were the very best. Anyone else will be less so, and I want only the best for Maggie."

"There are many competent governesses, my lord, who would be eager for a position in a viscount's household."

He raked his hand through his hair. "Yes, but you see, *Alexandra* sent you. Understand? If you leave, she'll blame *me*."

Her brows furrowed. "Why should she?"

"Because she believes I am the worst excuse for a father since King Herod. You should have read the letter she sent me, outlining everything I was doing wrong. And I have been doing absolutely *everything* wrong. I know that; I've only been a father for six months, and I was a pirate for nineteen years."

"Pirate—?"

"I have never had any training for the job. I only saw what the missionaries had done, and I swore to God I'd do the opposite. They never broke her spirit, but they certainly tried."

Mrs. Fairchild said, "Oh," but Grayson barely heard her.

He remembered the tight politeness of Alexandra's

note explaining that daughters of lords in Mayfair should neither wear breeches nor soiled pink concoctions that had been made for ballrooms several seasons ago. Grayson had not had a chance to explain that he'd bought the pink frock in Jamaica in a fit of rage. He'd purchased it because the garment was the direct opposite of the horrible gray dress they'd stuffed Maggie into. Maggie should be wearing the loveliest gowns money could buy and should be smiling and laughing, not dour and quiet, like the missionaries wanted her to be.

The lady shoppers in the secondhand clothier where he'd so incompetently searched for the gown had found him amusing. They'd taken pity on him and helped him find the sweet pink thing they'd said a young girl would love. They had been right. Maggie had been so pleased with the gift that she'd refused to take the dress off for days.

Alexandra had written, stiffly, that Maggie needed morning dresses and walking dresses and dresses for rides in the park, for outings to museums, for visits to the theatre with her father or herself—not, he noted, both of them together. She also needed a proper and well-trained governess, not to quash her, but to teach her how to become a graceful and lovely young woman.

If Mrs. Fairchild left him, Alexandra would write him another letter equally as polite and pointed. Or she'd stand before him, bathing him in a sorrowful look, and express her disappointment in him.

He eyed Mrs. Fairchild, who looked a bit stunned. "Will it help if I beg?" he asked.

"My lord—"

He abandoned the polite viscount, who was doing him no good, and resurrected Captain Finley, terror of the seas. "Mrs. Fairchild, I do not have time for histrionics.

You and Mr. Jacobs will have to talk through your problems and reach some conclusion. But do not let it distract you from taking care of Maggie. Make her your first priority. Understand?"

Mrs. Fairchild's stare was a mix of amazement and outrage. "But, my lord—"

"No buts, Mrs. Fairchild. Dismissed."

She gazed at him for one more astonished second, then snapped her mouth closed. Giving him a look that told him King Herod was a pleasant and forgiving gentleman compared to him, she turned on her heel and strode out the door.

There, Grayson thought as he closed it behind her. *I am not as bad at this as Jacobs thinks.*

"M'lady, I vow to you, there are no pins to be had!"

Alexandra looked into Mr. Priestly's red and exasperated face and barely contained her glee. She sat demurely at Grayson's desk in his cabin perusing an out-of-date lady's magazine. "Do you mean, Mr. Priestly, that in the entire Thames estuary, not one shop possesses ladies' dressmaking pins?"

"I give you my word, I looked!"

She heaved an aggrieved sigh. "Mr. Priestly."

"M'lady," he almost wailed.

She shook her head. "My silk became torn last night when his lordship rescued me. I cannot possibly mend it with implements for repairing sails. I must have pins, silk thread, and the thinnest of needles. Why is this so impossible?"

Priestly mopped his brow. He'd worn a haggard look all afternoon, and the last time she had ventured on deck to summon him, he had actually fled her.

"M'lady, my men went up and down, searching. They

asked; they looked in shops. They found no pins and no needles and no silk thread."

Alexandra smiled secretly at the thought of Grayson's rough-looking pirates shambling through the streets asking for ladies' dressmaking pins. Still keeping her expression dark, she feigned a heavy sigh. "I suppose it is not your fault. Someone will simply have to send to Town for another gown. Or I will have to go."

His lips thinned. "M'lady, I was ordered explicitly by Captain Finley himself that I am not to let you off this ship."

"Yes, indeed," Alexandra said. "He also ordered you to obtain for me whatever I needed. Did he not?"

"Yes, but—"

"I *need* a change of clothing. I cannot possibly wear my theatre gown all day and all night. Perhaps you can send your men into town again to a secondhand clothing shop. They will have ready-made garments. I will write down my measurements."

"I do not think," Mr. Priestly said carefully, "that the sailors will obey an order to go into a shop and purchase lady's clothing."

"And a nightdress, if I am to sleep here. And a few pairs of stockings, and some garters." She tapped her cheek. "That young man called Thomas is about my height and girth. Perhaps he could try on the gown, make certain the fit is right—"

"No!" Priestly shouted. His voice filled the room. A sailor above peered in through the opened skylight. Priestly balled his hands, shaking, his face red. "Mrs. Alastair, I can take no more. I have brought you ribbons and combs and oranges and magazines—"

"None of them *Le Belle Assemble*," she put in.

"M'lady, I could not find one! All I could find was *Le Beau Monde*. And I do not speak French."

She tapped the journal on the desk. "It is three months out of date. And they are all in English, Mr. Priestly."

"I do not read ladies' magazines," he said desperately. "You have made me and my men a laughingstock. You sent us out for oil of jasmin, and I do not even know what that is!"

She gave him a severe look. "Really, Mr. Priestly, there is no need to shout at me."

"There is need. I am at the end of my tether. What the devil do you want me to do?"

"Restrain your language for a start, sir. I am only asking for the accoutrements I will need if I am forced to stay here. Surely the viscount does not expect me to shiver in a torn garment and exist on grog and biscuits."

"He expects *us* to," Priestly muttered.

"I do not believe the viscount thought it through when he ordered you to keep me here."

"No," he agreed fervently. "But I can't let you go ashore, m'lady. He'll peel the skin off my hide and hang it up to dry, then nail the rest of my body beside it."

His lips were white, his breathing fast. A little foam flecked the sides of his mouth.

Alexandra felt pity for him, but she could not relent just yet. "Then I must have a change of clothing. You see that." She sighed. "Or you will have to take it up with the viscount." She frowned, pretending to think. "Please tell young Thomas that I am particularly fond of yellow."

Priestly stared at her, fists tight. Then he cried "Gaahhh!" and stormed from the cabin.

It had grown quite dark by the time the viscount returned to the *Majesty*. The stars were out, thick and bright against the dark throat of night. Alexandra gazed at them from the quarterdeck. In Town, so many lights from houses and passing coach lanterns, not to mention the smoke from chimneys and the fog or clouds that habitually hung over the city, obscured the stars. Here, the wind parted the clouds and allowed the beauty of the night to shine through.

Alexandra smoothed the cotton of her yellow gown, proudly brought to her by young Thomas. She'd relented in her suggestion that he try the clothes on for her, and had written a note with her measurements for Priestly to give to a clothier. The gown did not quite fit, but it would have to do.

She sighed and continued to study the stars. Stargazing always reminded her of home, of the rolling green swards of Kent, of happy summers spent lying in sweet grass, feeling as if she were falling upward into the stars, dreaming dreams great and glorious.

A heavy step sounded behind her, and presently, she sensed him next to her, his bulk of warmth and his masculine scents of musk and the night. He leaned on the rail, his strong arms taking his weight, the wind from the sea lifting his blond-streaked hair.

She did not, as she longed to, fling her arms about him and joyfully cry his name. She continued to watch the stars and the horizon, as if it made no difference that he'd joined her.

"Alexandra," he began. His baritone flowed over her like cool water in the heat. "I have been captaining ships since I was eighteen years old. I have faced frigates that outgunned me and hostile islanders ready to boil me up for supper and the fiercest pirates on the seas. And never once in that long career have my men disobeyed my orders or threatened a mutiny." He turned his head and looked at her. "Until today."

She felt her face heat, but she kept her voice innocent. "I only asked for the things I needed, my lord."

Grayson choked back a laugh. The battle between her and Priestly must have been fierce. Only months ago, he had seen Priestly boarding a frigate, pistols blazing, a cutlass in his teeth, fighting like mad and roaring obscenities. But this afternoon Priestly's face had been tinged gray, and his dark-circled eyes wild with terror. "She sent us off for women's undergarments, sir. And cream to keep off wrinkles. She hasn't got any wrinkles! And she told us the wrong name, so we had to keep asking and asking."

Grayson had worked hard to keep from bursting into laughter. He imagined his men running from shop to shop desperately seeking wrinkle cream and garters. He had known that Alexandra, with her independent spirit, would chafe at her confinement, but he had anticipated her trying to climb over the side and attempting to steal a boat and row it by herself. Her choice of how to fight back was delicious.

"How long do you plan to keep me prisoner, my lord?" she asked primly.

He looked out over the water again. The ship rocked a little at its anchor. "The danger is so great, Alexandra."

"Well." She traced patterns on the varnished wooden rail. "You could simply send a few guards to my house while I prepare for my soiree. Which is in two days, by the way. They could make themselves useful hanging garlands and carrying tables about."

"I do not think they'd like that any more than buying wrinkle cream. Did you really ask Thomas to try on gowns?"

She looked contrite. "I decided I would not at the last."

"I imagine he was thankful."

He could stay away from her no longer. He closed the distance between them and slid his arm around her waist.

She looked up at him, her eyes soft. "I must go home."

"But I want you to stay."

"It is impossible."

He drew his hand up to cup the swell of her breast, and leaned to the fragrant curve of her neck. She closed her eyes. "But perhaps," she murmured. "I could stay a little longer."

She smelled so good. How he could have ever thought another woman would satisfy him, he did not know. Sara had been a bird made to fly away. Alexandra was made of sterner stuff, though she appeared frailer than the robust Sara. But Alexandra would keep her feet firmly on the ground, stand at his side. Sara had been a wild spirit, true to none but herself. Alexandra would remain steadfastly loyal to whatever man she chose.

Lucky man.

It had been not even a full day and night since he'd made love to her, but his body was still hungry. His hands wanted to tumble her hair, to soothe the heat of her skin, to slide over the curve of her hips. He wanted to taste her mouth and her female places and let his tongue drive her to madness once more.

His cabin was only steps away. He could grow fond of his cabin.

He slid his hands beneath her hair and slanted his mouth across hers. He could taste her anger, her frustration, but despite this her lips softened for his, returned his gentle pressure. At last, with a small sigh of surrender, she dropped her head back and closed her eyes. Her hands came up to rest on his chest, fingers curled.

So little time. Only a few weeks to know her, to explore her, to love her. And then the chaos of his life would come to a head and he and James Ardmore would meet a final time.

Too soon. He had not known what gifts life would give him. He'd never dreamed he would grow to love his daughter until every breath she took was his breath too. He never knew his heart could expand like this, never knew such feelings could find their way into the cynical, hard-bitten Grayson Finley. He only knew he wanted to tarry here a while, with Alexandra and this newfound hunger.

"Grayson, please," she whispered.

"It is I who will be begging, love." He pressed a kiss to the line of her hair, where fire met white. "Let me bed you again."

She shook her head, her ringlets brushing his lips.

"I beg you," he said.

She shook her head again, still not looking at him.

The correct thing to do when a lady rejected his advances was to swallow his pride, give an uncaring shrug, and depart. He remained in place, tracing circles on the base of her neck. "My pride is trembling, Alexandra."

"I am confused," she said. "You so confuse me."

He kissed her cheek. "I want you. There is nothing confusing about that."

The wind stirred her skirts and strands of her long hair. "I wish to marry. But you tumble me like a tavern girl and sequester me on your ship. I do not know what you want."

He traced her cheek. What did he want? Her, he knew that. Happiness? Maggie. Time. He drew a breath. *Peace*.

"Do you want me, Alexandra?" he asked in a soft voice.

"Yes. If you must know the truth, I do."

His heart leapt.

She held up her hand. "But am I to be your mistress? I cannot be. Or will I be a pirate's lady and sail away with you? I believe your crew truly will mutiny if I do that."

His lips twitched, but he suppressed his smile. "I told you, I am not leaving England."

"Because of Maggie."

Mutely, he nodded.

"Good. She does need you, Grayson. From what I gather, she did not have a proper upbringing." She smiled, a shining light of glory. "I am pleased that you shouted at the missionaries."

He bit back a laugh. "She told you about that?"

"Yes. And that you bought her all kinds of absurd presents. And shaved off your pirate's whiskers for her. You are a good man, my lord, a fine gentleman. Even though my feelings toward you are extremely wrong and a bit distressing, I do see the goodness in you."

He looked down at himself. "You do? Where?"

"Here." She laid her palm flat against his chest. She looked suddenly puzzled and lifted her fingers away.

Grayson unbuttoned his coat. Beneath it stretched a leather bandolier that held his pistol in its holster. He shrugged off the coat, unbuckled the bandolier, and laid it and the pistol on the bench under the starboard rail. He spread his arms. "Better?"

"You so confuse me."

"I am what you see. Nothing to confuse you."

He reached for her. She stepped away, smoothly sliding from his outstretched fingers. His hands closed on emptiness.

"For heaven's sake, Grayson, you are a *pirate*."

"Private merchantman. The charge of piracy is pending. And, if I find the French king, it will be dismissed."

She made a noise of exasperation. "It does not matter what you call yourself. I know nothing about your world." She waved her hands at the ship around her. "You have battles with ships and you have been sliced open and shot. I only know drawing rooms and at-homes and balls and operas. I have ladies and gentlemen coming to call— and pirate hunters do not try to murder my next-door neighbors. You—" She pointed a slim finger at him. "I do not know what to make of you. You still have not told me what you want."

"I want to know you," he said softly.

She shook her head, her ringlets dancing. "You want to come to my bed and make me feel all wild and strange. I want to lick your skin, and I have never in my life wanted to do something so wicked."

He smiled slowly. "You want to taste me? I am pleased."

She wagged her finger at him. "No, do not smile at me like that. You make me all confused inside. You make me long to say 'Yes, please, Grayson, let us tumble on the bed as we did last night and throw caution to the wind.' "

Warm sensations pricked his loins. "It was not entirely on the bed."

"Do not interrupt, please. You want to ravish me like a common tart, or a lady passenger who is no better than she ought to be."

He stopped. "Lady passenger?"

"Yes. That is what pirates do, is it not? You enter a lady's cabin, seduce her, and steal her jewels. While you are sinking the ship, of course."

Mirth danced in him. "Is that what you were thinking last night?" His desires began to rampage. "Well, if you would like to play such a game, Alexandra, I am willing."

She glared at him, but her cheeks turned a beautiful

pink. "Do not be ridiculous. Besides, it is not my game. It is Mrs. Waters's."

He frowned, lost. "Mrs. Waters?"

"You met her in my reception room last week. Before the accident outside my house. You remember—the woman in blue with very black hair."

His memory brought the event into focus. He remembered a large woman with a doughy face and small brown eyes, her hair unnaturally black. She had batted her lashes at him and blatantly roved a hungry gaze up and down his body. Alarm touched him. "Good lord. *She* thought that about *me?*"

"You must have done such things as a pirate."

He lifted his hands. "Alexandra, I assure you, if I had ever attacked a passenger ship, and if I even suspected that Mrs. Waters was onboard, I would have fled in the opposite direction."

"It makes no difference. I have behaved like a common—lady passenger. And you did steal my jewels." She glared accusingly.

"I remember you begging me to take them."

"I cannot imagine what you wanted with them. Maggie says you have emeralds, and you said you have opals. Why did you want my ugly diamonds?"

He smiled a little. "It is a surprise." Indeed, he had surprised the Bond Street jeweler that afternoon when he'd strode into the shop and flung down the diamonds and the handful of opals, five perfect stones, and said, "Do something with these." The jeweler had gaped, then the artist in him had taken over and he'd lifted an opal to peer at it through his glass. "Exquisite, my lord, most exquisite. Yes, yes, I can make quite a fine setting. Your lady will be most pleased."

Grayson's whole awareness at the moment had narrowed to pleasing his lady. He took up her hand and placed it on his chest. Her palm was warm through his linen shirt. "Perhaps you could be a lady passenger in the captain's cabin," he said, his heart beating fast and hard. "And I, the wicked pirate, could find you there."

Her lips parted, her eyes clouding in confusion. "No, I—"

"Or on deck will do just as well. It is dark, and my crew is all below."

"Grayson—"

She had firmly drifted from calling him "my lord" to using his given name. Good. He wanted her to know him, inside and out. The viscount was definitely on the outside.

A sudden sharp gust blew across them, cutting the summer air with the chill of the North Sea. Alexandra, in thin cotton, shivered. "Perhaps we should go in." She gave him a sharp look. "But only because I am cold."

He smiled and led her there.

Chapter Sixteen

Inside the warm cabin, Grayson drew her into his arms. They rocked a little together, swaying with the gentle motion of the ship.

After a time, Alexandra shifted, but her arms stayed firmly around him. "I think—" She paused. "I believe, Grayson, that I shall not allow you to bed me anymore." She nodded. "Yes, I believe that is the correct thing to do."

He smiled into her hair. "I would be more convinced if you were not hugging me so tightly."

"I cannot seem to let go."

He understood. She needed someone to hold, someone to put her arms around, someone to comfort her. He kissed the silk of her hair, let his palm stroke the soft warmth of it.

How strange the civilized world was. On board his ship or in port taverns, he had but to slip his arm about a woman's waist, and all would understand the signal. She was *his*. Not to be touched. Rules were a bit different in fashionable London. There, if a woman was yours, you very carefully did *not* touch her, at least in public. He cared nothing for such ridiculous strictures, but she did. She lived her life by rules that made her miserable. He sensed, though, that she would be even more miserable if she broke those rules.

He skimmed his lips across hers. "If you do not wish me to bed you, then we shall do something else."

To his delight she looked slightly disappointed. "What?"

He loosed her hold, then strolled away from her, across the small room to his bunk. "Well, my lady, let us suppose *you* are a pirate, and *I* am a passenger."

Her lips parted.

He laid on the bunk and stretched out his arms and legs. The bed had been constructed to fit him so that he would not be flung about in stormy seas. His right leg and arm hung over the wooden side, but so be it. He half closed his eyes. "Do as you will, my lady."

And please do not turn and run from me, leaving me lying here like a fool. She had already battered his pride into tiny pieces. She had the power to break him completely.

Slowly, slowly, her slippers whispered across the board floor. His heart began to pound. He counted the steps— five, six, seven. Through his lashes he watched her pause at the bedside. Her hair tumbled over her shoulders, damp and curled from the river-sea air. Her cool eyes riveted to him, her thick lashes shielding them as her gaze swept down his body.

Every one of his muscles tensed as that gaze roved him. He willed himself to lie still, not to leap from the bed, seize her, drag her to him.

She touched his shirt. He held his breath, certain that

if he moved one fraction of an inch, she would stop, overcome by lady-like impulses, and run away.

Alexandra took hold of one drooping tape that tied his shirt and softly pulled it. The tape slithered through the knot, and the lacing parted.

Sweat pricked him, cooling his skin from the hot fires that raced through his blood. He forced himself to wait, to see what she'd do.

Gently and slowly, she pushed the loosened shirt open. She looked upon him for a long time, her gaze tracing his chest. She reached down, her fingers landing on the round bullet scar on his left shoulder. She traced it, her fingers moving over the jagged hole that, long ago, had rendered him unable to prevent the murder of Ardmore's brother.

She whispered. "I do not wish to bed you. You understand that?"

"Yes, my lady," he said obediently.

She looked relieved. He suppressed a laugh. She leaned down, her fragrance dancing over him, and pressed her tongue to the hollow of his throat.

"Love," he moaned.

Her tongue brushed fire over his skin. She kissed his throat, then his chin; then she raised her head. "Your whiskers feel strange." She touched the tip of her tongue to them again. "I like them."

He liked that she liked them. He hadn't shaved since early that morning, so his face must be like sandpaper. She seemed to find this fascinating.

He closed his eyes, willing himself to lie still and enjoy every moment. His shirt opened wider. Her tongue touched the cutlass scar on his right shoulder. Ardmore had given him the wound while Grayson had still been trying to recover from the gunshot. The sword cut, delivered in Ardmore's grief and rage at his brother's death, had laid Grayson low for weeks. He'd raved like a madman in his fever, while Oliver had nursed him as though he'd been a helpless boy. He'd sensed death's wings beating near, but Oliver had pulled him back to life.

Thank God he'd lived so that he might lie on his bunk while a most beautiful lady tasted him.

She let her tongue trace the path of the old injury. She glided over his ribs down to the hard muscles of his stomach that had ached for months until he'd rebuilt their strength. Down farther to stop, barricaded, at his waistband.

His fingers moved of their own accord to the buttons of his breeches. "Let me assist you, lady."

Her head came up. "No, I don't want—"

Buttons popped under his shaking fingers. He forced himself to stop, to stretch his hands once again to his sides. He willed his desire to stay inside, out of sight, where it could not hurt anyone. "Do as you will," he murmured, his voice cracking.

She knelt over him for a long time. Her eyes were dark, pupils widened, her red-brown hair fanning like a cape over her yellow-clad shoulders. And then, sweet girl, she very carefully drew the flap of his breeches aside to expose his hipbone and the end of the scar.

She dipped her head to him and took up where she'd left off. Her tongue moved from his abdomen to his hip, to the knotted white skin where the cut ended. Air touched him, cold, where she licked him. He shifted his weight, trying to still his arousal. It would escape his control and take her of its own accord if he did not contain it.

She lingered for a moment, her face hovering over his hip, her warm curls tangling across his stomach. He wanted to hold her, gather him to her, encourage her to continue.

But if he did, she might fly away like a frightened bird. *Do not hold on*, Sara had told him. Let go, and see what would be.

He knew somehow that losing this woman would be entirely different from the regret he'd felt when Sara had left him. Alexandra had already changed him. She'd touched him deeply in the short while he'd known her, and that change would not be easily forgotten.

Alexandra peered at the pale skin that showed in the square of his opened breeches. Slowly, timidly, she pulled the flap all the way back.

His arousal sprang out and landed heavily on his abdomen. Large, stiff, and not very happy, it lay there waiting for him to do something. He balled his fists.

She stared at it for a long time, her head bent so he could not see her eyes. Her lips moved slightly, as if she were speaking, but no sound emerged. Moments slid by. The candle in the lantern above flickered, sputtered in melted wax, and flickered again.

Ever so lightly, she licked the tip of him. He gasped and squeezed his eyes closed.

Her warmth moved. "Does that hurt you?"

He took several breaths, trying to slow his heartbeat to only a frantic pace. "No, love. Quite the opposite."

And please, please, please do it again.

What she did was kiss it. The light cushion of her lips pressed daintily to the tip. He clenched his fists so hard his nails drove into his palms. And still he willed himself to lie still, to say nothing. Any quip or teasing word might frighten her away, and then she'd go and so would this incredible feeling.

She delicately touched him with her tongue. Then she

kissed him again. She grew bolder, playing a little, never giving him more than the briefest touch. She obviously had no idea how to pleasure a man, knew nothing of the studied methods of courtesans. She did not know how to take a man into her mouth, how to draw the maximum of pleasure from him.

And he did not care. What she did was more erotic than anything he'd ever felt before. She had already driven him closer to madness than any of Sara's sexual games ever had. The tickle of Alexandra's long hair, the sweet perfume of her, her light touch sent him into spirals of ecstasy. He pressed his hand to his face and stifled another groan.

What are you doing to me Alexandra Alastair?

He needed to be inside her right now. Inside and happy. But folds of fabric hid her, and he would never be able to fling aside the gown and pull her on top of him in time.

It was too late. He dragged in a breath, then groaned aloud. His seed spilled, scalding hot, onto his skin.

He opened his eyes in time to see her spring away in surprise. She came to rest at his feet, sitting back on her knees, her eyes wide. "What happened?"

"You happened," he said between his teeth.

He groped in his pocket for a handkerchief, half embarrassed, yet flushed with joy. He wiped up the mess, then closed up his breeches again. "My sweet, you cannot be so beautiful and then touch a man so and expect nothing to happen."

"Are you angry?"

He broke into a grin. "No, my love, my beautiful love." He reached for her. She came into his arms, a shy smile on her face but a small glow in her eyes, the glow of a woman who finally understood her power. He gathered her against him and kissed her hair. "You have made me very, very happy."

He slept with her. Alexandra thought he would perhaps continue their tumble in bed, but he simply stripped off his clothes and burrowed under the covers and invited her to join him. She did, still in her yellow dress. He lay on his side and tugged her back against him, circling one arm about her waist. She lay in the cradle of his body, feeling herself droop with tiredness.

He slept before she did. The candle in the lantern burned out and darkness filled the room. Behind her, his sonorous, even breathing lulled her. She drifted off soon after that, feeling wanted and happy and *wicked*.

When she awoke, he was still there. She'd imagined he would slip away in the dark, rising and dressing and disappearing back to Town and leaving her imprisoned again. But he only bellowed to Mr. Priestly to bring them some coffee and bread, and hurry up, they were hungry. After that, he dressed and took Alexandra home.

Two days later, Alexandra rubbed her sore fingers and frowned at the papers piled on her writing table. She'd spent the time since Grayson had brought her home in frantic last-minute preparations for her soiree, made more difficult because Alice, her very proper lady's maid, had given notice.

Jeffrey and Annie and Amy had been quite impressed that Alexandra had been abducted by pirates and rescued by the viscount. They begged her for the story, of which she gave an edited version. Even Cook did not seem dismayed at her adventures, but then, she'd already struck up a friendship with Mr. Oliver herself. But Alice had packed her bags and departed. *No better than she ought to be*, the maid's tight-lipped expression had betrayed, and Alexandra supposed she was right.

Today, Alexandra's difficulties mounted. The wrong flowers had been delivered, and she was waiting impatiently for the correct ones to arrive; and all the ices had melted because Jeffrey had not stored the containers in the right place in the cellar. The Duchess of Lewiston had written to express her regrets that she could not attend, and Alexandra had paced the sitting room carpet a good hour wondering frantically if her behavior was now the talk of the town. But no other letters telling her the invited guest was suddenly ill or called away came, and eventually, she calmed. Of course, no other cancellations could mean that all wanted to come and examine her through quizzing glasses and lorgnettes, the Mayfair lady who had become a pirate's mistress.

But dear lord, how beautiful it had been to touch him! He'd tasted so hot and so exciting and so wicked. He'd filled her with longing, and she'd been utterly fascinated by him. His body was so well-formed, a sculpture of lithe muscle and sinew. It seemed a shame not to gaze upon it, to touch it, to taste it.

He'd lain tense under her fingers and tongue, his breathing swift, his pulse rapid. How scalding hot his arousal had been, how firm and stiff, and yet, how velvet soft. She'd never touched a man before, certainly not her husband, who had simply poked at her in the dark and then departed, leaving her numb.

Grayson's hands had balled to tight fists, his eyes had closed hard, his muscles had hardened, as if he'd been holding himself in with great effort. And yet, he'd lain still and let her touch. He'd not demanded a thing.

She laid down her pen and rubbed her temples again. If he had continued to plead with her, would she have been able to resist? When he'd said in his low voice, *I beg of you*, she had been hard-pressed not to fling herself into his arms, no matter they had been standing on the quarterdeck at the time, in full view of the ship.

His siren call was clouding her reason. She was Alexandra Alastair and she wanted a respectable marriage and motherhood, not a tumble with a handsome pirate. Did she not? She craved a child more than anything. She could not have one without a proper marriage to a gentleman who would be a proper father. She could not allow Grayson, however handsome, to steer her from that purpose. She had failed the first child of her body. She would not, she *must not* fail the children to come.

She laid her head down and let out a heartfelt sigh. She had not thought a single sensible thought since Grayson Finley, Viscount Stoke, had moved in next door.

"Madam?"

Alexandra quickly raised her head. Jeffrey stood in the doorway, watching her anxiously. "A gentleman has called to see you, madam."

Alexandra drew a handkerchief from her sleeve and dabbed her wet eyes. "What gentleman, Jeffrey?"

"Don't know, madam. I put him in the reception room."

She waited, but he was no more forthcoming. "Did he not give you a card?"

Jeffrey shook his head fervently. His wig stayed in place while his head moved back and forth. "No, madam. But he told me his name." A silent moment passed. "Except I've forgotten it."

Alexandra hid a sigh. At least facing her frustrating footman had dried her tears. It was not easy to wallow in sorrow with Jeffrey in the room. "Is he one of the viscount's men?"

171

"Don't know, madam."

Alarm touched her. She recalled Grayson's warnings about Burchard. She thought about Mr. Ardmore and his dangerous rage, which had already caught her in its crossfire twice.

Jeffery offered, "He *is* a proper gentleman, madam. Came in a proper carriage. With proper horses." His tone grew admiring.

"Think, Jeffrey. Is it Mr. Burchard?"

Another vigorous head shake. "No, madam."

That left Mr. Ardmore. Alexandra drew herself up. "Please tell him I am not at home."

He hesitated. "Don't like to, madam."

"Jeffrey, it is part of your duties to turn undesirable callers away."

"I know, madam." He twisted his large, gloved hands. "Only he was very insistent. And he *looked* at me so. He called me a good lad when I finally said I'd fetch you."

"For heaven's sake, I have already been abducted once. I have no wish to repeat the experience."

"He doesn't look like a pirate, madam. He wears a proper gentleman's clothes, all fine and respectable like. Goes to a proper tailor. And has golden spectacles, all shiny."

Alexandra's heart missed a beat. Mr. Henderson. *In her house.*

"Jeffrey," she said quietly. "Bring the poker."

Mr. Henderson was pacing the oriental carpet in the front reception room, his head down, his hands behind his back. He wore his usual subdued black suit, looking once again like a vicar without a collar. Fading bruises outlined his left eye and the left side of his mouth.

He looked up as Alexandra entered. His eager smile

froze when Jeffrey stopped beside her with the iron poker in his beefy hand.

Alexandra gave him a cold stare. "You are not welcome here, Mr. Henderson."

Mr. Henderson held his white-gloved hands palm out. "I give you my word, Mrs. Alastair, I did not come to harm you in any way."

"What am I to think, sir? Our last two meetings caused me much harm. What will you do to me this time whilst apologizing for the previous two indignities?"

He winced. "I promise—on my honor as a gentleman— I am quit of Captain Ardmore and his schemes. I told him so. Any moves against you will be made without me."

"I am not certain that comforts me, Mr. Henderson."

"What I mean to say is that I want to keep you from all harm. He has no right to pull you into his games with Finley."

"Viscount Stoke," she corrected.

His expression turned pained. "Captain Finley is nowhere near good enough for you. He is a barbaric pirate who has not set foot in England since he was a lad of twelve. He sees, he wants, he takes. He does not abide by any rules but his own."

So she had noticed. "His lineage is an old and respected one," she pointed out. "Or he would not have become the viscount."

"He may have the family connections, but he knows nothing of our world. His parents died violently—I do not know the story, but I know that his mother was murdered. He ran away to sea right after—can't really blame him."

"Yes, I had heard that." He was confirming Mrs. Tetley's rumors. She imagined a young lad, no older than Maggie, confused, heartbroken, utterly shocked by his sudden and terrible loss. Her heart wrung for him.

"He had no upbringing at all," Mr. Henderson went on. "Unless you count being captured by pirates and trained to be one of them an upbringing. I, on the other hand, stayed safely in Kent and went off to Oxford."

"I come from Kent," Alexandra replied, for something to say.

"You see? I am English through and through. Finley, for all he is a viscount, is an outsider all the same." He paused. "You would not happen to have heard of the insignificant village of St. Mary's Newbridge, would you? My family has a house near there."

She blinked. "Good heavens. I lived only two villages away, in Little Marching."

His smile beamed, wide and straight-toothed. "We are neighbors then. I know Little Marching well. I visited my cousins there in the summers, and we made nuisances of ourselves chasing sheep and clambering about in the mud. Do you remember Fox Hollow?"

Her caution thawed slightly. "I do, indeed. I learned to climb trees there."

"I learned to fall out of them."

Alexandra permitted herself a smile. "I do not remember a family called Henderson."

"They were my mother's sister's family. Name of Bancroft."

Memories rose. "Oh, yes, I do remember. My mother and Mrs. Bancroft were on quite friendly terms. The boys were a bit unruly. They both went into the army, I believe, and are now splendid officers."

"Randall and Cecil, yes." He grinned. "I was the horrible little tow-headed cousin who ran after them."

"Come to think of it, I might remember you, after all. I used to run and hide from the three of you."

Mr. Henderson clasped his hands. "I am so pleased we discovered this. I must write Randall and Cecil and tell them I have met you."

"That would be splendid. Remember me to them, of course." She glanced sideways at Jeffrey, who looked a bit confused, then said, "The fact that we are truly neighbors does not make me trust you, Mr. Henderson. Nor does it explain why you are here."

He smiled a bit ruefully. "I came to talk to you. You did tell me that if you saw me again, you would speak to me."

"That was before you abducted me and made me breathe that awful concoction. And I did not give you leave to call on me."

He held his hands out. "I am here now. Please let me speak with you—a real conversation, just as if we were old acquaintances from Kent." He motioned to the chair near the window. "I can sit there. And you can sit all the way over there." He pointed to the divan on the other side of the room. "And your lad here can remain ready with the poker." He glanced at him. "If you must strike me, Jeffrey, please try not to tear the coat. My tailor only delivered it this morning. Oh, and not the face. The honorable Viscount Stoke has already managed to render it almost unusable."

Jeffrey studied Mr. Henderson's bruises with professional interest. "His lordship did that?"

"Indeed, he did."

The hero worship in Jeffrey's eyes rose to new heights. "He's a dab hand at boxing then, is he?"

"Following no rules but his own, yes."

Alexandra broke into this male exchange. "Mr. Henderson, do not be ridiculous. We cannot have a conversation shouting across a room."

"Then give me leave to call on you properly. To—to take you driving in Hyde Park, like an old family acquaintance might do. Please."

His words rang with longing and sincerity. She reminded herself that his apologies outside the theatre had also been profuse, just before he'd wadded the handkerchief into her face. Although—her thoughts went back over that conversation, clearer now after a few days of rest. He had not promised then that he would not help Mr. Ardmore. He'd only expressed regret that he had. Today, on the other hand, his first words had been a promise—on his honor—that he would never harm her again. A true gentleman never broke his word.

But was he sincere, or was he only pretending to be a true gentleman?

She sighed. Two weeks ago, her life had been predictable, structured, compartmentalized. And then Viscount Stoke had moved in. And now up was down and right was wrong, and she had no idea whom to trust. Mr. Burchard had transformed himself from respectable acquaintance to pirate villain; now Mr. Henderson was trying to move from villain to respectable acquaintance.

"I am uncertain why you even wish to continue to see me, Mr. Henderson."

He slanted her a sheepish look, which he tried to soften with a faint smile. "Because I find myself in love with you, Mrs. Alastair. Completely and hopelessly in love. I have never met a woman like you."

Chapter Seventeen

Alexandra stared at him in pure shock. "Mr. Henderson, you forget yourself."

His look was anguished. "I have no right to say these things, I know, but I cannot help myself. The way you confronted Captain Ardmore—and me—was little short of astonishing. You have won my greatest admiration."

Alexandra glanced at Jeffrey. Jeffrey had lowered the poker and looked not at all displeased with Mr. Henderson's declaration. In fact, he looked a little teary-eyed.

"Mr. Henderson, I hardly think—"

"I know. I know. I do not deserve to ask for your love or even your friendship, but please give me a chance. Just a chance to prove myself worthy of you. Please."

"If this is another trick of Mr. Ardmore's I think it a poor one."

"No—never. I swear to you. Upon my honor. Would I be more convincing on my knees?"

"No, do not—" She flushed. "Please get up, Mr. Henderson. You look silly."

He remained kneeling on the carpet, staring up at her adoringly. "I beseech you, Mrs. Alastair. I have behaved badly. Let me try to make it up to you. Give me that at least."

Oh, dear. Jeffrey's lip was trembling now. She had no doubt about whose side *he* was on.

"If you will please get up before someone sees you and sit down like a sensible person, I will think about it."

Mr. Henderson smiled in enormous hope. "Anything you like, my most darling Mrs. Alastair. I am your devoted slave."

Jeffrey choked back a sob. Mr. Henderson climbed to his feet, but he did not sit down. He remained standing, wearing a look of abject devotion.

Alexandra said, "Grayson—the viscount—said that Mr. O'Malley was Maggie's devoted slave. Is he correct?"

Mr. Henderson nodded, seemingly unsurprised by the abrupt change of subject. "Oh, yes, you should have seen him on the *Argonaut* when we crossed from Jamaica." He looked faintly amused. "She wrapped him around her little finger. He'll do anything for her. I say that it is because they are both of one height, but O'Malley claims that they are both outsiders, striving against the restrictions of the bloody English." He stumbled to a halt. "Beg your pardon. His words."

"I see." Her curiosity rose, despite her misgivings. Mr. Henderson was in the position to explain many of Mr. Ardmore's cryptic statements. She had given up trying to obtain a straight answer from Grayson. Whenever she asked questions of Grayson, he would kiss her or suggest she sleep naked, and her resolve would simply depart.

"Maggie traveled on Mr. Ardmore's ship? Why, when the viscount has his own ship?"

Mr. Henderson lifted his brows. "You do not know?"

"No," she said cautiously. "We should sit down and discuss it. Jeffrey, tell Annie to bring tea. You may leave the poker with me."

Jeffrey, looking slightly disappointed, departed on his errand. The poker was heavy in Alexandra's hand. She carefully set it on a polished table near the door, close enough to snatch up if need be, but far enough away to let Mr. Henderson know she was willing to trust him—if he made no sudden moves.

Mr. Henderson gave her a sage look. "You want to pry information from me? Well, no matter. You deserve to know."

She motioned him to sit, not at the chair next to the window, but on the divan where she and Lady Featherstone had reposed the day of the accident, the day Mr. Henderson had so rudely kissed her. She perched on a chair near the center of the room, positioning herself between him and the door. "Please proceed," she said, inclining her head.

Mr. Henderson laced his gloved fingers and darted a glance about the room as if for inspiration. "Finley brought Maggie back to England courtesy of Captain Ardmore. You did know that?"

"I know very little. Excepting that Captain Ardmore is terribly angry at Grayson, mostly over Maggie's mother. And did I hear Captain Ardmore accusing Grayson of murdering Captain Ardmore's brother?"

Mr. Henderson nodded. "It is a sad tale. I am not certain I understand it all myself. I signed on with Ardmore after it was all over, so I was not there to witness it." He blew out his breath. "But I will tell you what I know.

Captain Ardmore had a younger brother named Paul. Ardmore rather doted on him. From what O'Malley tells me he just about raised him, as their parents passed away when Ardmore was only fourteen. Well, Paul married and had children. His wife and two daughters had traveled by ship from Charleston to Roanoke, in Virginia, to visit her family. On the way back to Charleston, the ship was boarded by pirates, and all aboard were murdered."

Alexandra touched her lips. "Oh, dear."

"Paul nearly went mad with grief. He had taken up a seafaring career as a merchant captain. He sold his ship, and purchased a refitted frigate, which he called the *Argonaut*. He sailed up and down the coast hunting pirates for ransom or simply sinking their ships and killing them. I do not know if he ever found the pirates who had murdered his wife and children. My Captain Ardmore, who had already quit working with Finley, eventually joined him."

Amy entered the room at that moment, bearing a tea tray. She set it down on the table near Alexandra, shot Mr. Henderson a flirtatious look—he reddened—then she departed.

Alexandra was too absorbed in the story to reach for the tea. She said, "So Captain Ardmore truly is a pirate hunter?"

"He is. That is why I joined him. We search for pirates, overcome them, and turn them over to whatever government wants them most. When we come upon them besieging a ship, we show them no mercy." His words were clipped.

She hid her shiver by reaching for the tea, warming her suddenly cold fingers on the pot. "What happened to Captain Ardmore's brother?"

Henderson rose to accept the cup Alexandra handed

him. He remained standing, fingering the cup's handle. "One day, Paul Ardmore decided he would bring in or destroy the crew of the *Majesty*, Finley's ship. He was a bit mad by that time. He knew that Ardmore and Finley were enemies; or at least, deadly rivals. Ardmore was not with him. He might have stopped him." Henderson's voice went soft. "I think Ardmore is torn between blaming Finley for what happened and blaming himself."

"What did happen?" Alexandra asked, her throat tight.

Henderson looked at the cup in his hand as if just remembering he held it. He abruptly seated himself on the nearest chair. "Disaster happened. Paul Ardmore, as I said, was a bit mad. Finley warned him off, or at least that's what Finley claims he did. But Paul should have known better than to approach Finley. Finley is—I beg your pardon—a mean mother's son when he is provoked. Only a fool would try to take him." He sighed and lifted his teacup, correctly crooking his slender fingers. "But Paul was a fool by then, so I am told."

Alexandra gripped the arms of her chair. "Grayson sank the ship?"

Henderson shook his head. "*He* says he veered off, knowing it was Ardmore's brother and not wanting to engage him in battle. But Paul drove straight at him. He had the wind on his side, and he rammed the *Majesty*. There was no chance to avoid him." He took another absent sip of tea. "They fought, ship to ship, man to man. In the end, Ardmore's brother died, shot through the heart. Finley has always maintained that he himself was shot early on, and that he spent the entire battle writhing in agony on the deck. He says he had no idea what went on in the fight. Ardmore, of course, doesn't believe him."

"He carries the scar," Alexandra said, staring into the middle distance. She touched her fingers to the place just under her own left shoulder, where the jagged round mark rested on Grayson. "Of the bullet. Just there."

She heard in her mind the frantic shouts, the boom and roll of cannon, the crack of a pistol shot, the stink of gunpowder and smoke. She could see Grayson crumple to the deck, his linen shirt stained red, writhing in pain, helpless.

There was a marked silence. Alexandra returned her gaze to Mr. Henderson. His gray eyes behind his spectacles told her he knew perfectly well under what circumstance she'd seen the bullet scar on Grayson's chest. Her face heated. He remained still, his eyes hard as polished stone. She reminded herself that for his innocuous looks and his curate-like clothes, he hunted pirates for a living. Hunted them, and won.

She went on hastily. "How did all this lead to Maggie returning to England on the *Argonaut*?"

Mr. Henderson's look did not thaw. He had changed from the decorous gentleman who knew how to hold a teacup to a dangerous man who shared his master's hatred. "Ardmore finally caught up to Finley again this past December in Jamaica."

Alexandra connected the pieces. "After Grayson had found Maggie."

"We caught him alone, Ardmore and O'Malley and Forsythe and me." His lips went tight, his eyes remote as he watched a distant memory. "I am not terribly proud of what we did to him, but we did not know about Maggie then."

Chill spread through her body, coursing through every limb, cooling her blood to her very fingertips. Her closed, protected little world recoiled at this invasion of violence and black hatred. She remembered the tension in Captain Ardmore's cabin, the quavering moment when Grayson had stared with hot rage into Ardmore's eyes, and Mr. Henderson had trained a loaded pistol on Grayson. One wrong word, one wrong movement, and death would have descended upon them.

"Captain Ardmore let him go," she said, with difficulty.

Henderson nodded once. "Because of Maggie. Finley used her to bargain himself out of a tight spot and save his own worthless skin."

Anger stirred in her. "He would do anything for Maggie. I know that. The bargain must have been hard for him."

Silence fell between them like a crackling curtain. Outside, hooves clattered and carriage wheels rumbled, and the shrill cries of street vendors sounded over them. "Of course he would not have told you," Henderson said finally. He drew a quick breath. "Captain Ardmore agreed to help Finley get Maggie to England. And in return—Finley forfeits his life to Ardmore."

Alexandra's jaw dropped. Horror rose through her, along with a surge of anger and grief. *"What?"*

The door swung open. Jeffrey came trotting in, oblivious of the tension in the room. "Her ladyship, madam."

Lady Featherstone bustled in behind him, her gray eyes sparkling. "Alexandra, I—" She broke off, catching sight of Mr. Henderson, who had sprung up to stand stiffly in the middle of the carpet. Her plucked brows rose. "I beg your pardon."

Alexandra's heart pounded so hard she thought she would be sick. Forfeit his life? Those were the unspoken words he'd kept from her. The same words Mr. Ardmore had not said to her. They'd known the truth, all of them—Mr. Jacobs and Mr. O'Malley and Mr. Henderson. Grayson's daughter had traveled safely to England aboard

Mr. Ardmore's ship, and Grayson had promised to lay down his life for it.

She clenched her shaking hands and turned blindly to her friend. The correct polite words tumbled from her lips. "Lady Featherstone, this is Mr. Henderson. He is an old acquaintance from Kent."

Lady Featherstone's gaze became thoughtful. Alexandra could almost hear the words rattling in the lady's head: young, handsome, old family acquaintance—married?

Mr. Henderson bowed. "Pleased to make your acquaintance, my lady."

"How excellent to meet you. You are attending Alexandra's at-home tonight, are you not?"

He gave her a half smile. "I do not have the pleasure of an invitation."

"But you must come. An old acquaintance, so happily found again? Alexandra would be glad to see you there." She darted a meaningful look at Alexandra.

Cornered, Alexandra could only reply, "Of course, Mr. Henderson. If your duties do not prevent it, I would be pleased for you to attend."

Mr. Henderson bowed again. "I would be most honored."

"Excellent!" Lady Featherstone exclaimed. "We begin at nine o'clock."

Jeffrey banged the door open again. "Viscount Stoke!" he bellowed.

Grayson walked in leisurely, calm as you please, taking in Mr. Henderson and Lady Featherstone without surprise. But of course, he would have seen them arrive. He seemed to know all the comings and goings of her house.

Lady Featherstone gave a surprised yelp, then recovered and extended her hand. "Oh. Your lordship, how delightful."

He advanced, smiling his lazy smile. Only an hour before, that smile would have melted Alexandra to a quivering puddle, but Mr. Henderson's story had left her rigid and cold.

"The delight is mine," Grayson said. He lifted Lady Featherstone's ring-studded hand to his lips and pressed a brief kiss to it.

"My word." Lady Featherstone almost simpered. Grayson slid his gaze to Alexandra, lowering his right eyelid in a half-wink.

His shirt was laced, his dark coat buttoned. His bronzed throat showed in the V where his cravat should have been. He wore smooth leather gloves on his large hands and polished boots on his feet. His sun-streaked hair was pulled back in a neat queue. His blue eyes, despite his wink, his heated smile, told her nothing.

Lady Featherstone beamed at him. "Lord Stoke, you are certainly attending Alexandra's at-home."

"Indeed, I would not miss it." He slid Alexandra another difficult-to-interpret look.

Lady Featherstone trilled happily. "This will be a most interesting evening. Alexandra, you will be the first of the *ton* to host a gathering that Lord Stoke attends. The Duchess of Lewiston will be green with envy." She gave Grayson a flirtatious look. "We have missed you until now, my lord. I trust this will be the first of many times we see you?"

He inclined his head. "Business has filled my time, my lady. I hope to amend that."

"I am pleased to hear it."

Mr. Henderson cleared his throat, cutting through their polite exchange. "I will detain you no longer, Mrs. Alastair. *My lord*, perhaps you will be so kind as to walk me to my carriage."

Grayson studied him a moment, brow raised. "Certainly, Henderson. I see how you might get lost from here to there."

Henderson's expression was cold, tense. Lady Featherstone looked from one to the other in obvious glee, certain she was seeing jealous rivals taking up stances over Alexandra. Alexandra's dry throat ached.

Grayson's deep timbre cut through the silence. "Mrs. Alastair." He casually crossed the room to her. "I apologize for interrupting you." He stopped beside her, his back to the others. He withdrew a small package from his pocket and slipped it into her hand. "Wear them tonight," he whispered.

She clenched the package, feeling something hard and sharp beneath the paper. He backed away and made an overly formal bow. "Good afternoon, ladies. I look forward to seeing you later. Mr. Henderson?"

He turned and strolled out of the room. Henderson shot him a look of annoyance, then bowed to Alexandra and Lady Featherstone and scurried after him.

"Goodness." Lady Featherstone jumped as the front door banged. "Two such handsome gentlemen in your reception room, looking daggers at each other over you, you lucky girl."

Chapter Eighteen

Alexandra did not feel lucky in the least. What Mr. Henderson had told her had drained her of feeling—and made her angry beyond measure. All this time Grayson had known of his diabolical bargain with Captain Ardmore. And he had made her love him anyway.

As for Captain Ardmore— She longed to see the man again and tell him just what she thought of his so-called bargain. She understood his grief about his brother, she was no stranger to the loss of loved ones, but he'd taken it a bit too far.

Lady Featherstone came to her. "What did he give you?"

"What? Oh." Alexandra looked down at the package. "I do not know."

"Well, open it, silly."

Alexandra lay the gift on the small Sheraton table and unwrapped the folds of paper. Inside was a black velvet cloth. She opened it.

She and Lady Featherstone gasped together.

"Good heavens!" Lady Featherstone said, her hand to her heart.

Lying on the cloth, glittering like stars against the night, was a strand of diamonds. The pattern was intricate, yet simple. In the middle of the piece, held by clasps of beaten silver, were five opals, each about a half-inch across, polished and shining white.

Alexandra recognized the diamonds. They had been part of the hideous necklace Theo had given her, the one Grayson had stolen from her the night they'd made love aboard his ship. He must have had them cut apart and reset. But the opals—

She remembered his voice, the touch of his hand: *I have opals that would shine like white fire in your hair.* Here they lay before her.

Lady Featherstone looked up at her, her face still. "You did not tell me," she said carefully, "that you and Viscount Stoke were engaged."

Alexandra swallowed. "We are not."

The lady's face went a bit white. "Why else would he give you such a gift?"

Alexandra made herself fold the black cloth over the jewels, shutting out their starry sparkle. "I cannot imagine."

From the look on Lady Featherstone's face, she obviously could. "Have a care, my dear," she said. "Tongues in the haut *ton* can be very cruel." She brightened. "I know. Perhaps this is his way of announcing he intends to propose." She pressed her hands together. "How delightfully romantic. You and a viscount, right next door to one another, falling hopelessly in love."

"Yes," Alexandra sighed, folding the papers. "Hopeless."

*   *   *

She repeated the word again later as she stood at her dressing table and waited for her new lady's maid to put the finishing touches to her hair.

The lady's maid, Joan, a plain woman with brown hair scraped into a painful knot, had proved competent and quiet spoken. She'd had references from a baroness and a countess, and said she preferred a quiet household. Alexandra had bitten the inside of her cheek, crossed her fingers, and said that her household was quiet—most of the time.

The jewels lay on the black velvet before her. Her first thought had been to hide them away, but she could not bring herself to do so. The tiara was so beautiful. She'd never liked diamonds, finding them cold and harsh, but the jeweler had made these beautiful. Using Grayson's opals he had transformed a rather gaudy piece—purchased by her husband only to prove that he could afford such baubles—into one of elegance and grace. It seemed a shame to hide it.

"Will you wear it, madam?" Joan asked behind her. She'd already expressed approval for the jewelry, though she'd not asked where it came from. She must have believed it part of Alexandra's collection from her husband.

Alexandra jumped. "Hum? Oh, no. No, I do not believe I will."

Joan's square, stoic face registered disappointment. "But it would look so good on you, madam. You have just the right coloring to set it off."

Before Alexandra could protest, Joan lifted the jewels to Alexandra's hair.

The lady's maid was correct. The opals shone like white hot stars against Alexandra's dark red hair. The diamonds glittered like more distant stars, visible when they caught the light. It took her breath away.

"Please consider it, madam. It will go well with your new gown."

How she wanted to wear the jewels. Grayson had had the tiara made for her, had given her a princely gift.

But why? She had been convinced at first that he meant to make her his mistress. Lady Featherstone was now convinced he meant to make her his wife. But after her conversation with Mr. Henderson, she realized that Grayson had told her the truth from the beginning. He had said with regret that he could not marry.

Anger coupled with her confusion produced outrage and grief. He was going to let Captain Ardmore murder him. She fumed at the pride and arrogance of men, who left women and children to grieve for them. She fanned her irritation, because it kept her fear at bay. This bargain had to be stopped. And it would be, if she had anything to say about it.

Her thoughts raced from one to the next, emotions tumbling through her. She had some ideas about what she could do. None was very practical at the moment, such as running Captain Ardmore to the ground, giving him a good talking to, and threatening him with arrest if he did not leave Grayson alone. Shouting at him appealed to her, but she reflected that it probably would not have much effect.

She turned over possibilities in her mind, her breath pushing her breasts against the hard bones of her stays. She became aware of Joan's brown eyes regarding her steadily in the mirror.

Alexandra picked up the tiara. "Yes," she said calmly. "I shall wear it."

Vanessa Fairchild paused before the mirror in Alexandra's bedchamber, smoothing the last of her dark curls beneath a hairpin. The soiree had already begun; guests poured in through Alexandra's front door, and carriages jammed Grosvenor Street as coachmen tried to halt as close as possible to the red carpet that led in the short space between door and carriage stop. The reception room blazed with light. The rear reception room's doors had been thrown open to make the two rooms one, and the carpet had been taken up so dancing could commence. Upstairs the sitting room and dining room had likewise been opened, making one long room where guests could linger, chat, and eat.

Maggie would be entering with her father. Vanessa smiled a little as she studied her subdued gown in the mirror. The viscount wished to show off his daughter. Vanessa would wait upstairs for the hour when Maggie drooped or the viscount tired of her and deposited her in this quiet corner. Of course, Vanessa thought indulgently, having observed the viscount's obvious love for his daughter and Maggie's unfailing spirits, that hour could be long in coming, if ever. But she, as a good governess, would wait to take her charge.

Robert Jacobs was also in the house. Her trembling fingers knew it. He came ostensibly as a guest and friend of the viscount's, but his true purpose was bodyguard to Maggie. For the last three days, he had been Maggie's constant companion, and therefore, he'd also been Vanessa's.

Did he sense the fire that shot through her every time he drew near? Did he know that she had to slow her panicked gasps whenever she looked upon his face? Did he know that the desire she'd had for him all those years ago had never waned?

Possibly not. He remained entirely businesslike, watchful and alert when they went out, quiet and unobtrusive when they stayed home. Maggie liked to include him in their conversations, and he answered questions or made comments in a friendly way. But he never spoke directly to Vanessa.

Today, for the first time, Vanessa had seen a sign of the danger from which the viscount wanted to protect Maggie. She had taken Maggie to Hookham's to introduce her to the world of novels, which Maggie knew nothing of. Robert had accompanied them on the errand, as he did on all errands. Afterward they had walked up to New Bond Street and looked in the shops. On a sudden, Robert had herded them away from a glovemaker's and shoved them both into a tiny, deserted passage.

They'd hovered there, in the shadow of the tall buildings, while Robert had shielded them both from the street with his body. They'd watched, tense, while a gentleman who looked no different from any other gentleman strolled by, looking right and left as if trying to take in all the wonders of mercantile London.

Robert had later explained that the gentleman was called Burchard and that he was a dangerous pirate. He had a vendetta against Captain Ardmore and would not hesitate to mow down Captain Ardmore's associates, current and past. At the time, however, Robert had told them nothing. He'd simply stood against her, with Maggie sandwiched between them, his nose nearly touching Vanessa's hair. She'd held Maggie, arms around the girl's slim shoulders, and tried to find a safe place to rest her gaze. But all she could see before her was his throat, swathed in a crisp neck cloth, and his chin, tinged with new beard. His broad chest in waistcoat and coat was below that, rising and falling with his quick breath. The scent of him had washed over her, so masculine and desirable. The five minutes they'd spent in that passage had stretched to an eternity.

Now as she looked into the mirror, she touched the cameo at her throat. She looked so respectable, a widowed woman making her way in the world as governess to a viscount's daughter. An enviable position. His lordship was very handsome himself, although anyone with eyes could see that he was obviously madly in love with Alexandra.

On the outside, Vanessa was neat and respectable. On the inside, she churned with emotion. She was simply a woman who desired a man, who could think of nothing but a forbidden passion of five years before.

The door opened. Supposing it to be Alexandra, Vanessa did not turn. She lifted her gaze to the mirror again and saw Robert Jacobs standing behind her.

He did not speak. He closed the door and stood looking at her. Their gazes caught and tangled in the glass. He must have come to tell her that the viscount had arrived or that he needed her to take charge of Maggie. But he only crossed the room slowly, saying nothing.

He stopped behind her, an arm's reach away. If only she could turn and face him.

"Vanessa," he said. "I have never stopped loving you."

"Robert—"

White lines etched the corners of his mouth. "No, let me say what I came to say. I loved you then, and I love you now. It has not changed. You may think me young and a fool, but I love you with a man's love, not that of a callow boy."

She put her hand to her throat, fingers touching the cold cameo. "Do you believe that I did not love *you*?"

The dark depths of his eyes caught her. "I believe you

could not accept that I could truly love you. As a man."

Vanessa spun around. The lock of hair she'd been pinning loosened again. Dear lord, he was so handsome. He stood close to her, and yet a mountain range might have separated them. His dark hair caught the light from the chandelier above. Rich brown highlights burned into the silk of it, beckoning her fingers. In contrast, his severe suit shut her out. He dressed as she did, respectable, subdued, firmly keeping the outside world away.

"I told you to go because I would ruin you!" she cried.

"You did ruin me," he said tightly. "I never loved another woman after you, Vanessa. Never. God knows I tried." He smiled a feral smile, and her heart turned over. Of course he would have gone to other women. It had been five years, after all. But she had not expected that the thought would tear her in two.

"If you had been free," he asked, his voice savage, "would you have come with me?"

She shook her head. "I do not know. I was ten years older than you."

"You still are," he said. "And I still love you."

She tried to take a step back, but the dressing table impeded her. "What do you want me to say, Robert?"

His dark eyes went hard. "That you never loved me. That I will never have a chance. I want you to tell me so I can be quit of you at last."

He was offering her peace. She only had to say that what they'd had in Oxford had been nothing—a lonely professor's wife taking her amusement with a handsome lad. Then they could freeze into mere acquaintances and put the past behind them. She opened her mouth to tell him so.

"I loved you." The words spilled out before she could stop them. "I loved you so much, Robert. You taught me how to open my heart and love as I had never loved before. It killed me to send you away. I did it because I feared scandal would cling to you when you were just starting your life."

His chest rose and fell. He reached to her, then clenched his fist. "And now?"

She touched his closed hand. His fingers were so cold. "I love you," she whispered. "I always have. I will never stop."

He studied her for a long moment. Then he made a raw noise in his throat, as if a rage and longing that he had kept bottled for too long had suddenly burst free. He seized her, his grip like iron, and crushed her to him. She closed her eyes in surrender. Sweet desire and hopelessness crashed over her as his strong mouth covered hers.

Downstairs, Grayson entered the main reception room, leading his daughter by the hand. Maggie had dressed in a new gown of light pink silk, courtesy of her previous shopping expedition with Mrs. Alastair. Her black hair had been woven into loops and braids, courtesy of Mrs. Fairchild. Light shimmered through the facets of the huge chandeliers high above like fire through a jewel box and rained a rosy glow to the company below. A trio of violins played madly in a corner partitioned by potted palms. Jeffrey, stiff in red livery and a new powdered wig, bellowed into his ear: "His lordship, Viscount Stoke and the Honorable Miss Maggie Finley!"

All heads swiveled. Quizzing glasses and lorgnettes rose, conversation dipped. Even the violins squawked to a halt. Grayson and Maggie stopped, just inside the doorway.

The glittering crowd looked their fill, from those who glanced at Grayson in mild curiosity to the obvious gawpers who stared and nudged their neighbors. Ladies began fluttering fans and smiling covertly. The plump, black-haired Mrs. Waters sent him a come-and-get-me smile, her eyes promising that she'd changed her bedchamber into a passenger's cabin. He suppressed a watery chill and made a small bow to the collected company.

To his disappointment, he did not see Alexandra. He caught sight of a few gentlemen the duke had introduced him to at White's, but apart from Mrs. Waters, no one else looked familiar. He was a stranger here, despite the fact that he was technically one of them. Grayson had been thrown among people exotic and plain all over the world, had met officers of naval and merchant ships from France, Prussia, America, England, Corsica, the Netherlands, China, Siam, and India. However, unlike those sailors, who knew they'd encounter a wide circle of people in their business and had cultivated a polite but wary mask, the people in this room stared in open curiosity that bordered on rudeness. This was their territory, and he had entered it. They had let him in, but they would judge whether he was embraced or merely tolerated.

The only other person in the room Grayson recognized was Alden Henderson, who lounged near the tall fireplace, a glass of champagne in hand. He gave Grayson an ironic half smile and sipped his drink.

As Grayson turned to search for Alexandra, the Duke of St. Clair was announced. He gave Grayson a welcoming smile and extended his manicured hand. "Stoke. So pleased to see you."

The duke dressed in what Grayson's tailor had said was the height of fashion—dark suit, white cravat and collar, silk stockings, and pumps. The tailor had desperately tried to talk Grayson into ordering not one, but six such suits. Grayson had quelled the man's enthusiasm and ordered subdued coats and trousers, much to the man's despair.

But since Grayson had originally come to him in leather breeches, collarless shirt, and long duster, the tailor had sighed and gotten on with the order.

The duke greeted Maggie with formal politeness, and she smothered a titter as she curtseyed.

"Is Mrs. Alastair about?" Grayson asked the duke as the three of them strolled from the room.

"I assume she's receiving upstairs. I have yet to greet her myself. Shall we?"

Chapter Nineteen

They walked together to the main staircase, which had been swathed in silver and gold ribbons. Gold satin streamers dripped from the wall sconces and the chandeliers high above. The landings were lit with candles, and more silver and gold ribbons fluttered from every railing. A stream of people wound up the stairs to the first floor. This was Alexandra's world—softly shimmering, elegant. Light glowed over it all, welcoming, friendly, as soft as her smile.

Memories, vague and wavering, as if he looked at them through water, stirred in his mind. He seemed to see himself as a wee lad, standing behind the banisters on the top floor of a tall house, peering surreptitiously down through the railings. He could still feel the cool carved posts under his palms. Below him stood his mother, elegant in lace and satin and fashionably powdered hair. She held out her dainty hands to perfumed guests who fanned in a long line down the stairs, waiting to greet her. He remembered his swell of pride that so many people liked his pretty mother. Every once in a while, she would glance to the top of the stairs and give him a covert wink. It had been amusing, this game they'd played, keeping Grayson's truancy from his scolding nurse.

Grayson now lifted his gaze to the top of Alexandra's stairs, where his mother would have waited. Alexandra stood there, dressed in silver and gold. His childhood memory dissolved and faded.

Maggie squeezed Grayson's hand. "Mrs. Alastair is very beautiful, is she not?"

She was, oh God, yes, she was. Her silver-and-gold gown skimmed her shoulders and cradled a modest amount of bosom. A gold satin ribbon circled her neck. Her riot of red-brown curls had been caught back at her nape, then made to spill over her shoulders. And in her hair, sparkling like white stars, as he'd known they would, were his opals. He had obtained the stones in Siam, a gift pressed on him by a prince grateful to Grayson for rescuing his kidnapped bride-to-be.

She was wearing them. His blood beat hot. He knew in that moment that Alexandra filled a place inside him he had not known was empty. The loneliness of years gone by faded suddenly to nothing.

"She is easily one of the most elegant ladies in society," the duke was saying.

"I want to be just like her," Maggie declared.

"You could have no better model, Miss Finley."

Grayson did not answer. He agreed with them wholeheartedly, but he could not banish the memory of the Duke of St. Clair's name in the premier position on Alexandra's list. With all those exclamation points and crosses. She'd listed no defects for the Duke of bloody St. Clair. He ground his teeth. Perhaps when they reached the top of the stairs, the duke could stand just close to the banister and Grayson could accidentally topple him off—

But Alexandra was wearing the opals. *His* opals. He wondered if she had a code on her list for that.

Their progress up the stairs was impeded by all the other guests eager to greet their hostess. Strangely, they seemed equally as eager to stop and be introduced to Grayson.

"H-h-how do you da-da-da-do," a young man with an affable smile and ingenuous blue eyes said.

"Mr. Bartholomew," the duke intoned.

Grayson shook his hand and gave the man a hard look. Bartholomew was another name on Alexandra's list.

All those honored on her list were there. He met Mr. Carrington, Mr. Wesley, Lord Hildebrand Caldicott, who had been present for Henderson's earlier trick. Each gentleman was near to thirty, well-dressed and well-groomed, and knew every polite phrase in existence. They talked horse and sport without effort and behaved with exquisite manners to any lady who passed.

They were the most boring, innocuous lot Grayson had ever clapped eyes on. There was absolutely nothing to disparage in any of them. He found that fact the most irritating of all.

At last they reached the top of the stairs. Alexandra stood, resplendent, next to Lady Featherstone and a middle-aged gentleman, presumably Lord Featherstone. The couple hovered like a pair of chaperons and helped Alexandra to greet guests. Grayson shook Lord and Lady Featherstones' hands. He forced his lips into a smile. Then, at long last, he was allowed to turn to Alexandra.

She gave him a challenging look from beneath her lashes. Her brown-green eyes sparkled and danced in high fury. What was the matter with her? He stopped, forcing the crowd to bump to a halt behind him.

"I am delighted, Mrs. Alastair," he said neutrally. He sent her a wicked wink, then lifted her cool hand to his lips.

"Lord Stoke." She tried to tug her hand away.

"Your beauty is dazzling, Mrs. Alastair," he said softly. "More so than any jewel."

Her eyebrows rose as if to say, "What are you doing?" She tried, again unsuccessfully, to withdraw her hand. She turned to Maggie and bathed her in her sunniest smile. "I am pleased to see you, Maggie. I hope you will like the refreshments in the dining room."

Maggie curtseyed as taught by Mrs. Fairchild and won another beaming smile from Alexandra.

Grayson only garnered another frown. He searched his memories of their last encounter for what he had done to so displease her. He could think of nothing. She was certainly glaring balefully at him, but then, she was wearing the jewels. Most confusing. Had she forgotten how eagerly she'd run her tongue along his shaft, tasting the length of him? He squeezed her fingers. "I believe *I* have found the finest place in the house."

She scowled. The duke said good-naturedly, "Let the rest of us have a chance, Stoke." He extended his hand. "Mrs. Alastair."

Alexandra snatched her hand from Grayson and turned quickly to the duke. "Your grace."

The duke bowed. "Our hearts sigh in contentment in your presence, Mrs. Alastair."

She flushed, smiling sweetly. "You are too kind."

Grayson rolled his eyes.

The duke continued. "As you can see, Stoke and I are both smitten. But alas, we will have to make due with canapés and champagne in the dining room. We will drink to your honor." He clapped Grayson on the shoulder. "Come on, Stoke, let us allow some other poor wretch his turn."

Grayson looked pointedly at the opals shining white against the russet of her hair, then lifted the corners of his mouth in a light smile. He let his gaze send suggestions. She reddened.

He turned and led Maggie back down the stairs after the duke. Behind him, Mr. Bartholomew began, "Pa-pa-pa-pleased to s-s-see you in good h-health, ma-ma-ma-Mrs. Ala-st-st-stair."

By the time Grayson regained the crowded lower floor, his mood had soured and he damned all society protocol. He and all the other guests had journeyed here with the sole purpose of speaking to Alexandra, yet it seemed that they were only allowed to spend a minute and a half in her presence. He wanted to spend many more minutes than that. A lifetime of minutes.

Instead, he found himself in the company of the duke and likely to remain in his company all night. A poor second choice. Maggie, on the other hand, seemed to find everything delightful. She kept up a steady chatter of praise for Mrs. Alastair and the decorations until they reached the dining room.

The morsels laid out in fine porcelain on the table were elegant, tasty, and tiny. Maggie left his side and circled the table like a predator, her dark eyes happy. A young gentleman busily piled macaroons and light pastries on a platter and bustled past Grayson to present them to the slightly petulant young lady sitting against a wall. The young man plopped down beside her and watched with adoring eyes while she lifted a macaroon and nibbled it without thanks. Maggie watched her, then lifted a macaroon and tried to copy the girl's dainty nibbles.

The duke put a canapé into his mouth. Grayson eyed a macaroon and balanced it on a plate. "It is pleasant, you know," he remarked. "To eat food you don't have to inspect for weevils."

The duke choked, coughed, and swallowed. "Good lord, Stoke." He caught Grayson's grin and returned one of his own. "How does it feel to be a landsman now?"

"Strange." He missed the feel of clean wind, the crack of sails, the rise and fall of the ship beneath his feet. Wouldn't he love to show Alexandra his world, exotic ports beckoning his restless feet? But he had Maggie to consider now.

"Admittedly, there's not much adventure in London," the duke said ruefully. "Unless you consider gambling your entire fortune on the turn of a card to be adventure."

"I favor dice. Pure chance. No second guessing. Unless, of course, the dice are weighted. In which case you are a fool for not noticing."

The duke smiled uncertainly. "I know plenty of houses that will welcome you. Unfortunately, most are disreputable."

Grayson took a sip of champagne. It was sweet and smooth. "Dice and disrepute. Sounds interesting."

The polished and manicured duke, a product of Harrow and Cambridge and a sheltered upbringing, could have no idea of the disreputable places Grayson had come across in his travels, places so foul even someone like Burchard would fear to enter them.

"We can retire to St. James's after making our social rounds tonight if you like," the duke said. "I'll take you to a new place where you can play dice to your heart's content. Along with other—um—fascinations."

Grayson nodded noncommittally. He'd heard of the

gaming hells in St. James's and other places, though he had not yet had the opportunity to frequent one. He'd told his officers to stay out of them on pain of flogging. Tavern games were one thing, games with elegant men of fortune were something else. He did not need to bail his officers out of the Fleet prison or rescue them from duels when they lost all their money.

"Or I can simply tell you all I know now," Grayson offered.

The duke took an alarmed look around. They stood in a relatively empty corner, away from the grazers who circled Alexandra's table. "Perhaps we should find somewhere more private," the duke said.

Grayson shook his head the slightest bit. "That would cause people to wonder what we had to discuss so covertly. Just listen carefully."

In a low voice he explained about the shop near Marylebone Street and his conviction that the king had been rowed to a ship waiting in the middle of the Thames.

The duke swallowed. "I can have the shop searched, the proprietor questioned."

"Later. The girl there let drop a few names while she was trying to be ever-so-French and impress her English customer. I recognized those names, and I'd like to pry around a little longer. Then you can loose your men and search every ship on the Thames."

The duke sucked in his breath. "We need him soon, Stoke. News will leak."

"A day," Grayson said. "If I cannot pinpoint his whereabouts by day after tomorrow, search away." He did not like the idea of the duke turning out mobs of the Royal Navy to search ships from here to the Channel. His own ship was out there, and he did not want certain things about it coming to the attention of the Admiralty—like its secret holds and its lovely capacity for smuggling. Maggie could make a fortune with the *Majesty*, and Grayson wanted nothing to stand in the way of that.

He glanced around as Henderson entered the dining room, spectacles gleaming. He was chatting with Lord Hildebrand Caldicott.

"St. James's, eh?" Grayson said in a normal voice.

To his credit, the duke caught on at once. "The usual crowd will be there," he said, pitching his voice to match Grayson's. "Chaps you should meet."

Henderson approached, talking in a relaxed way with Lord Hildebrand, as if he were on friendly terms with every gentleman in London. But this was Henderson's territory. Like the duke, Henderson knew the ins and outs of social rules—where what not to say was as important as what *to* say. Henderson could happily fall in with the plan to migrate to a gaming hell, while Grayson had no interest in watching the cream of London's gentlemen slumming. The ladies there, he imagined, would be well-dressed and well-versed in the art of pleasuring—elegant and expensive. Just the type Henderson liked. Maybe Henderson would get lost there and leave Alexandra the hell alone.

Grayson introduced the duke to Henderson. Henderson, he noted, had used powder to cover the remnants of the bruises on his face. Henderson also watched him in slight trepidation. He liked that.

As the duke, Henderson, and Lord Hildebrand greeted one another and began comparing notes on who they knew, Grayson wandered away, snaring a glass of champagne as he went. He'd come here tonight to watch Alexandra and to keep an eye on Henderson, to make certain Ardmore did not try anything annoying, like kidnapping her again. He'd also simply wanted to gaze upon

Alexandra, so beautiful and elegant in her silver and gold, with his jewels in her hair. He could look at her all night. Perhaps when the last of the guests departed, he would linger—

Her suitors did not seem to take much interest in her. Terribly honored, they'd claimed, but they were content to talk about horses and sport and gaming and to stay well away from Alexandra. And she wanted to marry one of them! Good God.

His own name was on that list. An idea began forming in his mind, one he was not certain Alexandra would accept. If he played it right, she would not have a choice in the matter. But it would give her what she wanted, as well as himself some peace of mind—that is if peace of mind were possible near Alexandra.

"Lord Stoke, forgive me."

Grayson looked up, his thoughts scattering. A gentleman with silver hair and a quiet face stood before him. The man half lifted his hand, then clutched it into a fist and let it drop. "Forgive me for approaching you without introduction. My name is Gordon Crawford."

His gray eyes focused on Grayson intently, as if he expected Grayson to know the name. Grayson offered his hand. "Mr. Crawford."

Crawford shook it hesitantly. "You do not remember me."

"No."

"It is no matter. You were a child. You—" He dragged to a stop, his gaze raking Grayson's face. "You so have the look of your mother."

Grayson's heart ceased for an instant. "You knew my mother?"

"She was—a dear friend to me. Many years ago."

Grayson felt cold congeal inside him. Try as he might,

he could not call up a memory of the man's face or voice, but he had the feeling he knew what Crawford wanted to tell him. He noted the formal elegance of his frock coat, the slick neatness of his gray hair, and the sadness in his eyes.

He said abruptly, "Were you my mother's lover?"

Crawford faced Grayson like a recalcitrant schoolboy. "Yes."

Grayson looked away, hiding his thoughts. A link to his past. Standing before him. The fact that his mother had taken a lover didn't surprise him in the least. The poor woman would have needed comfort while living with his father, a brute of a man. He looked back at Crawford. The man looked unashamed, and a touch defiant. "Did you love her?" Grayson asked.

"Yes. Truly and deeply." He paused. "You have her eyes."

Grayson shielded them. "She never spoke of you."

"I would not think so. She was terrified of your father."

"With good reason," Grayson said, his words clipped. "Why did you approach me?"

Crawford hesitated. "I do not know. I suppose I wanted to meet her son, the only thing left of her. To see if—to see if you were like her."

Grayson swallowed. Anger, grief, and anger again spilled through him. He said quietly, savagely, "If you loved her so much, why did you not help her, in the end?"

Mr. Crawford looked stricken. "What recourse did I have? She was your father's wife. What could I have done?"

"Taken her away." His voice was flat. "Taken her away from him. Far away."

"In disgrace and scandal? I could not do that to her. You would have felt that disgrace as well, all your life."

"But she would have lived."

They studied one another. "He did kill her, then?" Crawford asked quietly.

"He did. He shot her."

Crawford flinched.

"Right in front of me," Grayson said.

Crawford looked up in horror. "Good God. You were there?"

Chapter Twenty

The memories that Grayson had tried, and failed, to banish since five minutes after the incident occurred suddenly flooded him. He smelled the smoke of the pistol shots, heard the worried voices of the servants beyond the drawing room doors, saw his mother touch the red stain on her bosom in bewilderment. Her gaze—sad, blue, confused—found Grayson's an instant before she crumpled to the floor.

It had been Easter, and Grayson had returned from Eton to his father's country house in Gloucestershire. The afternoon of his arrival, his mother had sent for him to visit her in the drawing room. When he'd sought her there, she'd smiled at her son, and, because they'd been alone, dared to embrace him. For a brief moment, Grayson had felt a boyish bubble of happiness.

All happiness had shattered when his father had burst into the room from the garden. He'd been riding, and he'd carried two pistols because he liked to shoot at grouse, in season or out.

His father had closed the door and ordered Grayson away from his mother. Then Archibald Finley began raving, as he'd done many times before, accusing his wife of unnatural behavior with her own son. The only thing unnatural, Grayson reflected now, was that his father had never allowed his mother to show Grayson any kind of affection. Affection and attention made a boy soft, he'd said. He must be hard and cold to survive in the world. Any mother who wanted to embrace and touch her son was disgusting, and filled with sin and weakness. His mother had been forced to creep to the nursery to see her rambunctious child, and bribe the nurse to secrecy. Even as Grayson grew, becoming taller than his mother at age eleven, they had had to plan covert meetings to even speak as mother and son.

One shot had slain her. The other had been meant for Grayson himself. But Grayson, in grief and fear, had leapt to his father and wrested the second gun from him. The subsequent shot had been fired straight through his father's heart, with Grayson's finger on the trigger.

His motions had seemed dreamlike at the time, but they returned now with startling clarity. Grayson had pushed the pistol into his father's hand and fallen down beside him just as the servants had broken open the locked door to the hall. Dazed, he had explained to the shocked footmen that he had wrestled with his father for the gun, and the gun had gone off.

The servants had accepted his story at face value. To this day, Grayson had never been certain if the footmen had broken down the door right before or right after he'd pressed his father's fingers around the second gun. He had not lingered to ask. After the inquest and the double funeral, Grayson had fled England, never to return.

"You are right," Crawford said brokenly, "I should have acted."

"It was a long time ago." The past dissolved again, and Alexandra's elegant dining room came back into focus. "You were not there that day. I was, and I could not stop it."

His throat felt thick and tight. Damn the man for making him remember.

"I searched for you," Crawford said. "For a long time. Thought I could look after you—as a favor to her."

Grayson gave him a dry smile. "You are not going to say anything dramatic, like you are my true father, are you?"

Crawford did not return the smile. He shook his head. "When I met her, you were already seven years old."

"Pity. I have only known you ten minutes, and I like you better than I ever liked my own father. But you would not have been able to find me in any case. I was long gone. Shipped out on a merchantman sailing for India only days later."

"I cannot blame you for running away. You must have been terrified out of your wits. What I wonder is—" He paused. "Why did it take you twenty years to return?"

Grayson idly drew his finger around the rim of his champagne glass. "I meant never to come back at all."

"But then you came into your title. Is that why you returned?"

"Not exactly." He lifted his gaze to Maggie. She had finished the macaroon and was eyeing the tray of bubbling champagne that a footman had just carried in. Grayson motioned to her. "Maggie, love, come here and meet someone."

Maggie abandoned the champagne and went to them,

her eyes alight with curiosity. Grayson stood her in front of him and placed his hands on her shoulders. "Crawford, this is Maggie. My daughter." He paused. "My reason."

Whatever Maggie thought of this statement, she gave no sign. She held her hand out. "Pleased to meet you, Mr. Crawford."

Crawford stared at her in mild shock. He gently shook her hand. "She is so like her."

Grayson nodded. He remembered his own staggering surprise when he'd first looked upon Maggie's face and seen the eyes of his own mother looking back at him. Grayson the boy had been seconds too slow to save his mother from dying. But Grayson the man could save Maggie. And he was going to, damn anyone who got in his way.

Crawford said to Maggie, "I was a friend of—of your grandmamma's."

Maggie looked interested. "Truly? Will you and Papa tell me about her? Perhaps Mr. Crawford can come for tea. Mrs. Alastair and Mrs. Fairchild are teaching me how to pour tea."

Crawford nodded, hopeful. "I would like that."

Grayson looked him up and down. He wondered whether speaking to this man about the past would erase the hurt or make it worse. But Maggie appeared interested and eager. So did Crawford. He had run away from his mother's memory; perhaps he owed it to her to keep the memory alive through his daughter.

Before he had a chance to answer, something happened that altered the entire evening and made Alexandra Alastair's end-of-season soiree the talk of London for years to come. Over Crawford's left shoulder, Grayson saw Zechariah Burchard quietly walk past Alexandra's dining room door, sipping champagne.

Bloody hell.

Henderson and the duke had left the room. Only the young girl and her eager suitor and a few frail old gentlemen who seemed determined to eat everything in sight remained.

Grayson discarded his glass and shoved Maggie at Crawford. "Stay with him." As he crossed the room, he assessed the weapons he carried—only a small dagger in his boot, deadly, but meant for a last-ditch effort, not an all-out attack. Calmly, he stopped at a sideboard, took up a silver candlestick, and removed the candle. He blew out the candle, tossed it down, then left the dining room, candlestick in hand.

Burchard was heading for the staircase. He was not hurrying; he simply let his lithe form dodge through the guests.

Alexandra still stood at the top of the stairs, greeting her admirers. Burchard climbed toward her.

Henderson was holding court in the reception room door, closer to the stairs. But his back was turned, his attention engrossed in his new friends. He had not seen.

"Henderson!"

Henderson started and looked around. Grayson charged for the stairs.

Henderson looked up and saw Burchard. His face went white. Hastily excusing himself, he mounted the staircase, his hand dipping inside his coat. He'd probably brought a pistol, but the man couldn't use it *here*. He might hit one of the open-mouthed, bewildered guests, or worse still, Alexandra.

Grayson pushed people out of his way as he hit the staircase, letting politeness go hang. Burchard climbed ever higher, Henderson just after him. The throng, damn them, impeded Grayson at every step.

Burchard reached Alexandra. She saw him. Her mouth opened.

Grayson's fears ground through him. He saw his mother's death all over again, only this time it was Alexandra falling limply to the floor, Alexandra's bodice stained with her own red blood. A savage snarl sprang from his lips.

Burchard passed Alexandra and ran lightly along the landing. Grayson desperately shoved his way to the top of the stairs and managed to reach them at the same time Henderson did. Burchard reached into his coat and pulled out a pistol.

Lady Featherstone saw it. She screamed. The scream echoed up and down the stairs. Other ladies took it up. Gentlemen began to swear. Everyone below came running to see what was happening.

Burchard spun and aimed right at Grayson, who stood exposed on the landing. The eyes above the pistol were hard and remorseless.

"Grayson!" Alexandra dove at him, shoving him hard. Grayson toppled into Henderson, who toppled into another gentlemen. Like dominoes, the four of them tumbled to the floor, just as Burchard fired. A statue in a niche behind them exploded as the bullet hit the stone. Shards of marble rained over the guests.

Henderson kicked and shoved himself to his feet. Grayson untangled Alexandra from him and pulled her upright.

Burchard spun away and ran up the next flight of stairs. Alexandra started after him. Grayson pulled her back. She fought him. "Mrs. Fairchild is up there!"

Grayson cursed. He pushed Alexandra into the caring hands of Lady Featherstone. Then he and Henderson charged to the next flight of stairs. They reached the bottom just as Burchard gained the top.

A door burst open above them, and Lieutenant Jacobs sprang from the doorway. He carried a curved cutlass in one hand and wore nothing else. His bronzed torso glistened with sweat, and his long dark hair tangled to his shoulders. Several female guests dropped into gentle swoons.

Burchard halted in surprise. Jacobs charged him, naked body gleaming. Grayson and Henderson flung themselves up the stairs. Burchard slammed his body between Henderson and Grayson, and the two men got in each other's way trying to grab him. Burchard broke free. Grayson brought the candlestick down on Burchard's narrow back. The man stumbled but kept running.

Henderson drew his pistol, but the alarmed and curious crowd now filled the landing. Behind them Jacobs, oblivious of his nudity, shouted, "How the *hell* did he get in here?"

Burchard grabbed the nearest female, Mrs. Tetley, Grayson thought her name was, swung her around, and threw her at Henderson. Henderson caught her like the gentleman he was, giving Burchard the lead.

Grayson had no such scruples. He charged on, candlestick ready, flinging aside the unfortunate young lady Burchard tried to throw at him. She shrieked, and two young men rushed to her rescue.

The guests seemed to catch on and started pulling the ladies out of the way. The gentlemen, on the other hand, got in the way trying to catch the man themselves. Burchard was quick. He twisted and turned to slide through the crowd like a snake, where Grayson's bulk found no passage.

And then the man reached Alexandra. Something

glinted in his hand. Alexandra flung herself toward him, ready to stop him.

"*Alexandra, no!*"

Grayson's shout was swallowed by the crowd. A blade flashed. Scarlet blood splashed the silver and gold of Alexandra's gown. She stared at the blood, surprised. Then her face whitened, and she slowly crumpled to the floor.

Burchard reached down and ripped the strand of opals and diamonds from her hair.

Lady Featherstone lunged for Alexandra. Lord Featherstone lunged for Burchard. Burchard scrambled onto the staircase railing, balanced himself for a breathless second, then lightly dropped to the open hall of the floor below. Guests screamed and scrambled out of his way.

Henderson raced past Grayson's stunned figure. He set his backside on the rail, swung his legs over, and vaulted down in Burchard's wake.

Another set of footsteps thudded past—Jacobs, with his cutlass, ran unsteadily by. He'd donned white cotton underbreeches that clung to his hips and did little to hide the dark hair on his loins. He descended by the more common means of the stairs, scattering ladies and gentlemen before him. A few more ladies, and one slender gentleman, swooned.

Alexandra lay in a heap at the top of the stairs. Blood soaked through her gown and her silver and gold bodice. Grayson, his heart beating in hard, aching blows, discarded the ineffectual candlestick and dropped to one knee beside her.

She looked up, her face a mask of pain. Lady Featherstone held Alexandra's arm. A deep gash slashed the white skin of her forearm, just under the lace of her sleeve. Blood splashed from the cut, dripping and running, rivulets flowing to stain her gown and puddle on the floor.

"Grayson," she whispered. "He took the opals. I am so sorry."

He touched her hair, tangled where Burchard had yanked the jewels from it. "Hush, sweetheart." He gently took her hurt arm. *Stop bleeding, stop, please.* Too much blood, and it would not stop spurting. The man had cut an artery.

He yanked at his cravat, tearing the knot and pulling the strangling folds from his neck. His thudding heart made him sick to his stomach. He pushed up her satin sleeve, ripping the lace out of his way. He brushed against another hand holding her—Lady Featherstone's. The lady looked on in consternation, her own thin face white.

"Get me towels," he commanded. "Fetch her maid. I need to stop the bleeding."

The lady rose without arguing. Grayson decided he liked her. As she sped away, her husband took her place. "Surely it is better to let her bleed. It will wash away the ill humors."

Grayson bit down on his response. He wound the cravat around her arm and knotted it tight, twisting the knot with his strong fingers. Alexandra made a soft sound of pain.

"I know it hurts, love," he said. "But it will help you."

Her pulse beat strong beneath his hand. She fluttered her fingers a little as the feeling went out of them. The spurts of blood slowed.

He heard noisy breathing beside him. A woman in maid's garb, her cap half hanging over her face, dropped to her knees beside him. "Madam," she said breathlessly. She held towels. Grayson grabbed them and pressed the folded pad of them over the slash in Alexandra's forearm. Alexandra closed her eyes.

"Stay awake, sweetheart," he said.

"Give her laudanum," someone else offered. Others concurred. Grayson ignored them. He glanced at Lord Featherstone.

"Go next door and get my man, Oliver. Tell him what happened."

"We should send for a doctor," the man replied.

Grayson definitely preferred the man's wife. "Oliver is a surgeon. I want him. Now go."

"I'll go," a breathless voice said. It was Henderson. Face white, chest heaving, spectacles bent, he appeared at Grayson's elbow.

"Good. Hurry."

Henderson gave Alexandra a longing look, then sped away.

Legs and skirts moved aside and Jacobs stumbled into view, followed by the duke, Lord Hildebrand Caldicott, and Mr. Bartholomew.

"He's gone, sir." Jacobs panted heavily, holding one arm across his abdomen. "Ran across the garden. Then just vanished."

Grayson looked up angrily. "How could you not find him? Henderson was right on top of him."

Jacobs shook his head, eyes worried. "I don't know. He didn't go through the gate. There was a lad just outside it who said no one ran through. He hit Henderson pretty hard, and then he dashed into the shadows and just vanished."

Grayson swore in the foulest sailor's language he could muster. Another lady swooned.

"He might have climbed over a wall," the duke offered. "I did not see where he went after he struck Mr. Henderson. We were hard on his heels, but—" He made a futile motion with his hands. "Who the devil was he?"

Mr. Bartholomew spoke. "Hu-hu-he da-dropped this." He held out the strand of sparkling diamonds. The opals shone softly.

Alexandra reached for it, her face lighting. "Thank heavens." She pressed the glittering handful of diamonds to her lips, then cradled them against her breast. "Thank you, gentlemen," she whispered.

Then she fainted.

Chapter Twenty-one

Alexandra convalesced for two days after the soiree. Her arm remained stiff and painful, but she found herself able to leave her bed on the third day and resume her normal activity.

But everything had changed. Alexandra's adventurous soiree was the talk of Mayfair. Several newspaper articles furnished lurid descriptions of it and boasted interviews with eye witnesses. Alexandra read a few of the articles, and concluded that the anonymous sources must have been trapped in the reception room for the duration and missed everything. According to these stories, several shots had been fired upstairs and then a hoard of pirates had descended from above, several of them naked, all of them carrying murderous-looking weapons. Their purpose, to rob all and sundry. The quick thinking of Viscount Stoke, the Duke of St. Clair, and several other gentlemen had saved the day, and the pirates had been chased from the house.

Speculation about who the pirates were varied widely—from French spies to discontented English deserters to the viscount's old enemies. The rumor that Viscount Stoke had once been a pirate, the notorious Captain Finley, was dredged up and splashed across the newspapers. Amazingly, the conjecture that the attacker was an old enemy was dismissed by most as being fanciful and unlikely. Alexandra, on the other, knew it to be utter truth.

The mystery of why Mr. Burchard had been admitted to the house at all had been easily solved. Lady Featherstone had sent him an invitation long before Grayson had revealed to Alexandra that the man was a murderous pirate. Alexandra had left the guest list to Lady Featherstone, and she'd been far too busy to check it herself. Lady Featherstone had been startled and annoyed by Mr. Burchard at the theater, but perhaps had changed her mind and not withdrawn the invitation. Though Alexandra had made it clear to Jeffrey that Mr. Burchard was no longer welcome as a caller, the man had been on the guest list, which, in Jeffrey's mind, was as sacrosanct as the Bible.

Why Mr. Jacobs had been in Alexandra's bedchamber, naked, was more of a mystery. Mrs. Fairchild, white-lipped, had called on Alexandra the next day and had tried to take the blame. Alexandra learned, to her surprise, that her beloved Mrs. Fairchild had once had an affair with Mr. Jacobs. The lady was clearly very much in love and quite ashamed. Alexandra's heart went out to her.

Mr. Jacobs had arrived looking for her. He'd charged into the bedroom, and stated angrily that the fault for the night before was all his. Mrs. Fairchild had wept. Grayson had come in after both of them, and the three had argued heatedly in the middle of the room while Alexandra watched from her bed. Mrs. Fairchild had tried to resign as Maggie's governess. Grayson had growled that he refused to let her go. Mr. Jacobs also proclaimed he'd resign, and Grayson threatened to flog him.

Then Maggie arrived, with Mr. Oliver in tow. Jeffrey and Annie and Amy had peered in, curious about all the fuss.

Mr. Oliver, surprisingly, had taken charge. He was backed by Cook, who'd been drawn out of her kitchen by the noise. Cook ran them all out of the bedchamber saying that her lady needed rest—yes, even you, your viscount lordship; wasn't it your lot what got her hurt in the first place?

They'd gone. Not to return. Whether because of her dragon guardian or some other reason, not even Grayson had returned in the intervening time to speak to Alexandra.

So she was a bit surprised to find that her first caller the day she descended to her drawing room to resume her routine was Mr. Henderson.

Alexandra received him in the first-floor drawing room. Jeffrey bowed him in, then look disappointed when he was dismissed. Mr. Henderson's spectacles were straight and clean, his dark suit was perfect, and every hair was in place. He was too perfect, she reflected, too studied. Grayson's hair was always easily mussed, and it felt like silk beneath her fingers.

Mr. Henderson came to Alexandra, gently lifted her hurt arm, examined the bandage, then brought her hand to his lips.

"I tried to call on you three days running," he said. "Your footman would not admit me. The cook's orders, he said."

222

So it *had* been a dragon guard. "I was resting." She slid her hand from his grasp.

"I know." He wandered from her, distracted. "I have been hunting for Burchard everywhere. I made Finley tell me the name of the hotel he'd tracked the man to, but he has not been there in days. Small wonder. Finley has been hunting him too, but without success."

"Why?" Alexandra burst out. Henderson raised his brows in surprise. She massaged her temples. "Why do you try to find him if he is so dangerous?"

"He hurt you, Mrs. Alastair. He must pay for that. Even your duke friend has hired Bow Street Runners to track him down. London will be too hot to hold Mr. Burchard."

"The duke is conscientious," Alexandra said.

"No, he's potty in love with you." Mr. Henderson smiled crookedly. "As I am."

She made a faint moan and rubbed her temples harder. "Mr. Henderson do not say such things to me."

"What, tell you I love you? I cannot help myself. I fell in love with you an instant before—well before that incident on your doorstep." He paused. "I hope—I sincerely hope—that one day soon you will let me erase what I did by showing you how gentle I can be."

Alexandra tried to retain her composure, tried to be merely a lady who must gently turn down a hopeful suitor. But she was tired, her arm hurt, and her composure crumpled like wax under flame. She let out a frustrated cry and plunked down onto a chair.

"Oh, God," Henderson said. "The thought cannot be that awful, can it?"

"Mr. Henderson." Alexandra clasped her hands and spoke between tight lips. "I have been trying to think of ways to erase the events of the last two weeks from my mind. But what happened at my soiree now makes that impossible! I am the talk of the town—I am ruined. All because you pirates, and pirate hunters, decided to carry out your private war in my house." She let her hands fall against her skirt. "My life used to be peaceful." *Dull*, a tiny voice echoed. "Like clockwork." *Plodding*. "Everything in its place." *Predictable and staid*. "Until you—" She jabbed a finger at him. "Kissed me on the street, *in front of my neighbors*, and Grayson Finley asked me to sleep without clothes, and Mr. Ardmore abducted me to his ship. And then, at my soiree, I completely betrayed myself by crying Grayson's name when I thought him in danger and weeping when the jewels he'd given me were stolen. I am certain the next time I open a newspaper, I will see myself in caricature with Captain Pirate Viscount Stoke, probably naked in his arms, with some clever words coming out of our mouths in balloons."

She ran out of breath and sank back into the chair, spent.

Mr. Henderson came to her, his face a study of misery. He dropped to one knee and took her uninjured hand in his. "Mrs. Alastair—Alexandra—I so hate myself that I hurt you. You have no idea. I want to make everything up to you. I adore you." He pressed a wet kiss to her fingers.

"Please, Mr. Henderson," Alexandra groaned. "You are only making things worse."

"Tell me how to make it better."

"Put back the clock." She gave him a weary smile. "Can you do that?"

He lifted her hand to his lips again, and she was too tired to pull away. "I would if it would make you forget you ever met Finley." He sighed. "I am going to speak openly. Please forgive me if I offend you. Finley is a barbarian. He does not understand your world. You say you do not like violence—Finley lives in violence. I know in my heart that he has already taken you as his lover. He does not wait when he wants something. But he will never be your husband."

Alexandra felt as if she were falling. Any moment she'd crash right through the floor and land in her reception room. "Husband—"

"He has his agreement with Captain Ardmore, above it all. Finley actually has some honor. He will present himself for his execution."

Alexandra's breath hurt her. "You cannot let Mr. Ardmore do it. You must stop him."

"Me? Stop Ardmore? He stops for no one. Even Madame d'Lorenz cannot control him—he is using her, even though she thinks her schemes are so secret. But I imagine Finley has something up his sleeve. He generally does."

"Are—are you saying you believe Grayson will *not* let Mr. Ardmore kill him?" She seized on the hope.

"I have no idea what Finley will do. He's always been difficult to predict." He squeezed her hand. "What *I* want is to take you away from all this. I am quit of Ardmore, and will return to Kent. I have plenty of money; you would never have to worry for anything. We can settle near your old home, have a fine life together. Children, dogs, anything you want."

Anything she wanted. She drew a breath. "I think, Mr. Henderson, that I no longer know what I want."

His look turned pained. "I know what you want. You want Finley. What I cannot fathom is why."

"I do not know." She did not. *Because he makes me feel joy, because he understood when I grieved for my son, because he took my husband's horrible necklace and made it into something beautiful.* Such feelings were beyond explaining. Certainly not to Mr. Henderson. Mr. Henderson was bound to Captain Ardmore, much as he tried to tell her otherwise.

"I am sorry, Mr. Henderson," she said softly.

He clasped her hand. "Do not refuse me quite yet. At least consider my offer. I will leave you alone to think. You can send for me at the Majestic Hotel when you are ready. Let me hope, even if it is a futile hope."

She watched as he kissed her hand again, but she barely felt the press of his lips. She knew that she could give him no hope. Her heart had been lost to the man who had agreed to give up his life for the sake of his daughter. Which meant she had no hope at all.

"Mrs. Fairchild is taking me riding in the park," Maggie announced. "Will you come?"

Grayson turned from the garden door as Maggie entered the dining room. She was dressed in a light-colored riding habit and wore a small bonnet that framed her beautiful face. Her eager smile lit her eyes.

"Unfortunately, no. I have work to do for the pox-rotted Admiralty," he replied, seeing no reason to keep his feelings from her. "Tomorrow, perhaps."

Her smile dimmed. "When we were on the ship, we were always together. Remember, you and Mr. O'Malley taught me how to climb the rigging?"

Amusement touched him. Maggie had been an eager pupil, and fearless. Ian O'Malley, forty-five years old, had gone white-faced a time or two at her antics.

"I remember."

She came to him, her feet whispering softly on the bare board floor. "Papa, when we were aboard, I thought Mr. Henderson and Mr. O'Malley and Mr. Ardmore were friends. But since we've reached London, that has all changed." She gave him a look that was too intelligent for her twelve-year-old face. "Something is wrong. What made them become your enemies?"

He noted the use of *your*. O'Malley, who reported to Ardmore, was still enchanted with Maggie and she with him.

"They have been my enemies for a long time," he said slowly. "We agreed to put that aside, just for the crossing."

"I wish you would have told me."

He rested his fingers lightly on the table. "I did not want to frighten you. I must have been frightening enough."

The look in her eyes pierced him to the heart. "You did not frighten me. I knew you were my papa the moment I saw you, and that everything would be all right. I was much more frightened of staying alone forever. Even Mr. Ardmore was not as frightening as that."

"I will tell him you said so." He let his gaze rove her. She was so heartbreakingly fragile, and yet, at the same time, so strong. "I am glad you don't fear him. He can never defeat you, then." At her puzzled look, he stopped. "I will never leave you behind, Maggie. You have my word on that."

She nodded once, as if she'd had no doubt he would be there for her forever. She announced, "Mrs. Alastair's cook says she is much better. Mrs. Alastair, I mean. She says I may visit her tomorrow." She gave her father a knowing smile. "Will you visit her, too?"

He had a sudden vision of himself lying under Alexandra's inquisitive gaze in his cabin on the *Majesty*. How her fiery tongue had traced his muscled torso, how her soft lips had pressed the tip of his arousal. He smothered a groan. "Yes, I will be visiting her." Every day. For the rest of my life.

"Good. Perhaps we may go together." She came to him, gave him a brief hug, and hurried back to the door.

The warmth of her childish embrace lingered long after she'd pulled away. He said, "Maggie."

She turned, inquiring.

His entire heart went into his question. "You know that I love you, don't you?"

She hesitated, and he held his breath. She broke into a warm smile. "I love you too, Papa." She gazed at him for a heart-rending moment, then turned and was gone.

Grayson found Ian O'Malley in the kitchens with Oliver and Mrs. Dalloway, Alexandra's cook. He drew O'Malley aside and gave him a series of messages to deliver.

O'Malley whitened. "You want me to tell him *that?* Why don't I just commit me own murder and be done with it?"

Grayson's impatience chafed. "Deliver the messages in that order. I want Madame d'Lorenz as soon as you can get her. If I haven't returned by the time she arrives, keep her here. Have Oliver sit on her if you have to."

O'Malley scowled. "Damn your soul, Finley. I am second in command on the most feared ship on the seas, not a messenger boy to a trumped-up English bastard."

Grayson pushed his face close to the wire-haired man's. "Here in London, you're simply a nuisance Irishman with ties to the '99 rebellion. I am certain the Admiralty would be interested in speaking to you about that."

"That's blackmail, that is. Breaks me achin' heart, Finley, you'd even say such a thing. After all we've been through."

"Just do it," Grayson snarled, and then stamped away to Marylebone.

* * *

Grayson was pleased to find Miss Oh-So-French waiting on customers again that afternoon. He seated himself in a chair and absently studied the wares on the shelves behind her counter while she assisted another Frenchman. After a time, the Frenchman left the shop, nodding almost cordially to Grayson as he passed.

The girl looked upon him and smiled. The smile told him that though he might ask only to inspect the jewel boxes, he could easily ask to inspect something else, and be rewarded.

Grayson stuck to jewel boxes. He examined three prettily gilded and painted ones that he thought Maggie would like. He laughed silently at himself. Each time Maggie unnerved him he bought her a present. At this rate, she'd have to rent a warehouse in which to store them all.

Miss Oh-So-French smiled encouragingly as he lingered over his choices. "Zis one," she said, fluttering her dark lashes and pointing to the costliest of the three. "Your daughter will find it lovely, all filled up wiz her jewels."

The girl wore the thinnest of muslin gowns that put very little between the herself and the world. The pink bows of her chemise were clearly visible against her bodice, and the outline of her nipples pressed the thin cloth.

"Were you born in England?" Grayson asked her casually.

She bathed him in a smile. "I was, yes. But my parents, zey are French. Zey fled ze Terror. In France ze are great aristocrats."

Grayson doubted that. Most aristocrats tended to continue living as aristocrats, although in reduced circumstances. Some of the minor gentry eked out a living as shopkeepers, reduced, definitely, from their days of glory, but unlikely to have been in the king's inner circle.

He toyed with the enameled lid of the expensive box, which was trimmed with gold filigree. "You mentioned a Madame d'Lorenz when I visited before."

"Oh, yes. A great lady. She likes our boxes and zings for 'air dressing table."

Grayson rested his elbows on the counter. "Then would you be surprised, mademoiselle, if I told you Madam d'Lorenz was a French agent? In the employ of Napoleon's government?"

Chapter Twenty-two

The change in the young woman was remarkable. Her studied flirtation and her winsome smile vanished, to be replaced by a wide-eyed stare. "What? That cannot be true. Not Madame d'Lorenz." The French accent had nearly disappeared.

"I am in a position to know," Grayson said.

"How can you?" She blinked, shook her head, then seemed to realize she'd dropped her persona. The French accent returned. "No, she cannot be. She is so loyal to ze king. She would do anyzing for him." She leaned to him, her face worried. " 'ow can you be certain of zis?"

He made a little shrug. "I was once her lover. There is little about her I do not know."

She straightened, confusion warring in her eyes. "Oh, monsieur, zis is terrible what you have told me."

"Yes, you perhaps should reconsider selling her your jewel boxes."

"What?" Her brow furrowed. Then suddenly she wiped

231

her expression clean and nodded. "Yes, it shall be as you say. No more sales to Madame d'Lorenz. Now, monsieur, have you made your choice? I have zo many zings to do."

Alexandra remained in her upstairs sitting room a long time after Mr. Henderson had left her. The ormolu clock ticked quietly in the corner, and a faint breeze stirred the drapes at the open window. The fragrance of roses beckoned her, but Alexandra only sat, hands in her lap, following a gold twist of pattern in the carpet.

She could sense her writing table standing calmly by the window, its satinwood gleaming like burnished gold. Inside its drawer lay her list of suitors. The foolish, foolish list. How could she have supposed she could choose a husband by listing his qualities, as if she were buying a piece of furniture? The list and the guidelines that she and Lady Featherstone had chosen seemed woefully silly now. The trouble was, only a few weeks ago she'd have been perfectly content if a gentleman like Mr. Henderson had proposed. She could have married him, moved to Kent, and happily continued her prosaic life.

Everything had changed when old Viscount Stoke passed away and a younger viscount took his place. A blue-eyed pirate had moved in next door, and her entire existence had shattered.

When the sun's shadows touched the potted palm in the corner, Alexandra at last rose and left the room. Annie and Amy were dusting in the downstairs hall, as she noted over the banister. Jeffrey lounged at his place by the front door, dozing. She ought to scold him, but she did not have the strength. All seemed quiet from the kitchens—Mrs. Dalloway must be visiting Mr. Oliver next door.

The upstairs hall was still. Strange, when it had been

so frenzied the night of the soiree. She paused in the very spot where she'd seen Captain Burchard turn and aim a pistol at Grayson. She'd thought her heart would stop. The dim memory of her scream lingered in the hall, as did the roar of the pistol, the sharp stench of the smoke.

And then Mr. Jacobs had come running out of the bedchamber above, stark naked. Well, her guests had been quite entertained, at least. Mrs. Waters in particular had looked most pleased.

She turned her back on the spot and climbed the stairs to her bedchamber. She opened the door, stirring the dust motes that danced in the warm sunshine. Joan was no-where in sight; she was likely resting or running an er-rand. Alexandra crossed to the window, reaching for the catch to let the summer air into the stuffy room.

The door behind her closed. The lock clicked softly. Alexandra swung around.

Standing just inside her bedchamber door, his green eyes holding the chill of winter, was James Ardmore.

Her heart began pounding frantically. She opened her mouth to scream, but no sound came from her bone-dry throat.

Before her stunned senses could rally enough for her to run for the bell-pull, he was upon her. His large body blocked her escape; his grip pinned her as tightly as if he'd wrapped her in chains.

She stared up at him in fear. His swarthy face was dark with beard, his eyes a bit wild around the edges. When she'd faced him under the influence of the substance Mr. Henderson had given her, she had been foolishly unafraid of him. Now she saw his ruthless anger, one that could easily break her and any person who ran to her assistance.

She drew a ragged breath. "How did you get in? Jeffrey would have announced you." She recalled Jeffrey dozing by the door and a sudden suspicion touched her. "Where is Joan?"

His eyes flickered. "Sleeping. Do not blame her. It was not her fault."

"No, I blame *you*, Mr. Ardmore. What do you want?"

"I came to talk to you. Our last conversation was so rudely interrupted."

"We have nothing to say to one another, Mr. Ardmore," she announced coldly.

"Oh, I think we do, Mrs. Alastair." As Mr. Henderson had, he lifted her arm and studied the bandaged wound. His fingers were calloused and rough on her skin. "Burchard did this."

"He did. He is another gentleman I am not happy with."

Ardmore did not reply. He began gently working loose the tie of the bandage. Alexandra held her breath, fearing to jerk her arm from him—it still pained her so.

He parted the white cloth and examined the gash. A row of neat stitching, dull and red, cut across her arm. His fingers drifted above it, but he did not touch the wound. "Oliver's work."

She nodded. He wound the bandage again, as gently as Mr. Oliver had wound the first one. "You are fortunate. He is a competent surgeon."

He did not release her arm, but loosely clasped her hand in his.

She swallowed. "You lied to me."

"Did I? I do not recall."

"Well, you did not tell me the truth, anyway. Neither did Grayson. I am most put out by the pair of you. Mr. Henderson had to explain things to me."

He stood too close to her. The smell of London coal smoke mingled with a sweet smell that she now knew came from the act of coupling. Evidence that he had casually tumbled her maid to bribe his way into the house made her fury grow.

"He told me about the terrible bargain you and Grayson made," she went on. "How could you? How could you do such a thing to Maggie?"

His grip, which had been gentleness itself, suddenly tightened. "Understand, Alexandra. We made the agreement because of her. At least I did. Finley is unworthy of her. But I will see to it that she lives a good life, with all the honor she deserves. The best thing Finley can do for her is die."

Alexandra recoiled. "She loves him! And he her. Anyone can see that."

"He used her, Alexandra, to save himself. I saved Maggie—*I* did."

"I do not believe you."

He curved over her, the warmth of his body smothering her, the cloying scent of lovemaking choking off her breath. "I *had* him. He knelt on my deck with no one to help him, not his loyal Oliver or Jacobs or his other misguided crew. He knelt there, at my mercy, and he begged me for his life. Do you know what he said?"

Alexandra, trembling, shook her head.

"I asked him why the devil I should not kill him. And he looked up at me, bleeding and pathetic, and said, 'Because my little girl would miss me.'"

"Maggie," she whispered.

His smile was cold. "I actually withdrew my sword. I had been one instant away from running him through and ending his miserable life. And yet, I stopped. I asked him what he meant. And he told me. He told me that the woman I had loved most in the world had given birth to a child. *His* child." His eyes blazed, "Not mine."

Alexandra could not answer.

"When I saw Maggie," he went on, "I knew the truth. She looked so like Sara. But she had the look of Finley, so much so that there was no doubt she was his."

"Why did you help Maggie? If you hate him so?"

Ardmore did not seem to hear her. "Did he tell you I was there when Sara died? I held her hand when she drew her last breath. She was so thin, Alexandra. Her fingers were like twigs, and her beautiful, beautiful face was sunken and wasted. She asked me to make sure Finley looked after Maggie. She asked me to make certain she was safe." The lines on his face deepened. "Then she told me she had always loved me."

His hold was strong, and his eyes shone with crazed grief. What he meant to do, she could not say. She knew she could never fight him, but she must not let him prevail—she must not. She reached inside to the anger burning deep beneath her fear and tried to kindle it into a bonfire.

"Mr. Ardmore, you should not delude yourself. You must know she lied. If she had loved you at all, she would never have left you in the first place."

His eyes glittered. "I know that. But I loved her. I loved her enough to bring Maggie back to England and make certain she grows up safe. And I will kill Finley to do it."

"She loves him."

"She barely knows him. Neither do you. You have no idea what a black-hearted monster he is."

She stirred the anger building within her. "You do not know him very well yourself if you believe that," she blazed. "He has a large and generous heart. He loves Maggie like his life's blood—he has decided to sacrifice himself to you for her. You are blinded by your anger and your own misguided love for Sara, and your grief over your brother."

She'd known when she began that speech that she'd say too much. His face lost its etching of pain and turned hard with fury. He caught the hair on top of her head and forced her body backward, taking her down to the carpet. She fell onto her back, trying to twist from the pain, and found him full-length on top of her. He gripped her face, fingers biting into her flesh.

His breath was hot on her face. "He is a liar, Alexandra. He's charmed you with his lies. He loves no one—not you, not Sara, not Maggie. And he murdered my brother, as sure as he pulled the trigger himself."

Alexandra tried to shake her head. "No. Grayson was injured. He could not stop it. It was not his fault."

"Dear God, listen to you bleat your defense of him. He *says* he was not to blame, and his besotted crew chimes in and agrees with him. But the truth is there. He murdered my brother, and he loves nothing. Learn that."

Fear churned her, but she hardened her will. "I will not let you bully me."

"God's blood, woman, I am trying to save you from him."

"No. You want to turn me against him, as you have turned against him. I will not."

He pressed his face close to hers. "Do you want to save him, Mrs. Alastair? Do you want to know how you can save him?"

"Yes." Her whisper was cracked.

His fingers bit deeper. His breath washed over her, hot and brandy-scented. "Marry me, Alexandra. Become my wife, not just in name, but in every way. Marry me, and I will leave him alive, and leave England."

Chapter Twenty-three

Alexandra could not breathe. "Marry—"

"Yes." His eyes were fevered. "Leave with me. I will take you to Charleston. I have a fine house there, and you will want for nothing. You have so little here—there, your beauty and grace will be celebrated. You will live a fine life. I promise you."

"Mr. Ardmore—"

"My name is James. I know you hate me, but I will work to change that. If you come with me, I will let Finley live. I will quit England and never return. He wishes to stay here with Maggie. We will never meet again."

Which meant Alexandra would never see him again. Or Maggie. Her heart burned. "You would leave him alone? You would give me your word?"

"My word, Alexandra."

She shook her head in despair. "But you break your word. You tried to kill him that night."

"Because I thought he'd broken his. What was I to believe when I learned he was entertaining the Admiralty in his own house? I thought he'd betrayed me to them. I still am not certain he did not."

"He is a man of honor." The words tasted bitter. "He will keep the bargain."

His grip on her face tightened anew. "Your devotion to him wearies me. Marry me and I spare him. Refuse me and I kill him. The choice is yours."

Her voice was hoarse with tears. "How can you ask this of me? You know I will always hate you."

"But I could grow to love you. You are a fine and beautiful woman, Alexandra. Finley is nowhere near worthy of you."

He yanked her head back and kissed her. She shut her mouth and twisted away, but his lips followed hers. His tongue scraped her mouth.

"Leave me alone."

He lifted his head, breathing hard. "If I leave you alone, he dies."

"Let us at least discuss this reasonably."

He laughed, a brutal sound. "There is no reason where Finley is concerned."

"He said that about you."

"Did he? Then maybe the truth is we cannot be reasonable about one another. What is your answer?"

She squeezed her eyes shut. His hot breath on her face, his fingers twisting her hair, would not allow her to forget his presence. To marry him, to save Grayson's life— She opened her eyes. "How do I know that you will not go back on your promise and simply murder him once we are safely married?"

His smile frightened her more than his words ever had. "Because it will kill him to see you with me. It will kill him every day. And for me, that will be far, far more satisfying than stringing him up and watching him die."

He was wrong. Alexandra fought a hysterical desire to laugh. Grayson would be angry, yes, but hardly devastated. They had tumbled together and loved each other's bodies, but he had never said one word to make her believe his affection went beyond that. His deep love was for Maggie—she saw that. Alexandra was no more than a passing distraction.

With a word, she could save his life. She knew Mr. Ardmore would adhere to his promise. She would make him adhere to it, whether he liked it or not. Even if she had to chain him to the wall.

She took a deep breath. "Very well, I will marry you, Mr. Ardmore." She held up her hand. "But only if you promise that we sail from England the moment the deed is done."

His eyes sparkled with sudden animation. "We will sail even before that. I cannot come out of hiding to make a marriage in England. You gather what you need and tell Henderson to take you to the *Argonaut*. We will quit England, and then we will marry." His terrible smile widened and he bent to her lips.

She stopped him with a hand on his chin. "What about Madame d'Lorenz?"

He frowned. "Madame d'Lorenz? What about her?"

"What will she say to you marrying me?"

"Madame d'Lorenz has nothing to do with this."

"It is likely she will not feel that way, if she is in love with you."

He made an impatient noise. "Madame d'Lorenz loves France and Napoleon. In that order. I am far down on the list."

"But—" She wrinkled her brow. "You told me—you

told me that she would never give the king to Napoleon. That she could not have kidnapped him."

"No, I told you that an émigré would never do that. I never said that Madame d'Lorenz was an émigré. Her exile is self-imposed, until Napoleon is completely victorious in Europe. Until then, she'll do what she can to see that it happens."

"Do you mean you are harboring a French *spy?*"

He shook his head impatiently. "She is using me, and then she will go. The sooner you marry me, the sooner she goes back to France."

"I will need a little time—"

"No time, Alexandra. No prancing off to the Admiralty, no dealing behind my back with Finley. Pack up what you want, and I'll send Henderson to fetch you. I will not let you on board the *Argonaut* if you are with anyone but him."

Her heart sank. "Mr. Henderson will not wish to help you with this."

"Because he's besotted with you himself? He will. He knows what will happen to him if he does not. Besides, he would not be happy for the Admiralty to investigate his past either. We all have skeletons to hide, including your precious Finley."

"I—"

He pressed a hard kiss to her lips, cutting off her words. "You have given your promise, Alexandra," he said in a soft, deadly voice. "An engagement in England is just as binding as marriage. I will hold you to it."

He rose to his feet with the same leopardlike ease she'd observed in him before, then reached down and pulled her up. "Henderson will arrive this evening. Busy yourself packing."

One last time, he kissed her. She did not respond, but

hung in his grasp, numb, unresisting. Her first marriage had existed in unfeeling misery. She had vowed, so desperately vowed, never to be caught in such a marriage again.

After Ardmore strode from the room, she stood in the middle of it, clenching and unclenching her hands, nausea in her stomach. She glared at the closed door. "Binding only if witnessed, Mr. Ardmore," she whispered.

"The famous Madame d'Lorenz," Grayson said, folding his arms. "Welcome."

The red-haired woman glared after Mr. Oliver, who had just led her to the dining room. "What do you want, Grayson? I am busy." The gown she wore was fine—pale muslin adorned with loops of ivory ribbon. A light summer shawl encircled her arms and she wore white kid gloves. Her face was heavily rouged, and her lips were painted bloodred.

"Busy deluding poor French émigrés?" Grayson suggested. He leaned his hip against the scarred table. "Making them believe you are helping them restore Louis Bourbon to the throne? Cruel."

She went very still. "I have no idea—"

"Don't bother telling me you don't know what I am talking about. How did you convince the French king to go along with your plan? From what St. Clair told me about him, he is most careful with his person."

Her lips whitened under their paint. "You know nothing."

"I know you, Jacqueline." He favored her with a half smile. "I wondered right away if you were involved, and then I discovered that you are indeed in England—on Ardmore's ship, no less. Then I discover that you frequent the shop where poor King Louis was last seen. Anyone who knows you would put the two together."

She was silent a long moment. She glanced at the door, as if ready to flee. Grayson knew that Oliver waited right outside, as he'd been instructed, ready to seize her. Jacqueline must guess that as well.

"What do you want?" Good. No long and tedious denials. "Is it money?"

She had not changed, he thought with weary amusement. "I have my own fortune. I inherited a title. Or hadn't you heard?"

"I know all about your damned English aristocratic title. I never thought *you* would join their scum."

"Always the republican. How many assassinations did you witness during the Terror?"

"Not enough," she said, her lips tight. "They still think they will recover France with their pathetic Louis Bourbon at its head. You still have not told me what you want. My body?"

Grayson choked down a laugh. "No. I want the king."

She looked annoyed. "Well, you cannot have him."

He smiled. "It was cleverly done, even for you. I've thought it all out. Louis went into the shop, but he never came out. The person who emerged and climbed back into the carriage was a decoy. Later, the loyalist French shopkeeper rowed Louis to a ship. But here is the curious thing. If a decoy climbed back into the carriage, Louis's entourage would have known right away, or at least very soon, that this man was not really the king. That meant that either they were in on the plot, or that Louis himself had never really been abducted at all. It was some time before I realized that both conclusions were true. The entourage was in on the plot to get Louis back to France, and Louis does not realize he has been abducted." He paused, then finished curiously, "What does he believe?"

Jacqueline snorted. "The fool believes he is returning to France covered in glory. That while Emperor Napoleon's armies are busy trying to conquer Europe, Louis will usurp him from behind." She shook her head, trilling a sharp laugh. "He was so easy to convince."

"Kings are not always known for their intelligence. England's are no better than any other country's."

She brightened. "You agree with me, then. A man of intelligence must rule. A great man like the emperor. Not a silly excuse of a man, not a king who is foolish and weak."

Grayson shook his head. "You misunderstand me. I prefer my monarchs weak so that I can get on with my business unimpeded. In truth, Jackie, I don't give a damn about your plot, or about your monarch, or about France. I want Louis, and you are going to take me to him."

Her eyes narrowed. "Then you do not know where he is."

"I have several good ideas. But I am in a hurry. Much easier on me if you simply take me to him."

She gave him a scornful look. "Why do suppose I will do such a thing?"

"You know what I am capable of." His voice went quiet. "I am sure you remember."

Fear flickered in her eyes. She rubbed her right wrist, where, under the long sleeves of her fine muslin gown, she must still carry the scars of their last encounter. "I cannot," she said woodenly. "I must take him to the emperor."

"So he will reward you? Or so he will take you as his lover again. Both, perhaps?"

Her red-dyed curls jiggled as she shook her head. "I would never dream to ask for the privilege of becoming his mistress. If he wishes to bestow it on me, so be it. But I do it for him, and for France."

"Well, you will have to do something else for France. I need the king." He smiled again. "Which would you prefer, Jackie? To lead me to the king, or to lead the Admiralty to him? I want only the king. They would want your neck."

She went dead white. He watched her realize that he was not going to let her go. Oliver was just outside the door. Unless she had brought a dozen armed French spies to watch her back, as she had that long ago day in Barbados, she would not get away. But he had seen no shadowy figures skulking about in the street near the house. No doubt she had come alone, believing herself able to charm Grayson into her way of thinking.

She gave him a contrite look, as if ready surrender to him. Then suddenly, she ripped a long and needlelike dagger from her glove and lunged at him.

Grayson had expected something like this. He expertly caught her arm and twisted it. The dagger clinked to the bare floor. She snaked her arm about his neck. He flinched, expecting another weapon, but she simply pulled him to her. "Please, Grayson, for old times."

"The old times when you tried to use me for your French schemes?" he said without humor. "No."

"I truly loved you. I did." Tears stood in her dark eyes. She dragged his head down and squashed a kiss to his parted lips.

He tasted bitterness like old coffee on her tongue and the anguish inside her. He did have pity for her—her dream of becoming Napoleon's courtesan and the vanquisher of his enemies drove her every deed. Once he had thought her attracted to him, but that had dissipated when he had refused to help her in her plots for France.

And he'd refuse to help her now. The Admiralty wanted the king, and he wanted the Admiralty's good graces so that Maggie could grow up without the taint of his crimes on her. Maggie's life was more important than Jacqueline's sad attempts at greatness.

The dining room door burst open. Grayson tried to shove Jacqueline from him, but her lips clung firmly and her fingers clamped his neck, nails driving into his flesh.

Alexandra stood on the threshold, breathing hard as if she'd been running. Lovely red-brown hair straggled from under her lacy cap, and her eyes were wild. "Grayson," she said breathlessly. "I must speak to you. It is very important!"

Then she whirled and was gone.

Chapter Twenty-four

Grayson pried Jacqueline's hands from his neck and forced her lips from his. She stumbled back, then reached for him, tears streaking her face. "Grayson, I need you. I need you by my side. Please!"

"Sorry, Jackie. I am busy."

"Grayson!"

Grayson set her aside and made for the door. Madame d'Lorenz wailed, but he ignored her.

Alexandra was nowhere in sight when he emerged, but Oliver and Jacobs were waiting in the dark hall. "Front sitting room, sir," Jacobs said.

"Good. Oliver, take Madame d'Lorenz downstairs and get her some water. Or, better still, port. Keep her there. Jacobs, I want you watching her as well. And for God's sake, don't let her near the knives."

He pushed past the pair of them and made for the sitting room.

His senses tingled. Three days had passed since he'd

seen Alexandra. His need for her, his cravings for her, had only grown. At last she'd come to him, at last she'd sought him—only to find him locked in another woman's arms. Damn, damn, damn.

"Sir."

Jacobs's sharp word halted him in his tracks. He swung around.

Jacobs gave him a look. "Your mouth, sir."

Grayson touched it. His hand came away red. Not blood, but the painted color of Jacqueline's lips. He made an impatient noise and wrenched a handkerchief from his pocket. Angrily wiping his mouth clean, he strode to the sitting room.

Vanessa stepped from the staircase as the door banged closed. Robert caught sight of her and motioned Oliver to carry on without him for a moment. As he neared her, she marveled anew that she had spent a glorious hour this morning in his arms, while Maggie visited Mr. Oliver and Alexandra's cook in the kitchens. Robert had loved her without fevered heat, but with a slow, delicious savoring. He had thoroughly stolen her heart.

She gestured to the closed sitting room door. "Have they gone to talk it out?"

He clasped her hand lightly. "Talk it out?"

"They are so obviously in love with each other, do you not think? Alexandra says not a word, but I see how she looks at him."

Robert grinned. "Never seen the captain so besotted myself."

"Should we help them?"

He pursed his lips. His fingers traced a slow pattern on her palm. "Captain Finley is a good captain. But he's stubborn. Lord, he is stubborn. He needs to think things are all his own idea." He paused. "But we can always nudge him along if he doesn't move swiftly enough." He looked at her, his eyes filling with sudden warmth. "He can follow our example, for instance."

Her face heated. Goodness, how she blushed like a schoolgirl whenever he was near. "Our example?"

"When we marry. That is, if you will have me."

His look was quiet. So unlike it had been that day five years before when young Robert Jacobs had confessed his love and begged her to leave her husband to run away with him. That declaration had hardly shaken her more than this one. Then she had seen the folly in such an action, had tried to explain to him that they should break off their affair rather than following it to ruin. He had raged and cursed at her, and her heart had broken into a thousand pieces.

But now— He waited silently for her answer, a calmer man than the youth she'd met at Oxford, one who loved her from the depths of his soul rather than with desperate passion.

"Robert," she whispered.

He raised his brows. "Is that a yes or a no?"

She pressed her hand to her heart. "It most decidedly and certainly is a yes, dear Robert."

He took her into his arms, and she kissed him, and at long last, knew happiness.

Alexandra waited for him near the front window, the late afternoon sunlight haloing her hair. Her dark-red curls fell to her neck, straggling over her pale yellow bodice. Her eyes were red-rimmed in her paper-white face.

He closed the door and said, "Stand away from the window. It is not safe."

She took two agitated steps to the center of the room,

and halted. "Grayson," she said, her voice strained. "I love you."

He stopped, arrested. His heart began to pound, slow and hard.

"I love you." The words burst out as if they hurt her. "I am certain you do not wish to hear this, but I must tell you, even if I am like every other love-struck woman who falls at your feet."

He moved to her, his footfalls soft on the just-cleaned carpet. She stood her ground, hands clenched. The top button of her bodice was open, as if she'd forgotten to fasten it in her agitation.

She had been crying. He touched the dried tears on her cheek. "Sweetheart."

"I love you," she whispered, desperation in her voice.

"Shh." He stroked his thumb across her lips.

"I want to tell you."

His need to be near her drove everything else away. To hell with Jacqueline, the French king, and the Admiralty. He wanted—he needed—Alexandra.

He bent and kissed her. Her soft mouth trembled beneath his. He gathered her into his arms, drawing her shaking body close. He tasted the sweetness of her, letting her spice and honey erase the bitterness of Jacqueline's assault.

She twisted away from him, her face fevered. "Grayson, I want—"

"Love." He traced her cheek. "You may have anything you want."

She stared at him a moment, eyes glittering, as if unsure what she really wanted. Then suddenly, she reached for the ties that closed his shirt and started to jerk them apart.

"Sweetheart," he said, pleased. "You want me?" *Say yes, oh God, say yes, my love.*

The laces caught. She made a growling noise and yanked at them hard. One tape tore completely off. Her fingers shook as she forced the shirt open, baring his chest to the warm, stuffy air of the room.

He bit back a laugh. "Alexandra—"

She dipped her head and pressed her tongue to his skin.

"Alexandra," he murmured, his tone deepening.

The shirt slid from his shoulders and dragged down his arms. She licked the round, ragged bullet scar beneath his left shoulder.

He freed himself from the shirt and laced his fingers through her hair. Her pretty white cap fluttered to the floor like a white bird. Madame d'Lorenz and her information could wait. The king of France could wait. The whole damned British Admiralty could wait. He pressed a kiss to her fragrant hair while she skimmed her lips to the hollow of his throat.

"Mmm." He lifted his head and let her play. "You were crying, love. What has happened?"

She looked up at him, her brown-green eyes full. "I love you." She raised on tiptoe and kissed his mouth.

He gathered her in. He let the kiss deepen. He scooped his tongue inside her, tasting the heat of her. Her fingers twined in his long hair, reminding him how she'd twisted and pulled it when he'd teased her with his tongue so many nights ago.

The little open button of her bodice beckoned his fingers. He flicked open the button just below it, then the next, and the next. He ran out of buttons quickly; they ended at the sash tied just beneath her breasts.

He eased his lips from hers as he parted her bodice. He found her chemise, a white, practical garment with only a few satin bows to decorate it, very unlike the gaudy, lacy thing he'd glimpsed beneath the gown of Miss Oh-So-French at the shop.

The chemise laced in the back. He parted the tapes, spreading his hand over her bare skin beneath. She wore no stays today. He wondered if she'd taken them off in preparation for coming here, and his arousal tingled.

He kissed her bared shoulder as he slid the chemise and bodice away. Her skin was tender and smooth, like white roses. What about this woman made him want to be rough and playful yet slow and gentle at the same time? She smelled faintly of lemon, tasted a little of orange marmalade. He smiled into her skin.

Her hands moved down his bare back, frantic, shaking, molding to his flesh. Her fingers were hot, her nails scratching him slightly. He worked the sash of her gown loose and pushed the bodice and chemise from her. Yes, at last, her warm skin against his, her body to his body. He pulled her to him, resting his cheek on her hair.

"Grayson," she whispered into his neck. "Please."

"As I said, whatever you like, love." He stroked her tumbled curls, savoring their scent. The stuffy air of the room clung to his skin, beading sweat. Oliver had just finished readying the room for use, and a long chaise, open-backed with scrolled ends, stood conveniently dust-free and waiting.

She lifted her face to his. "Do you love Maggie?" she asked. Her lips trembled, and he saw in her eyes that his answer was terribly important.

Fortunately, it was also easy. "Yes. With all my heart."

"Why?"

He blinked. Why did he? Because her laughter touched the loneliness deep inside him? Because he'd found a part of himself, a thing that was missing, in her? Or simply because she was his child? "I do not know," he had to answer. "I just do."

"Good," she said fervently. Her eyes shone like bright gems. "Good."

He'd given the right answer apparently. She threw her arms about his neck and kissed him again. Her lips were hot, her tongue moved, her teeth nipped and played. Her hands slid swiftly down his back, to his waistband, to the buttons in front. She popped one open.

He pushed her away, chuckling. "Slowly, sweetheart. Let me savor you."

His arousal did not like that answer. It was happy with her quick, firm hands and the kisses that fell upon his skin like raining sparks. She kissed him again, harder, her hair falling in warm waves over his arms.

He disentangled her from him and swept her into his arms. He carried her to the open-backed chaise and laid her down on it. Her yellow cotton bunched in frothy waves about her knees. He leaned to her and he kissed her throat, the curve of her shoulder, her breast. He slid his palm to her other breast, moving a soft circle over her skin. She reached for him again, her touch almost desperate.

Her breath smelled of tea, her mouth tasted slightly sweet, as if she'd drunk a beverage laced with honey. He licked the honey from her lips, from her tongue. She stirred fires in his soul, a passion that beat through him like waves over rock.

He covered her breast with his mouth. She arched to him, pressing into him, her nipples beading beneath his tongue and his fingers. He suckled her has he traced his hand down her abdomen, kneading the soft flesh there.

The folds of her skirt kept him out. He wadded the skirt in his fists, pushing it up over her thighs. He laid himself over her, fitting his arousal to her, seeking her hot places through the supple leather of his breeches.

"Please, Grayson." She almost sobbed it.

He slid his fingers between them. She was hot and wet and ready. He rose from her, his body unhappy as it left her warmth, and seated himself at the end of the chaise to remove his boots. Short work stripped himself of those and his breeches and underdrawers. Naked, he came to her and lifted her again from the chaise.

She started to protest, but he silenced her with a kiss. He laid down on the chaise himself and lifted her to straddle him. Her gown softly brushed his thighs as he pulled her down. The tips of her breasts were taut and dark, her hair tangling about them. His hands on her waist, he lowered her gently onto him in one smooth stroke.

She whimpered. Her head dropped back, her eyes closed. She took a long, ragged breath, her chest expanding beneath his hand. She began to ride him, her body instinctively rocking to drive him deep into her. He lay still, letting her pleasure herself, letting his arousal become hot and happy.

Her fingers sank into his chest, sharp points of pain, as she rocked forward. She opened her eyes and bathed him in a dark, dreamy smile, curls straggling across her flushed cheeks. "Love you," she whispered.

"Sweetheart," he said. "You are beauty itself."

She made a sound of delight, and Grayson's excitement soared. He could hold back no longer. He thrust up into her, hard, groaning his pleasure.

He would never let her go. Sara had been wrong. He must gather this woman to him, neither smothering her nor pushing her away. Holding on did not mean depriving her freedom. It meant growing together, sharing lives, sharing love. Sara had simply not wanted to share any of herself. This woman gave and gave and gave. He craved all she had to give, and he wanted to give everything of himself back to her.

She cried his name. Her voice echoed to the high ceiling, mingling with dust motes and heavy summer air. Her climax took her. She wriggled tight on him, gasping her pleasure. Grayson held her waist, his hands brown bands against her white skin.

She collapsed, breath ragged, onto his chest, her climax easing, her eyes heavy. He drove himself upward, sweat slick between their bodies. His control shattered.

"Alexandra. My lady." His seed shot from him, up into her tight, slippery heat. And then it was over.

He exhaled, his body easing from climax into warm, afterglow contentment. He gathered her to him and pressed kisses to her temple, her hair. "Alexandra," he whispered. "My lady. Mine. Only mine."

She nestled against him and gave a little sigh. Two hot little droplets touched his chest, but he was too swamped with warm feeling to ask if they were tears.

Alexandra drew her fingertips along Grayson's broad chest, tracing the path of the long scar that split his torso in two. Her limbs were heavy and tired, her body so warm, blood still tingling through her. She lay across his body, and beneath her ear, his heart thudded in long, slow beats.

May I stay here forever? she wanted to ask. He was still inside her. She would have to rise and go soon, straighten her clothing, continue with what she planned to do.

Odd that she had found Madame d'Lorenz here. The poor woman had been kissing Grayson so desperately. He had stood against her, stiff and unresponding, rather like

Alexandra had been under Captain Ardmore's assault. She shuddered, holding Grayson's warm body a little bit tighter. Women might swoon over Captain Ardmore's handsomeness, but Captain Ardmore had a deep coldness that Grayson lacked. Both men had born loss and grief, but Grayson had emerged with a piece of his heart still intact. Captain Ardmore had lost his altogether.

She kissed his chest, melding her lips to his curve of muscle. He lifted her tangled hair, letting cooling air touch her neck.

"Grayson," she whispered. "You must leave England. Take Maggie and go."

His breathing slowed, but the pulse in his throat beat harder. He scraped his hand along her jaw and lifted her head. His blue eyes were dark. "Why do you say so?"

The tears she'd fought to contain now spilled from her. They wet her face and dropped to his skin. "Mr. Henderson told me what you'd promised Captain Ardmore. Grayson, you must not let him. You must not finish the bargain."

He stroked the pad of his thumb across her cheek. "Sweetheart. I have no intention of letting him kill me."

"But you promised—"

"Of course I did. He had his sword at my throat and a rope around my neck. I would have promised him anything if he'd only keep me alive so I could protect her." He stroked her hair. "I have in my life been afraid, deeply afraid, but I had never been afraid *for* someone. But you should have seen her, Alexandra. She was so small, so thin in those damned awful clothes. That's why I bought her that ridiculous frock. I wanted to see her alive, not half dead like they tried to make her." He drew a breath. "I would have sold my soul to Ardmore to keep her safe.

I had not felt that protective of anyone since—" He stopped. "Well, since my mother died."

She spied the pain deep in his eyes, one that echoed in her own hollow heart. "I know that your mother was killed. I am sorry."

He lifted her from him, his softening erection sliding from her. He cradled her in his arms again, gliding his hand beneath her hair. "She was younger than I am now. She was so fragile. I hope my father is rotting in hell."

She flinched from the anger in his voice. "Perhaps he felt remorse," she offered. "He shot himself, did he not?"

"No." His jaw hardened, the light in his eyes going bleak. "I killed him."

Alexandra's breath stilled. "You could not have."

"I could and I did." His eyes were even colder than Ardmore's had been. "I had to. He was going to shoot me."

Alexandra shivered. She thought of her own father, a genial, kindly gentleman who had loved reading and his gardens. She could not imagine him lifting a pistol and shooting anyone, let alone his own wife and child. "I am sorry."

He regarded her without heat. "The inquest ruled he committed suicide. But I think the servants suspected. They told me to go. In case anyone guessed the truth."

"And you became a pirate?"

He moved his shoulders in a shrug. "Not right away. I began as a simple sailor on a merchantman. Nimble and light enough to climb the lines. I learned a great deal about sailing long before the pirates caught up to us."

"And you joined them?"

He shook his head. "They captured me. And the rest of the crew. I was young enough and strong enough to work, so they kept me alive. Most of the others they murdered or drowned. I watched friends be put to the sword, while I tried to pretend I was too callous to care. I had killed my own father, hadn't I? But I would have died of despair if it had not been for Oliver."

"Oliver, your manservant?"

"He was not my manservant then. He was the pirate's cook and surgeon. He took me for cook's mate, thus saving me from the drunken, sodomite captain." His lips twisted into a wry smile. "He nearly killed me with work, but he taught me how to survive. When the frigate rescued me a few years later, I begged them to keep Oliver alive. Then, when the time was right, Oliver helped me get rid of the idiot captain and take over a fine frigate loaded with guns." He grinned.

"You did not murder the captain, did you?" she asked fearfully.

"Set him adrift. All trussed up." He stroked her hair softly. "He was a fool, but I am not a murderer. I did not believe in torturing or killing. Waste of time." His lips twitched. "I built myself quite a reputation. I heard that crews longed for me to board their ships so they could have harrowing tales to tell their grandchildren. Well, I obliged often enough."

She traced the ridge of his collarbone. "Did you ravish the lady passengers?"

The chill in his eyes dissolved, and he shook with baritone laughter. "Oh, love. No, sweetheart. Only you."

Her heart pulled. "Don't."

"Laugh? Why not? You make me laugh for the delight of you."

She touched the swell of his lower lip. "Please do not make me love you."

His smile turned wicked. "I want you to love me. I want you to touch me. I want you to sleep bare for me.

I want you to beg me to take you against a wall, my lady passenger." He nipped her fingers.

She withdrew her hand. "Grayson." She cast around for an easy way to open the subject. None came to her. Outside, a carriage rumbled past, very near to the house, and somewhere upstairs, a clock chimed, sonorous and slow.

There was no way to tell him. Not easily. She looked into his eyes, savoring the deep blue warmth there, the warmth that she would erase with her next words. She drew a deep breath. "Grayson," she said. "Captain Ardmore asked me to marry him."

Chapter Twenty-five

Beneath her, his body stilled. As she had feared, the warm contentment left his eyes and they became fixed, hard and glittering.

"He what?" His voice was low, savage, more frightening than if he had shouted. "When?"

"This afternoon. In my house."

He sat up abruptly, lifting her from him and shoving her onto the empty space at the end of the chaise. He rose to his feet and stood over her, naked, every muscle in his body tense. "He came to you."

She nodded wordlessly. She clutched her crumpled bodice to her bare breasts.

"You let him in?" he asked, his voice deadly quiet.

She shook her head. "He just appeared. He tricked my maid into admitting him. I ought to scold her, but I don't have the heart."

He swung away from her and marched to the door. Still

naked, he yanked it open and bellowed into the hall. "Jacobs!"

In a few short moments, she heard booted feet on the stairs, and then Mr. Jacobs appeared in the doorway. He betrayed no surprise to see his captain standing there nude, or Alexandra sitting on the chaise, clutching her bodice to her breasts.

Grayson did not even try to hide himself. He jabbed his finger at Jacobs, his bronzed arm a contrast to the pale flesh of his backside. "Ardmore entered Mrs. Alastair's house today. Tell me how the hell he got past my guards."

Jacobs blinked. His dark eyes swam with fear. "I don't know, sir. I—"

"Pull the guards and have them flogged."

"No!" Alexandra flung out her hand, then grabbed her bodice as it slipped. "It was not their fault. He must have tricked them, too. I am certain they were no match for him."

"True, sir," Jacobs said hastily. "If anyone should be flogged, it's me. I should have noticed. I was—not paying sufficient attention."

"I set you to take care of Maggie," Grayson snapped. "You cannot be eleven places at once, though I believe I know what place you *were* in." Jacobs flushed. "Never mind, Jacobs. Just take care of it."

"Yes, sir." Jacobs saluted, pivoted, and was gone.

Grayson closed the door. When he turned back to Alexandra, his eyes had chilled, and his face was rock-hard. She had never before seen him completely enraged, excepting when he'd come to take her from Ardmore's ship. She'd witnessed him frustrated, fond and loving to Maggie, teasing, seductive, charming. Now she faced a man filled with cold, ruthless anger.

He came back to her, stood over her. Part of her delighted in his nakedness, in the perfect blend of muscle and sinew that made up his body. The other part cringed before his fury.

"Alexandra," he said evenly. "What did you tell Mr. Ardmore?"

She lifted her chin. She would be brave. "I answered that I would marry him. If he promised to let you live."

For a moment he only looked at her, his face hard and quiet and bleak—the face of a pirate captain who had kept a crew together and uncaught for seventeen years. She saw in a flash that Ardmore had underestimated him by a long way. So had the Duke of St. Clair. Here was a man who played by no one's rules, a man who would be a deadly and merciless enemy. She wondered if she had just made him hers.

"You will not," he said, still cold. "You are mine."

On the other hand, she mused, his high-handed arrogance could be quite grating. She drew herself up. "Are you the only person who is allowed to sacrifice himself, Mr. Pirate? He wants to kill you. I want you to live."

He glared at her. "By going to him? You think that will save me?"

"He promised."

"Only because he knows that you are more important to me than my own life."

Her heart pounded. "That is not true. You tease me, yes, and you make me fall in love with you, but I am only the woman who lives next door. A passing fancy. I will go out of your life, and you will forget me and watch Maggie grow up and be happy."

He stared at her as if she'd run mad. "A passing fancy? You?"

A tear rolled down her cheek. "I know perfectly well

you have loved other ladies. There was Maggie's mother, for one, and Madame d'Lorenz, and others. You are accustomed to moving on. I will be like—" she cast around for a thought—"like a bird on your hand. You enjoy looking at it, then let it fly away."

His eyes flared blue rage. He closed the distance between them in a flash, leaning to her and seizing her arms. No loving embrace. His hands crushed her. "Do not ever say that. It is not the same thing. Do you understand me?"

She stared. "Not really."

"Understand this, Alexandra. If you go to him, I will kill him. I don't care if you are wrapped in his arms; I will murder him and think it a good day's work. I am not afraid of Captain bloody Ardmore."

She whispered, "Grayson."

"You want to love a pirate?" He tapped his chest. "*This* is what a pirate is. I do what I please and I obey my own laws. I will not allow anyone to touch those under my protection, and I will cut down any enemy who tries."

She forced herself to look into his eyes. "I was right about you. You decide how things should be, and then you toss over anyone in your way to see them done. No matter what."

"I know. I have just said that."

She reached to brush his shoulder. His bronzed muscle jumped under her touch. "Including me. You must not finish the bargain, Grayson. Maggie needs you."

"I thought you understood. I have no intention of letting him take my life. He broke the damned bargain as soon as he dragged you into it. He could not resist the chance to twist the knife. He is vengeance-mad. Just like his brother."

"Poor Mr. Ardmore."

He gave her an irritated look. "Do not waste pity on

him. He is a vicious mother's son. He is feared for a reason."

She sniffled. "Mr. Henderson said that about you, too."

A feral grin lit his face. "Did he? I am glad he thinks so. Keeps him in his place."

"He proposed to me, too."

Grayson stopped. His gold lashes hid his eyes once, twice; then the blue gleam of them returned to view. "Henderson. Proposed to you."

"Yes. His offer was much better than Captain Ardmore's. He comes from Kent, as do I. He offered me a home in the country with dogs and children." She broke off wistfully. "It is so beautiful there, Grayson. All green hills and gentle skies. I was happy there, and I did not even realize it."

He took her hands in his. "Is that what you want? A home in Kent?"

She shook her head. "I do not know anymore. You cannot be a child again, can you? With people to love and protect you—so well that you do not even notice it." She looked away. "I am not certain what I want."

"Did you accept Henderson, too?"

"No."

He relaxed slightly. "Good."

"I told him I would think about it."

His grip crushed her again. "Alexandra, good God. How many other men proposed to you today? What about Jacobs and Priestly? Don't tell me Ian O'Malley wants you, too."

She gave him a look of reproof. "I have barely spoken to Mr. O'Malley, though he did once pay me a compliment. Mr. Jacobs seems to be in love with my Mrs. Fairchild, and I am certain Mr. Priestly dislikes me intensely." She paused thoughtfully. "Perhaps I should send him a small gift by way of apology for abusing him so."

The scar at the side of Grayson's lip pulled his mouth down. "You will not send Priestly gifts. And you will tell Henderson your answer is no."

That high-handedness again. She said, "I know he is not on the list, but he does have all of the necessary qualities. The right breeding, a good taste in dress, his own fortune. Additionally, he is rather handsome—"

"He wears spectacles."

"Yes. They give him an air of seriousness, don't you think?"

"No, I think he looks like a fish."

"That is uncharitable, Grayson. He has been quite kind to me—apart from kissing me and abducting me, of course, but that was only on Mr. Ardmore's orders."

He brought his face close to hers. The heat of his anger and his passion touched her. "Alexandra, you are not marrying Henderson. He is loyal to Ardmore and will not desert him, no matter what he tells you. All Ardmore's men worship him, God knows why."

"He *is* rather compelling. Mr. Ardmore, I mean."

His grip tightened. "Tell me you will not marry either Ardmore or Henderson."

She gave him a challenging look. "I will not marry Mr. Ardmore if you promise you will not let him murder you. If you will take Maggie and flee him."

"I told you that I have no intention of letting him kill me. Or of leaving England." He paused. "I notice you did not mention Henderson."

"I will consider Mr. Henderson's offer. Unless I am given a better one."

He growled low in his throat, rather like an annoyed bear. "Alexandra, I have many things to do. I have a French agent in my kitchen and Burchard running about

London like a loose cannon. Not to mention Jacobs and your governess making sheep's eyes at each other in my upstairs rooms. I have plans in motion that need attending." He leaned to her again. "But after that, you and I are going to have a talk. A long talk."

"That would be a nice, for a change."

His eyes narrowed. "A change from what?"

"Whenever we converse, we usually end up kissing. We never finish our conversations, I have noticed."

His smile returned, hot and sinful. "I had noticed that, yes."

"Did Madame d'Lorenz tell you where the French king was?"

He stared at her a moment, then let out a barely breathed curse. "And how do you know about Madame d'Lorenz and the French king?"

"I drew the conclusion. Mr. Ardmore told me she worked for Napoleon, and he lied about her when I first met her. Or did not tell the whole truth anyway. Mr. Henderson said something about her trying to use Captain Ardmore for her schemes. I imagine that the king is on Captain Ardmore's ship, awaiting transport to France." She shook her head. "Why you men believe this is all so secret, I do not know."

He scowled. "A *very* long talk."

"If you wish, but I am quite busy myself. I will have to shut up my house for the rest of the summer, whether I marry or simply return to Kent with the Featherstones."

A muscle moved in his jaw. "I will have everything resolved by tomorrow. And then we will converse." He paused. "But first, I want to kiss you."

She looked up, her pulse speeding. "Should you not go and speak to Madame d'Lorenz about the French king?"

"Yes, I should." He leaned down, nuzzling the curve of

her neck. He touched his lips to her throat. She closed her eyes. "On the other hand," he whispered into her skin, "she can wait a little while longer."

Excitement laced through her. She bunched his sleek hair in her hands and sought his lips with hers. His arms came around her, and he lowered her to the chaise, his warm, hard body molding to hers once more.

Alexandra returned home via the garden and the gates that connected to the mews. She fervently hoped that no stray stableman or night soil remover would choose that moment to use the path, as she scurried through the gate and across the green patch of lawn to her back door. The twilight air hung heavy with the scent of roses, and the fountain trickled a soothing stream.

Her body felt loose and supple, as though she could stretch like a cat, then curl in a ball and drift to happy sleep. But unlike a cat, who could choose when it liked to repose on a hearth rug, Alexandra had things to see to. Mr. Ardmore had said he'd send Mr. Henderson that evening. If so, Alexandra could have a firm talk with Henderson and persuade him to help her. It was all very well for Grayson to vow he would never let Mr. Ardmore kill him, but what Ardmore could do in retaliation worried her very much. She really needed to speak to Mr. Henderson.

First, however, she must bathe and change her dress. She had not yet spoken with Joan about her letting Mr. Ardmore into the house, and the thought of doing so wearied her. Mr. Ardmore did as he pleased, just as Grayson did. Poor Joan was as much Ardmore's victim as was Alexandra.

She lifted her crumpled skirt and glided upstairs to the sitting room. Grayson had helped her back into her chemise and bodice, but the gown was wrinkled beyond hope. Her hair, she saw in the hall glass, was a mess. Anyone glancing at her would guess what she had been doing.

As she passed the sitting room on the first floor landing, she thought again about her list of suitors reposing there in the drawer. Such silliness. Why hadn't she remembered that many a couple in the fashionable world chose their mates by a careful set of criteria, to their mutual unhappiness? Their lists were satisfied, but their hearts were not. No wonder so many men took mistresses and so many ladies took lovers.

She would destroy it. Determined, she opened the sitting room door.

Mr. Bartholomew and Lord Hildebrand rose from their respective chairs and faced her.

She stopped, stunned. As one, the two men looked her up and down, and she blushed to the roots of her hair. Why hadn't she first hastened to tidy herself? At the soiree, her suitors might have suspected that she and Grayson had become lovers; her dishabille now would remove all doubt.

"Madam," Jeffrey called up the stairs. "His lordship and Mr. Bartholomew came to call. I put them in the sitting room."

Alexandra winced, suddenly understanding why Grayson became so enraged with guards who let enemies slip past them.

Mr. Bartholomew was studying her, looked slightly shocked. Lord Hildebrand raised an ironic brow and made a delicate sniff. Alexandra felt as though she were boiling inside. She remembered the scent of lovemaking that had clung to Mr. Ardmore. No doubt the same scent clung to her now.

She could run. She could scream and dash up the stairs and lock herself in her room. Or she could square her shoulders and face them. Perhaps she could claim she was climbing trees with Maggie. They would believe that, would they not?

Would climbing trees explain the mark Grayson had left on her neck when they'd made love a second time? A love bite, he'd called it. She'd never heard of such a thing. But she'd seen it on her throat, stark and nearly purple, as she'd buttoned her bodice before the mirror in his drawing room. Did her loose hair cover it sufficiently? Did she dare pull the locks over her shoulder to make certain?

She made her choice. She squared her shoulders and entered the room.

"Gentlemen," she said, giving them her best duke's-granddaughter stare. "To what do I owe this unexpected visit?"

Mr. Bartholomew's face screwed up with effort. "Wa-wa-wa-we—Th-that is—"

"What he means to say," Lord Hildebrand broke in smoothly, "is that Mr. Bartholomew desired to call on you. I agreed to accompany him, to speak for him."

She inclined her head, then turned to Mr. Bartholomew. "What is this about?"

Her calm voice belied her trembling knees and the slick sweat on her palms. She hoped they didn't notice she was about to crumple to the floor.

Mr. Bartholomew opened his mouth, then shot a helpless look at Lord Hildebrand. Lord Hildebrand took the cue. "Mr. Bartholomew wishes to convey that he very much admires you, Mrs. Alastair."

She swallowed. "Thank you, Mr. Bartholomew. You are kind."

Mr. Bartholomew blushed.

"And that he has rented an elegant townhouse in Cavendish Square," Lord Hildebrand continued, "but he will understand if you wish to remain here."

Her pulse began to throb in slow, painful beats. "Remain—I do not understand."

Lord Hildebrand smiled. "Actually, I have begun paying half the rent on the house. Only fair, if I am to act as his speaker, that I should get a proper share."

Little chills made their way up her spine, dampening the sweet, relaxed looseness. "Lord Hildebrand," she said. "Tell me what you mean and please tell me plainly."

Mr. Bartholomew had gone very red. Lord Hildebrand's smile deepened. "Mrs. Alastair. We are in love. We both submit ourselves humbly, at your feet. If you will agree, we would be happy of your company in the Cavendish Square house." He glanced about. "Perhaps Bartholomew could meet you there, and I could meet you here." He added dryly, "And if it is jewels you like, we can certainly furnish you a supply."

A scream welled up from the depths of her, but only a dry croak emerged from her open mouth. She regarded them with horror. They were *propositioning* her. They were standing in her elegant sitting room, so carefully appointed with graceful furniture and costly paintings, and asking her to become their mistress. *Both* of them.

She was going to be sick. She covered her mouth with a shaking hand, tears of rage pricking her eyes.

A voice sounded behind her. "I believe, gentleman, that you should both depart." The Duke of St. Clair glided into the room and bathed both guests with a reproving glare. "If you remain, I will be forced to ask my seconds to call on you."

Chapter Twenty-six

Mr. Bartholomew's flush deepened to brick red. Lord Hildebrand merely looked annoyed. For the first time, Alexandra was grateful for Jeffrey's habit of admitting visitors he was too timid to turn away. The duke stood between her and the other two gentlemen like a guard dog protecting its mistress.

"I-I-I, wa-wa-we ma-meant—"

"I heard what Caldicott said," the duke said sharply. "I advise the pair of you to leave. Now."

Mr. Bartholomew, looking ashamed, made a jerky half bow, and nearly fled from the room. His harried footsteps rang on the stairs. Lord Hildebrand remained. "Only dukes and viscounts for you, eh?" he said, raking an impudent gaze over Alexandra. "I suppose they can give you better jewels."

The duke's gaze hardened. "Please name your seconds, Caldicott."

Lord Hildebrand's look turned slightly alarmed, which

he hid with a sneer. "Dueling is for fools. Good evening, Mrs. Alastair."

He moved past the duke and into the hall. The duke, muttering something under his breath, closed the door.

Alexandra felt suddenly ready to burst. She wanted to scream and rant and say colorful phrases like Grayson did. At times, being a lady was reprehensibly inconvenient.

Her gaze fell on her writing table. With a smothered scream, she dashed to it, yanked open the drawer, and snatched up the list of suitors. She ripped the innocent paper into shreds and hurled the pieces to the floor. "Men!" she snarled. She dug her heel into the creamy white pieces, grinding them into the gold and ivory oriental carpet.

The duke watched her in surprise. She sank into the nearest chair, her legs shaking uncontrollably, and pressed her face into her hands.

She heard the duke cross to her, sensed him drop to one knee before her. He did not touch her. "Mrs. Alastair, are you all right?"

No! she wanted to shout. *Of course I am not all right! They insulted me horribly.* And the worst part of it was, they were right. They believed her a doxy, and she was. She had so gladly let Grayson tumble her, had so eagerly run to his arms. And she would do so again and again, so willingly becoming his whore.

She drew a long breath before she looked up. "Not really, your grace. But I thank you for arriving when you did. I did not know quite what to do."

His usually mild eyes were filled with anger. "They are boors. And fools. Good God, I thought Bartholomew had some manners."

Alexandra did not want to talk about Mr. Bartholomew. She had also supposed him kind and somewhat foolish, but even he had decided what he'd seen at her soiree. And then she had come dashing in today, all flushed and tousled from her lover's bed. What else were they to think?

Shakily, she wiped her eyes. "How did you know I wanted you to come, your grace? I hadn't sent for you yet."

His brows drew together. "You meant to send for me?"

"Yes. It is most convenient you have come on your own."

"Is it?"

"Yes." She struggled to sit up. "Now all we need do is wait for Mr. Henderson."

Grayson amused himself bullying Madame d'Lorenz for a time, then let her go. She would go straight to Ardmore, he knew that. But while she kept Ardmore busy with her frantic worries about what Grayson would do, Grayson could carry out his own plans.

"Jacobs," he said as he emerged into the hall again after sending Jacqueline on her way. "I need you for this one."

Jacobs raised his brows. "What about Maggie and Mrs. Fairchild?"

Grayson peered up the dim staircase to the where both Mrs. Fairchild and Maggie watched over the banister, listening to every word.

He decided to be plain. "Oliver will remain here and look after them, and also keep an eye on Mrs. Alastair's house. They will be safe here because anyone dangerous will be chasing me. I need you on the *Majesty*. She needs to be ready to sail on an instant. I already have Priestly readying her. For my first errand, I only need Ian O'Malley."

Jacobs was not listening. He was already skimming his way up the stairs to Mrs. Fairchild. He held out his hands to her, and she came to him. He kissed her lightly, without heat, and pressed his face to hers. All under Maggie's delighted scrutiny.

"I will try to be quick as I can, love."

"Be careful."

"Yes." He kissed her again.

A longing tugged at Grayson's heart. His first officer was saying everything to his lady that Grayson longed to say to Alexandra. He looked up at Maggie. "I will be home again, soon," he said. "And then we shall never be apart. Promise."

She grinned down at him. "I know, Papa. You are very smart. And very brave."

His heart swelled. His daughter was proud of him.

He realized, as Jacobs hurried downstairs to join him again, that he was grinning like a fool. He clapped Jacobs on his shoulder. "You and Mrs. Fairchild," he said. "Me and Mrs. Alastair. I would say things are working out well."

Jacobs returned the grin. At that moment, Ian O'Malley came waltzing in the front door without knocking. He gave them an impudent smile.

Grayson scowled at him. "You are late."

"I know." His smile turned smug. "I fell in love with a barmaid," he said. "Decided I'd linger. I think I'll marry her."

Jacobs gave a short laugh. "You, too?"

Ian gave him a puzzled look, and Grayson, growling now with impatience, shoved them both out of the house.

The duke looked puzzled. "Mr. Henderson?"

Alexandra nodded. Her shaking had subsided a bit, now that she could focus on her plans again. "Yes. I need to ask him a question. Then I will reveal to you what it is all about."

The duke looked nonplussed. "Very well." He hesitated, then he reached out and gently lifted one of her hands. "In the meantime, may I tell you what I came here to say?"

She blinked. "Of course. How rude of me. You must have arrived for a reason."

"I did." He lifted her hand and pressed it to his chest. The stiff ends of his cravat touched her fingers. "Mr. Bartholomew and Lord Hildebrand made you a dishonorable proposal," he said. "I mean to make you an honorable one." He looked straight into her eyes. "Mrs. Alastair, please tell me you will make me the happiest man in the world. Become my wife."

Dizziness swamped her and her head throbbed and ached. "Your grace—"

"I have admired you for a long time, Mrs. Alastair." He gave her a self-deprecating smile. "I must have given myself away a dozen times over."

Given himself away? What was he talking about? The duke had never slanted her a smile full of sin, had never begged her to sleep bare for him, had never given her gems gleaming with the fire of his eyes. Possibly she had not noticed the duke's attentions because the poor gentleman had been completely eclipsed by Grayson. Since the dratted pirate had moved in next door, she had not been able to focus on any man but him.

She drew a shaky breath. "You have taken me by surprise, your grace."

"Have I? I had thought my admiration so obvious." His fingers tightened. "We would do well together, I am certain."

She had once been certain of that herself. "Your grace, I sincerely wish you had spoken to me three weeks ago. If you had, my answer might be different."

He began to whiten. "Three weeks? Why three—" He broke off. "Ah." His voice went bleak. "When Lord Stoke moved in."

"I am truly sorry. But my answer must be no."

Lines tightened about his mouth. "I had fooled myself into thinking you rather fond of me."

"I am. You are one of the kindest gentlemen of my acquaintance. You were at the top of my list."

"But you have lost your heart to Stoke," he finished for her. A grim light entered his eyes. "I will be plain with you, Mrs. Alastair. I know you are Lord Stoke's lover. Has he asked for your hand in marriage?"

She had to shake her head. Her hair tickled her neck where Grayson had nibbled her flesh.

"Then you would do as well to accept me, to save your honor if nothing else. I will not ask you to love me."

Her heart constricted. "I cannot. Please do not ask me. It would not be fair to you." She straightened her spine, letting her shielding hair fall behind her shoulders. Let him see what he would see. "It is true he has not spoken to me of marriage, but I am not ashamed of loving him."

The duke looked unhappy, but he did not release her hand. Alexandra hurried on. "I have a confession to make, your grace. I had planned to send for you to arrive at the same time Mr. Henderson did. I know where the French king is."

It was the duke's turn to be surprised. He stared, alarm building in his mild brown eyes. "Good lord. Did Stoke tell you about that?"

"I overheard a conversation I was not meant to. But I have learned many things in the meantime. Grayson— the viscount—actually discovered the king's whereabouts. Do I understand correctly that in return for his help you will erase any deed he and his crew did against the crown far away in the Pacific?"

"I did make that promise," he answered glumly.

"Regardless of what you think of him concerning me, he does have a child to take care of. Please promise me you will not go back on your word."

He frowned, rubbing his lip, then sighed. "Of course I will not. If I were a cad, I would force you to marry me in return for releasing him." He shook his head. "But I could not live with myself if I did that. I do not want you to come to me under coercion."

He seemed to be the only one, she mused. Captain Ardmore was perfectly willing to coerce her into all kinds of things.

The duke bowed his head and at last withdrew his hand. When he looked up at her, his eyes were clear, businesslike once more. "Please, Mrs. Alastair. Tell me where the French king is."

"I will take you to him." She cocked her head, listening. "And if I am not mistaken, Mr. Henderson has arrived. We will need him to show us the way."

Grayson was waiting in the sitting room of Zechariah Burchard's lodgings when the slim gentleman opened the door and stepped inside.

He stopped short, his eyes widening in sudden panic. He swung around, ready to flee, but Ian stepped in front of the door, closed it, and locked it.

Burchard swung back around. "Finley." He filled the word with more venom than a viper imparted to its victims.

Grayson folded his arms, enjoying Burchard's discomfort. "I reasoned you must return sooner or later to these rooms. My informer watching this hotel told me this morning that he'd seen you. You would need your clothes. It would be difficult for you to go to a tailor without causing a stir, am I correct?"

Burchard's lips pulled back into a snarl, but his face whitened. "What the devil do you mean?"

"I recognized you," Grayson went on calmly. "When I

finally saw you at close range at Alexandra's soiree, I realized who you were. I was so amazed that I let you get past me. What has it been, fifteen years?"

Burchard's eyes narrowed to hard black agates. "Fifteen years and I still hate you, Grayson Finley. And Ardmore."

Grayson was not certain if he should feel revulsion or pity. "It should be Ardmore and I with a grudge against you. We've never lived it down. O'Malley makes certain he tells the story to every sailor who joins us."

"Aye," Ian chuckled.

Grayson gave the Irishman a nod. Smoothly, Ian came forward and seized Burchard by the arms. Burchard struggled, twisting his slim body, but Ian was wiry and fast. He pinned Burchard's arms behind him, dragging the fluttering hands out of reach of weapons.

Grayson approached. He kept a wary eye on Burchard's feet, in case the pirate employed a dirty trick like a knife blade in the toe of his boot. But Burchard did not kick, and Ian held him well off balance.

Grayson stopped in front of Burchard and looked into the smaller man's enraged face. Giving him a faint smile, he reached down and ripped open Burchard's trousers.

The man screamed. Grayson thrust his hand inside. He came out with a roll of soft linen clutched in his hand.

He held it up before Burchard's desperate and enraged eyes. "You seem to be missing something, Mr. Burchard."

Burchard snarled and spat.

"Recognize her, O'Malley?" Grayson said. He tossed the linen roll to the carpet.

"Aye, that I do. Laughed meself sick, I did."

"You ruined me," the woman who was Burchard hissed. "I swear I will kill you."

Chapter Twenty-seven

Grim satisfaction touched Grayson. He had not been completely certain until he'd held the proof in his hands. Here was the answer to how Burchard could simply vanish and reappear months later without anyone seeing him in between. Simple if all he had to do was transform himself back into a woman and walk away. Few people noticed a washerwoman or a maid or a servant girl getting about her master's business.

"Wasn't it enough that you made utter fools of us?" Grayson asked calmly. A humorless smile tugged his lips. "The arrogant team of Ardmore and Finley—trussed up, stripped naked, and robbed blind by a slip of a girl. Helpful that we were dead drunk at the time."

They'd found it amusing to discover that the young "man" teasing the barmaid in a Jamaican tavern had in fact been a woman. Burchard, or whatever her name had truly been, had accompanied them to the inn readily enough. Small wonder she had, when she'd known she would have no trouble stealing everything from the two cocksure fools. They'd been forced to send the landlord for O'Malley and Oliver because, of course, they'd had no coin to pay for the room, nor any clothes in which to leave it.

"Waking up stark naked and tied to James Ardmore is not a memory I treasure." Grayson pursed his lips. "No wonder it was always so difficult to capture Zechariah Burchard."

Ian chimed in. "So who was it Ardmore killed in that ship battle? Some poor hapless decoy dressed in your clothes?"

Her face pinched. "He was well rewarded."

"Pity he never lived to collect it," Grayson said dryly. He looked her up and down. She kept her hair close-cropped, and she was flat-chested, narrow-hipped, and plain-faced. She needed very little to disguise herself, just a well-tailored suit of man's clothes and a bit of rolled-up cloth to keep her breeches from being too suspiciously flat.

The fact that she was female did not keep her from being dangerous. This woman had caused the murder of countless seamen and other innocents who got in her way. Once, Burchard had come upon a slaver, taken what she wanted, then burned the slaves alive. The act had driven Ardmore to pursue her and to attempt the same fate on her. Except that Burchard had thwarted them all. Until now.

"I came here for a reason," Grayson said. "You want Ardmore dead. I am tired of him myself. I believe we have something to offer each other."

He tamped down his misgivings as he said the words. He was taking a grave risk making this move, but he wanted Burchard out of London. He saw his chance to seal Burchard's fate, finish the Admiralty business, and resolve his bargain with Ardmore all in one blow.

If he did not destroy his own life in the process.

He took a deep breath, said a heartfelt prayer, and began to talk.

Mr. Henderson glowered in the corner of the hired carriage, arms folded, brow furrowed. The duke, sitting next to him, pretended to peer out the window at the darkness beyond.

It had taken all of Alexandra's powers of persuasion to obtain Mr. Henderson's consent to take them to the *Argonaut*. He had arrived at Alexandra's house with the sole purpose of carrying her off to Kent to marry him. He was no longer willing to be party to Ardmore's schemes, he said.

When he'd understood that Alexandra wanted him not only to take her to the *Argonaut*, but to betray his captain's whereabouts to a duke highly involved with the Admiralty, he had raged. The black fury in his usually apologetic eyes reminded her once more that Mr. Henderson was a dangerous man, able to turn from affable dandy to ruthless pirate hunter in a moment.

The compromise they finally reached was that they would hire a carriage, and the duke would accompany them alone, without his servants, coachmen, or any other entourage. He would allow them to fetch the French king—about whose fate Henderson cared nothing—but he would not lead the duke to arrest Ardmore.

The duke expressed dislike for the proposal and threatened to arrest Henderson on the spot. Henderson turned upon him a look of mild scorn and told him the duke would have to lend his coat because Henderson's coat was new that morning and he did not want to ruin it in New-gate.

Alexandra had to step rapidly between them, but she managed to persuade the duke that his only chance of reaching the French king was to follow Mr. Henderson's plan. Mr. Henderson had arranged for the carriage and so forth with his usual cool aloofness, but when he'd handed Alexandra into the carriage, he'd turned a look of naked anger upon her. She was using him, and he knew it. He would not forgive her for it.

But she had to. The duke desperately wished the return of the French king. And once the duke knew the location of the *Argonaut*, James Ardmore would have to flee. Grayson would be safe, and Grayson would earn the Admiralty's gratitude. The duke had thoroughly swallowed the story that Grayson had told her where the French king was hidden and that she should lead the duke to him. What young Mayfair woman would act on her own?

Mr. Henderson, by his expression, had guessed the truth. Why he had at last agreed to help her, she did not understand, but she felt no compunction to demand an explanation.

They rolled through the night. The sky was lightening when they reached Gravesend, and the silent land was chill. Cold wind blew from the east, from the mouth of the river and the sea beyond. They rolled into Gravesend and mingled with the foot traffic of fishermen putting out for the day, servants shuffling past with heads down into the wind, dogs barking wildly at the carriage, wagons passing with loads from whatever ships were in the docks.

Alexandra scanned the wide river, but it was a confusion of masts standing black against the early sky like winter tree trunks. She was not certain she would recognize Ardmore's ship in any case—she had been half insensible when she'd boarded the *Argonaut* the last time.

Mr. Henderson directed the carriage to stop at the end of a dock, one empty and forlorn and in disrepair. Farther down the shore, mighty ships—merchantmen and East Indiamen—unloaded, but this dock was relatively deserted. A dinghy floated at the end, its one mast small and bare.

Mr. Henderson paid the carriage driver and told him to wait. In clipped tones, he ordered the duke and Alexandra to follow him, and he led them to the little boat. The duke helped Alexandra in, while Henderson raised the sail and cast them off from the dock.

The sun rose as they sailed east. Light touched the ships, burnishing them golden. Billowing sails on an outbound Indiaman haloed white and gold against the faint blue of the sky.

Tucked behind a cluster of smaller merchantmen was a narrow, sleek ship with two square masts and a triangular jib. It rode high in the water, but it was slightly smaller than the merchants, nearer the size of the naval frigates that sailed past in escort of the Indiaman. Seen alone, the ship might earn a second glance—it was obviously neither merchant nor warship, but Captain Ardmore had chosen to moor it among sloops and other smaller craft so that the ship's size blended with the others.

As they drew near, Alexandra saw that the vessel was called the *Carolina*. The duke frowned at it.

The smaller boat bumped the larger. Mr. Henderson lowered the sail. A face appeared at the rail above them, one of a sailor Alexandra had not seen before. He peered down at them, took in the three of them, then disappeared.

Alexandra held her breath. Here was the test. Captain

Ardmore had said he would not let her aboard if she arrived with anyone but Henderson. As soon as he knew the duke had accompanied them, he would know that Henderson—and Alexandra—had betrayed him.

After a long moment, a pair of brawny hands rested on the rail, and Ardmore himself looked down at them. Mr. Henderson flushed under his scrutiny, but he stood straight and said nothing.

Captain Ardmore's gaze burned Alexandra through the distance that separated them. He studied her for a long time, then turned to the sailor, gave a nod, and walked away.

Alexandra was hoisted aboard by a harness similar to the one that had lifted her onto Grayson's ship. Mr. Henderson and the duke climbed a rope ladder that the sailor unrolled to them. Henderson marched to the stern cabin, but the duke waited to escort Alexandra aft in the wake of the sailor.

Ardmore waited for them. He leaned against his desk, arms folded. He wore a midnight blue coat buttoned over his bare torso and faded black breeches and boots. The darkness of his dress made his light green eyes stand out like pieces of jade on a jeweler's cloth.

The cabin was as barren as she remembered it. The long bench curved beneath the windows, polished and gleaming. A few pillows would soften it, she thought critically. The stern wall was too big for drapes to affect it much, but a nice valence, perhaps.

The duke murmured to Alexandra, "Stay near me, Mrs. Alastair."

Ardmore ignored him. His gaze pinned her. "Alexandra. Why did you bring me a member of the Admiralty?"

The duke bristled. "How dare you, sir? Address her with respect."

Ardmore shot the duke an ironic glance, then raked his gaze over Alexandra's ragged hair and crumpled gown. "Mrs. Alastair." He drew out the name with an exaggerated drawl. "This afternoon Mr. Henderson told me and my schemes to go to hell. Now he stands before me again—leading you and a peer of the realm." His lips lifted in the faintest of smiles. "You are the damnedest woman."

The duke reddened. "Sir, you are a brigand and an outlaw. You will not speak to a lady in this manner."

"You may call me out at anytime," Ardmore answered without heat. "My seconds are Ian O'Malley and Henderson, when he's speaking to me."

The duke opened his mouth, but Alexandra threw etiquette to the wind and stepped quickly in front of him. "None of this matters. We came here, Captain Ardmore, to fetch the French king."

He looked at her, unsurprised. "I see."

The duke spoke shrilly, "Then you do not deny that you kidnapped him?"

"I did not kidnap him," Ardmore said mildly. "He may leave at anytime."

"So you say. Where is he?"

Alexandra made an impatient noise. "Madame d'Lorenz tricked the king into coming aboard. Am I correct?"

Ardmore nodded once. He looked, if anything, very uninterested in the entire discussion.

Alexandra tapped her lips in thought for a moment. She looked at the two doors that led off the main cabin, one on each side. During her brief stay several nights previously, Madame d'Lorenz had emerged from the right-hand cabin, and the sailor had brought her a dipper of water from the same.

She gave a decisive nod, turned to the left-hand door, and pulled it open.

A long-legged, obese man with close-cropped gray hair was folded into a sitting position on the narrow bunk. He lifted his head and blinked large eyes over the folded page of a newspaper. Across the narrow cabin, Madame d'Lorenz sat on a sea chest, chewing her nails. The duke peered over Alexandra's shoulder. "Your majesty!" he exclaimed.

The king rose. He was tall and rotund, and his bulk filled most of the tiny cabin. He gave the merest nod. "Your grace."

"Good lord." The duke switched to French. "You have been here all this time?"

The king answered in the same language. "Three weeks, your grace. Not long from now, I will return to France."

Alexandra blessed Mrs. Fairchild's French lessons, and formed phrases in her head. "I am afraid Madame d'Lorenz has tricked you, monsieur."

He shook his head. "No. All is ready. I will return to France, and the emperor will be ousted. I am assured."

Ardmore said nothing, though his expression left no doubt that he'd understood every word. The king tossed down his newspaper and emerged from the cabin, looking neither fearful nor uncomfortable. He motioned to Madame d'Lorenz, who followed him out, her black brows pinched together. Thoughts warred behind her eyes, and she shot Alexandra a venomous look.

"Madame has been a great comfort to me," he said.

Ardmore made a neutral gesture in her direction. "She is a French agent."

The king stared at him. "No indeed, monsieur. She is the emperor's enemy, as surely as I am."

"She was once his lover."

The king gave Madame d'Lorenz a swift look. His face changed as he began to believe. "God help me."

Alexandra reached to him. "It is all right, monsieur. His grace will see you are returned safely home."

He opened and closed his mouth. "But France. They are waiting. They will return me to the throne. I have been assured."

"She's always been an excellent liar," Ardmore said.

Madame d'Lorenz screamed. She lunged at the king, a knife in her hand. "Vive le France!" she shouted. "Vive le Republic!"

The king stared in horror, transfixed. Ardmore did not move. The duke pushed Alexandra aside, trying to throw himself in front of the king. Mr. Henderson, at last stirring from the black quietness he'd subsided into since they'd entered the cabin, grabbed Madame d'Lorenz and jerked her backward. One competent squeeze to her wrist and the dagger dropped to the floor. She raged and swore, but Henderson's grip was unbreakable.

Ardmore motioned to the duke. "Take her and the king and go."

"Yes." The duke brushed off his coat. "I am afraid I will have to place you under arrest, madame."

"You bastard!" Madame d'Lorenz spat at Ardmore. She reverted to French. "You traitorous, evil bastard. You told me Finley would not have him."

"And he does not." Ardmore slanted a glance at Alexandra. "The Duke of St. Clair has that honor. Henderson, take her out. Please."

Henderson, grim-faced, dragged her from the cabin. She still shrieked and swore, vowing vengeance and other gruesome fates for Mr. Ardmore.

The duke blew out his breath. "Your majesty." He

made a little bow. "A boat is waiting below, and I have a hired carriage that will take us back to London."

The king, looking shaken, nodded.

"As for you, Captain." The duke gave him a stern look. "I will also place you under arrest—for pirating and other crimes against the crown."

Again, Ardmore smiled that thin, faint smile. "I remember Finley telling me that you would grant him amnesty if he helped you locate your French king. I have delivered him to you. Should not that amnesty extend to me?"

The duke spluttered. "You abducted him yourself!"

"This was Madame d'Lorenz's plot, her actions. I merely provided a comfortable place where he could hide. If I had let her take him to one of her French patriots, they would have torn him apart before you even noticed he was missing. Here, he was safe."

The duke stared. "You have great audacity to ask me that, sir. You have boarded countless English ships, sunk frigates, had the captains *flogged*, for God's sake."

Ardmore's voice turned hard. "English ships that have dragged away Americans and other innocents to feed their war."

"They were English deserters!" the duke said heatedly.

"Even the ones who had never set foot in England? Even the lads from Pennsylvania and the Carolinas? Who barely know where England is?"

"Even so." The duke sounded less certain. "You sank our ships. You are an outlaw."

"So I've been told." Ardmore folded his arms again. "Take your king and get off my ship."

The duke's fists clenched. Alexandra cleared her throat. "I believe, your grace, that we should go. Before he changes his mind."

The duke blinked, then looked hastily about the cabin, as if just remembering that he'd come there alone, with no soldiers or even a strong footman to help him. He closed his mouth and made a nod. "We will go then. Come along, Mrs. Alastair."

"Mrs. Alastair stays."

The duke stopped. He swung around. "What?" Alexandra's heart began to pound. She had known when she came here what she would have to do. But it frightened her all the same.

"I will give you the king," Ardmore said clearly. "But Mrs. Alastair remains with me."

"What the devil do you mean?" The duke started forward, fists clenched. Ardmore straightened up. He pulled his arms apart to reveal a pistol in one hand.

"Make your choice, your grace. The king, or Mrs. Alastair."

The duke eyed the pistol warily. Anger glittered beneath his lashes. He looked slowly at Alexandra, then back at Ardmore. Finally, he let out his breath and turned an anguished gaze on Alexandra. "I am sorry," he said in a near whisper.

Alexandra gave him a reassuring pat. "It is all right. I will be well."

He caught her hand a moment. He gave her a long look, as if he wanted to say more. Then he bowed his head, turned away, and left the cabin.

Ardmore followed him, with Alexandra pattering anxiously behind. Outside the door Ardmore spoke to a passing sailor. "Hoist anchor as soon as they're gone. We're away."

"Aye, sir," the sailor answered, and jogged off, shouting to his fellows.

Ardmore turned to Alexandra. His green eyes burned

with sharp fire. "That is what you wanted, isn't it? To force me to leave. To keep your lover, Finley, safe."

Alexandra clasped her hands. "I am afraid so. I have used the duke and Mr. Henderson most shabbily."

"Nothing more than they deserved. I would almost like to congratulate you. I was not expecting such a move."

"Almost?" she repeated the word in trepidation.

His smile was cold. "Almost, Alexandra. You have not won yet. But you still might have a chance."

He turned his back on her and strode to the rail. When he reached the place where they'd boarded from the boat, he stopped and pointed the pistol straight down.

Alexandra dashed to him, her tangled skirts impeding her. She reached the rail the same time he did, and looked down. A damp mist rose from the river, curling around the mast of the little boat. The duke and king looked up. Madame d'Lorenz, her hands shackled, also looked up.

Mr. Ardmore, his face fixed, aimed and shot Madame d'Lorenz through the chest.

Chapter Twenty-eight

Alexandra screamed. The pistol shot echoed into the dawn, the acrid smoke mixing with the mist.

"Why did you— How could you—"

Ardmore seized her and dragged her back to the stern cabin. He did not close the door. Henderson entered behind him, looking shocked. "Sir?"

"Are we underway?" Ardmore asked, as if he just hadn't murdered a woman in cold blood.

Henderson nodded. "Forsythe is taking us out. But— was that necessary?" He was white around the lips.

Ardmore laid the spent pistol on the desk. He opened a drawer and removed a box, which, when opened, revealed a small cask of powder, white wadding, and round lead bullets, all tucked into neat compartments. He lifted a cloth fitted to a rod, then slid it into the barrel, cleaning the pistol. "What would your English Admiralty have done to her? Taken her to Newgate? Tortured her for the names of her fellow agents? They will kill her in any case.

And how are traitors and spies killed in this country?"

Alexandra's face drained of blood. Traitors were tied and their abdomens slashed. They were kept alive to watch themselves be disemboweled. Sometimes, she had heard, they lived for a long time.

"Even if she escaped them," he went on, as he tapped fresh powder into the pistol, "she has tipped her hand to the French émigrés. Would they let her live?"

Alexandra swallowed. "I suppose not."

"I will give the English back the French king," he said. "But I will not hand them an easy victory. They will have to fight the war themselves, without benefit of all Madame d'Lorenz's secrets."

Alexandra watched, mesmerized, as he dropped a lead ball into the barrel and followed it with a small wadding of cloth, tamped down with the rod. Then he cocked the trigger and carefully tapped more powder into the pan.

"If Napoleon invades England—" she began.

"He won't. Your navy is far too strong, despite my efforts. And I truly do not care if he does invade England." He looked up at her. "Because you will be with me."

She nodded. "Yes. I promised to marry you."

Henderson glared in fury. Ardmore closed the box and slid it back into the desk. "You did. But I no longer wish that. The game has changed."

She stared. "It has?"

He lifted his eyes to her. She saw dark amusement dance in them, the amusement of a man about to play his trump card. "It has." He lifted the pistol and pointed it at her. "Please remove your clothing, Mrs. Alastair. All of it."

Both she and Mr. Henderson stopped dead. "Sir, no!" Henderson choked.

The pistol did not waver. "Please begin, Mrs. Alastair."

Alexandra looked into the deadly dark hole pointed straight at her. "Or—or what? You will shoot me, too? I am not afraid to die." She lifted her chin, trying to pretend she was, indeed, not afraid.

"No," he said. He moved the pistol and leveled it at Henderson's chest. "I will shoot Mr. Henderson."

Henderson went sheet white. "You son of a bitch."

Alexandra met Mr. Henderson's eyes, wide behind his spectacles. No matter what Alexandra thought, Henderson at least believed that Ardmore would kill him.

She bent a glare on Mr. Ardmore. "Oh, very well," said the haughty duke's granddaughter once more. Under his pinning green gaze, she reached for the buttons on her bodice, and began to unhook them.

Grayson watched the *Argonaut*, whose sails were almost as familiar to him as those of the *Majesty*, making swiftly for the mouth of the Thames. He lowered the spyglass and stepped back to Ian O'Malley who held the wheel.

"Looks like your captain sailed without you, lieutenant."

O'Malley looked resigned rather than alarmed. He took the glass and moved to the side of the boat.

Grayson took his place at the wheel. The morning wind lifted his hair. He adjusted his stance automatically to the tilt of the deck, the ship pulling hard against the leaning sails. The power of the ship came to him through the tiller, the pull of the water, the rise and fall of the deck, the wind that could either aid or hinder.

He belonged here. He knew it with his heart. Here, not in gray and brown Mayfair with unmoving cobbled streets and stifling smoke-drenched passages. He belonged here, giving orders to the sailors who scrambled to furl sails, working with precision among the myriad lines that criss-crossed the ship from the masts, tying off every few feet along the gunwale. He belonged at the tiller, steering his precious ship through dangerous waters; he belonged in his chart room bent over a table, drawing lines where lines had never been drawn before.

He had brought Maggie to London for her own good. He should have known better. Alexandra knew. She sensed what he did, that Maggie would have an impossible time against the rigid codes of Mayfair. Maggie had adored sailing across the Atlantic. She also adored Alexandra.

To hell with it. Grayson held the wheel against the tug of the wind, aligning the ship in a straight path with the fleeing *Argonaut*. He would finish with Burchard, whose ship hung just aft, finish with Ardmore, and deliver the French king to the Admiralty. Then he'd take Alexandra and Maggie away. To anywhere in the wide world. He would marry Alexandra and he would have a family. After so many, many years of solitude, he would have a family. A heady thought.

At the rail, Ian suddenly fixed the glass on something moving astern. His jaw dropped. "Oh, me sainted mother."

Grayson glanced at him. "What?"

Ian snapped his mouth closed. "Ah—nothin' in particular."

Grayson shouted for Jacobs to come and take the wheel. When the young man had done so, he stepped to Ian's side and pried the glass out of his hand. He lifted it.

What he saw was a dinghy, slicing haphazardly about in the water. At its tiller sat a corpulent man who obviously knew damn-all about steering a boat. Wrestling with the sails was none other than the Duke of St. Clair.

In the bows, blood scarlet against her dove-colored bodice, lay Madame d'Lorenz. Her eyes were fixed, staring at nothing.

"Jesus Christ."

"I knew you wouldn't want to look," Ian breathed.

"Jacobs! Come about."

Jacobs, without questioning, obeyed. He bellowed orders to the sailors. Ponderously, the ship turned, slowing. They drew alongside the foundering dinghy. St. Clair looked up. His face was harassed and as white as the sails he struggled with.

"As I live and breathe," O'Malley said. "I believe that's Louis, king of France, a-manning that tiller."

Grayson stared at the large man, then at the duke. "What the hell happened?"

"Stoke," the duke panted. "Thank God. Mrs. Alastair led me to the king, as you asked. But I'm afraid she's in a spot of trouble. Ardmore still has her."

As I asked? The words flitted through Grayson's mind, and then dissipated before the hard anger that filled him like water pouring into a dry well. "Ardmore has her?"

"Yes. I could do nothing to stop him."

Ardmore had her. The words beat through his brain. He had her. She had led the duke to him. She had gone to him.

Sudden fear touched him. She had not gone to betray Grayson. She had gone to betray Ardmore. To save Grayson's worthless hide. Because she loved him.

A grim iciness settled over him.

Ian called down to the boat. "Did you shoot the lady?"

"I did not." The duke's voice was shaking. "Ardmore did it. He's a madman."

"Well, you don't need to be tellin' me that," Ian shouted back. He clucked his tongue. "Well, well, an English duke and a Frenchie king. In a conundrum." He gave them a cheerful wave. "Hope you sink."

"Jacobs," Grayson heard himself say. "Dispatch someone to help him sail that bloody boat to shore."

Ian looked mournful. "You take away an Irishman's sweet pleasure, that you do, Finley."

Grayson frowned. "Full ahead, Jacobs. I want to speak to my old friend, Ardmore."

Ian's eyes narrowed. "I thought the plan was to double up and take down Burchard."

Actually, the plan had been to distract Ardmore with Burchard and then rescue the French king, all the while giving Ardmore a good pounding. Grayson had seen no reason to share that information with Ian.

"The plan has changed. He has Alexandra. He wants me to come after him." He smiled a bleak smile. "So I will."

"I'll be obliged to stop you, you know," Ian said.

Grayson's smile stretched wider. "You can try," he said.

Alexandra shivered as Mr. Henderson locked the cold chains about her wrists. His mouth was hard, his face drawn. But he was not disobeying Ardmore's orders.

Ardmore had made her remove every stitch, even down to her silk stockings. She stood barefoot, and the boards of his cabin floor were cold under her feet. Her skin prickled with the cool breeze blowing through the skylight, but she held her head high and refused to give way to embarrassment.

She frowned at Mr. Henderson as he clicked the manacle in place. A long chain stretched between her wrists and lay cold against her abdomen. "I am ashamed of you, Mr. Henderson."

His eyes were still, though she sensed slight dismay

behind them. "We all make choices, Mrs. Alastair."

"That may be true," she replied. "I simply disapprove of yours."

Captain Ardmore still held the pistol. "Have her clothes been dispatched?"

Henderson gave him a weary glance. "Aye, sir. Robbins took them, the poor, unlucky fool."

"I will reward him well." He gave Mr. Henderson a nod. "Leave us."

Henderson stiffened. "Sir?"

"Leave, Henderson. I would be alone with the lady."

Henderson drew a breath. "You are using her to lure out Finley, sir. That is all."

"Thank you for the reminder, lieutenant."

Henderson swept a glance down Alexandra's bare body, his spectacles glinting. He tightened his mouth, shot a hard look at Ardmore, and finally departed. The click of the door closing sounded loud in the stillness.

Alexandra had been raised to be a genteel lady. Her well-trained governesses had reared her to rise to every occasion with aplomb. She thought it unlikely any of them, even Mrs. Fairchild, had ever dreamed Alexandra would be standing in the cabin of a pirate-hunter's ship, unclothed, and in chains. A lesser woman would have swooned or wept or hidden herself in trembling fear. Alexandra straightened her spine and swept Captain Ardmore a glare worthy of a princess dressed in silks and a tiara, who stared down at her supplicants from a royal balcony.

Captain Ardmore did not seem impressed. He looked her over carefully, from the tangled red curls on her head, down over her bared breasts, to her abdomen so pitifully exposed, to her thighs, calves, and stockingless feet. It was not a lustful glance, or a glance of frenzied evil, but the calm scrutiny of a man who wanted to fully examine a prize he had just won.

What he thought of his prize, he did not say. He simply looked at her, and in his eyes she saw grim satisfaction.

She drew a breath and broke the silence. "Your lust for vengeance has driven you a bit mad, I think, Captain Ardmore."

His eyes flickered. "I went mad a long time ago, Alexandra. You can't change that. Neither can Finley."

She ventured. "I am certain Grayson did not mean for your brother to die. I know that."

He was not as unemotional as he tried to appear. His large hands curled, his knuckles whitening. He had a naked woman standing before him, and yet, his eyes held only anger and pain. "How do you know, Alexandra? How do you know what Finley meant to do? You weren't there. *I* was not there. I was not there to stop it."

"I know," she said. "It was beyond your power."

His fist struck the desk in a sudden, explosive blow, shattering his calm. "I did not *want* it to be beyond my power. When my brother lost his wife and child, I hurt for him. He was lost in his grief until the end of his life. All his smiles, all his happiness, gone." He came to her. "And Finley, your precious Finley, took away my last chance to help him heal."

She stared at him. Tears beaded on his black lashes. Behind the tears lay the grief of a man who could not bear to feel grief.

"I swear to you," she whispered, "he never meant that."

"It does not matter what he meant. Paul died. And I could do nothing."

Her heart twisted. "I am sorry."

The pain in his eyes was raw. "He was still alive when I reached him. Do you know what it felt like to watch him die? To know I had failed him—again? I failed him, Alexandra. I have never in my life been able to make up for that."

"You cannot blame Grayson." She lifted her hand, the chains clinking, and touched his shoulder. "You cannot make him pay for that. It is not his fault."

He stared at her a moment as if he'd forgotten her presence. Then he seized her arms, his fingers biting her flesh. "Dear God, he does not deserve you. You are completely in my power, and yet you stand here and tell me I am mistaken and misguided. A man could fall in love with you."

"Please do not. I have had enough declarations for one day."

He laughed, a harsh sound. "Well, mine is the last. I believe I will enjoy life with you, Alexandra. I will make it worth your sacrifice." He touched her cheek. "After Finley catches up to us."

She flinched from his touch. "How do you know he will bother to follow? I should be more worried about the Duke of St. Clair, were I you."

He chuckled. "St. Clair knows where his duty lies, the poor bastard. In his world, the French king is important, the fate of a widow he admires is not. That was a hard choice he made, a choice between worlds. He will not pursue us."

She bit her lip. "Oh."

"Finley, on the other hand will come. When Robbins hands him your gown and stockings, he will roar like a bull and come charging after us."

Alexandra imagined the sailor called Robbins handing the pile of clothing to Grayson. Robbins would either be innocently unsuspecting or trembling with fear. Poor wretch. She wondered whether Grayson would shrug and say that he had finished with Mrs. Alastair, or whether he would slam Mr. Robbins to the ground. "The poor man," she breathed.

"I will make it up to him." Ardmore traced her lower lip. "I am much looking forward to our marriage, my dear."

Alexandra swallowed. She did not tell him that she had come here only to make certain Grayson was safe, and with no other purpose. She would do anything she had to do. Her ancestors had fought for the English crown when it had been threatened a hundred and fifty years ago. They had been just as bold and ruthless as Captain Ardmore ever was. And their blood beat in her veins.

Ardmore leaned to her and kissed her lips. She did not respond. He did not seem to care. He kissed her again and lifted his calloused palm to her breast.

The cabin door slammed open. Alexandra jumped. Ardmore straightened up slowly, taking his time. He turned to the panting boy who stood on the threshold. "What?"

The terrified lad's gaze did not waver from Ardmore. Alexandra might not have existed. "He's here, sir. Mr. Henderson sent me to tell you. Captain Finley's behind us. And he's brought another ship. It looks like Captain Burchard."

Chapter Twenty-nine

Ardmore did not move. The cabin boy stood, white-faced, waiting for orders. Alexandra also waited, her legs shaking, the chain between her hands clinking slightly.

At last Ardmore spoke. "Good." He drew the word out, his Charleston accent becoming pronounced. "Then I don't have to wait for him."

"Sir?" The boy's voice trembled.

"Get back to your post. We'll come about."

The boy scampered away. Ardmore swung on Alexandra and seized the chain. "Time to go."

Alexandra tried to resist, tried to fight him, but he simply dragged her along behind him out onto the deck.

"He's coming about!" Jacobs shouted.

Grayson watched as the *Argonaut* turned. Ardmore's ship moved swiftly, sails bent to the wind, the prow slicing water.

"Burchard is signaling, sir," Jacobs continued.

Beyond the polished ship's rail, the gray river rolled behind them, wide and misty between the flat, faraway banks. Burchard's ship, sails wide, tread in the *Majesty's* wake.

"Send this back," Grayson said. "When we reach the *Argonaut*, we split. I'll go starboard, Burchard turns port."

"Aye, sir."

Ian O'Malley continued to stare ahead through the spyglass, watching his own captain's ship cut toward them. "We're leavin' the plan far behind, Finley."

"As far as I have to."

Ian lowered the glass and glared suspiciously. "You going to cross-cut the *Argonaut*? Broadside her from both sides?"

"Not with Alexandra aboard. No one lights as much as a candle until I get her away from there."

He grinned. "Ooo, captain, I do believe you're smitten."

"I am more than smitten, Mr. O'Malley. I'm madly in love." He gave the Irishman a faint smile, then held out his hand. "I'll relieve you of your pistol now."

The Irishman started. "You'd leave me defenseless? Burchard is out there. The one who's peeved at me and me captain for sinking her ship."

Grayson's calloused palm remained steady. "Your pistol, Mr. O'Malley. Or you spend the next hour locked in my hold."

"You don't trust me?" He sounded hurt. "After all I've done for you."

"You are Ardmore's man, first and last." Grayson said dryly, "No, I don't trust you."

Ian regarded him for a long time. Then he sighed, dipped his hand beneath his coat, brought out his pistol, and plopped it into Grayson's hand.

* * *

"Prepare to fire on my mark," Ardmore said, his voice hard.

Cold wind lifted Alexandra's hair and burned across her skin. The chain between her wrists was wrapped around Ardmore's hand. He held her against him, his bulk at least cutting some of the sharp breeze from the sea.

The other officers on deck—Henderson, the pilot called Forsythe, and a Frenchman she had not seen before—averted their eyes at her nakedness. But the fear within her erased most of the humiliation she might have otherwise felt. Ardmore was truly mad, and he would certainly kill Grayson.

Ardmore watched the two ships approach, his face set. The *Majesty*, riding high in the water, cut right, swinging around to the left, or port side, of the *Argonaut*. The second ship, a little behind, began to veer to the *Argonaut*'s right.

The *Majesty* neared swiftly. The two bowsprits passed, not a shiplength away. The dark wooden hull of Grayson's ship slid by, then the stern came into view, and the quarterdeck. Grayson stood firmly on the deck, his blond hair loose, one booted foot braced on the deck's bench.

Ardmore positioned Alexandra in front of him, and pressed his pistol to her temple. The cold circle touched her skin. "Signal him. Tell him to come aboard. Unarmed."

Henderson turned and gave the abrupt command. The *Majesty*'s stern slid past, slowing as the *Argonaut*'s sails blocked the wind. The French lieutenant shouted through a speaking tube. After a few moments, an answering shout came from the *Majesty*. "He's on his way, sir," Henderson said.

Grayson's ship turned neatly and came alongside the *Argonaut*'s starboard side now. The second ship veered to give it room. The sailors grunted and strained, furling sails. Officers bellowed orders, calming the ships and drawing them quietly together. On the quarterdeck of the second ship stood the slim form of Mr. Burchard, hands on the wheel.

Alexandra gasped and looked quickly at Ardmore to see if he'd noticed the man, but Ardmore's gaze was fixed on the myriad lines of Grayson's ship, and the grappling hook that grabbed the rail of the *Argonaut*.

"Just you, Finley," Ardmore called across the sliver of water. "No one else."

Grayson did not answer. In economical movements, he stepped to the rail, caught a line, and swung easily onto the deck of the *Argonaut*.

Ardmore dragged Alexandra around. Grayson mounted the steps to the quarterdeck and stopped.

They faced one another across the rocking stretch of boards. Grayson's face was hard as granite. If the anger that filled Ardmore made his hands shake, made sweat drip in rivulets down his face, Grayson's anger was bottled, contained. The stiff breeze blew hard from the water, whistling through the lines, the only sound on the suddenly silent ship.

"Let her go, Ardmore." Grayson's voice was deadly quiet.

Ardmore's grip on the chains tightened. "Why? When she is so lovely?" He leaned down and casually bit her ear.

Grayson made a sudden move forward. Ardmore shoved the pistol into Alexandra's temple, and Grayson stopped, as if he'd hit a wall.

A second man swung onto the deck from the *Majesty*, the small Irishman, Ian O'Malley. He took in his captain, Grayson, and Alexandra. Unlike the other lieutenants, he did not avert his gaze, but raked it up and down Alexandra's naked body. His look was troubled.

"Let her go," Grayson repeated.

Ardmore jerked the chain. "Did you let my brother go?"

Grayson remained still. "I told you what happened."

"Many times." Ardmore pulled Alexandra back against him, holding her in a bizarre parody of an embrace. "You've told me so many times."

"You know I did not shoot him." Grayson yanked open his loose shirt to reveal his bronzed shoulder. The white bullet scar stood out on his tanned skin. "Because of this. I was down. I was dying."

Ardmore did not seem to be impressed. "Tell me, Finley, if one of my sailors harmed *her*—murdered her—who would you blame?"

Grayson did not answer. Ian O'Malley looked on, his lined face expressionless.

"Let her go," Grayson said again. His eyes fixed on Ardmore, clear and blue and crystal sharp. "Face me alone."

Alexandra felt Ardmore's heart beat, swift and hard. "I want you on your knees, Finley," he said with strange hunger. "You once begged for your life. Now beg for hers."

Ian O'Malley drew a breath. Mr. Henderson remained at the rail to Ardmore's right, his face frozen, fixed.

Grayson never looked away. Slowly, silently, as if stiff strings pulled him down, he lowered himself to one knee. His eyes glittered with suppressed fury. His posture might be submissive, but he never would be. "Please, let her go."

"Do you love her?"

Grayson's mouth tightened. He said nothing. Alexandra's heart beat rapidly. His eyes were so grim, so angry.

Ardmore dragged her a step forward. "I said, *do—you—love—her?*"

"Yes," Grayson roared. He leapt to his feet. "I love her. With all my heart and with every breath. Now leave her the hell alone."

Ardmore chuckled, a mad sound. "Do you even know how to love? Do you know how to care so much that if one thing happened to her, you would grieve for a lifetime?"

He shoved the pistol against her cheek. Alexandra yelped. Grayson remained rooted in place, his fists at his side. "You hurt her, you are dead before you take a step."

Ardmore did not seem to hear. "If you love her so much, Finley, ask her to marry you."

Again Grayson said nothing. A muscle in his jaw tightened.

"What?" Ardmore hissed. "I hear nothing. Did you plan to make her your whore? She is a lady. If you cannot make her honest, she will have to remain with me."

"Please," Alexandra said, shaking all over. "Stop."

"Alexandra," Grayson said. "Will you marry me?" His baritone grated on the harsh wind.

Tears stung her face. She shook her head the slightest bit. "No," she said.

Grayson stared at her, not certain he'd heard correctly.

His rage barely let him see straight. Around the red edges of his vision, he saw only Ardmore, tall and towering, his face dark with fury, and his blue-coated arm wrapped about Alexandra's middle. He saw the pistol shaking in Ardmore's hand, and his enemy's fingers white on the chain. Ardmore dwarfed Alexandra's slim body, which was covered with the sweep of her red-brown hair. The tips of her breasts were dark and tight with cold. Her long, slim legs were bare, shaking; the swirl of hair at the join of her thighs exposed for all to see.

Her white skin showed no bruising, no marks of Ardmore forcing himself upon her. Just the rust-red manacles circling her wrists and the heavy chain between them. But her eyes held terror.

He gave her an incredulous look. "No?"

"No," Alexandra repeated, her voice sweet and shrill above the wind.

What was the matter with her? "Alexandra—"

She lifted her chin. "I will not accept a proposal forced upon you by Mr. Ardmore. You would not be happy if I did. You would always wonder."

"Whether you meant it? Right now, I am not inclined to care."

"You see?" She glared at him with her lovely brown-green eyes.

Ardmore smiled above her head. What he had in mind, Grayson was not certain. Ever since the day he'd pulled Ardmore from the rat-infested cage on that pirate ship, the man had been unpredictable and untrustworthy. Whether he intended to kill Alexandra in front of him, or make him believe so until he turned that pistol on Grayson, Grayson did not know. He did not want to guess wrong.

"Alexandra, say yes now. Quibble later."

She shook her head. "There is no quibbling about being drawn into a loveless marriage. I cannot let you."

"It won't be loveless. I've just said that I love you."

"Only because Captain Ardmore forced you to. Because you are trying to save my life."

"Because it is the truth!" he shouted. He felt the eyes of the sailors and officers upon him. He fought to rein in his temper. "I love you, Alexandra. I loved you the moment you dashed into my bedchamber to rescue me. I love how you look away when I tell you you're beautiful. I love how you blush when I kiss you. I loved you when I found that blasted list you made. I even loved you when you went behind my back and finished my mission for me." He paused. "We will discuss *that* later."

Her eyes shone with tears. "Grayson," she whispered. "You truly love me?"

"Yes! Even though I am at the bottom of your damned list of suitors. With the query mark."

"I tore up the list."

He smiled grimly. "I am glad of it. Do you love me, Alexandra?"

She gave him a watery smile. "Yes. With all my heart."

Behind him, Ian O'Malley murmured, "Oh, ain't it a grand thing."

"Then marry me."

"No."

God's teeth. "Why the devil not?" he bellowed.

"Because Captain Ardmore will never let you live. Please go, Grayson."

"The hell I will."

He started forward. Ardmore snatched up Alexandra and swung her onto the rail. He held her there, balanced precariously between deck and sea. "Stay where you are, Finley."

Grayson's heart pounded until he felt sick. Alexandra's face had drained of color, her eyes dark and terrified. *No,* he cried inside. No. *Not this time.*

"Sir!"

Henderson's voice brought Grayson out of his dark well of fear. The lieutenant was standing a few feet from Ardmore. He had a pistol in his hand.

Ian took a step forward. "Henderson. Leave it."

Ardmore neither moved nor took his deadly gaze from Grayson. "As you were, lieutenant."

Henderson's voice shook. "I am not going to let you harm her, sir. I must draw the line."

"This is not your fight, Henderson."

"Yes, it is, sir. Let her go."

Grayson's breath hurt. "No, Henderson. You might hit her."

"I'm a dead shot," Henderson said. "The captain knows it."

Grayson assessed the distance between Henderson's outstretched arm and Ardmore's head. Henderson might be dead on, but pistols were unreliable. And there was wind. One miscalculation and it would be Alexandra who was dead.

"Henderson," he said again. "No."

Laughter, high and shrill split the air. Grayson jerked his attention from Ardmore. Burchard's ship had completed its circle, and was now drawing to the *Argonaut's* side. Burchard stood on the stern deck, her head flung back.

"Finley and Ardmore," she shouted, still laughing. "Together again. And at each other's throats. How delicious."

Ardmore glared across the water at the tossing ship. Burchard cupped her hands to her mouth. "Just how I like you. Bosom enemies. And now, you die." She turned and shouted down to her crew, her voice filled with harsh glee. "Fire!"

Cannon fire roared, deafening. Ian O'Malley whirled around. He swore hard. "She's cutting the rigging!"

Grayson knew he meant that she'd fired not lead shot but bar-shot, which were small iron bars, weighted on the ends, that twirled with ripping speed through the rigging. Destroying the lines meant crippling a ship so she could be boarded or sunk.

Grayson tore his gaze from Alexandra and Ardmore. His own ship was moving to circle Burchard's; Jacobs was attempting to pinch Burchard between them.

Henderson abandoned them and hurried with Ian to the main deck. Ian bellowed, "Fire!" to the waiting gunmen below. Flint was struck. Cannons roared, belching pale fire into the morning.

Jacobs continued to turn the *Majesty*. Shot crunched into the side of Burchard's ship, tearing down the railing and blasting a gaping hole in one side, above the water. Screaming and shouting sounded from the hurt ship.

Alexandra cried out. Grayson swung around. Alexandra was struggling with Ardmore. Ardmore had his arm firmly around her waist, and she teetered on the rail, fighting like mad. Grayson sprinted toward them. Ardmore snapped his pistol to him. "Do not come any closer, Finley. I'll drop you here and now."

He meant it. Grayson stilled, his heart pounding. Ardmore would shoot him, and Grayson would die, knowing that Ardmore had Alexandra. Or he could walk away and leave Alexandra to him, and live the rest of his life knowing that. Just the thought of living a moment without her made his heart bleed. Ardmore truly knew how to exact the cruelest revenge.

"James," Grayson said. "Please. Not this time."

Ardmore's eyes burned all the way across the deck. "Sorry, old friend." His finger closed on the trigger.

Alexandra screamed. She flung herself at Ardmore, lunging for the pistol, just as it fired. The gun roared, mingling with the noise of the cannon from the three ships. Alexandra and Ardmore balanced on the rail for a sickening moment, then toppled from view, out of sight, down to the waiting sea.

Grayson gave a cry wrenched from the depths of his soul. Primal and uncontrolled, it welled up from a hot core of pain and echoed over the gunfire and the shouting of pirates and Ardmore's men.

He closed the distance between himself and the rail, leapt upon it, and launched himself overboard.

Chapter Thirty

Grayson heard Alexandra screaming and screaming, and then the screams stopped with sudden and deadly abruptness. Grayson hit the water a moment later. The *Argonaut* rode fairly low, and the impact was not as harsh as it might have been. Men had broken limbs when falling from high ships—the least of their troubles if they survived drowning.

He could think only of the heavy chain hanging from Alexandra's wrists, a weight that would drag her down, down, into the greedy sea. He broke the surface and gasped for air. His boots had filled, and he wriggled free of them. In shirt and breeches, he tread water, searching the dawn-lit sea for the silhouettes of Alexandra and Ardmore.

Water fountained not five feet from him, and Ardmore emerged, gasping and coughing.

"Where is she?" Grayson shouted.

Ardmore shook his head.

"Find her!" Grayson screamed, but Ardmore was already diving. Grayson gulped air and plunged downward, kicking hard. He forced his eyes open, letting the salt and muddy water sting them. He could see little. The depths were murky, dark, and kept their secrets.

He grabbed at a shadow moving past, but came away with only a handful of brown seaweed. A rush of water ahead and to the left revealed only Ardmore's kicking feet. Grayson's breath ached, his lungs cried for air. He kicked to the surface, dragged in another breath, and dove again.

There. Was that—? He did not wait to find out if he was right. He swam hard, driving deep, and snatched at the shadow.

He found his hands full of Alexandra's long hair, which flowed as if she were standing in a gentle breeze. His heart nearly burst with relief. But she was sinking, her struggles slowing.

Willing himself to hold his breath a moment longer, he groped down until he found her face, her neck, her arm. He grabbed.

The chain was heavy. It pulled against him, adding to her weight. If he could only get to the surface, breathe life-giving air, he could hold her up, save her from the sea. He kicked. The drag between the tide and the current that pulled the Thames swirled against his legs, sucking him down.

The load suddenly lightened. Ardmore had grabbed Alexandra's other arm, adding his strength to lift her. Together the two men swam mightily upward, pulling Alexandra between them.

With a suddenness that dizzied him, he broke the surface. Water rushed away and air poured over him. He gasped, letting it flow into his lungs.

Alexandra coughed weakly. The chains still pulled her down, their weight the way to her death.

Ardmore broke the surface beside her. Together, they held her high, keeping the waves from swamping her while she coughed and hoarsely gulped air. Her eyes were closed, and she hung unresisting in their grasp.

They had to get her out of the water. But shore was so far away, and the three ships nearby circled each other like menacing animals. Burchard fired wildly every time the *Argonaut* or *Majesty* tried to turn to the three overboard.

Grayson moved her to rest against his broad shoulder, keeping her nose and mouth above the surface. The chain swung between her bare legs, pulling. He grasped one of the manacles. "Key," he grunted.

Ardmore shook his head. One lock of his dark hair was plastered to his cheek. "On board."

"You sorry bastard."

"She wasn't supposed to jump."

Grayson glared at him. If Alexandra had not needed him, he would cheerfully have taken the time to strangle the life out of Ardmore. He'd hold him down under the waves until Ardmore and his threats were out of his life.

But even beneath his turmoil, Grayson had a glimmer of understanding. Ardmore was a man slow to love. The few things he had truly loved—Sara, his brother—Grayson had had a hand in taking from him. Sara, because Grayson had not realized what Ardmore felt for her; his brother, through unfortunate happenstance. Grayson embodied all of the pain in Ardmore's life. Small wonder the man hated him.

But he was well on the way to receiving more pain. If Alexandra died, Ardmore's life was forfeit.

Grayson's arms and legs were already tiring in the cold

water. Ardmore's own breathing was labored. Even if they managed to make shore or be fished out, she might well die of freezing.

"Boat," Ardmore said suddenly. He jerked his chin at something over Grayson's shoulder. Grayson risked a look. The cutter that usually rested on the *Majesty*'s main deck bobbed and foundered on the water. Jacobs had made time to at least get them that. No one manned it; it rocked on the swells, drifting back from the wake of the *Majesty*.

Without speaking, he and Ardmore made for it, towing Alexandra between them. They matched each other stroke for stroke, balancing their pulls automatically so Alexandra would not slip underwater.

An explosion rocked the morning. The *Majesty* had fired all guns, right into Burchard's ship. Dimly Grayson heard Burchard screaming. Her ship survived, limping around to launch another volley at the *Argonaut*.

Ardmore reached the boat. It swung perilously, but he grabbed it with a white-knuckled grip and held it hard. Grayson seized the gunwale, and with the other hand pushed and boosted Alexandra up and into the boat. Her torso and backside were ice-cold under his hands, her slim legs unmoving. She landed in the bottom of the cutter with a clank of chains.

"Get in," Ardmore rasped.

Grayson launched himself with the last of his strength into the boat. He rolled over the gunwale and landed next to Alexandra, gasping like a fish on dry land. He coughed and coughed, his loosened hair sending rivulets of water back into his mouth.

Alexandra lay curled in the bottom of the boat, her lips blue, her limbs shaking. She had landed on a pile of blankets, supplied no doubt by Jacobs. A wine skin lay

on the stern bench. Grayson sent his first officer a silent
thanks.

Ardmore's hands and torso appeared over the gunwale,
then dropped out of sight again. Once more, he heaved
into view, his face strained, his eyes half-closed. He was
running out of strength. Grayson crawled past Alexandra
to the bows. He leaned over, grasped Ardmore by the
waistband, and hauled him into the boat.

Ardmore fell to the bottom and lay still, his breathing
hoarse. Grayson left him there. He stripped off his own
sodden shirt, then stumbled back to Alexandra. He lifted
her from the blankets, and wrapped one around her, co-
cooning her limbs in the thick, warm wool. He held her
close, pressing her to him, the blanket prickling his bare
chest. She breathed heavily, eyes closed, but she had
stopped coughing.

He leaned to her, tears stinging his cheeks. "I love you,
Alexandra," he whispered. "I love you."

Alexandra returned slowly from the place of darkness and
fear. She felt strangely warmed and content for someone
who was drowning. Solid arms wrapped her, and heat
touched her ear. "I love you," came the whisper.

It warmed her to her toes. "Grayson," she murmured.
"I saved you."

"Sweetheart?"

Alexandra opened her eyes. She stared, perplexed, at
the side of a wooden boat and the rocking sea beyond,
but Grayson held her safe in his arms.

"Sweetheart," he said, his voice breaking. "I thought
I'd lost you."

"I am right here," she said. "Is Captain Ardmore dead?"

"No."

The captain's voice rumbled from the other end of the

boat. She lifted her eyes, an action that hurt very much for some reason, and found Captain Ardmore in the bow, slumped against the gunwale. He'd peeled off his shirt and lay limply, his bronzed torso gleaming with water. "Why the hell did you push us in?" he croaked.

"I had to stop you murdering Grayson." She lifted her chin. "And I will stop you again."

Ardmore gave her an incredulous look. "She is a dragon, Finley."

Grayson's laughter rumbled. "She is *my* dragon." He had a wineskin in his hand. He pulled off the top, and the sharp scent of brandy drifted to her. "Drink this."

He set it to her lips. Alexandra had never drunk spirits in her life, let alone out of a wineskin. She had learned so much since meeting the pirate next door. How to drink from a dipper, how to climb from a ship, how to make wild love in a narrow captain's bunk—

Warm, tingling brandy flowed into her mouth. The liquid made her cough, but it also burned a bright path down to her reeling stomach. She felt just a little bit better.

Grayson passed the skin to Ardmore. He drank deeply, wiped his mouth, then drank again, before handing it back.

A bang that sounded liked the end of the world exploded just behind them, and Alexandra yelped. Ardmore jumped from his seat and quickly unlashed the oars that had been tied to the bottom. Grayson dragged Alexandra to the stern seat. He settled her in the corner, kissed her briefly, then took up the tiller beside her.

The *Argonaut* had turned again, using the wind to put her level with the third ship, where Captain Burchard stood ramrod straight on the deck. Their little rowboat was right in the *Argonaut*'s path, and the *Argonaut* was not swerving to avoid them.

Without exchanging a word, Grayson and Ardmore began working to move out of danger. Ardmore pulled hard on the oars, and Grayson fought to keep the tiller steady on the tossing waves. Grayson's broad arms bumped Alexandra as he moved the tiller back and forth. Ardmore's muscles bunched and stretched as he rowed with mad frenzy.

Alexandra huddled into the blanket and watched them. She remembered how Grayson's undress had unnerved her the first night she'd met him. Now she realized just how beautiful his body could be and knew she'd never have her fill of looking at it. His blond hair, dark now with water, curled onto his tanned shoulders, and the morning sun shadowed the hard muscles of his torso. Scars criss-crossed his forearms, lost in the sun-touched hair that grew there.

The two men worked together silently, easily, as if slipping into a routine they'd worked out years and years ago. As hated enemies, they were powerful. She wondered how much more powerful they would be as friends.

The boat skimmed across the water, and the *Argonaut* slid by. Henderson hung over the rail to watch them, the sun glinting on his blond hair and spectacles. Alexandra untangled her arm from the blanket and waved at him. He'd redeemed himself in her eyes, stepping in at the last minute to defy his captain.

Captain Ardmore rowed them well out of the way of the circling ships, then hoisted the oars. Both he and Grayson turned to watch the battle, each of their gazes locked on their respective ships.

The *Majesty*, proudly unmarked by gunfire, bore down on Burchard's ship, forcing it to turn. The *Argonaut* came about swiftly, despite having two sails hanging limp. The ship picked up wind and raced across the short distance, head on toward Burchard.

Ardmore shouted, "Damn it, Ian, what are you doing?"

"He's going to ram her," Grayson said. "Good."

"*Good?* That's my ship!"

Grayson clutched the gunwale and watched, eyes gleaming. The *Argonaut* charged on. Burchard screamed orders. Desperately Burchard moved the ship forward, trying to slip between the two and perhaps cause them to ram each other. But the proud captain was too slow.

The *Argonaut*'s bowsprit struck the stern of Burchard's ship. The groan of splintering wood came to them, then the soft explosions of shattering glass, and screams of the crew. Fire suddenly crawled up one of her masts. Burchard's cannons tried to fire, but the gunpowder caught fire and exploded with an upward thrust of flame.

Ardmore stood up in the boat. "Ian, get out of there!"

The *Argonaut* swung to the right, tearing the remainder of Burchard's stern with it. It dove past the burning, listing boat, out to open sea. When it was clear of the flames, Ardmore sat down and blew out his breath.

The *Majesty* marched toward Burchard. Now it was Grayson's turn to half-stand, his knee on the seat, and hold his breath while his ship gracefully pivoted and blasted all guns. With a splendid and fiery *whump*, Burchard's ship went up in flames. Sailors dove over the side, desperately swimming from the burning wreckage. Boats began lowering over the *Majesty*'s side, sent out to fetch the survivors.

Grayson sat down hard on the bench and seized the tiller. Ardmore lifted the oars again, and dipped them in the water, turning with Grayson's pull to come about.

The *Argonaut* slid by them again. A dark hole lay like

a stain just below the railing in the bow. The bowsprit was shattered, a large piece of it dangling like a huge broken arm.

Ardmore made an anguished sound. "Damn you, O'Malley."

Grayson laughed into the wind. "Cheer up. It's still floating. A few repairs and you can run back to South Carolina with no worries."

Ardmore set his mouth and did not answer.

Sailors in the boats from the *Majesty* were picking up foundering sailors. The wet men seemed subdued, content to let Grayson's crew take them in.

Grayson's eyes narrowed as he spotted something on the waves. He swung the tiller and motioned for Ardmore to row. Ardmore did, his face grim. The waves danced and rippled beneath them, shreds of foam forming and hissing under the bow.

As the boat skipped forward, Alexandra caught sight of what Grayson had seen. A body floated just beyond the others, out of reach of the *Majesty*'s boats. As they drew near, Alexandra saw that it wore a dark blue coat. Ardmore rowed to it. At the last minute, Grayson dropped the tiller, leaned over, and dragged the body into the boat.

It was Burchard, alive. He coughed and choked, then doubled over and vomited water onto the deck. He hunched there, wet and miserable, then slowly sat up.

Alexandra gasped. Burchard's blue coat had parted, and the white shirt beneath had torn from neck to waist. The gap revealed small, firm, woman's breasts, nipples pinched tight with cold. "Good heavens," Alexandra breathed.

The woman's short hair lay flat upon her head. With her plain, square face, she could easily pass as a man; her breasts were small enough to need little binding.

Grayson betrayed no surprise. He had known, the rat. Ardmore, on the other hand, stared as if he'd been struck. His stunned gaze roved up and down the woman's body, and then he said, "God's breath."

"You remember me then," Burchard said, her voice ragged.

Ardmore only stared.

Burchard swung her glare to Grayson. "I knew you would betray me." She smiled an evil smile. "I also knew you and Ardmore would never be able to fight together, even against me. You had to both be overboard before your lieutenants could act." She looked from one to the other, her gaze sliding right past Alexandra as if she were invisible. "Even if you kill me, I will die happy, knowing I've had my revenge."

"Have you?" Grayson asked dryly. "Your ship is sinking."

"What do I care? I purchased it in a hurry and hired an idiot crew. When I got word that Captain Finley had become a viscount, I had to come to London to see how he fared." She gave him a look of scorn. "I should have known that you'd fall right in with the Admiralty, you hypocrite. But then I learned that it had put you at odds with Ardmore again. Excellent news."

Ardmore's dark brows lowered. "What is she raving about?"

"She nurses a hatred for us," Grayson answered, his voice calm. "Because we embarrassed her all those years ago."

"*We* embarrassed *her?*"

Grayson nodded, his grin incongruously cheerful. Alexandra stared at him in surprise, hoping he would explain. But to her disappointment, he did not continue.

"You humiliated me," Burchard said in a hard voice.

"It took me years to pick up the pieces after that night."

Ardmore growled. "Having all our money, clothes, and sundries must have helped."

Alexandra truly wanted to hear *this* story. "Grayson," she began.

Burchard turned her dark gaze fully on her. "You," she snapped. "I thought I could get to Finley through you, but you proved useless. You are one of them."

Alexandra still did not much understand what Burchard was talking about. "Why did you not tell me you were a woman?" she asked. "You were courting me." She looked at Grayson. "She was on my list!"

"What list?" Burchard demanded.

"Um—never mind."

Burchard ignored her. "All this is worth seeing Ardmore and Finley together again," she said. She glanced at Ardmore. "I can see that you hate him with great intensity. I like that."

Ardmore glowered. "I do not need you to make me hate him."

If anything, Burchard looked slightly hurt. "No, I did it. I drove the wedge between you."

Ardmore shot her a skeptical look. "You did not tell Sara to go to him. He stole her from me all by himself."

Burchard threw back her head and laughed. The teeth in the back of her mouth were black. "I did tell her. I was there. I saw the two of you and her in Tahiti. I saw her smiling at Finley. I told her that if she went to Finley, he'd make her wealthy beyond her wildest dreams—take her back to England, let her live in a gilded castle." The wild laughter again. "And she believed me."

"What?" The hard, angry word was drawn from Grayson. His eyes went as cold as the gray sea around them.

Burchard hugged herself. "She persuaded you to marry

her, how delicious. You must have disappointed her; that's why she ran away so soon. If she had been patient, she would have become a viscountess."

Grayson's gaze should have burned a hole right through her. Alexandra hung on to the side of the boat, her heart beating swiftly.

Ardmore broke through Burchard's laughter. "It does not matter. He still took her."

"It was a trick," she said gleefully. "And I thought of it."

Ardmore's look turned dangerous. "Did you murder my brother, too?"

To Alexandra's horror, the woman nodded. Her eyes gleamed, the morning light making her pale skin nearly waxen. "I did it, James Ardmore." Her face split into a wild grin. "I told your brother that Finley had overpowered a slave ship and was taking the slaves to Barbados. That Finley had butchered the ones he had no room for. He was so ready to believe the worst about Finley that he fell right for it."

Ardmore stilled, his eyes cold as an ice storm. Burchard, looking delighted, went on. "So easy to arrange one of my men to join Finley's crew. So easy to convince your stupid brother to ram the *Majesty*. So easy to have my crewman shoot and kill him. *I* did it. I broke the famous captains Ardmore and Finley. Me. And I have loved watching you at each other's throats ever since."

Grayson's hand clenched the gunwale until his fingers were white. Ardmore remained still, his gaze fixed.

Alexandra could bear it not longer. "You stupid woman!" she shouted. She clenched her fists, her fury so great that she spluttered. "Why on earth would you want to do such a thing?"

Burchard's red-rimmed eyes blazed. "Because they took

me, my dear sweet Mrs. Alastair. Your fine Lord Stoke, and your fine Captain Ardmore. They took me, and they raped me, and they—"

"Alexandra is right," Grayson broke in, his words clipped. "You are a stupid woman. Why not tell the truth for a change? We never touched you. What we did was expose you for a woman in that tavern in Jamaica, and you never forgave us. I think you're a bit confused yourself, despite the roll of linen you shove in your trousers. Was humiliating us not enough? I had never seen Ian O'Malley laugh so hard. Then or since."

Foam flecked her lips. "No, it was not enough! Do you know what you did to me? I had to quit my ship, find another crew. I had to go back to being an anonymous sailor, and eat maggot-infested bread and work my fingers to the bone before I could rise again. All because of you."

She spat. The spittle struck Ardmore on the chin, and dropped to his wet chest.

He lunged with the suddenness of a snake. Burchard gave him one surprised look, then found herself locked in his powerful arms. She struggled, hands trying to reach for weapons, but Ardmore pinned her, sinews working in his bare arms.

The boat rocked sharply under their struggle. Grayson steadied it with the tiller. Alexandra remained glued in place, her mouth open.

"You murdered my brother," Ardmore hissed, his voice deadly. "You murdered my brother, for your *pride?*"

"For yours," she gasped. "For your stupid pride and your game of exposing me."

He roared. He lifted Burchard in his powerful arms. Grayson dove at him, but a second too late. Ardmore got his huge hands around Burchard's neck. The woman screamed.

Alexandra heard it, audible and sickening, the snap that ended Burchard's life. She saw the woman's head fall, saw the terrible fear in her eyes suddenly fade to nothing.

Burchard's body went limp, eyes fixed and staring. Ardmore looked down at her for a long moment, his breathing ragged. Then, with another snarl, he hauled the body over the gunwale and flung it into the waiting sea.

Silence descended in the little boat. In the distance, Burchard's ship crackled and roared, flames hungrily devouring it. The *Majesty* was turning, slowly; the *Argonaut*, smaller and faster, floated out of its way.

Ardmore watched the ships for a moment, his face stark and drained of all emotion. Then he turned his broad back on Grayson and Alexandra and sank onto his hands and knees.

A choking, horrible sound reached Alexandra. She thought for a moment that Captain Ardmore was sick, but she realized a moment later that he was weeping.

Her heart wrenched. He was hurting—the truth had hurt him, had taken his vengeance from him. Perhaps he was regretting the ending of his friendship with Grayson, the thousand injuries the two had done to one another, the hatred that had been built so needlessly. She clasped the blanket around her and started forward.

Grayson put a heavy hand on her arm. "No. Leave him."

She frowned at him. Men always believed no other man could possibly want comfort. She shook off his grasp and climbed forward to the bows.

"There now." She patted Ardmore's broad, shaking shoulder. His fist was pressed to his face, his eyes squeezed shut, tears wetting his cheeks. She glanced back at Grayson. He remained in the stern, his face still, watching her with a resigned look.

She returned her attention to Ardmore. "It is over," she said softly. She touched his hair. "You can put it all behind you and go on. It will be a new day tomorrow, Mr. Ardmore. A new life. A new step forward."

Ardmore raised his head. He looked, not at Alexandra, but back at Grayson, his green eyes wet. Grayson, strangely, only gave him a shrug.

"She is yours," Ardmore said.

Grayson nodded once, his smile curving his lips. "She is."

Alexandra patted Mr. Ardmore's shoulder again. "The ships are coming to get us. I hope they hurry. I am so cold."

Despite the blanket, the wind bit like ice on her limbs. Ardmore wiped his eyes with the heel of his hand. "She's going to freeze," he said to Grayson.

"I know," Grayson said. He started forward. "We need to keep her warm."

Ardmore nodded. The fire had gone out of him. He no longer looked a fearsome man, but one lonely and defeated.

The boat listed as Grayson climbed into the seat next to Ardmore. Alexandra gave herself into his arms, and he gathered her close. His wet, bare chest was cold, but she did not mind leaning into it.

After a moment, she felt Ardmore behind her. She looked up at Grayson in alarm, but he only shook his head. Then she understood. They would try to warm her between them. Ardmore pressed his torso protectively over her, effectively sandwiching her between the two men. The change was immediate. Their bodies, large and solid, warmed her, and her shivering lessened. They took the cold wind on their backs, working together to shield her from it.

The awkward position put Grayson and Ardmore very close together. Ardmore had to rest his hands on Grayson's arms to lock Alexandra into their protective bubble. Grayson's leg had to rest across Ardmore's thigh.

Grayson grinned, his laughter rumbling. "Ah, James," he said. "It has been so long."

"Finley," Ardmore growled back. "I really hate you."

Chapter Thirty-one

Grayson remembered putting Alexandra to bed in his own cabin, and the next thing he knew, he was waking up beside her. Her lithe body rested in the curve of his arm, and her fragrant hair tickled his nose.

After boarding the *Majesty*, they had washed and rubbed themselves dry, and Jacobs had poured hot coffee down their throats. Grayson had thought himself perfectly aware and awake, but when he'd lain down next to Alexandra—just for a minute—the exhaustion, cold, and tension had taken over and he'd fallen into a dark pit of sleep.

He touched Alexandra's bare shoulder, enjoying the silken feel of it under his fingers. She murmured in her sleep but did not waken. She smelled so good. This woman, and the entire delight of her, had changed him profoundly and deeply. After his mother's death, he had decided never to love completely again. He had kept that vow until Maggie, and now Alexandra, had forced past his barriers and taken up refuge in his heart. He knew he loved them; he could acknowledge that now. Fear of that fragile love touched him, but he closed his eyes against it. Grief could come so quickly, he knew, but he was willing to love now, to build up joy against that inevitable day.

He also tasted triumph, which made him smile. He had Alexandra. Ardmore had not succeeded in taking her. Even when Alexandra had gone to him, she had made it clear that her love and her heart belonged to Grayson. Not Ardmore, no matter how much he'd tried.

Those thoughts reminded Grayson of business unfinished. Carefully he eased his arm from beneath Alexandra's head, settling her on a pillow. Her eyes opened a crack, but immediately closed again, her breathing deepening.

Grayson pulled on a dry shirt and breeches and left the cabin. Outside, the sun was setting, stars just breaking through twilight. He stared at the sky in surprise and rubbed his eyes. He must have slept for at least twelve hours.

The *Majesty* was at anchor again, drifting not far from shore. He recognized the town of Blackwall, its dockyards filled with naval vessels whose naked masts pierced the evening sky. He scanned the river and the horizon, but nowhere saw the familiar shape of the *Argonaut*.

Jacobs kept watch on the quarterdeck, leaning lazily on the rail. Grayson joined him. "Where is he?"

Jacobs did not have to ask who. "Gone, sir. A couple of frigates started strolling toward us, no doubt wondering what all the fuss was about. Last thing I saw was the *Argonaut* heading back to open water. Haven't seen her since."

Grayson knew with strange finality that Ardmore was

gone. He was an outlaw in England; he could not risk repairing his ship at a dockyard where the Royal Navy prowled. No doubt he'd try to make for France or the Netherlands. The *Argonaut* had been wounded before, worse, and had survived.

But Grayson regretted the chance not to speak to Ardmore before he sailed. Burchard had cleared Grayson's guilt in the death of Ardmore's brother, but there was still so much in the way. Or perhaps they had never been meant to be friends. Even their young camaraderie had been laced with rivalry—who could shoot the straightest, sail the fastest, catch the attentions of the prettiest woman. Burchard had very easily pitted them against each other. If their friendship had been deeper, she never would have succeeded.

Grayson turned back from the horizon. He outlined his plans to Jacobs, then went back below to his snug bed and the warm woman waiting there.

St. George's, Hanover Square, that September was the site of the most curious wedding London had witnessed in many a year. The bride was the widowed Alexandra Alastair, daughter of Lord Alexis Simmington and granddaughter of the Duke of Montcrief. The groom was the dashing and handsome Viscount Stoke. Such a society pairing should have been ordinary, but this one was not. Journalists lined the street eager to glimpse the odd wedding party, ready to capture the most exciting story since the pirate invasion of Mrs. Alastair's soiree.

The bride's guests came from the top of society. The wealthy and titled had returned to town in droves in this unfashionable month to vie for invitations to the most interesting wedding of the year. Among the guests were the lofty Duke of St. Clair, the amiable Lord and Lady

Featherstone, Lord Hildebrand Caldicott and his sister, the Hon. Mr. Bartholomew, and even, astonishingly, Louis Bourbon, the king of France in exile, accompanied by an entourage of Hussars.

On the groom's side—well, some said they were pirates, others simply merchantmen hardened by their world travels. They certainly *looked* like pirates, as both the *Times* and the *Gentleman's Magazine* reported. They were a collection of bronzed, brawny, and fierce-looking men, some even missing eyes or limbs, many giving the ladies on the other side of the aisle leering grins. One journalist swore that the respectably married Mrs. Waters spent the entire ceremony actually batting her lashes at a particularly virile-looking gentleman called Mr. Priestly. Whether this developed into a full flirtation, the writer could not tell. It was rumored the pair were seen in deep conversation at the wedding breakfast, during which the young man was reported to have worn a hunted look.

The bride was attended by the Honorable Miss Maggie Finley, the viscount's daughter, a black-haired, foreign-looking child, but one who promised to become a great beauty. The new Lady Stoke was also attended by the former Mrs. Fairchild, a widow of an Oxford *don* who had quietly married a Mr. Robert Jacobs at the end of June. Mr. Jacobs stood up with the groom, and reportedly the two of them exchanged much good-natured banter and laughter.

The bride was radiant in a gown of cream satin. White rosebuds were embroidered on the gown and the bride's long gloves, and her sash was yellow. In her hair lay a lovely strand of diamonds laced with opals, reputedly a gift from the viscount himself. Lady Stoke smiled her way through the ceremony, as did Miss Finley, though the new Mrs. Jacobs wept for joy.

Once the ring was on the bride's finger, and the groom had kissed her—a kiss rather longer than was proper—the groom's guests erupted into a loud cheer and threw out rather bawdy and inappropriate suggestions. Several ladies on the bride's side reportedly swooned and had to be carried outside.

The wedding breakfast took place in two houses in Grosvenor Street, the viscount's and the one Mrs. Alastair had inhabited next door to it. The breakfast commenced in Mrs. Alastair's exquisite cream and light green dining room, done in the Adam's style, presided over by a young footman who became so excited that he stammered and neglected to serve people.

The festivities then moved to the viscount's townhouse, opened for the first time to eager eyes. Much redecorating had been completed. Mrs. Tetley told *Le Beau Monde* that though the old-fashioned dark paneling remained, it had been polished until it gleamed, and the huge dining room had been softened by Constable's paintings, a slender-legged Heppelwhite table, and an oriental carpet of dark green silk.

The feasting here continued throughout the day, the wedding breakfast becoming a wedding supper. Guests lingered, mingling with the piratelike men who mustered together instruments and began dancing with the mystified and delighted ladies of the *ton*. The festivities were presided over by a large and fearsome-looking man with dark skin, who went silently about his duties with a smile hovering about his mouth.

The dancing and merriment continued as the sun went down, and did not stop even when the discovery was made that the bride and groom, their daughter, and Mr. and Mrs. Jacobs had all disappeared.

*   *   *

Aboard the *Majesty*, Grayson groaned aloud as he thrust into Alexandra again and again. She clasped him in the darkness, her heart thudding with joy, arching to him, needing him. They climaxed together, his fevered hands tumbling her hair, his lips bruising hers.

After a long time, he settled back into the bed. "Alone at last," he murmured.

Alexandra snuggled against him, feeling sleepy and achingly happy. "It was fine to see our friends having such enjoyment," she said, smiling in the dark.

"Hmph." His large hand skimmed her breast. "I put off having you for three months so they could enjoy themselves."

Alexandra's smile widened. He certainly had not waited patiently. He had complained every single day that he wanted to marry her and get on with the fun. Once she had changed her "No" into a "Yes"—about half-way into the second time they'd made frantic love in his cabin the evening after their wet rescue, he had wanted to marry immediately. Obtain a special license, marry on the spot.

Lady Featherstone, hearing the good news, had told him *absolutely not*. He was the new and intriguing Viscount Stoke, Alexandra was a respectable lady, and they could not behave as though they were scandalous and illicit lovers. Even when Grayson informed her that the whole point was that he and Alexandra wished to *be* lovers—forever—she would not yield. But she did blush a bit.

The planning, the decorating, the wardrobe, and the invitations took much time and energy. Lady Featherstone said it would be a miracle if they got it all done even by September. But Grayson had been adamant. September, and that was final.

During that time, they'd seen not one sign of James Ardmore, the *Argonaut,* or lieutenants O'Malley or Henderson. They were truly gone.

"Grayson." Alexandra touched her husband's arm where it rested across her warm abdomen. She had been wanting to ask this for a long time, and perhaps now that he was tired, happy, smiling—"What *did* Burchard do that so humiliated you and Captain Ardmore?"

He stilled. He slowly stroked his fingertips across her skin, drawing fire. "That is not a tale I care to share with my wife."

"It was a long time ago."

"I was about twenty years old and very full of myself. I do not want to talk about when I was twenty years old. Now is better."

Alexandra had to agree. Her heart swelled with the greatest happiness she had ever known. Only one thing more would complete her joy, and perhaps, after tonight, her greatest dream would come true. In any event, trying to reach her dream was proving to be quite pleasant.

"It's all right," she said, patting his arm. "Mr. Jacobs told me."

He came up on one arm, scowling. "What? That impudent, be-damned— I'll throw him overboard."

Alexandra rolled over and wrapped her arms about his waist. "Do not do that. He and Vanessa seem so happy."

"Besotted, more like. They couldn't keep their eyes off each other during the entire wedding. At least Maggie liked it."

Maggie had been quite happy with all the weddings. She'd thrown herself into planning Alexandra's, which won her Lady Featherstone's admiration. Every one of her new friends should be happy, Maggie said. Their happiness would spill onto her. Alexandra gave a small, wistful sigh in the dark. In a few years, Maggie, who had taken to calling her "Mama Alexandra," would be ready to look for happiness of her own.

Mrs. Fairchild—Vanessa, she now begged Alexandra to call her—had announced her engagement to Mr. Jacobs only days after they'd returned from the harrowing sea battle. She and Alexandra had hugged and wept, and Vanessa had proudly showed her the ring Mr. Jacobs had given her, a lovely, square-cut ruby that had been handed down through his family. They had married as soon as the banns had been read, a quiet ceremony with only their closest friends attending. Alexandra had seen something new in her former governess's eyes, a deep contentment that had been entirely missing before.

She thought she understood what that deep contentment felt like.

"Speaking of besotted," Grayson continued, his voice soft and sleepy. "I went down to the cellars to find more port. What do you think I saw when I passed through the kitchen?"

She pressed a small kiss to the bridge of his nose. "I haven't the faintest idea."

"My man Oliver. And your cook. Kissing."

Alexandra giggled, delighted. "Love is in the air. I believe Jeffrey is quite smitten with Joan. She seems relieved to have an ordinary young man interested in her, after I explained about Mr. Ardmore. It really was too bad of him to seduce her, poor thing."

"He is ruthless. When he wants something, he will do what it takes to get it." He paused. "As do I."

"But your heart is filled with kindness." Alexandra touched her hand to his smooth chest, tracing the curve of his muscle. "And much love. Perhaps out there on the oceans, Mr. Ardmore will find his own special lady. One who will at last teach him what love truly means."

Grayson snorted. "I doubt it." He grew quiet again. "He loved Sara, and Sara alone. I understand what he felt for her. I knew it when I saw him with you on his deck."

She shivered. "Let us not speak of it. Perhaps there is hope for Captain Ardmore."

Grayson rubbed his cheek against hers, then rolled over so that he lay full-length on top of her. His warm weight soothed rather than oppressed; he made a comforting and cozy blanket. "What I hope now," he said, "is to show you some more how much I love you. I don't think you quite believe me, yet."

"Well, Captain Ardmore did have to force you to say it."

"Captain Ardmore be damned. I love you, Alexandra. I love the freckles on your nose and your beautiful hair and your eyes that I want to drown in." He paused, his voice becoming husky with desire. "Shall I tell you about the other parts I love?"

"Goodness, no. I will blush."

"Then I will show you instead."

He lowered his head and nipped her neck. She stretched, arching to him once more. He kissed his way down her throat and drew his tongue over the swell of her breast. "I love you," he whispered into her skin. "Forever."

"I love you, too, Grayson," she murmured. She smiled into the night. "My pirate next door."

Epilogue

The warm winds of June again blew through the garden, stirring the riot of roses that climbed the bricks of both houses. The fountain trickled a soothing melody, and a dozen sparrows began a cacophony of chirping in the tall trees. Alexandra reposed on one of the benches in the shade, tired, but happy. The smell of green things and earth and flowers wafted on the friendly breeze, refreshing and delighting her.

This was her first venture into the garden since her confinement. She had stolen this moment to bathe in wonder at her happiness. Her ordeal was over, her immediate fears assuaged, although she now realized that a mother never really put all fear behind her.

Mr. Jacobs had purchased Alexandra's house and had moved in with Vanessa. During the intervening months, they'd pulled down the garden wall separating them, turning the green oasis into one large garden for all to share. Alexandra and Vanessa had planned and overseen the installation of walkways, flowerbeds, benches, trees. Grayson and Mr. Jacobs had glanced at the piles of plans, glanced at each other, and fled.

Grayson and Maggie were upstairs now with the twins, no doubt gurgling and burbling at them. Charlotte, named for Grayson's mother, had red hair and deep brown eyes. Alexis, named for Alexandra's father, had hair of gold, and his eyes were blue, like his father's. Grayson, ever since the hour he'd walked into Alexandra's chamber and beheld his tiny, perfect daughter and son, had behaved like a man obsessed. He'd held them and talked to them and promised them all kinds of absurdities, and in short, behaved like a dazzled papa. This did not mean he ignored his first child, Maggie, whom he doted on without abandon. Maggie, for her part, seemed as besotted with the twins as he.

Motherhood and wifehood had made Alexandra's life in the last ten months both harried and content. She supposed that happiness was all about mingling chaos and delight. The future could hold more darkness, but the bright times would exist as well. Life, in its complex array, would go on.

The shadows moved. Alexandra sat up and peered into the patch of darkness beneath the beech tree that stood near the far wall. Her pulse quickened, and she wondered if she should call for Grayson or Mr. Jacobs.

After a moment, she saw him. He stood in the shadows like darkness himself, his midnight blue coat, black hair, and swarthy skin nearly hidden in the lace-patterned shade. He did not move, only watched her with glittering eyes as she rose and glided to meet him.

Shadows closed about her, bathing her in soothing coolness. He had chosen the one spot that could not be viewed by either house, and she knew he had not done it by chance.

She reached him. She looked into his ice-green eyes, so unchanged. His face was as hard, his mouth as severe, as they had been the previous year.

"I am pleased to see you, Mr. Ardmore," she said softly.

He regarded her a long moment before he answered. "Are you?"

"I am," she replied. "Grayson would be as well."

"But I do not wish to see him. He will want to reconcile. I do not."

She frowned. "Surely everything has been resolved between you. You should be friends again."

The look he gave her held amusement. "Old friends make the best enemies, Alexandra. Grayson and I have seen too much of each other's weaknesses, of each other's cruelties. Those can't easily be forgiven, even if the blame for the actual events lies elsewhere." He paused. "It is much too complicated for a simple I'm sorry."

She bit her lip. Ardmore's voice held finality, telling her that she could plead until she was hoarse, and she would not move him. "I think you give up the chance of happiness too easily. But then, at this moment, I am adamant for everyone to be happy."

He actually smiled, though his eyes did not warm. "You make a good match for him. Finley has always, even with the tragedies that have struck him, been filled with the joy of life." The smile faded. "I, on the other hand, find no joy in it."

His words made her heart twist. "You sadden me, captain. May I pray for you? Pray that someday, you will find someone who will bring you happiness."

His eyes softened. "Pray all you like. I don't mind."

"May we at least be friends, then?" She offered her

hand. "Put everything behind us? Although I am still a bit angry at you for Joan. You might be happy to know that she married my footman and the two of them are setting up housekeeping in his father's inn."

"How excellent for them." He took her hand, but instead of shaking it, businesslike, he clasped it softly. "I had come today to beg for your forgiveness. I hurt you. I never meant to. I had to leave England last year before I could tell you that. The fact that you are now happy—even with a man like Finley—pleases me."

"You hurt Grayson, too."

He laughed softly. "You may have noticed that Finley bounces back with astonishing resilience. How long did it take him to recover from our last adventure?"

"Um—perhaps a day."

"You see? He doesn't need my prostration. And I'll be damned if I give it to him. We both hurt each other. We're about even."

She tried to withdraw her hand, but his grip, though loose, did not release. "At least, if you cannot be friends, you should put it all behind you. Go on with a new challenge, new adventures. Will you at least do that?"

He gave her an ironic look. "You take the cliché of turning over a new leaf to its utter limits, my lady. To reassure you, I am not skulking about London brooding over my lost friendship with your husband. I am here on completely different business, and took the chance of finding you. I have already begun new adventures, new challenges."

She regarded him skeptically. "Are these challenges some our Admiralty would approve of?"

"Very possibly not." He at last disengaged his hand from hers. "I ask that you do not run to your husband or the Duke of St. Clair until I have the chance to clear England."

She decided not to answer that with a promise. "How is Mr. Henderson?"

The flicker in his eyes indicated he had not missed her evasion. "Henderson will recover. He has had many things to occupy his attention."

"You forgave him then? For trying to turn against you?"

"Let us say that I need him. I might forgive him later."

"Tell him—" She stopped, casting about for something that would not be hurtful. "Tell him I am grateful to him for his help. And tell him good-bye."

Ardmore inclined his head. "If you wish." He stopped for a moment, then reached down and took her hand again. He pressed it to his lips. "Good-bye, Mrs. Alastair," he said softly.

She started at the use of her old name, but just then, Grayson's voice boomed out from the house. "Alexandra!"

She withdrew her hand, turned, and hurried back into the sunshine. The June air chased away the chill of the shadows, as did the sight of Grayson emerging from the house, a bundled baby on his arm. He wore no coat, just his shirt and breeches and boots, the same as the first day she'd met him. Maggie trailed behind him, crooning something to the babe she carried.

"There you are, love." Grayson crossed the grass to her, leaned down and kissed her lips. The kiss was no less fiery for little Alexis's coo of protest. "They missed their mama. So we came to find you."

Alexandra accepted the bundle from him. She dropped a kiss to Alexis's downy head. Maggie stopped beside them. Grayson draped an arm around his first daughter's shoulder and teased his second daughter's fist with a scarred finger. Charlotte opened her hand, seized his finger, and squeezed tight.

"Gooble, gooble, gooble," Grayson said.

Maggie gave him a look of thirteen-year-old dignity. "Papa, please."

Grayson tweaked Maggie's nose. "Gooble, gooble, gooble."

"Papa!"

Grayson's gaze moved past Alexandra to the shadows of the trees. His eyes narrowed. But she sensed, without turning, that James Ardmore had gone.

Grayson's gaze met hers again, the blue undimmed. His eyes held knowledge. He looked at her for a long moment, then smiled, warm and dazzling. "We are having fine weather," he said. "Why don't we take the *Majesty* out for a short voyage? Around the Channel to Cornwall?" He wriggled Charlotte's hand. "The twins need to gain their sea legs."

Maggie laughed. "They cannot even walk yet, Papa."

"Never too early to learn. Besides, my crew is getting lazy. A nice run won't hurt them."

Alexandra smiled into his eyes. "I would like that."

Their gazes met, held. His look told her he'd guessed every moment of her encounter with Ardmore. It also told her he loved her, and that his old rivalry with Ardmore would never change that.

Alexandra touched her husband's hard and handsome face. "Once the twins gain their sea legs, then perhaps we can sail farther?"

He lightly kissed her fingers, his lips warm. "Where did you have in mind?"

"Tahiti."

Maggie stared up at her, wild hope in her eyes. Grayson looked amused. " 'Tis a long and dangerous voyage."

"But we will have the great Captain Finley to guide us. He can sail anywhere."

He tried to look modest. "True." He gazed down from his height at his two ladies and the two infants. "Very well, then, we'll sail for Tahiti."

He gathered Alexandra into the circle of his arm and kissed her, long and warm and loving. Alexis made a happy noise, and Charlotte followed suit.

Grayson chuckled. "Every sailor on the seas feared one Finley before," he said. He smiled into her eyes. "Now, they must face *five*."